IN PLAIN VIEW

J. WACHOWSKI

writes stories, screenplays, school excuses and anything else that pays.

She lives with her family on the midwestern edge of civilization, but is often sighted lurking at www.jwachowski.com.

IN PLAIN VIEW

J.WACHOWSKI

CARINA
PRESS™

For Rob,
Ryan & Sophie
Sine qua non

CARINA PRESS™

Recycling programs
for this product may
not exist in your area.

ISBN-13: 978-0-373-06237-9

IN PLAIN VIEW

First North American Publication 2010

Copyright © 2010 by Splendide Mendax, Inc.

www.CarinaPress.com

Printed in U.S.A.

IN PLAIN VIEW

Acknowledgments

A story is a dream until it has an audience. Many people helped me realize this dream as my first readers and steadfast supporters.

L. Longford, M. Watson, S. Phillips, K. Hannah, C. Linz and the Creativefest Braintrust;

J. Clark, H. Hughes, S. Lariz and the Arrowhead Book Group;

Melissa Johnson, Angela James and the avant-garde entrepreneurs at Carina Press;

Ron and Lynne Wachowski, Lana and Karin, Laura and Pete, Andy and Alisa, Sandy, Peggy and Sandy Eakins;

Miriam Norton and Grams.

It is a great joy to thank you all in a book.

SFX: Ker-flush

That's the sound of my career going down the toilet. Three months ago, I was *the* freelance reporter to call for full-color images of an international crisis.

Now? I'm stationed at the far edge of the Chicago fly-over as a disappointing mother-sub to my eight-year-old niece and the babysitter for a newsroom College Boy.

Camera still: a man in Amish clothing hanging from a tree. Dead.

One photo of the lifeless man was all I needed to see—there's more to this story than anyone wants to admit. Especially Sheriff Jack Curzon, with his death-ray eyes watching my every move. I have a feeling that man wants more than my cooperation.

Quick-cut, pan, tilt and—run.

Someone is hiding, just out of sight. And I'll do whatever it takes to protect my new family.

Seeing the truth can be dangerous…

…when evil is In Plain View.

Dear Reader,

Thank you for purchasing this Carina Press launch title. During our journey these past months to acquire manuscripts, develop relationships with authors and build the Carina Press catalog, we've been working to fulfill the mission "Where no great story goes untold."

If you'd asked me what I'd be doing a year ago, I never would have conceived I'd be working with the brilliant team behind Harlequin's digital program to bring you a new and exciting digital-first imprint. I have long been a fan of Harlequin books, authors and staff and that's why I'm so pleased to be sharing these first Carina Press launch titles with you.

At Carina Press, we're committed to bringing readers great voices and great stories, and we hope you'll find these books as compelling as we do. In this first month, you'll find a broad range of genres that showcase our promise to Carina Press fans to publish a diversity of content. In the coming months, we'll add additional genres and continue to bring you a wide range of stories we believe will keep you coming back for more.

We love to hear from readers, and you can e-mail us your thoughts, comments and questions to: generalinquiries@carinapress.com. You can also interact with Carina Press staff and authors on our blog, Twitter stream and Facebook fan page.

Happy reading!
~Angela James

Executive Editor, Carina Press
www.carinapress.com
www.twitter.com/carinapress
www.facebook.com/carinapress

AUDIO (VOICE-OVER): "A mystery solved is a fine remedy for death. It suggests there is sense, or justice, in the messy unraveling of mortality. It presumes to clean up ragged edges, explain all events and sell it back: case closed. Such a nice feeling—while it lasts."

THURSDAY

10:00:00 a.m. Sign-on

Bad days are the raw material of life. Good days are earned. Apparently, I was undeserving as well as unemployed.

"Sorry, Rich. I'm solo."

"Not anymore. Not if you want this job," Richard Gatt shot back at me. Picture your typical Midwestern fire-plug of a guy—shiny head, white button-down oxford and a blunt, booming voice.

I could feel my interview smile warping into a grimace. Must have made for a fabulous ensemble, with my current suicide-blonde-in-leather-pants look. My fingertips worried the seam across my knee. My lucky pants.

News flash: the pants weren't working either.

"Come on, Richard. Why tie up resources? I'm a one-woman show. It's part of my charm." I attempted the smile that once got me out of a cardboard box and into a bullet-proof truck in Somalia. Works pretty well on bartenders, too.

Gatt ducked his chin into his collar. I caught a tinge of blush on his unprotected forehead. He pulled a handful of sugar packets out of his desk drawer. "We can help each other out here, O'Hara. But if you want this job, you gotta train my kid."

"Kid?" The sudden déjà vu resulted in serious stomach acid.

News of Gatt's job opening was whispered in my ear by a friend at the tippy-top of the network-TV food chain who owed me a favor. WWST was a small sister station camped in western suburban Chicago Land. Not exactly top ten, but Gatt was the only program director in the state looking to hire a producer for a position that offered both salary and benefits. People in jobs that sweet sat tight until ratings offed them or they actually died.

It wasn't my dream job. But I'd stopped feeling picky two months ago. Too long between gigs. Every freelancer knows the feeling that creeps over you as the jobs spread thinner, the fear that what you've got inside—all your dreams and abilities—no longer match what's happening outside. If you aren't working, you're a fraud.

My stomach issued another warning shot.

Gatt pretended not to hear it. He ripped the tops off three sugar packets and dumped them all into his cup at once. "We want stories with a local slant. Warm-fuzzy Midwest shit. Local, but with national appeal."

"Sure," I said. Local but national. Oxymorons are Television Marketing 101.

"How much do you know about this area, O'Hara? They told me you're local."

"I grew up in the city. But my parents brought us out this way occasionally. My dad used to race dirt bikes when I was a kid. We'd always end up picnicking at that war museum out here where you can climb on tanks while you eat your tuna sandwich… You know the place I'm talking about?"

"Cantigny." Gatt nodded.

It was one of many grand summer homes dotting the farm county, built by Chicago's landed gentry of a century ago. Cantigny's owner survived France and the First World War. His house was a monument created to display the souvenir tanks-cum-lawn-ornaments he'd brought home.

My grandfather survived that same war. He claimed all he'd been allowed to bring back was a bad case of foot rot.

"Nice spot."

We did the mutual *yeah*.

My eyes kept straying to the window behind him. The view from Gatt's office was the visual definition of horizontal. Farmland at the horizon blended into a field of grassy weeds that ended at the black-topped parking lot.

War. Tanks. Foot rot and flatland. Unfortunately, local story associations weren't looking very warm and fuzzy.

Gatt bent his mouth into something like a smile. "Born and raised in the city myself, O'Hara, and I'll tell ya, this ain't Chicago. But it has its moments, you know? Small town. People know people. Sometimes reminds me of the neighborhood." He raised an eyebrow and opened his palm, the regional gesture for *your turn*.

"Grew up in Longwood." The far south side neighborhood I hadn't seen in years.

"Then you know what I'm talking about. Neighbors help each other out."

Translation: the kid Gatt wanted me to train was a favor. Payback.

The best way to think of a Chicago neighborhood is like a clan designation. Clans are all about relationships and alliances. Favors are the currency most often traded. *I might know somebody; I'll make a call* is Chicagoan for money in the bank. Who you can call is the last best measure of the good life, whether you need a driveway plowed, a ticket fixed or a special-order birthday cake from a really good German bakery.

Out on the East Coast, it's all about the pedigree. On the West Coast, it's only about the pay stub. Here on the Third Coast, it's the clan pact.

From the look on Gatt's face, the only way I was getting this job was if I agreed to train his kid.

Settling deeper into the chair, the faux leather protested with the kind of rude noises my pants would never dream of making. "First things first, Richard. Let's hear what you've got."

Exactly what the man was hoping I'd say. "Network's launching a new magazine show, half-hour format. It's a late-season fill but they'll go sixteen weeks if it gets any kind of numbers. Most of it'll come to us in the can. They're leaving a hole for each market to drop in a local story."

"How long?"

"We get four to six minutes," Gatt said.

I nodded. Six minutes was a hell of a lot of network time. "What's the time slot?"

"Pre-prime or first half hour. They want to see if we can pick up viewers drifting from the news. You'll produce one story a week. Schmooze the network crap as necessary." Gatt spun the scenario without fuss. "Deliver the story to engineering before we pick up the satellite feed and that's it. You don't even have to cut me promos. Those assholes in promotion need to stay busy, or they start bitching about what kind of doughnuts they're getting free every morning."

Free? Any money bet, most of those people didn't clear 30K a year for the privilege of working here at the crap-end of the business.

"What's the angle?" I tried to sound like it didn't matter. Like I hadn't spent the last ten years building a reputation. "What kind of stories they looking for?"

"Crime, sex, local movie stars. Whatever you get that captures a 'Midwest sensibility.'" He put little air quotes around the words. "New York will help set you up."

"The 'Midwest sensibility' on crime, sex and movie stars?"

He shrugged, *what can you do?*

Sound effect: *Ker-flush*. That would be my reputation going down the throne in the name of health benefits and geographic stability.

I smiled.

There aren't a handful of women in this world who make a living freelancing in international crisis scenes. It took me years to earn the respect that would buy me access. Years before I got the chance to take the picture people remember, be the one that shouts, *Look at this! Do something!*

And one phone call is all it took to send it down the tubes.

"But—" Gatt raised a finger in the air. "I don't care how many New York big-shits you get to blow smoke up my ass, O'Hara. You want this job? Train my new guy. He can camera for you. Drive the truck. Whatever."

"How 'new' is this guy?"

Gatt made a show of adding another pair of sugar packets to his coffee mug. "First job. Got his card last month."

"Just got his union card?" I almost laughed. "A college newbie who doesn't know an f-stop from— No way. That's not going to work."

The man flopped backward in his chair. He was so short it made him harder to see behind the cluttered landscape of his desk—three years of flip-page calendars, a dozen remotes for the monitors behind me, piles of color-coded files, a tower of old black tape boxes and a phone that could double as a NASA console.

"Let's be honest, O'Hara." He spread his hands. A classic how-bad-do-you-need-it move. "I'm willing to offer you a nice predictable gig, but I don't want the station left high and dry if, or should I say *when,* you decide to blow."

He had a point. "I'd have to meet this kid first."

"Sure you do." Gatt hit a button on his phone. Nothing happened. He jabbed at a few more, grumbled a few expletives in the back of his throat, then stood up, which didn't really make a lot of difference to my overall view.

"Barbara! What the hell is going on here?" he shouted in the direction of the door. "Barb's my assistant. My absolute right hand. Make her happy, she'll take care of you. Make her unhappy, everybody suffers. Barbara! Damn it, I'll be right back." He walked as far as his office door, flung it wide and shouted, "Barbara!" at the top of his lungs.

I could see from where I was sitting, there was no Barbara at the nearby desk. Gatt disappeared through a side door to the WWST reception area, a time capsule of early '80s—retro with a touch of grunge. Dark paneling and mirror tiles on the walls, olive-colored carpet with a plastic runner, and orange burlap upholstery on the lobby chairs. A stunning first impression.

The nasal drone of the receptionist drifted this way.

"I don't care if her entire family has Ebola. You promised me coverage from nine 'til five, Monday through Friday. Either you get someone in here to answer my phones or I tell Mr. Gatt we're doing an *ex-pose-ay* on a certain local weasel who runs a temp agency."

It was a voice you didn't forget. On the way in, the woman had looked me up and down and assumed I was a courier. Didn't care for the biker boots or the leather pants. The boots might be a little butch, but the pants were my mother's finest Gold Coast Goddess knockoff. What's not to like?

"Barbara," Gatt whined. "What the hell are you doing at reception?"

"What does it look like I'm doing? And I will tell you right now, Richard, I go on break at ten. I don't care if this whole switchboard crashes."

"Where's Katie?" he asked.

"Schmed's got her unpacking boxes."

Gatt grumbled something I couldn't hear. "Leave it. Go find the boy. Please," he added with some effort.

"You don't pay me enough for this, Richard," she threatened. "I am serious."

He came back into the office rubbing the top of his shiny head. "Okay. Ainsley's on the way."

"Ainsley? Are you shittin' me?"

"No, Ms. O'Hara, I am not 'shitting' you." He plopped

back into his chair and answered deadpan, "It happens to be an old family name. Ainsley Prescott is my sister's kid, so I'd appreciate you keeping it clean around him."

"Your sister's kid?" My mouth stayed open. Possibly from the foot I'd inserted there.

Maybe it's the same everywhere, but the majority of men in the television business seemed to have only recently evolved from the single-cell organism. Behind the scenes, we've got the engineer geeks who think it high-end comedy to splice beaver shots into color bar preroll, and behind the closed doors upstairs we've got skanky VP executives waving their standing invitation to lunch. Talk about something that'll put a girl off her feed.

You learn to cope or you get out. Harassment is CDB—cost of doing business—if you're a female in Television Land. A little garbage mouth helps. I learned early how to do the boy patter, what would help me pass and what wouldn't. Most of the women I know in this business cuss like soldiers, skim the sports pages enough to blend and would personally scoop out their eyeballs with plastic spoons before they shed tears in public.

What was Gatt expecting me to teach this kid?

A quick knock was followed by a bright blond head around the door. "Hello?"

"Come on in, buddy." Gatt took a swallow of his candied coffee and waved.

Welcome, Ainsley Prescott—poster child for the Aryan nation, all flaxen haired and sweet smelling. He flashed me a mouthful of sparkling teeth and popped out his hand to shake.

I turned back to Uncle Gatt. "I don't work with stand-ups."

The kid's perfect smile down-shifted from eager to encouraging. The offer of his hand was not retracted.

"Ainsley's not talent," Gatt assured me. "He wants to camera."

"I want to *produce*," he corrected and pumped up the output on his Kegel-watt grin. "But I'm willing to start with camera."

"Sure you are." I forced myself to smile back and take his hand.

Nearly six-foot in my boots, I'm tall as the average American man and could probably bench-press him too, if he'd stick around long enough. I usually get a pretty good feel for a guy by eyeballing him in the clinch and watching for flinch.

Ainsley didn't flinch. He tipped his head nearer my ear and in a private voice added, "Cool pants."

Gatt beamed, the picture of a satisfied matchmaker. "Look, Ms. O'Hara, you want this job, Ainsley gives the tour, shows you to the truck and you two go get to work. Our first feed is next Wednesday. So there's—"

"—less than a week to produce the story." Typical.

"That's right." Gatt started making himself busy sorting his stack of phone messages. I was being dismissed. He had me and knew it. "You don't want the job, say so now. I got a conference call in five minutes."

I looked the kid over again. He wore razor-pleat khakis and a white button-down shirt so squeaky clean-cut it hurt my teeth. Most camera jocks lumbered around in size double XL athletic wear. Ainsley barely topped six feet, had the beanpole build of a young man who hadn't fully grown into his feet and the smooth blue-eyed complexion of the perennial ingénue. How was he going to handle fifty pounds of camera equipment at a jog?

Ainsley's head flipped back and forth between Gatt and me, looking for one of us to say something. His smile faded on a sigh of resignation. He stuffed his hands in his pockets, elbows locked, exactly the way my eight-year-old niece, Jenny, does when she's worried.

What the hell. I'd made a career of specializing in disasters.

"All right. I'm in." I accepted Gatt's deal with a grim nod.

Gatt looked relieved. "Great. You're hired. I'll get Barbara going on the paperwork. You have a look around. Make some calls. Like I said, we need something in the can by next Wednesday."

Looking at Ainsley, all I could think was I'd have to change my damn hair color. Side by side, we'd look like the freaking Bobbsey twins.

"Awesome," Ainsley said. The smile was back.

"Go show her around, buddy." Gatt winked. The boy's charm wasn't lost on the uncle. "O'Hara, I'll set you up with the GM for a meet-and-greet later, and get your offer finalized today."

"Anybody pitched you a story idea for this week?" I asked.

"Nope. Network's got some ideas. You'll want to call them first. Reminds me—I logged a weird call this morning, right before you came in. Out west somewhere, Amish land. People love those Amish-in-trouble stories. Why don't you go check it out?"

"Amish? There are Amish people out here?" I tried

not to sound panicky. "I thought they only lived in remote rural areas."

Gatt's cockeyed glare begged the question, *what's your point?* "Get going, you two. I got work to do."

11:41:12 a.m.

Hanging around the office waiting for Network to call back and pitch me a "crime, sex or movie star" item did not sound like a good plan to me. Seeing Ainsley the Wonder Boy in action might be a good idea before a real shoot landed on us.

It didn't take long to pin down the necessary details. Ainsley was happy to lead the way. "Our Amish community isn't really that nearby," he assured me. "It's actually way out to the edge of the county, at least a half-hour drive west and south."

"A half hour?" I repeated, trying to adjust to the thought that I now lived closer to an Amish settlement than the city. It took an hour to get into downtown from out here, when the traffic didn't suck. "That far?"

"Few miles past the Wal-Mart. But there's a Mennonite church right over in Lombard if you're looking for something closer. You want to see the remote truck first? It's pretty sweet." Ainsley pointed me up the hall. "I knew this one Amish guy who got special permission to go to my high school. He was there a year. Had to ride a bus for an hour and thought it was the greatest. Hard to believe, huh?"

We turned a corner and walked past the cubical shantytown that housed sales, accounting and the promotions departments. Ainsley offered a *good morning!* to every person we passed, along with a quick introduction.

Maneuvering our way through the building, the kid pointed out the station's highlights. "Through here's the kitchen…doughnuts…pop machines…oh, and the bulletin board where we keep the take-out menus."

"College boys are walking stomachs."

"No way," he told me. "I'm no college boy. I'm done with school."

"Really? Where'd you go?" There were a couple of good schools nearby. A credential I could trust would be nice.

"Pretty much everywhere." His confession melted out, sticky and sweet. "I, um, had a little trouble in school."

"You flunk?"

"Not exactly." The words stretched twice their usual length, long enough to include a whole range of possible mischief. "Got kicked out. Twice."

"Twice." I nodded. "That takes some effort."

"Yeah." He didn't seem too upset about it. "Nothing for you to worry about though. I finished all the core courses in broadcasting and camera. I'm fully trained."

"Sure you are."

Freelancing a new job, I usually feel excited, ready to dig in, ready to work. It was different to be filled with thoughts of doom.

Ainsley, on the other hand, could not believe his luck. Taking out the remote truck on our first day. He scored points for loading the cameras with the proper awe. The remote "truck" was technically a van, with a decent bank of machines inside—playback, switcher, monitors. Some of the places I've worked would have considered it a state-of-the-art editing bay. He was right, it was sweet.

"Looks good. Let's get going, College." I slammed the

rear doors after a quick inspection and climbed in beside him on the passenger side. "Stop in the front lot on the way out, would you? I need to grab my cameras."

I always carry both still and video camera equipment to a shoot. I started as a photographer, which is unusual these days. I never set out to be on-screen talent. I prefer to let the pictures tell the story. Sometimes on location, I can get straight photos where I can't get tape. With a splice of quick-cut, pan-tilt, I'll incorporate the photos into the final story. It's a distinctive look, one of my signatures.

"If the Amish thing doesn't heat up, you can show me around town. But I do need to be back at the station by say, two-fifty this afternoon. You know where we're going, right?"

"Sure. I've lived in Dupage County my whole life," Ainsley admitted without a trace of embarrassment. "Wow. Is that your motorcycle?"

"Yeah."

"How old is that thing?"

"Older than me," I answered flatly. "Older than television."

"No way," he whispered reverently.

"Watch it, kid." Peg had been my grandfather's, before she was my father's, before she was mine. I pulled my camera gear out of the saddlebags and gave her a pat goodbye.

Peg's always my first choice of transportation. In the city, she was fairly practical—what with my frequent travel schedule and her fabulous parking profile. But I haven't had many chances to take her out on the road lately. Practical transport has been redefined for me.

"Where'd you get it?"

"My bike is not an *it*. My bike is a *she*." I tossed my gear into the truck. "Her name is Peg."

"Oh. Sorry." Boy didn't stay down long. "How'd you and Peg meet?"

"Grandpa O'Hara worked at the Chicago Schwinn factory back in the old days."

"The bike company?"

"They made motorcycles back in the '20s and '30s. Fastest motorcycles in the world—including the Excelsior Henderson Super X." I waved a hand of introduction. "Back in those days, boys named O'Hara needed to travel fast."

"Why?"

I frowned. "Gangs. Chicago in the '20s? The mob was Irish."

"Oh, right." That got a nod and a furtive glance as he compared me to his mental picture of an Irish mobster's granddaughter. "Mind if I drive?"

Was he razzing me? "Knock yourself out, College Boy."

"Cool," he replied.

No sooner were seat belts fastened than he gunned the van across three lanes of divided traffic into the left lane.

My hand welded itself to the oh-shit bar above my door. When the truck settled into a straightaway, I used my free hand to secure the camera on my lap. "Network usually hires me a driver. Someone who can translate and handle a weapon."

"A weapon?" he scoffed.

"Mostly small arms, though one guy preferred the Uzi. Whenever I traveled with him, I didn't have to worry about a bodyguard."

I made a show of giving him the once-over and nodded a tentative approval. Honestly? Most of my employers were too cheap to hire a driver. And if I needed a translator, I had to pay him out of my per diem. But the boy and I were bonding; he didn't need to know that.

"You're a lightweight but I'll bet you could keep somebody occupied long enough for me to get into the truck and call for back up, right?" I gave him a friendly shot to the arm. "You study martial arts or anything?"

His eyes jumped sideways. He rubbed his shoulder where I hit him. "Uh, no."

"We'll have to stay out of trouble then, won't we?" I flashed my best buddy smile.

Given something else to think about, his driving mellowed considerably. I pried my hand from the grab bar and dug around behind the seat for my camera bag.

The light was beautiful. I wanted to shoot a few prints to play with later. I always carry a couple of bodies in my camera bag, both digital and print. Old school.

Approaching the entrance to the highway, we stopped at an intersection that presented exactly the same kind of reality shift you get on a Hollywood back lot. Behind us lay a long procession of strip malls—to the right sat a Wal-Mart, to the left a Home Depot. Beyond the shadow of the highway overpass lay fields of feathery yellow grass on one side of the road and a farmhouse with an honest-to-god rusty red barn on the other. I felt as if I was looking through a time machine at the view of before and after.

"What are they growing over there?"

"Where?" Ainsley made a quick check out the window. "What?"

"The yellow stuff over there. In the field."

"Are you kidding?" He checked my face. "That's hay."

"Oh." I tried to explain. "I never saw it growing. All together like that. It's pretty."

I made myself busy testing my equipment in the silence that followed. There was half a roll left in the camera. It didn't take long to check my lenses, so I dug out my notebook to brainstorm a few story ideas. No storms came to me; all was dry. Very dry.

"Done much location work?" I asked after a few more miles of silence.

"A little cable stuff. Uncle Rich, uh, you know—Gatt—he helped me get some freelance work last summer, so I could get my union card. The station hired me about three months ago." He did some very elaborate mirror checking, his face turned away.

Not a shock to me. The entertainment industry is just as incestuous as it's ever been—theater, vaudeville, movies, television—it ran in families like eye color and a tendency toward mental illness. Shakespeare had probably had two uncles and a chorus of cousins on the payroll. As long as the boy did his job, it didn't matter to me.

We traveled straight west on the interstate, and then a relatively short hop south through stubbled farmland. Once we hit the exit, Ainsley got behind a state police cruiser with its lights flashing and ended up following him the rest of the way. It surprised me PD was still en route.

A crowd of assorted rescue vehicles appeared beyond a rise. Everybody's lights were flashing like a cheap Christmas display. Police and a few bureaucrats were milling around the edge of a grassy field. Fire department was there, as well. They'd driven a ladder truck as close as the pavement could get them to the base of a huge spreading oak. Farther away, the fenced field, the white barn and simple farmhouse made a perfect country backdrop.

"Pull over, College." I rolled down my window, switched to my longest-range telephoto lens and shot the rest of my print film as the van rolled to a stop. I prefer to shoot both print and digital when I have both cameras handy. I trained on print. Digital cameras try to do the thinking for me. It's annoying. "You ever worked with police on a shoot before?"

"No."

With my finger on the camera's trigger, I rattled off some basics. "When we get out of the truck, go ahead and pull a camera box, but stay behind me. Wear your credentials on your shirt. Keep your ears open and your mouth shut. Don't try to set up the camera until I say it's a go—got it?"

"Got it." He didn't sound happy about it. "Can you see any better with that lens?"

The tree must have blocked his view from the driver's seat. It's hard to miss a body with a crowd of public servants standing around gaping. The FD couldn't have been more than twenty or thirty minutes ahead of us to the scene. I caught the shot of the dead man being lowered into the arms of a firefighter.

"Hanging." My voice had gone flat. The working voice. The voice I use to face the world. My lousy luck was running true. I hate suicides.

"What?" Ainsley asked, that long, slow Midwest version of *huh?*

"The dead guy was swinging from that big oak

tree. Look at all these guys. Half the public servants of the county must be out here. Fire, EMT, sheriff—" I dropped the camera to peek over at my college boy. "Did you just say 'Eeeuuu'?"

His pretty face was crunched up, one part *uh-oh,* and two parts *yuck.*

There's something else I forget. In these Great United States, plenty of people get all the way to full grown without ever seeing death any closer than roadkill from the car window.

"Maybe you better wait in the truck."

"No way." He worked to smooth out his expression. "I'm fine."

I looked into those clear blue eyes and felt myself caught between two minds. Part of me wanted to toughen him up—get him out there and force him to meet reality. Part of me didn't want to be the one that popped his corpse-cherry. I'd seen enough of the world to know innocence had a value that was always underrated.

"It's your choice. No problem if you want to wait." I made my voice as neutral as possible while rewinding and reloading. The film can got stuffed deep in my front pocket, out of sight. Old habit—I always hide exposed film. I switched to digital to give me electronic options—easy translation to the web and satellite feed.

"I want to go with you." Ainsley nodded as he spoke, convincing himself.

He didn't use the high-volt smile this time and I liked him better for it.

"Come on then. Follow me."

We hopped a fence and strolled across the field. Broken rows of corn bristled all around us. The unfortunate oak was perched on the far side of a small rise. As my sight line improved, the corn stretched toward the horizon, creating the illusion of perspective. Except for the dead guy, it was a pretty view.

With the fire truck unable to get close enough to the tree, the guys had carried a regular extension ladder over to lean against the limb where the rope was tied. The fireman I'd photographed remained at ground zero, hunched over the body. The fireman at the top of the ladder was busy slicing through the last of the rope with a small hacksaw. From his higher vantage point, he was the first to see Ainsley and me approach the edge of the action. The man on the ladder shouted to the men below. The guys beside the body stood up and stared.

I'm not sure why, but I suddenly felt protective of my camera and my college boy. I shifted the strap to hide the lens in the crook of my arm.

"Stick close, kid. These guys aren't too happy to see us."

12:53:22 p.m.

Shit. Shit. Shit. What was Maddy O'Hara doing here?

There was a shit smell coming from everywhere: the farm downwind, the body on the ground and the men jockeying around it for a look.

"Watch it!"

"On three. Up!"

It took four men to lift the body and set it on top of the bag. The head lolled toward the shoulder at a nasty angle. The guy had known his knots; knew just where to place it so the fall would snap his neck.

"Camera Press over there," somebody whispered.

"No shit," he said. "Get me the cardiac monitor. We should record *asystole* before we bag him."

"Not here." The sheriff stepped in, all puckered up because the press was on site. "I want this body in the ambulance and en route—now."

"Yes, sir. I'm on it."

"Then quit staring at that woman. *Move.*"

The sheriff's men weren't happy to see us either. A big bouncer type who stood guarding the perimeter backed us off before I even had a chance to make our case. We hung out for a few minutes trying to get someone to talk to us without any luck.

"What now?" Ainsley asked as we retreated to the roadside.

"We're on a bear hunt, College." I scanned the perimeter and started toward the shrub line. "Can't go through 'em. Can't go over 'em. Got to go around 'em."

I walked along the road to where the fence line ended, then turned up a small side road that seemed to follow the boundary of the property.

Ainsley matched my pace, breathing heavily with the camera case in tow. "Where are we going?"

"Don't know. I'm looking."

Not far from the turn, I cut back following a line of scraggly shrubs and small trees up a slight incline toward the farmhouse we had seen from the road. Every so often I popped through the bushes and held up my camera to check for a decent line of sight.

The college boy threw questions at my back the entire way. "Do you think we're trespassing? What if someone lives here? Is this legal?"

"I don't know," I answered. "Follow me."

"Wish you'd stop saying that."

Near the crest of a small rise, through the heavy barberry branches, I found a spot where the perspective on the action by the tree was perfect. Firefighters and police were milling around. The ladder was coming down. Some of the men were fascinated by a spill of cardboard boxes and paper where the body dropped.

"Okay, College Boy, this is it. Let's get a handheld shot. We're too far away for anything but the in-camera mic, but record it anyway. We may want to use the ambient sound—wind, leaves rustling, birds. See if you can get tight enough for a couple steady, close-up head shots of these guys. I want facial expression if you can get it."

Ainsley set the camera case down with a thud. His face glowed with a faint sheen of sweat from the effort of getting it there. He took a few minutes to organize himself. We'd prepped in the van, so it didn't take long. Once he had the camera rolling, I stepped back to give him some room. Behind me, I heard the rustle-crack of a scramble in the hedge, the sound of an animal trying to escape.

With two hands, I spread the leafy whippets of overgrown barberry. My camera bumped against my chest, swinging heavily from the neck strap. It took a second for my eyes to adjust.

At first, all I saw was her face and her fear. The white of the young woman's skin reflected light where her dark clothes disappeared into the shadow. Bits of contrast jumped out at me. She was wearing a hat, a black Amish bonnet to be exact, but she had a cell phone pressed to her ear.

"What the hell is going on here?" a man's voice rose behind me.

I admit I jumped. The branches I'd been holding snapped back into place as I spun around. Ainsley jumped, too, but he kept the camera up and running. The guy shouting was obviously The Man. From what

I could see, he was the only one wearing a decent suit and all the men around the tree stopped everything to watch.

"I thought I said *no* cameras!"

"The officer told us to stay as far back as the road, but no one said anything about no cameras." I smiled. Behind me, there was absolute silence in the bush. "I'm Maddy O'Hara, WWST. You're the man in charge, I presume?"

He was a fairly large guy, enough so I'd notice. Not a whole lot older than me. Sandy-dark hair with a thread or two of silver, maybe. Good sharp bones beneath the cheek and brow. He'd be a dream to photograph monochrome, except you'd lose the eye color—the pale green of a cloudy agate.

"Give me the camera," he said to Ainsley, ignoring me in the extreme.

"I'm sorry, sir," I pressed. "I didn't get your name."

"*Sheriff* Curzon."

Boy, I hadn't cheesed-off a local public servant this fast in years. Good to know I hadn't lost my touch.

Ainsley appeared mesmerized. He lowered the camera off his shoulder and shot me a quick, panicked look.

"It's all right," I soothed with a snicker. "You don't have to give him anything."

While I was busy being amused at the sheriff's bravado, Curzon reached over and grabbed the television camera, scanned the side quickly and pressed eject. He plucked the card right out of its slot. Ainsley stood there, face frozen.

"I am the man in charge here," Curzon announced.

"And I said, *no cameras.*" He looked at me and the 35 mm hanging from my neck.

I wrapped a hand around my Nikon lens and dared him to try.

He jabbed the little black rectangle of digital recording at me like a pointed finger. "Give me that card or I will arrest you. You can tell your story to the judge—tomorrow morning."

It felt like being clocked upside the head. Six months ago, I'd have gone to jail for my card with no hesitation.

My fingers opened the camera and handed him the memory card.

Of course, the fact that I had a roll of exposed 35 mm tucked in my pocket made it a little easier. "We heard there might be a story worth covering here, Sheriff."

"I don't think so, Ms. O'Hara. A man's dead. Sad, but nothing important enough to rate the television news."

I couldn't help it. This time I did laugh.

"Something funny about that?"

I was thinking, *then why bother?* But I said, "Just between you and me, Sheriff, around here, it's news when somebody's dog dies."

"Not from around here, are you?" he deadpanned. Was that a sense of humor? It didn't last. "There's nothing to see here, Ms. O'Hara. My office will provide a written statement to the press as soon as possible."

"Ah." I nodded, all understanding. "And when do you think that might be?"

"Couldn't say."

"Look, I'm just trying to do my job, Sheriff. Performing a public service, you know?"

His gaze dropped abruptly, taking in my leather pants.

He hesitated for half a second before he added, "Funny. That's what they used to say about prostitution."

I flashed the man a smile and winked. "And I'll bet people like you still do, *Sheriff.*"

Ainsley's eyes popped and he did a panic check— look left, look right, look down.

Now I'll admit I was overdressed for fieldwork. Compared to the girl in the bushes in the long dress and hat, I was looking more Saturday night on Rush Street than Monday morning on Michigan Avenue. But no way did Sheriff Curzon, in his fine suit, hold to an Amish dress code standard. He was trying to annoy me.

Oh, there was definitely something going on around here.

"What's in the bushes?" Curzon asked, stone-faced and heavy on the green-eyed death glare.

"What?" I asked him back.

"You had your head in the bushes. You drop something?"

"No." I felt the silent shadow-presence of the girl behind me. A little louder I answered, "No. Thought I heard a rabbit or something." I crossed my arms over my chest and shrugged. "You know us city girls, we'll do anything for a glimpse of wildlife."

He wasn't wholly convinced, but one of the other men down near the tree called out. "Time to go," Curzon announced.

"See you." I waved.

I caught the flavor of a grin quickly suppressed before he grabbed Ainsley's silver camera case with one hand and the boy's elbow with the other.

"Walk," Curzon ordered Ainsley.

It irritated me he never bothered to look back and see if I followed.

Curzon did not lead us into the area near the action; he edged the crowd and handed us off to a couple of junior dogs whose job was to shoo us back to our truck. As we crossed the road, I noticed a skinny guy in worn corduroy pants ahead of us. He stumbled toward an old Civic, head bent over a spiral notepad, pen flashing. A comrade in arms.

"Hey!" I jogged after him.

Ainsley followed slightly behind, camera case clunking with his long-legged strides.

"Excuse me?" I called. "You with the *Trib?*"

Mr. Skinny Guy looked back our way, his shoulders hunched. Beat reporters were kind of like B-movie undead; they always looked uncomfortable in the bright light of day.

"What?"

I jerked my thumb toward the truck and held out a hand. "I'm Maddy O'Hara, special assignment to WWST. We heard there was something going on here, but the cops won't let us near the place. Did you get anything?"

"Melton Shotter. I'm with the local daily—the *Clarion.*" He seemed a little disconcerted by my directness. "Did you say Maddy O'Hara?"

"In the flesh."

"I've heard of you." He shook his head in a wonders-never-cease kind of way.

Although Average Joes wouldn't know me from Adam, there were plenty of papers that ran my photos on occasion. Ainsley seemed to get a little thrill off my sort-of celebrity status.

"There wasn't much to get." Melton shrugged. "Suicide. What kind of story would WWST be doing?"

"Local human interest." I glanced across the road at the broken stalks of a stripped cornfield. "But you probably get a lot of suicides out here."

"There's definitely more to it—" He sounded like a kid with a secret. All I had to do was be patient. Reporters live to tell secrets. "But I couldn't get any kind of ID on the guy. They'll never let me run the story without more detail."

"What did you see?"

"The body was covered by the time I got close. Everybody had gathered round in a huddle." He leaned toward me and his voice dropped. "I did see porno mags on the ground. Spread out all over the place, like the guy'd been reading them before he jumped."

"No way."

"I kid you not."

"What?" Ainsley ambled into the conversation in confusion.

"Maybe it wasn't suicide." I felt that prickly tingle of discovery, the journalist's drug. "Ever heard of autoerotic asphyxiation?"

The reporter snapped his fingers and flapped his notebook open. "That's what I missed! I heard the sheriff mumble something before they chased me off."

"Really?" I grinned back at the scene of the action. "Now why would Sheriff Curzon tell us there was no story here? I may be from out of town, but I'd say when an Amish—"

"I don't think he could be Amish," Ainsley corrected me. "Maybe Mennonite—"

"Whatever. When a man of serious religious conviction offs himself publicly, in more ways than one, that's news."

Ainsley's face scrunched again—grossed out, sure, but also trying not to laugh.

Of course, when a sheriff steals your pictures, that's a pretty good indicator as well.

"Why do you think he was Amish?" Melton asked.

"The clothes." I pictured the girl in the bush wearing that dark bonnet, even before I thought of the man from the tree.

"She got some pictures with a long lens before we got out of the van," Ainsley clarified. "But that guy couldn't have been Amish. He looked too old to shave, and I heard one of the cops say the Honda over there must be his. Amish don't own cars."

"No cars at all?" I asked.

"Too old to shave?" Melton said, at the same time.

"Grown men wear beards," Ainsley told him. "It's a sign of maturity."

We experienced one of those awkward pauses in which I got caught staring at Ainsley's baby-smooth cheek.

"About those pictures?" Melton jumped in. "Could I get a look at those? The paper'd pay, of course. They'd run the story if I had a picture. Nothing too gruesome, though."

I thought about it for a minute, glancing back toward Sheriff Curzon. I didn't have a lot of time here. Auto-erotic asphyxiation was the kind of pseudoserious sex topic they would love at Network, a definite ratings grabber. The sleaze factor was high, but if I scored on ratings I'd definitely stay employed. Compromises like that guaranteed I'd be dining on antacids and acetaminophen for the foreseeable future. Yum, yum.

There was certainly more to this than a simple suicide. I could feel it, the way I'd felt the girl behind me in the bushes.

What was she doing there?

I needed to flush this story out into the open where it was fair game. It's not like my story would be competing with nightly news for a scoop. By releasing one of my photos to Melton, I could make the story public and redirect Curzon's fire toward the print media. Without heating up attention for the story, the sheriff would continue to stonewall me and chances were good I'd end up stuck doing something on the network's latest local promotional tie-in.

Time to take a gamble.

"I might be able to help you out with a photo, Melton. Let me take a look at what I've got. What's your deadline?"

"Eight o'clock." Melton passed me a card.

All of a sudden, I thought to look at my watch. It was past two already. "Damn. How long will it take to get back to the station?" I asked Ainsley.

"As long as it took us to get here, I guess."

Double that damn. I'd never get back to the station for my bike and home again by three o'clock. "We need to go."

"Back to the station?"

"No. I need you to take me straight…to my appointment."

Maddy O'Hara was going to be a problem.

"This is township ambulance number five, currently en route with a twenty-eight-year-old male, apparent suicide."

"This is County E.R. Can you repeat?"

He twisted the cell phone away from his mouth and shouted to the man driving the ambulance. "Siren? Can't hear a fucking thing back here."

The sheriff had sent a car to escort them to the hospital. With both vehicles blaring full lights and sirens, even the dead couldn't hear himself think.

What was she doing there?

He flipped the blanket back and tugged the zipper down. Some genius had decided to start making body bags white instead of black lately, because everybody knew what a black bag meant. Like it made a difference—black or white. What nobody could change was the sound of that big, thick zipper sealing everything up inside. Forever.

He peeled open the sides of the bag and forced himself to think in the impersonal terms of work. "Male patient...mottled skin...obvious lividity." Painting the picture for the dispatcher in the E.R. gave him time to reach down inside, open the rough, buttonless shirt and attach the cardiac monitor electrodes.

"Lead one—flatline."

Had she gotten a call, too?

"Lead two—flatline."

"Roger. Stand by," the dispatcher said.

The only personal effects the sheriff's team had

located on the scene were those fucking magazines. It was hard not to hit something just thinking about it.

There had to be a cell phone. He held his phone cocked against his shoulder, pulled off the electrodes with one hand and snaked the other hand down into the bag, along the body. It was cold already. There were damp patches where fluids had started to settle. He felt the change of texture and temperature through the thin casing of latex over his hands.

Nothing.

The phone wasn't the only thing missing that could get him into trouble.

"Everything all right back there?" his driver called out.

"Fine."

He had to find the sample bag. Everyone was watching him now. Thinking the worst. No matter how hard he tried to explain, to fix things, it never seemed to be enough. Nothing else could go wrong now or more people would get hurt.

She didn't know what she was getting into. He was not going to let her fuck everything up now.

The face lying before him wore a contorted grimace of pain and bruising.

He wasn't supposed to touch the body but he couldn't stop himself. He pounded down with both fists, hard, center of the chest, right over that guilty heart.

What did you do? What did you do, you dumb-ass farm boy?

"Hey! Whoa, what's going on back there? We're one minute away, man. Captain's going to be at the other end. Don't freak on me now."

"Okay. I'm okay."

There was no peace in death on that face. Only pain. And hatred.

Gently, he laid his hands on the face. He massaged the mouth, the jaw, the brow. He tipped the head and smoothed the expression.

At last, the face appeared peaceful.

He would do whatever he had to do to fix it, to smooth it over.

Everything was going to be fine. Just fine.

He zipped the bag shut slowly, so there was almost no sound at all.

It took forty-two minutes for Ainsley to drive me to the house that once belonged to my sister, Angelina O'Hara.

Jenny was waiting, sitting on the doorstep hunched by the bulk of her backpack, fiddling intently with her shoe. She's the kind of kid who looks like she's made of hollow straws and toothpicks, all held together by wire bread ties. Everything about her was either stiff or sharp.

I swear, we couldn't have been more than twelve, thirteen minutes late, at most.

"This is where you live?" Ainsley asked.

"Yeah." A squat, yellow-brick ranch house was not my idea of heaven either.

"Who's that?" Ainsley asked.

I had a sudden flash of the Boy Wonder reporting back to Uncle Rich all the details of my life story. Definitely not. Not before I signed the paperwork anyway.

I popped the van door open but didn't get out. "You're mighty curious, aren't you? Let's add research to your job description. Go back to the station and make some calls. See if you can find out why Sheriff Curzon hates us. I'd guess he's worked with the press before. See what you can find out. Then call the police station just before five. If they still won't ID the body, get a name on who owns the property where it was found. We ought to try to set up an interview first thing tomorrow. Early light would be nice. Call me at home later so we can set a schedule, but plan on picking me up around seven-A. You got my cell number?"

"Yeah. I got it." He sounded distracted. Or maybe it was pissed. Sensitive boy. Wasn't like I ordered him to pick up my dry cleaning.

"Oh, one more thing. Push my bike into the dock, would you? Night air isn't good for Peg." I slammed the door behind me. "See ya." I followed the van as it backed down the driveway, walking all the way out to the road so I could empty the mailbox.

Jenny never picked up the mail; Jenny never went near the road.

Three months ago her single mother—my only sister—was the hit part of a hit-and-run. She died.

Fucking boondocks.

I got the call between flights on my way to a natural disaster in Mexico—earthquake? Killer bees? Hell, I don't even remember. I got off one plane and onto another, and just that fast, the life I had was over. My new life consisted of a thirty-year-old ranch house, a ten-year-old Subaru station wagon and an eight-year-old niece. Jenny.

The school counselor told me it'd be a big mistake to move her right now. Said Jenny needed stability. Same house, same school, same friends. So, here I am in the no-man's land of the Chicago 'burbs. Harbor of White Flight. Republican stronghold. Protestant heaven. Journalist hell.

News flash: Jenny wasn't all that happy with me either.

I crouched down next to her on the concrete step. "Been sitting here long?"

She shrugged and continued staring at her shoes.

"Sorry I kept you waiting."

No answer. She leaned over and poked the tip of her shoelace into one of the lace holes.

"I got the job. That's why I was late. We don't have to move or anything. For now."

Thank goodness I had enough cash stashed away, I could afford to sit on my ass with her for the summer. Neither of us was in any shape to detail a life plan more complicated than dinner and the TV guide. But I'd told her from the beginning that couldn't last. Besides the money, I needed to work. It kept me in circulation.

It kept me from going insane.

Jenny finally tossed her head at me, *oh?* and her purple plastic barrette unsnapped. A curtain of fine, brown hair, straight as her mother's, drooped in front of her face.

"Guess we should get you a key or something," I offered. "So this doesn't happen again."

"Kids aren't supposed to have keys," she mumbled to her shoe laces. "Kids are supposed to have somebody."

"Right."

Our after-school routine was loosely based on her mother's plan of operation. We ate a snack, watched cartoons together, then she tackled homework while I ran through my weight program. Today, I scrapped routine. I threw the kid a bag of chips and went straight down to my darkroom to work, eager to see how my shots would develop.

I had turned a portion of the basement into a work area as soon as I'd arrived. One small window had to be blocked off, but there was running water and plenty of space to hang prints to dry. I tied lines to plumbing pipes, bought myself some heavy-duty shelves and a shop table at the local hardware store. Boom, I was in business.

Jenny hung around the first time I printed a roll. But she didn't like the smell of the chemicals, which meant I usually had my privacy in the darkroom. Another bonus. Sometimes the hardest thing about coming to live with Jenny was simply having her around all the time.

People are funny. If somebody said go into a damp, smelly basement and sit around for a couple of hours, it'd sound unpleasant to most, but I always felt refreshed after time in the darkroom. There's a certain level of concentration that must be maintained, steps that happen in a certain order, and in the end if you do it right, you get something beautiful.

Some people do yoga. I do photography.

Photographing a death scene is a special challenge. There are very few shots that will play as acceptable for prime time, although the boundaries of acceptable have expanded in the last few years. I got everything through two baths and hung to dry when I heard a knock. The shot with the firefighter was a beauty.

"Come on in." I was hunched over the table, checking a wide shot with a jeweler's loupe. There was a flare showing up in some of the shots that irritated me.

"I'm hungry, Aunt Maddy."

"Oh, right." I pulled myself away from the flare problem and cracked my neck. "What time is it?"

"Almost eight. You missed Scooby-Doo and SpongeBob."

"How many commercials?" I asked.

"Forty-two. Thirty-six promos."

If the kid was going to watch television, she'd better know what she was watching. Whenever she watched regular TV, I made her count. "That's a lot of commercial time."

"Old Navy is having a sale."

"Ah."

Jenny slid in next to me as I hunched over proof sheets searching for flares. She looked up at the drying prints. "What is that?"

I jerked upright and had one of those *whoops! Is this a fuck-up?* moments. The smallest possible answer was, "These are the pictures I took today."

"Is that guy dead?"

"Yeah."

She stepped close enough to the photo that I thought her nose would touch the paper. "Did he kill himself?"

"Yeah, he did." The guy had a rope as thick as my wrist hanging from around his neck; what else could I say?

"Why?" she whispered.

I guess I'd been holding my breath because the first sound I made was a whoosh of air. "I don't know. I guess he was sad." I knew that wasn't right, wasn't enough, so I tried adding, "Very, very sad."

She turned her nose toward me and stared long enough I counted three blinks.

"Hey, Jen, I need to run these downtown to a guy." I tried diversionary tactics. "Wanna get a hot dog for dinner?"

"Chili dog?"

"Sure." I gave her my best happy chuck on the arm, feeling like I'd dodged a bullet. "Be right up—you go grab my bag."

With a snap, I grabbed the picture Jenny had nearly

pressed her nose against. It showed the flare as well, but not in the same spot. I set two prints beside each other and realized the flare wasn't crap on my lens. It was something in the photo, something catching light in the open second-story window of the barn.

Making pictures is a fairly complex operation. A million tiny details, a million choices that contribute to the final product. Most of the choices are things I don't even think about anymore, things happening so fast I don't remember half of what I see. I crouch to shift the horizon. I frame so the picture will fit into a TV screen's rectangle. I put the light behind me.

With the sun slanting in above the van's roof, the lens recorded something my eye had missed—the flare of light on glass in a tiny, double comma. Because I'd spent plenty of time over the last five years taking pictures of soldiers on the job, it happened to be just the sort of flare I'd recognize.

Binoculars.

Somebody had been watching from the barn.

By the time her aunt was asleep, it was really dark everywhere. But Jenny didn't mind.

Lots of other kids were afraid of the dark.

Jenny knew for a fact that Lindsay still slept with a light on, because she'd slept over once last year when they were still friends. That was a long time ago.

Jenny didn't need a night-light anymore. Night wasn't bad. In fact, she liked it.

She stood in her doorway and listened. Her heart was pounding so hard it hurt to swallow.

Before the summer, before everything was different, she'd loved her house: the chair she always sat in to watch TV, the wall where her mom hung her pictures from school, even the bathroom, where the heater vent was right beside the toilet and in the winter it blew warm air on her cold feet when she woke up. Whenever Jenny walked in the door of her house, she always felt right.

Everything was different now. Her chair was lumpy. Aunt Maddy had put her stuff in Jenny's bathroom, like her toothbrush and this thing called a tongue scraper that was double weird and totally gross. Jenny never had time to warm her feet anymore. She had to hurry up, so her aunt could have her turn. The house didn't even smell the same, because her aunt hated the smell of Pine-Sol and bought new cleaner that smelled like oranges and made Jenny sneeze.

Jenny looked up and down. The hall returned nothing but a long, black silence. The pounding in her chest began to pass. Here in the dark, she felt safe. Invisible, she could breathe. She could finally do the thing she most wanted to do, the thing she craved through the whole long, bright day.

She tiptoed up the hall, sticking close to the wall where the floor didn't creak. Outside the guest bedroom where her aunt slept, she stopped again to listen.

Quiet.

Jenny held her breath as she passed the door. Her aunt's bare foot hung off the bed, her face turned away toward the wall. *Your aunt had big shoes to fill,* her mother always said and it was true. Aunt Maddy had big feet. *That's why she's bigger than life.* Jenny wasn't really sure what that meant, until Aunt Maddy came to stay. Her feet weren't the only big part. She was so tall she bumped the light over the couch almost every day. And she had a big voice, too. She yelled in the car at the other drivers, she yelled when she talked on the phone, sometimes she even yelled at the TV. Loud.

The last door in the hall was Mama's. It was closed, as usual.

Jenny slipped in and shut the door behind her.

At last.

With a pillow and lap blanket off the bed, she crossed the last threshold into Mama's big square closet. There was a place deep in the back where she'd cleared away all the shoes, and Mama's long skirts and dresses nearly dragged the floor. Snuggling back against the wall Jenny let the clothes brush against her face, her mother's scent, her mother's softness surrounding her. She closed her eyes, breathing in, in, in.

Mommy, Mommy, Mom-mee.

Sometimes everything didn't feel as bad when you were awake in the dark.

For a while, Jenny worried that Aunt Maddy would

take it all away, all her mama's things in the bedroom. She never did. She just put her suitcases in the guest room and that was that. It was kind of weird, actually. Her aunt had like, no *stuff*. Except the weights and the camera junk in the basement.

Jenny sunk deeper into the pillow and pulled the blanket around her shoulders. It wasn't usually so cold in the closet. Tonight, it felt cold.

She couldn't stop thinking about that picture her aunt had taken. The one with the dead guy.

It was scary. One of those guys looked sort of like somebody she used to know, maybe. It was hard to remember his face though. That was scary, too. Jenny didn't like the idea of forgetting faces.

She needed to get another look. Maybe she could find another picture. A long time ago there was one in her mom's bedroom, but now it was gone. Where could it have gone? Jenny didn't take it and Aunt Maddy never even opened the door to this room.

Jenny pushed her way out of the closet and thought for a minute. Maybe there was another picture somewhere. Her mom always had special ones tucked in her underwear drawer.

Slowly, quietly, Jenny searched.

When she found what she needed, she put everything else back exactly the way it was. For another time…like maybe tomorrow.

The trip up the hall was quick, but heading downstairs, Jenny had to be careful. The stairs were noisy and Aunt Maddy woke up at the least sound. She was a light sleeper. Jenny's mom used to say that people who slept well had no imagination or a very clean conscience, which seemed to explain pretty good about Aunt Maddy.

Some nights Jenny was glad her aunt woke up easily. Not tonight though. She didn't want to talk about this. Aunt Maddy didn't like her very much as it was.

All the grown-ups Jenny knew had gotten weird since the accident. Teachers stared at her. The neighbors pretended like they didn't see her. None of her mom's friends called anymore. Maybe they'd all forgotten her mom, and her. Even the special friend.

Her mom kept a flashlight on top of the fridge in the basement for tornado drills and storms. Jenny had to stand on a plastic box to reach it. Her aunt's photo work was on the table near the washing machine.

Jenny took the picture from her mother's room and laid it next to the ones her aunt had made that day.

Oh, yeah. Oh, yeah.

It was him.

Maybe his luck was changing.

The house was quiet and dark. He almost went inside. But this time he was watching very carefully. He saw the faint light click on and off in Gina's bedroom—a nightlight, or the closet light maybe? A few minutes later, a light popped up in the basement window.

One of the girls must be awake.

Good thing he hadn't gone there. He wouldn't have been breaking the law or anything. He had a key. But there was no sense getting them all excited until he'd had a look.

The right thing to do was wait. Wait and watch.

Sooner or later the house would be empty. Then, he'd go in and see if maybe Maddy O'Hara had found something that belonged to him. Something that might make her hot to play reporter.

Watching was the smart move.

From now on, he'd watch her carefully. And he'd know when she'd gone too far.

*VIDEO: reprint of news color photo tree/ladder/rope
visible. Crowd of men watch as body lowered. (Slow
zoom out)*
Newsprint caption. Super over photo. Roll as crawl:
*"Unidentified man in Amish clothing was found dead
yesterday in a field south of Route 289. Police and fire
department services were brought to the scene by an
anonymous phone caller."*

FRIDAY

7:03:28 a.m.

College Boy arrived on time and raring to go for our
first interview. Unfortunately, Jenny's school wasn't open
at the crack of dawn. Failing to anticipate the intersection of work and family can be fatal in my business.

On the other hand, the survival instinct kicking
in with a vengeance does add a certain edge to the
morning.

"This is my niece, Jenny," I said as we piled into the
truck. "We're taking her with us."

"Hi," Jenny said.

"Hey." He nodded hello and offered his hand to guide
her over a spaghetti pile of cables and stick bags, so she
could strap herself into the spare jump seat. "Wow. You
two are related?"

Jenny hit me with her big-eyed, blank look—the mask
of trouble. She resembles the female side of my family:
smooth brown hair, round dark eyes and the translucent
skin of an Irish elf. Even for a kid, she was small.

Looks-wise, I got my dad's package: the Viking strain
of Celtic blood, tall and broad, plenty of freckles, wild

hair which is politely known as red, but actually closer to orange, when I don't color it—which is never. I'd dyed it fatal-blond right before the job interview. I'm all for irony. Now Ainsley and I looked more like relations than Jenny and I.

"I'm the black sheep of the family," I said. "Let's roll."

Ainsley took a convoluted back route of smaller roads to get us to the site of yesterday's incident and avoid the morning rush hour. We passed fields, farms and for sale signs.

September was a good time to be in Chicago—another two months, we'd all be freezing our asses off. The rising sun cast a perfect yellow light on dead grass and reddened sumac leaves. I opened the window to snap a few pictures and the autumn air rushed me, crisp with the scent of endings and beginnings. The wind helped blow away the last of the dusty, creepy feeling that had followed me home last night. I was on my way to work. Life was good.

Since I was busy hanging my head out the window taking pictures, Ainsley focused on getting Jenny to chat. It didn't take long for the two of them to bond; they were practically peers. As soon as we parked, Ainsley set her up with something to watch in the back of the truck. What he was doing with cartoons in stock, I don't want to know.

It took twenty long minutes to prep for our quickie on-camera interview with Al Lowe, the man whose land had been the site of yesterday's tragedy. The fact that College Boy had managed to find the man and schedule an interview on such short notice was such a pleasant surprise, I didn't bug him about his pace. There were always other things to cover.

"Fill the frame with the subject. Don't try to shoot me. I hate reporters in the story. You've seen the kind of stuff I do, right? We'll cut around my questions and tie everything together with a narrating voice-over. Got that?"

I wanted the black skeleton of the oak tree behind the man being interviewed. It looked different today. More mysterious.

We heard Lowe's truck before we saw him. He went off-road and parked ten feet from where we stood.

"Thanks for coming out to meet us, sir."

I offered my hand as he slammed the door. Lowe was a perfect interview to get us started. He wore jeans, a Cubs jacket that had seen better days and a squared-off bill cap. His face and hands bore the weathered tan of an outdoor work life. Everything about him said farmer—pure, old-fashioned, regular guy. Whatever he had to say, people would believe.

"Beautiful view," I said.

"Yeah," Lowe replied. Midwesterners could pack more meanings into "yeah" than Eskimos had words for snow. This one meant, *sad. What a shame.*

Ainsley fumbled with the tripod behind us, trying to lock down an even footing for the shot I wanted. Not easy. The ground was all torn up by the cars, trucks and men that had been trooping around the day before.

Lowe kept his back to the camera and stared out across fields that came together like a quilt beneath the eternal-blue morning. It wasn't the kind of sky that recorded well on video. The technology could never get the color right.

I stood beside him and gazed unblinking into all that color until vertigo brought me back to earth. The view to the horizon held nothing but dirt and straw and the scalloped border of a tree line. I dug my hands into my pockets and tried for a happy quote. "Reminds me of 'the pleasant land of counterpane.'"

Lowe looked at me, surprised. In a grave, rusty, morning voice he spoke the words,

"I was the giant great and still,
that sits upon the pillow hill,
and sees before him, dale and plain,
the pleasant land of counterpane.

"My dad used to recite that one," he admitted with a bashful crook of his head.

"Mine too," I said. We were having a moment, so I didn't mention that I was full grown before I'd understood the word was *pane,* not *pain.*

"Almost ready," Ainsley said.

Farmer Lowe and I chatted about hay harvest and dairy feed, while the Boy Wonder locked and loaded. By the time we got to bovine hormones, Lowe was at ease; I was on suppressed impatience.

"Ready," Ainsley finally called.

Interviewing is part skill, part talent, part luck of the draw. When it works, you become the glass through which someone else is seen. Sometimes, you blend transparently. Sometimes, you reflect. Sometimes, there's an invisible wall. I ran down the establishing facts with Lowe quickly.

I could feel his resistance before I asked, "Were you the one to find the body?"

"No." Lowe studied his boots. Kicked over a clod of dirt. "The authorities knew before I did. I got a call from a neighbor who'd driven by, saw all the commotion."

"About what time was that?"

"Neighbor called as I was finishing my pancakes."

"Could it have been that neighbor—over there?" I looked across the field, beyond the fence and the line of shrubs even farther back.

The buildings appeared exactly as they were yesterday, the perfect icon of farm, like an illustration from a kid's picture book. The second-story barn window stood open. No sign of binoculars watching.

"Old Mr. Jost? I couldn't say," Lowe mumbled.

Ainsley popped his head around the camera. "Has he even got a phone?"

"There's a booth out back," Lowe answered. To me he said, "The Amish don't allow phones in their homes. It's one of their rules. No wires to the outside world on their homes. They get around it by putting the phone in a separate little building, like a phone booth, that's outside apart from the house."

"An Amish family lives there?" I couldn't help pointing. "In that house?"

"Yeah." Lowe turned away from me and the relentless stare of the camera.

"What about cell phones?" I asked, thinking of the girl in the bush. "No wires on a cell phone. Do they allow those?"

"No. Don't think so." He snorted. "They'd have to charge it somewhere."

"Oh, yeah." I laughed. Joke on me.

"Is that it?" Lowe's reluctance suddenly took a shape I recognized.

Gently I asked, "Did you know the man who died?"

His chin dropped to his chest. There was silence for a good twenty seconds.

"Suppose it'll come out sooner or later... Yeah, I knew him. Damn shame. Seemed to be getting along all right these past few years. Boy's name was Tom. Tom Jost. He was adopted by my neighbor over there—" Lowe jerked his head in the direction of the farmhouse "—years ago. Kid had a hard life and old Jost tried to do right by him. I respected him for that." He half turned his back to the camera, mumbling, "Some hard years for a while there. Teenage stuff mostly, not too bad. But Old Mr. Jost is religious, you know, so he didn't see it that way. Boy left the farm, never came back."

Except to die.

"Why'd he choose this tree?"

No answer.

"Do you know why Tom chose this tree?"

Lowe's whole face tightened and I wished he'd have been facing the camera, instead of looking over at Mr. Jost's farm. "Guess I do."

"Why?" I whispered.

The quick glance he shot my way held all sorts of implications, but I needed words for the tape.

"This going to be on TV, Miss O'Hara?"

"Yes, we hope so."

"The Amish don't care to be photographed, you know."

It was a warning. *Stay away from Old Mr. Jost.*

"Yes. I've heard that."

Lowe turned and pointed a finger at the oak. "That tree is over a hundred years old, you know. The town moved the road for that tree."

The morning sun was fully awake and the leaves on the sunny side were glowing.

"Seen a lot, that tree. It was worth moving the road around it."

I nodded. "It's a beautiful tree."

"I suppose that boy would have found himself another tree someplace else," he said and it was almost a question. The rest wasn't. "There are things worth trying to preserve, Miss O'Hara. Even when you can't."

I wasn't sure how to answer. He was speaking a local dialect of neighborhood history, a language I'd never understand without translation. I hesitated, searching for what to ask next and I lost him.

Lowe made his decision. He stuck out his rough, tanned hand and shook my own—goodbye. Interview over.

Damn. "Well, thanks for agreeing to meet with us, Mr. Lowe."

"That's no problem."

"Can I ask you one more thing?"

"No."

I'm not so young I can't remember back to the days when shame was still serious business. As a kid, I remember people averting their eyes at something awful, instead of reaching for their camcorders.

How many times did I hear the words, *hurry, don't let anyone see. What will the neighbors think?* Bad enough. But now the pendulum's swung so far the other way nobody can turn on the TV or open a newspaper without somebody flashing their streaky underpants in your face. How is that an improvement?

The problem isn't that it's so painfully tacky, it's that we have only so much time, so much compassion, for our fellow human beings. I want to focus on trouble that matters. Ending wars, and hunger, and the sickness we know how to cure if we'd only pay attention. If the freaks would stop distracting us.

Which is a long way of explaining that even though people like farmer Al Lowe made my job harder, I can't say I always mind.

I followed him over to his standard issue, rusty pickup. "Mr. Lowe?"

He climbed in the cab and slammed the door shut before he answered. "Yeah?"

That one meant *Don't push your luck, lady.*

"No camera. I'm just wondering, do you have any idea who alerted the authorities about the body? Could it have been your neighbor?"

"No. Had to be someone before that," Lowe said. "Sorry."

I said thanks, but it bothered me. Usually, it was easy to find the person who'd tipped the authorities on something like this. Even if it was a random bystander, they generally had an emotional stake in telling the story again. The thirty-second hero was an easy interview to bag.

"One last thing—have the police identified the body as Tom Jost?" I didn't want either of us getting into trouble for not passing along important information.

"Oh, yeah." Lowe hooked a hand over the steering wheel and his mouth registered a nasty-tasting frown. "They know."

Questions started popping in my head, but Lowe slipped the truck into gear and revved the engine.

I nodded and he returned the gesture. With the big bill on his cap, it looked like he was tipping his hat to me; a move that registered as perfectly Midwestern, formal and yet familiar. I bit my tongue and stepped back to watch the truck drag a line of dust into the air as he cut back onto the road.

"Keep it rolling," I told Ainsley. "I want the truck."

Jenny popped her head out the door. "How much longer?"

I started to say we were done, when I noticed action up at the Jost farmhouse. Somebody had come out to gather the laundry. A pair of little girls and a boy were dodging between sheets draped in rows, playing at hide-and-seek as the wind flicked the bed tails. If I strained to listen, I could hear the squeals as they popped in and out.

"Shoot it," I ordered Ainsley.

He looked around, shielding his eyes from the sun. "Those kids playing?"

"Yeah." And this one meant, *trust me.* "Quick, College. Before it's gone."

He zipped the camera off the tripod and propped it on his shoulder for the shot. I had a sinking feeling that we'd lose the image because he wasn't used to shooting handheld, or worse, he couldn't see the picture I wanted. Sometimes that happens. They just can't see.

"How much longer, Aunt Maddy?" Jenny whispered.

I was startled to find her right there, at my side all of a sudden. "I don't know. Not long."

"Oh, man!" Ainsley finished all his maneuvers and turned to face us, the camera still resting on his shoulder. He sounded pumped. "This was great. What next?"

I wanted to walk up to the farm and knock on the door, but Jenny was quietly pulling my sleeve to check my watch. I took the hint. "We better head back to the station. Check in with Gatt. And we've got to drop Jenny on the way. At school."

"Sure," Ainsley assured her with a smile. His sandy hair seemed to change color to suit his environment. In the morning sun, he was blond as a prom date.

"I'll help strike."

"No. I've got it."

I admit I was itching to help wrap the equipment. You learn to pack fast when the aftershocks are bringing the building down around your ass. Unfortunately, Ainsley's progress was about as urgent as the seasons changing.

By the time we delivered Jenny to school, then found a gas station with a quick mart, the best part of the morning was gone.

This is another thing I wasn't used to in my new life—the deadweight of other people's needs. On my own, I'd have a story half in the can already. It took my college boy twenty minutes just to fill the gas tank and buy us a newspaper.

"What the hell took you so long?" I crabbed when he finally returned.

"Not much of a morning person, are you?"

"I'm a busy person, College. Busy, busy, busy."

Ainsley shrugged the obvious. "Had to take a leak."

"Pee on your own time. When I'm waiting in the car, tie it in a knot."

"Easy there, Boss. Don't get your knickers in a twist." College tossed the newspaper onto my lap. "Take a look at page three."

Don't get your knickers in a twist? Bold talk. That was promising.

Above the fold on page three of the *Clarion* was a quarter-page reprint of the photo I'd left Melton: tree, ladder, rope and a crowd of men in uniforms. Most of the body was blocked by the ring of men. The caption read, "Unidentified man in Amish clothing was found dead yesterday in a field just south of Route 59. Police and fire department services were brought to the scene by an anonymous phone caller."

"Wonder if anyone else picked it up," I said.

"We could call the station. Ask them to check the wire and keep an eye on the noon news until we get there."

"Good thinking, College." My congratulations should have included letting him make the phone call. Reception put me straight through to Gatt.

"Where the hell are you?" my new boss blared.

"In the van with Ainsley 'Life Is A Journey, Not A Destination' Prescott. You remember my partner?"

"Cut the crap and get your fanny in here now."

"My what?" I cracked a grin. I hadn't had a fanny since I was ten.

"You heard me, O'Hara. I got some township sheriff sitting in my lobby threatening to get a subpoena and trash my office."

"Sounds like Curzon read the paper this morning," I reported aloud for Ainsley's benefit. "What's he want?"

"Photos of a crime scene. I thought Ainsley told me you didn't get any video on that suicide."

"We didn't get any video."

Gatt wasn't an idiot. The silence hung between us like a bad smell. "Just get in here and deal with him."

"On the way. Hey, Gatt? Remind me again, how'd you get tipped on the story yesterday?"

"Phone call," he spouted. "Civilian asked for me, so I assumed he'd called the network hotline and they'd put him on to me as the local contact."

"Weird." It made sense Network would call the crew that was closest to look into the story. But no network hotline on the planet turfed a call that fast—Ainsley and I had arrived within twenty minutes of the cops. Which meant Gatt had gotten his call within minutes of the authorities. This reminded me of Ainsley's homework assignment. "Later, Gatt."

"Sooner, O'Hara."

"Right, right." I pressed the button that made him go away. "What'd you find out about Sheriff Curzon, College?"

"Not much," Ainsley said. "I asked around but nobody knows why he might be shy about reporters."

"Shy? I'd call it hostile. Who'd you ask?"

"Guy I know on the city council." He shrugged his bony shoulder. "And my mom."

"Your *mom?* You called your mother to ask about Curzon?"

The tops of his ears turned red. "Yeah. I had to talk to her anyway, you know, about Mr. Lowe."

"No. I don't know."

"Come on. It's not like that guy agreed to be interviewed because he wanted to be on television." Ainsley snarfed. "I asked Mom if she'd, you know, vouch for you. She knows a lot of people. She's been involved in town politics for a while." He paused and seemed to think better of what he was going to say next. Which is why I was surprised to hear, "Oh, and she and Curzon's ex-wife go to the same hairdresser."

"Same hairdresser. Right. Stop there. You're scaring me."

Ainsley gave another friendly shrug to say, *whatever.* He concentrated on singing along with the radio for the rest of the drive while his ears cooled back to their normal color.

Small town politics—where political science meets the theater of the absurd.
Curtain up. Sheriff Curzon was awaiting my entrance.

We pulled into the rear dock at the station within ten minutes. Despite the lobby's visual clues to the contrary, WWST was on the cutting edge of the television business in a few significant ways. I'd been pleasantly surprised to discover the remote operations equipment was state of the art.

According to the trades I read, the entire office had been established as an experimental sister station to a downtown Chicago minor network affiliate. It began as a way to divide the grunt work it takes to run a station, while boosting the signal coverage. All the boring, space-consuming aspects of the business—like the video library and the accounting department—were routed to the hinterlands where real estate doesn't do such a ream-job on the bottom line. Over time, everything but the main news studio and the general manager's office had been shifted westward.

As far as I was concerned, if they could find a way to lose sales and promotion, it'd be an ideal work environment.

"Barb-A-Ra!"

Ainsley and I could hear the shout all the way to the back of the building. This time it wasn't Gatt calling her. It wasn't a voice I recognized.

"Barbara, I need you! Now!"

We came around the corner just as Barbara marched by, fists clenched and sensible shoes clomping across the linoleum like combat boots.

Ainsley blew out a breath and shook his head. "She hates when he does that."

"Who?"

"Jim, the sales manager. Barb works for Uncle Rich, you know. But Jim's such an—" Ainsley dropped his voice to a whisper "—asshole—his secretaries keep quitting. Barb gets stuck helping him out."

A door slammed, muffling the roar of battle. Ainsley grimaced.

Up and down the hall, a flurry of action ensued. Somebody called, "I'm on the phone, people." Another door-slam echoed. Another shout of "Keep it down." Then, from behind us, the deepest voice yet called, "Quit slamming the fucking doors!"

One big, happy family, as they say, just living the dream.

"That last guy you heard was Mick, one of the engineers." Ainsley threw a thumb over his shoulder pointing down the hall that led to the edit bays. "I'll introduce you later. You'll like him. Maybe we should go in the back way, to be safe?"

"Sounds good."

We entered Gatt's office through a back hall door. Gatt was seated in the same position I'd first found him in yesterday—phone against his ear, slouching deep in the chair behind his desk. "Tell him to kiss my hairy butt and call my lawyer. No way am I giving him two runs in prime." He looked up and saw us in the doorway. "Gotta go. Call me if you hear any more."

"We're here. Where's Curzon?" I asked.

"In my lobby." Gatt's phone rang again almost the instant he hung up. "Go talk to him. Be diplomatic." He snatched up the receiver and growled, "Hold on—I'm in the middle of something here." Then he called to

Ainsley, "Go with. Watch her. She screws up, come get me."

Diplomacy at its finest.

Sheriff Curzon almost seemed at home in WWST's retro-tacky lobby. Except for the fact that his suit was too fine—a dark summer-weight wool, lightly breaking cuffs, crisp white shirt, dark narrow tie—he looked like a cover model for an old *Detective Magazine*. Standing in the center of the room, with his cell phone pressed tight to his ear, his body language said he didn't want to get too close to any of the solid surfaces. Not that I blamed him.

Unfortunately, I hadn't worn anything particularly outrageous today, just my usual jeans and a nice black T-shirt. I'd thrown a blazer on over the shirt because it was cold and I knew I'd be interviewing Farmer Lowe outdoors. With a touch of evil glee, I slipped off the jacket and tossed it over the back of the receptionist's empty chair.

Did I mention I don't usually wear a bra?

As my daddy used to say, when dealing with a hard-ass, the best defense is hard offense. I think my nipples qualified.

"Sheriff, what a surprise." I stepped out around the counter. "I'd have been happy to come get that press release, you know."

He snapped his phone shut. His eyes flicked down, no more than a quarter second, but I counted a double blink and two-Mississippis of silence.

"I want the rest of the pictures," Curzon announced.

"What pictures?" See how diplomatic I can be?

"You were not authorized to take photos at my crime scene."

"From a public road?" I grabbed the plastic badge that hung around my neck and flipped it so the sheriff could read the large black type: Press. I smiled some more.

He took two steps toward me and bent at the waist so his face was level with mine. In a quiet voice he asked, "Where's that badge going to get you if the police department shuts you out, Ms. O'Hara? Zero cooperation from now on."

"And your cooperation's been such a big help to me so far, Sheriff Curzon."

"It can get a lot worse."

I spread my hands wide, palms up, innocence incarnate. "I do maybe two, three, stories a month for the next year, Sheriff, then—*poof*—I'm gone. I think I can stay out of trouble that long."

"Nothing but business to you, isn't it?" he asked, the words crisp with bitterness. "You don't care who gets hurt in the process."

All of a sudden it clicked. "But you do." I lowered my voice. "Who? Who are you protecting?"

He jerked back before he could stop himself, and then popped out in those little jaw-knuckles men get when they clench their teeth.

"We got off on the wrong foot here." I was suddenly sorry I'd baited him. Sincere-yet-pert is a tough look to pull off. He was worried about somebody and I'd never figure out whom while I had him at DEFCON 1. "Look, I'm not out to get anyone here. I only want to know what happened." I've heard the public ranks journalists right up there with plumbers and lawyers these days, but some of us do try. I crossed my arms in front of my chest, dropped my voice to something soft and private. "Can you help me?"

For a long moment, Curzon hesitated. Cynicism eventually bubbled to the surface of his expression, spoiling my view of his pretty eyes. "Any more of those pictures turn up in the paper, I know where to come looking, Ms. O'Hara."

"Happy thought, Sheriff. Any idea when you'll have that press release ready?"

He tried the death-ray look on me again.

That's when I noticed Ainsley creeping up behind me; I could feel him twitching.

I walked to the door and held it open. "Have yourself a great day, Sheriff," I said as Curzon stomped past me. "Come back anytime."

Good manners are the bedrock of diplomacy.

"Yeah, I heard you. Auto sex-something—sounds good. Sounds great," Gatt mumbled between calls. "Call the county hospital. They must have some of those head-shrinkers. See if you can get someone to expert witness on this. Somebody credible. And make 'em say it a couple times, so we get a decent promo. What is it, again?"

"Autoerotic asphyxiation," Ainsley offered helpfully.

Gatt looked pained. "Don't tell your mother I taught you that."

Ainsley rolled his eyes, one shoulder slouched against the wall. I couldn't figure out whether he was doing the brooding James Dean thing for his uncle's benefit or just avoiding sitting down 'cause it might wrinkle his pants.

"We're going to try and interview Mr. Jost, the adoptive father, later today," I told Gatt. "Maybe swing by the victim's place after we get an address. I still don't know what we're gonna use as visual on this. Ainsley says these people don't go to public school. No yearbook photos, none of the usual sources for a head shot."

"Keep looking," Gatt muttered. "Something'll turn up. And stay away from Curzon for a while."

"Yes, Mother," I droned.

"I'm serious. Let him cool down."

If I was right and Curzon was running interference, I'd have to go after him again. "Let me do my job, Gatt. That's why you're paying me the big bucks, right?"

"Fine. Speaking of which, I've got the GM coming in

for the weekly management meeting in an hour. I want you both attending the show from now on." He flipped his finger back and forth, pointing to Ainsley and me. "But your final contract meeting will have to wait until Monday, O'Hara. GM's got a conflict."

"Fine."

"That's it. I'm done. Get the hell outta here," Gatt said. "I got work to do."

I have no patience for most TV office politics. Once you've watched *World Wide Wrestling,* or read *The Art of War,* there are no surprises. Making me wait to review my employment terms was a standard opening ego-blow. Managers like to count coup on new employees. Happens all the time, especially with a reputation like mine. 'Til now, freelancing had kept me out of the worst of the fray. As a permanent hire, there was lot less room to maneuver. Pucker up, O'Hara. Life's a series of trade-offs.

Of course I hated being seen as a complete pushover.

"One more thing, Richard. When do I see my office?"

"What the hell do you need an office for? You're supposed to be out on location shooting and in here editing. I'll have Barbara find you a desk someplace."

"A desk? You want me discussing station business with Curzon—and any other concerned citizens I happen to meet—at some bull-pen desk?"

A growl roughed up the back of his throat. "See what I can do," Gatt answered. "Now get lost."

Ainsley seemed impressed. I smiled modestly.

Not bad. Second day on the job, and Richard Gatt and I had already established a rapport.

With no office to call my own, I went out to my car to make a few confirmation calls while Ainsley went to find us a room to view what we'd shot this morning. The social worker at Jenny's school helped me set up an after-school care scenario back when school started in August, so I'd have a place for the kid as soon as I got the work situation pinned down. All I had to do was confirm my new employment details over the phone.

Bad enough I had to ask Ainsley to chauffeur the kid around this morning; no way was I about to use the public office phone for these calls. The television business is a wild ride, fickle with her favors and always sniffing after the next, younger thing. I'm not saying it's right, but once somebody gets a reputation for putting business second—behind the kid, the lover, the mother, whatever—the business finds a way to claim her pound of flesh. Or she drops you cold. The only way I figured to keep this whole situation in hand was if my personal life remained as vague as possible within the station's walls.

It took some serious begging but I managed to get them to take Jenny into after-school care *immediamento,* paperwork to be finalized at pickup. The relief of not having to rush out and meet the kid by three o'clock eased the sting of the grovel. After another three calls, I'd nailed down addresses for all the Tom Josts listed in the phone book. Business was in hand. Life was good.

Ainsley had our raw material on standby when I tracked him through the building to the available editing bay.

Edit bays are the cold, dark, primordial wombs of electronic storytelling. Cold keeps the machines happy, and light creates glare on the monitors. All the walls are covered in dark egg-crate foam to absorb any stray sound waves. The rooms are usually small and made smaller by stuff—blocks of players in various formats, switcher technology, playback monitors, audio controls, oscilloscopes and miles upon miles of connecting wires. The finished product may be seen by millions but most of the work is done alone, with an engineer assisting on the final cut. Two chairs on wheels are all you need.

It's a slightly different kind of darkroom, but one I'd also learned to love. When I'm developing film, I can almost convince myself each photo is one hundred percent my creation. In the edit bay, I can never forget that creation is a team effort. Keeps me humble.

Well, most of the time.

"Staff meeting in sixteen minutes," I reminded Ainsley. "Let's see what you got."

He flicked a little glance over his shoulder at me, *are you ready for this?* and hit Play. I watched it all the way through once and felt myself flatline a bit with surprise.

"Again."

Rewind. Play. Same images.

Not bad, not half bad, is what I was thinking. What I said was, "Shit, College. You are awful tight on some of these."

He'd framed most of the interview as an extreme profile close-up of the farmer's face. I hit the freeze-frame. The close-up highlighted the rough skin and deep lines of Lowe's face and revealed the unique patina of the working man. He might not be Tom Jost's father, but it was clear he knew the cost of a young man's death.

"I like to shoot tight," Ainsley answered.

I released the freeze. "Unfortunately, you're out of focus every time he moves."

"I figured we'd work around it with B-roll."

"Did you shoot me any B-roll?"

B-roll is filler, supplemental shots, extra footage, whatever's left over. Right now, I didn't have enough A- or B-roll to even fill airtime.

"Um…"

"You have a reason for shooting tight?"

"I kind of like the way it looks." He shrugged and kicked back in his wheeled chair to stretch his long legs in front of him, like an oversize retriever relaxing into a sprawl.

"Not good enough." If he had a reason, I might listen. If he was just showing off— "I don't need artsy-fartsy, College. I need clean and clear. That means in focus. Got it?"

"Yeah." He turned his back to me and punched a few buttons. Hard. "Got it."

"Next time give me some headroom."

"Fine." He jerked his chin.

After thirty seconds of sulk, I tacked on, "I like the shot of the kids."

"You do?" He spun around on his chair, eyes bright, smile starting to glow. In the darkness of the booth, the contrast hurt my eyes.

"I said I did." I checked my watch. "Time to hit the staff meeting."

"Okay. I'm looking forward to this," he answered with gusto. "They cater these meetings, you know."

"Well, eat fast. We got a lot to accomplish today. I'm planning to blow out of this place as soon as we can," I told him as he led the way through the building, past the kitchen—Ainsley slowed but didn't stop—to the conference room. "I found a possible address for Tom Jost."

"Cool." Looking more eager than an address usually warrants, he added, "This is my first time at a manager's meeting."

In my experience, manager meetings are best handled like amputations. Strive to remain unconscious while the big shots lop off a few hours, and pray the whole thing doesn't cripple the entire remainder of the day.

I gave him a pat on the back. "It's never good the first time, College. But I'll remind them to be gentle."

The boy ducked his head, denying the rise of pink to his cheeks more so than the grin as we entered the conference room.

Gatt saw us and frowned suspiciously in my direction. I gave him the *what?* shrug. Ainsley paid no attention to this side play. He went straight for the counter with the bagel extravaganza and hot caffeine.

The guy standing next to Gatt stared me down. Typical sales guy: buffed nails, French cuffs and more teeth than a sports announcer. His cologne reeked from eight feet away. In my experience, any man wears that much perfume is full of shit and laying down cover.

"This must be our latest acquisition," the guy thundered loud enough for everyone in the room to hear. "Get over here. I want to shake your hand. Jim Schmed, sales manager here at WWST. You've got to be Maddy O'Hara."

"That's right."

"Love your work. Great stuff. How'd we get so lucky, eh, Gatt?"

Schmed gave me the Grip-o-Death handshake—the one they exchange right before the ref calls "…and come out swinging."

"Really great to have you on board," he schmoozed.

"Can't wait to see what you do for us once you settle in. Love to get some promo materials from you, soon as you're able."

Everybody's heard of love at first sight. In my case, hate at first sight is a lot more common. Sales guys never make me warm and fuzzy, but this was something else. My last name and my coloring come from my father. My first name—Magdalena—and my hostile intuition come through my mother's blood.

Schmed raised every hair on the back of my neck.

"Why would you need promo material from me? I thought the promotions department was going to work off my stuff." I turned to Gatt to clarify.

"No, no, not on the show. On you." Schmed winked at me. "You've made yourself quite a name, honey. And it's my job to sell that name to advertisers. Right, Rich?"

"That's right." Gatt rubbed the flat of his free hand across his bald head and frowned.

"I am not doing personal promos."

"Sure you are, hon." My resistance piqued Schmed's interest. He'd stopped scanning the room for admirers and focused all his attention on me.

"No—" I tried to make it sound equally cheerful "—hon, I'm not."

Schmed the Sales Shark and I played a quick round of who'll-blink-first.

Then he barked a laugh. "Is she busting my ass?" he asked Gatt. "She's been here, what?—five minutes—and she's busting my ass already? Are you kidding me?"

I wasn't thinking of the first five minutes, but of the five million to come when I forced myself to suck in a calming breath.

"I'm not busting your ass, Jim. I'm just saying, I don't do on-air. Never have."

Like any good predator, he kept his eyes on me and slowly edged in closer. "Why not? You'd be great. Pretty girl like you. Camera would love you. Camera would eat you up."

"Thanks, but no. That's part of my charm, Jim. I let the pictures and the people making news tell the story. I stay offscreen." It also made me unique in the freelance world. By staying off-air, I could produce a story for any network, any station that wanted to foot my bill. My face and voice never became the commodity. Only my work.

"Gotta have promos, O'Hara. How else am I gonna sell you? Make up for what-all you cost us, right, Gatt? Cost us a pretty penny to hire a professional with your reputation. Am I right? Jesus-Priest, I can't sell you if I don't have product."

Ah. Apparently, rumors of my potential salary had ruffled the Sales King's feathers before I'd even walked in the door. CDB, I reminded myself, cost of doing business. Nothing personal.

I started us off on a round of chuckle-chuckle.

Gatt looked back and forth, one to the other, before he joined the merrymaking. We all laughed together.

The sound faded.

As if I was full to brimming with good humor, with a last gasp of mirth I asked, "So…you renewing your contract soon then, Jim?"

Gatt cracked up. Schmed didn't.

It was the sweetest kind of return. Was I implying he was using me to leverage Gatt for a better contract?

Or was I hinting that in a fight between us Gatt would side with me?

Schmed looked like he was going to say something very un-funny, but Gatt interrupted. "You got a head shot, O'Hara?"

"Maybe something old," I replied suspiciously.

"Fine. Get us an eight-by-ten and your résumé reel. Promo department can figure something out. That's what I pay those assholes for. Which reminds me—Jim, Barb says you got both offices on that side of the hall tied up."

Keeping my face ever-so neutral at the mention of office space, I mumbled, "I'm going over to make sure Ainsley's not getting into trouble. Excuse me, gentlemen."

The room had crowded up. Nobody had taken a place around the long conference table yet. Ainsley introduced me to the usual cast of characters: woman from HR, woman from accounting, guy from engineering, guy from studio and the promotions director.

After another eight or ten minutes of chitchat, the door opened and a little *busha* in a business suit entered. She was fifty-ish, solid, glossy white hair and sensible pumps. Her Secretary-at-Arms followed, laptop in hand.

Most general managers are a bit like feudal lords. They command as far as the eye can see. They make continuous war on neighboring peers. The most successful of the breed trace their management style back to Genghis Khan. Ruthless is good. Bigger is better. Dead enemies are best.

"Right," she called out, hands on her hips. "Where's our new star?"

Everyone in the room turned and looked at me. Most of the faces were neutral. A few showed more than healthy skepticism. Jim Schmed looked like he wanted to try out his favorite WWF takedown on me.

Welcome to the family.

Ainsley gave me a little shoulder shove. "Here she is," he called proudly.

"Shirley Shayla." She chugged across the room on sturdy legs and gave me the mutual-respect shake—solid grip, taking my measure. She stood with her feet a bit widespread, her trunk tilted forward. The way you'd need to stand if people were always trying to knock you down. "Good to finally meet you, Ms. O'Hara. How are you settling in? Anything I can do?"

"Definitely."

GM's always ask *anything can I do?* the first time they meet you. The standard answer is, *thanks for the opportunity to join the team,* and other similar crap. No GM has ever asked me that question twice. Which is why it's a good idea to have a list ready.

"For a start, I need an office with a door."

She tipped her head and stared at me over the top of her frameless glasses. "I'll see what I can find for you, Ms. O'Hara. See what I can find."

He had to find it. Had to find it all. Now.

Being in the house like this was making his palms so wet, the cornstarch inside the gloves was congealing into lumps.

He searched the top of the medicine cabinet first, trying to think like Gina. She was compulsive about where she kept that kind of shit. She would never leave a bag of medical samples someplace the kid might get her hands on it.

Gina was a good mother.

Next, he searched the bedroom and bathroom. Opening the bedroom door had been a shock. It was like a museum in there. Nothing had been taken away, moved, even touched. There was dust on everything. Not that he was some kind of a clean freak, but he started sneezing the minute he opened a drawer.

Maddy O'Hara might be hot shit in TV-land, but she was a lazy bitch when it came to housework.

After an hour of careful searching, he was pretty certain Gina hadn't hidden the bag in her room. He put everything back exactly as he found it, but he hated the fact that the room was gathering dust.

Someone ought to do something.

That's when he'd opened the nightstand and discovered the stack of photos.

Months ago, right after the accident, he'd snuck back into the house and removed the obvious photos of himself—one from the fridge and one from her bedside. "Play it cool" was the plan, especially with a reporter in the family. He'd stayed away from the kid at the funeral.

Done everything he could to convince the guys that his relationship with Gina was short-term only.

Nobody understood how bad he felt. Nobody.

He picked the photo off the top of the pile—he was smiling, Gina was smiling, a birthday party?—and he sat down on the bed. Nobody appreciated what he'd done to keep things under control. His sacrifices. His feelings.

Maddy O'Hara was one selfish, lazy bitch all right. This sad, dusty room proved it.

If she continued to make things difficult, more sacrifices would have to be made.

But this time around, Maddy O'Hara was the one who'd be making them.

Ainsley kept shaking his head and shooting me side-long glances while he maneuvered the truck out into traffic.

"What?" I asked. I'd no clue what his problem was; pretty typical manager's meeting as far as I could tell. I snapped my phone shut. "No answer at any of the Tom Jost addresses. Let's try the farm. See if we can talk to somebody out there first."

"Oh, sure. Why not?" Ainsley said. He sounded a little on the sarcastic side.

"Just drive."

It didn't seem to take as long to get to the Jost farm this time. Either I was getting used to the distances or the absence of Ainsley's singing improved our wind resistance. He parked the truck on the road and said we should walk to the farmhouse from there. He made a point of mentioning, "It's considered polite not to park on their property."

"Okay, Miss Manners. Before we get too close to offend anyone, get me an establishing shot of the whole scene, a view downhill from here of the hanging tree and a nice tight shot of each of the outbuildings." It was the kind of stuff I could use with a voice-over, while recapping Tom Jost's childhood.

We went to work. I took my camera out and shot a few stills. The farm buildings were all weathered wooden structures, painted either white or dark red and grouped at the end of a winding drive. There were two black buggies parked in the gravel near the house. No sign of the usual ugly 1950s slab house beside an old picturesque barn, like most of the modern farms around here. There were no people to be seen but we heard children's voices when the wind carried from the right direction.

College hung behind me a few steps, but he had the camera up and rolling. As we came up the driveway a rangy-looking dog loped out to greet us, stopped fifty feet away and started barking his head off.

"Camera down," I ordered. I'll argue a person to the mat for the chance to hang around and shoot. Dogs don't negotiate. "Someone will come now. Let's see what they say before we shoot anymore."

"'See what they say,'" Ainsley mumbled to himself. "Right." He lowered the camera immediately. The old camera jocks I've worked with would never stop just because I told them to. Now there's a benefit to snapping the kid fresh out of college I hadn't considered.

"Rascal! Rascal, stop that." A young woman in dark fairy-tale clothes appeared in the doorway of a small outbuilding. Her face was obscured by the brim of her bonnet. "Rascal, come."

"Good afternoon," I called. "We're looking for Mr. Jost."

The girl took a half step back, into the shadow of the doorway, her long dress and hat cloaking everything but her face and the silver pail she carried in front of her. I knew her face. It was the girl I'd seen hiding in the bushes.

"Hello, again." I tried a smile.

She remembered my face as well. From her expression, I'd say she considered me unpredictable and potentially disease carrying. "Who are you? Police?"

"No. I'm Maddy O'Hara. We're from WWST, the television station. Do you watch television?"

She shook her head vigorously.

"Is Mr. Jost around?"

"I'm here," a man called from the doorway of the barn. He was dressed in the Amish uniform with suspenders to hold up his pants and a straw hat. Together with the wiry, gray beard covering the lower half of his face, he also resembled someone lifted from the pages of a Grimm's fairy tale. Another much younger man, his whiskers still black, appeared in the doorway behind Jost. On the porch, two women stepped through the front door. A small girl-child peeped curiously from between the folds of their long skirts. Another face appeared in the upstairs window. People seemed to appear from thin air, all eyes on Ainsley and me.

"Good afternoon, sir. I'm Maddy O'Hara with WWST. I know this must be a difficult time for your family. I'd like to ask you about your son, Tom."

"I have no son. You don't belong here. Please, you will leave."

"We were told Tom Jost was your adopted son. Mr. Lowe spoke very kindly of the way you took the boy in."

Jost's face shifted from blank to grim. "Lowe is a good man. He'd be a better one with his mouth shut."

"So Tom wasn't your son?"

"Go away."

"Father?" the girl called out from the shadowy doorway, her voice high and thin with concern. Inside the shed, a commotion of clucks and caws erupted. She was standing in a chicken coop; I'd never seen one before.

"No, Rachel. Not now." Jost turned his back and shuffled out of sight, back into the barn.

I thought about following him but the crowd of on-lookers was not encouraging. I nodded at them, and signaled a retreat to Ainsley. The men went back into the barn, the women into the house.

We had almost made it back to the truck when I heard the fast crunching sound of feet behind me.

Rachel ran toward us, bucket swinging in her hand to the rhythm of her stride. When I turned, she stopped short, as if afraid to approach too closely.

"You said…'this must be a difficult time.'" In the sunlight, her eyes seemed endlessly dark against her pale face. "You said…'was.'"

I've known since I was a kid, I was born to play messenger. It's the kind of calling that makes you tough, fast. Everybody knows it can get you killed. Not everybody knows it kills you pieces at a time. Still, I have to look them in the eye.

"Tom Jost is dead," I told her.

The pail in her hand dropped. Seed spilled everywhere.

Rachel backed away from me before she turned and ran.

"We should go," Ainsley called softly.

I watched her run toward the barn, toward her father. It was hard to make myself move.

Ainsley started back to the truck. I walked the other way. Righting the girl's pail, I tried to scoop the fallen seed back inside. I took out one of my freelance cards and scribbled my new home phone number on the back with the words *I'm sorry. Call me if you want to know more* and stuck it straight up in the chicken feed.

"What a bust," I groaned. "Let's try the phone-listed Tom Josts again. Even if they aren't home we could do a drive-by."

"I thought we did pretty well," Ainsley said.

"You need to set your standards a little higher than thirty seconds of establishing shot, College."

"No, really. Amish don't allow photography. I'm surprised we got all the way up the driveway with the cameras at all."

"What do you mean they don't allow photography? I've seen coffee-table books on Amish, College. They must allow some pictures."

"No, really. It's against their religion. Those rules they follow, you know. *Ordnung?* They told us this in school. People can take pictures from far away and stuff, but never of their faces."

"Are you kidding me?"

Ainsley shrugged. Inconsistency didn't bother him much.

"Amish living isn't on the curriculum where I grew up," I told him. "Give me the Cliff's Notes version."

"*Ordnung* is their law. Each community has their own. Some are *really* strict, some not so bad. The one near here is known for being pretty progressive—they've got those phone booths Mr. Lowe mentioned, and kerosene fridges. Some even have electricity for the dairy barns, I think. Not in the houses though."

"I thought they couldn't use electricity at all."

"There was some accident, years ago. Somebody died in a fire. Things changed after that, to make the barns safer. There was a big story about it in the newspaper when I was in high school."

"Nothing like death to effect a little change," I mumbled. "I'd like to read that article. Let's pull everything we can on the local Amish. Which of those characters back at the station works the library?"

"Mick."

"'Quit-Slamming-the-Fucking-Doors' Mick?"

"That's him."

The charming ones always end up alone in the stacks. Coincidence?

"Right, I'll talk to Mick. You search the periodicals online. I want copies of anything on the local Amish community. Check local weeklies, magazines and the *Clarion* as well. Which reminds me…" I checked my watch to confirm. "Time to call Melton."

"We're here." Ainsley pointed out the window. "This is the only address that's an apartment building. I thought we should try it first."

"Good idea." I checked my list again. "How did you know? There's no apartment number noted."

"I've lived in this county my whole life, remember?"

The address took us to an ugly prefab apartment building at the end of a cul-de-sac. It was two-stories high, not a single open window and surrounded by a scruffy vacant lot. At the back of the building, you could just make out a set of railroad tracks that cut toward the city. We parked in the front lot alongside a convention of rusty muscle cars.

The bumper stickers on the car we'd parked behind said, "You'll Get My Gun When You Pry It Out of My

Cold, Dead Hand" and "I Can Be One of Those Bad Things That Happen to Bad People."

Definitely the kind of place that could accommodate a suicidal depressive.

"Let's check it out," I said. I didn't sound thrilled.

"Camera?" he asked. He didn't either.

"Find out if it's the right address first."

"Good idea."

There was a sidelight window beside the steel security door entrance with the sign Attack Dog on Premises prominently posted. We stood out front for a while buzzing the bell; nobody came.

A young guy in a cloth coat and a Grateful Dead T-shirt came flying out and Ainsley grabbed the door. The kid never looked back. I walked in. Ainsley followed.

The buzzer label and a pile of junk mail helped me figure out which apartment was Tom's. Ground floor. Right in the middle. Worst spot in the place. Rent must have been nothing. I rang the bell. Twice.

"If the guy's dead, he's not going to be answering the door anytime soon," whispers Ainsley Wiseguy Prescott.

"Yeah, well, I don't want any nasty shocks when I peep in the windows."

"There are no windows," Ainsley said, inspecting the dim, grungy hallway.

"Not in here anyway." I waggled my eyebrows at him.

Ainsley stared back, computing that thought.

"See if anyone else is home." I pointed to the other doors on my way out. "Ask if they knew Tom. Tell them we'll put 'em on TV if they talk to us."

Knowing which apartment was the mysterious Mr. Jost's, I was able to tromp around the outside of the building and find his window. There was nothing to see through the small frosted-glass rectangle that I was guessing looked into the bathroom, but there was a sliding patio door. Luckily, the curtains weren't quite closed. I cupped my hands around my eyes and pressed them to the glass to cut the glare. It was strangely quiet out there and the act of peeping in on someone else fired up the prickle of my guilt-o-meter.

Feet came crunching through the grass.

I jumped back from the window, heart pounding. This place made me more nervous than it should have.

"Strike out," Ainsley called in his version of a stage whisper. "The super is only around in the evenings, according to the neighbor. What are you doing?"

"Looking."

"Looking for what?"

"Don't know until I see it."

Ainsley came alongside me to look.

Tom Jost kept a simple studio apartment, furnished in late-century garage sale—one folding chair, one Formica table, one lumpy recliner. The place was damn tidy. His small single bed was made up with brown blankets and military care. White walls. No posters. No art. The only personal item I could see was a photo of a couple in a paper frame, the kind you pay five bucks for after you get off a ride at the fair. I'd seen several of Jenny and her mother around the house.

"Go get my camera case from the van, would you?"

"Would that be legal?"

"Not for pictures, Mr. Worrywart. I want the telephoto."

It worked better than I expected. With my camera against the door and a polarizing filter, I could read the faces in Tom's photo. It took a second before I recognized her. Fairy-tale Rachel looked quite a bit different wearing modern dress with her hair down.

"Got him. This is our Tom, all right."

"Are you done yet?" Ainsley was doing the college boy's version of furtive: hands sunk deep in his pockets, head bobbing, *c'mon, c'mon, c'mon* as he glanced back and forth. "Let's get out of here."

"Wait. *Yes!*"

"What?" Ainsley tried to peek around my shoulder.

Tom had hung a bag of dry cleaning from the top of a door. Focusing on the suit, I caught a glimpse of the patches on what seemed to be a uniform. "Our boy was a public servant."

"Police?"

"Nope. Firefighter."

"So those guys at the tree yesterday…"

"Knew him." Some instinct told me to scan the surroundings again. That crawly feeling someone was watching tiptoed up my spine. "Farmer Lowe hinted as much. Good news for us, College."

"What?"

A shadow passed in front of the super's apartment window. I gave Ainsley a happy, distracting shot to the biceps, urging him to walk toward the van. "It means he's got a decent head shot on record somewhere."

"Right! But how do we get it?"

We climbed in the van and I used my elbow to casually trigger the automatic locks. "I'll bet my new best friend at the *Clarion* might be able to help. Mr. Melton Shotter."

Ainsley's face bloomed with relief as he started the engine. "Can you call from the van? There's a DQ right around the corner and I'm dying for lunch."

"I watched you eat three bagels in the staff meeting."

"They were minis," he said indignantly.

"Fine. You eat—I'll call." Oh, to live the metabolism of a college kid again. I watched the building as we pulled out. Even though I couldn't see them, I was sure someone was watching. "Get us out of here."

"With pleasure."

By the time Ainsley'd scored his Dairy Queen happy meal—with a large diet pop for me—we were miles from Tom Jost's place and I was deep into the newspaper's phone system trying to hook up with a real, live Melton.

"*Clarion*. Metro desk."

"Melton, my friend. You rolled over on me."

"Umm…who is this?"

"You're funny." My day had not been very productive so far. Easy enough to punch a little Irish temper into the words. "This is Maddy O'Hara, Melton. Sheriff Curzon was at the station before I was this morning."

"Uh—sorry about that."

"What'd you do, draw him a map after you gave him my name? Whatever happened to protecting a source, Melton?"

"I figured you, well—" He squirmed. "I'm sorry, all right?"

"Yeah sure, because I got a great idea how you can make it up to me, Melton. I need some research help."

"What kind of research?"

"Easy stuff. Everything you can find on a guy named Tom Jost—where he went to high school, adoption records, if he had a girlfriend, what he did on weekends besides whack off—"

Ainsley coughed his chocolate shake all over the steering wheel.

"It's that dead Mennonite!" Melton's lightbulb blinked on. "You got an ID?"

"Maybe. We think the guy was a public servant, a firefighter."

"No way," he said with glee. Salacious mysteries are meat and potatoes to reporters. "Where? What town?"

"Not sure. His apartment's in Warrenville. One thing, Melton, everything stays out of the paper until after I air on Wednesday." I heard a grumble. "Did I mention there's a possibility of credit in this for you? National, on-air credit. 'Research by.' Look mighty sweet on your résumé. Not that you deserve it after ratting me out to Curzon like that."

"All right," he whined. "Fine. I'll try."

"Great. Tomorrow morning good for you?"

"Jee-zus. Tomorrow? Tomorrow's Saturday."

"Don't go getting religious on me yet, Melton. The fun's just getting started."

We agreed on an early afternoon deadline before he hung up.

Things were getting done. I was feeling good. "Next item on the agenda—expert head."

"Whaaat?"

Without looking up from my notes, I continued, "Get your mind out of the gutter, College. We need a specialist. A doctor. A psychologist. Someone we can get to say 'autoerotic asphyxiation' fast enough to work into a ten-second promo head shot. That's an expert head."

"Right." He sounded embarrassed.

The parking lot of the DQ was filling up. A couple of teenagers in a rusty Volvo circled for the third time, hungry for our parking place.

"Use your phone. Try the biggest hospital in the area. I'll try the community college."

Ainsley took his phone in one hand, chocolate shake in the other, and bounced his thigh against the steering wheel to the beat of oldies rock, while I entered my own phone purgatory. Pressing. Holding. Pressing. With my free hand, I dug through both gear bags and realized I was low on important stuff.

"You got any aspirin?" I asked.

College nodded toward the glove compartment. "We've got our choice," he reported between phone-mail-to-live-human maneuvering. "Do we want an expert on suicide, an expert on sexual deviance or someone who studies Amish psychology?"

No question. "Sexual deviance."

"Okay." More conferring, then he says, "Guy's out of town and won't be back for a week."

"Suicide?" I asked, hopefully.

"…Uh, that guy can only be reached on Mondays and Wednesdays. But she'd be happy to leave a message with the service," Ainsley added.

"Shit." No matter how much I tried to turn this into something that would look like ratings-happy TV, it seemed the Amish were my destiny. The sad thing was I found it pretty intriguing. "Amish psychology is our winner. But ask her to leave a message for the suicide guy, to be safe."

After three and a half more minutes of listening to him try to pin down an appointment, I held out my hand. "Gimme the phone."

"What?" he complained. "She keeps asking me to wait."

The standard whiney operator came on the line. "Who you holding for?"

"This is Maddy O'Hara from WWST and I'm trying to reach the doctor for a television news interview."

"An interview? On TV?"

"That's right. We'd like to use the doctor in an investigative report we're doing on a local public suicide." I hit that detail hard. Nothing wins over a gatekeeper like a juicy nugget of gossip. "Unfortunately, I'm having trouble getting through to someone who can schedule us. Can you help?"

"Oh, I'm sorry you've had to wait. Hold just a moment."

I had the doc on the line in under sixty and we were cleared to interview in less than that. Ainsley shook his head slowly, part admiration, part disgust.

"Dues you must pay," I intoned in my best Yoda imitation. "Eat much shit, then you, too, can use the force over secretaries. Let's go."

3:09:13 p.m.

We followed a major strip-mall route all the way to the western edge of the universe where the county hospital barely held the line on civilization. From what I'd heard, this hospital served a clientele that included everything from the average yuppie heart attack to the pavement drunk with a tire-track headache.

My sister worked there for years before she died. There.

I'm not fond of hospitals.

"Your aspirin bottle is empty, College."

"It's not mine. Somebody left it in there."

"Right. Add this to your critical equipment list. Pain reliever—we don't leave home without it. We should be stocking ibuprofen, extrastrength Tylenol and Tums, oh and breath mints—in the glove compartment. Got it?"

"Why?"

That got a laugh. I hope that's why he asked.

It took us as long to park the van and wind our way through the Escher-like interior of the hospital as it had to drive to the edge of the county. Of course I had no reason to complain. Ainsley did all the hauling. Our doctor's office was tucked in a dead-end hallway. There were plastic chairs along the wall, a small side table and eight copies of the same 1998 issue of *Prevention* magazine, all labeled Do Not Remove.

The inner sanctum receptionist greeted us and buzzed the doctor.

"Ms. O'Hara? I'm Dr. Graham. Please come this way. We can talk in my office."

Dr. Graham was in her late forties. She had a cap

of silvery brown hair, thick wire-rim eyeglasses, and wore a shapeless sack dress, but she had a voice like an angel—resonant, modulated. Perfect V.O. material. She could sell anything in a voice-over.

She shook my hand, then Ainsley's. "Please understand, Ms. O'Hara, most of my practice is family therapy. My qualifications as an 'expert'—" she smiled as she drew little finger quotes in the air "—regarding Amish psychology are tenuous at best. If you want a referral, I can direct you to people in Pennsylvania and New York who are much more qualified."

"Whatever you can tell us will be a great help, Doctor," I said. "The hospital PR people told us it was your specialty."

"I've done some research that involved Amish subjects. I organized several studies on the effects of family size on individuals and society. The Amish make an excellent reference group, very homogeneous."

"Really?" I said, meaning "keep talking."

"Yes. The average Amish family has seven children. Almost a quarter have ten or more."

"Ten kids?"

"That's right. Quite a difference, isn't it? The birthrate in the U.S. still hovers around two children per family."

"One seems like more than enough to me," I tossed out, but didn't get the laugh. "Tell me more about your study."

She fussed with her desk drawers, opening and closing, peering inside as she spoke.

"'Effects of Large Families on Self-Actualization and Community.'"

"Oh." It came out as one of those stupid-sounding

oh's. Doctors make me nervous. I never get my best interviews out of doctors. I rallied with another, "Really?"

She seemed prepared for that kind of response. "I have it right here, if you'd like to read it." From out of the desk came a stack of paper four-inches thick and bound with a paper cover. She tossed it onto the desktop with a *whump* that rang of challenge.

"Great. Love to."

"Take it with you. I have other copies."

"Terrific." I passed the brick to Ainsley. He slipped it in my camera bag.

I looked around, concentrating on how we would shoot the interview. Her office was small and not exactly the visual background I wanted. There was the requisite bookshelf or three, chairs and a small couch. No diplomas or plaques boasting her credentials on the walls; only one large print of the dunes and Lake Michigan.

She must have noticed me frowning. "I do most of my work over at the university. I'm only in this office twice a week to see clients."

"Sounds like we were lucky to catch you. Thanks again for agreeing to the interview."

She tipped her head and the curvature of her eyeglass lens distorted her eye. She looked a bit like a cartoon character peering through a magnifying glass. "What is it you'd like to discuss?"

"As I said, we have a local death possibly involving autoerotic asphyxiation. We'd like you to explain the condition. Any insight you might be able to offer would help."

"All right."

I signaled to Ainsley to start setting up and he

grinned, happy to be useful. He popped open the titanium suitcases that held the gear and started to rig for an interior interview. Once I was certain he was on the right track, I took out my notebook and flipped to my questions.

"Oh, wait. I'm sorry." Dr. Graham looked apologetic. "You seem to have misunderstood. I can't speak on camera on that subject, Ms. O'Hara. Definitely not."

"Excuse me?"

"I'm happy to answer your questions, but not on record." She made an effort at earnest eye contact. "In fact, I plan to encourage you to reconsider or at the very least, address the topic with extreme discretion."

"This is network television, Dr. Graham. Not You-Tube. We can be discreet."

Her earnest look sharpened into incredulity. "Perhaps our ideas of discretion differ. The fact is, it could be extremely dangerous to flash this syndrome across the media."

"Why?" Ainsley chipped in. He hunkered down into one of her upholstered chairs, all ears.

"For one thing, we don't know enough about how the practice initiates. The available data indicates death is most prevalent among young men—teenagers and young adults—a population likely to be sexually active, as well as developmentally prone to risk-taking behaviors. If they hear about something like this, they may try it simply because it's new and dangerous."

"Increasing awareness should also help doctors learn more about who's doing it and why," I countered.

Ainsley frowned. I couldn't tell if he was unimpressed with my logic or miffed over Herr Doctor's dim view of his peer group. "I don't get it. I mean, what's so sexy about choking to death?"

Dr. Graham masked her face in clinical calm. "There are two physical mechanisms at work. The transient cerebral hypoxia combined with autoerotic manipulation create a very distinctive physiological sensation."

Ainsley created a distinctive facial expression.

I whispered, "I think she said, lack of air to the brain while whacking off feels weird."

"No doubt," he said.

"Of course, human sexuality is never purely physiological," the doctor continued. "This syndrome is a paraphilia—"

"A what?" Ainsley was barely keeping up.

"—a socially prohibited sexual practice—" she paused to define "—of the sacrificial type. The sense of physical helplessness and self-endangerment enhances the sexual gratification."

"Yee-ech," he replied. Hard to argue with that.

The doctor tried. "Quite ubiquitous, actually."

I gave College a subtle backhand to the biceps. The more he squirmed with repulsion, the more obscure the good doctor's vocabulary seemed to get. If he kept up with the Mr. Yuck routine, she'd be speaking Latin in a minute.

"The practice has been noted across cultures and throughout history. There's some evidence it was practiced by the ancient Mayan culture a thousand years ago. And of course, literary references occur in de Sade—"

"Big surprise there," I noted.

"—as well as Melville and Beckett."

"Beckett?" Ainsley repeated.

"Yes. In the play *Waiting for Godot*."

"I read that freshman year of college." He shot me a bug-eyed look.

"An accurate estimation of incidence is difficult to establish because the behavior is almost always conducted in absolute privacy. Most practitioners seem to make arrangements for self-release mechanisms."

"Really?" I stopped her. "Such as?"

"They pad the rope, use quick release knots, carry knives, those sorts of things. Of course, it's important to remember these are the things which have been noted at death scenes."

"So they're *failed* self-release mechanisms."

"Precisely." She crossed her arms over her chest. "But they are the clues that help rule out suicide as the cause of death."

I had to think for a minute. Our Tom hadn't padded the noose as far as I could tell. Had he managed to rig his rope in such a way he believed he'd walk away?

"What other elements would you see at a typical death scene?" I asked.

"Generally, pornography is noted—" she ticked off a mental list "—partial or complete nudity of the genitalia and an absence of a suicide note. There are complex physiological and emotional contributing factors here. I'm sure you'll agree it's not something easily pared down and digested for network television."

"What if it aired on *Frontline,* Doctor? Or CNN?" I tossed back. "One of the programs where you get *your* news. Would that make it acceptable?"

She pulled upright, as if I'd insulted her. "No. You miss my point. We need to limit all mass media exposure of the topic. Those most at risk for death due to experimentation are young people whose access to information is inversely proportional to their capacity for good judgment. Teenagers are going to take risks. The risks associated with imitative behavior, in this case, are quite simply, life and death."

People always have such sensible reasons for censorship.

"What about those adults who need education on the subject? The opportunity to raise awareness and prevent further suffering?" Dr. Graham was starting to get on my nerves and I could hear it coming through in my voice. Not the best interview technique.

"Unfortunately, I know of no television forum in which adults can speak with other adults without the risk of children listening, Ms. O'Hara. Do you?"

"Thought all you psychological types knew the story of the elephant in the living room," I parried. "It isn't going away because we pretend not to notice."

"Interesting," she commented softly, as though she were talking to herself.

Suddenly, I was very aware of her attention honing in on me specifically.

"Are there no circumstances under which you would consider keeping something out of the public eye, Ms. O'Hara?"

"There are no circumstances under which I wouldn't be damn suspicious of any such request, Dr. Graham."

"Really? How would you feel about your son or daughter watching your program?"

"I don't have a son or daughter." The words flew out of my mouth.

Ainsley's head turned. I ignored him.

"Exactly." The word resonated in her lovely voice as

a sort of challenge. She looked down at her watch and said, "I'm sorry. I have another appointment coming in a few minutes. You'll have to excuse me."

Ainsley interrupted with some polite noises and smoothed the moment over. Interview over—and I was three for three. Strikeout.

We wound our way out of the place as fast as I could follow the signs.

"You okay?" Ainsley said.

"Fine," I lied. My face felt hot. The curse of fair skin is transparent emotions. The doctor's words had shaken something that my sister's death hadn't even managed. I'd spent my whole life alerting adults to the trouble ahead—behind, everywhere.

I'd never doubted that work.

"Now what?"

I put my sunglasses on before we stepped outside. "We make some more calls. See if someone else is willing to do an on-camera."

Ainsley looked confused. "But the doctor said it could be dangerous."

"There's always somebody who doesn't want you to tell the story, College." The artificial cold of the hospital lingered in my voice. "Always. Sometimes they sound so reasonable."

The doors swept open and we walked out, shoulder to shoulder. Cold, hospital-scented air-conditioning evaporated into the dusty afternoon heat. I sucked in a lungful and tried to warm myself inside.

The boy didn't give up. "But…what if she's right?"

By the time we returned to the station, I'll admit I was looking for an excuse to drop on somebody. Two days on the job and I had barely ninety seconds of airtime covered. No photos, no sources, no cooperation from anyone—except my Boy Wonder.

I sent Ainsley to get us an engineering booth so we could load my stills in the computer and went to find out about my new office.

Barbara, Gatt's opposable thumb, greeted me with the carefully neutral face of someone who knows a lot more than she's telling you. I stood still for another once-over and she showed general approval of the absence of leather. When I asked about my office, she blinked her Raggedy Ann eyelashes, frowned and unwrapped herself from her phone headset.

"Follow me."

Swear—we walked three and a half, four minutes, tramping all through the building until we finally arrived somewhere deep in the old tape library. She pointed her finger that away. Crammed in a niche between two eight-foot tall stacks, at the farthest end of a corridor, was the ugliest work cube in the Midwest flatland. No chair. No computer. Oh, and no phone.

"Mr. Gatt said you needed something private. They'll install the phone next Monday or Tuesday," she assured me, all practicality. "PC should come in the week after."

"Great. Sure they will. You want to lead me back to Gatt's office, or was I supposed to drop a trail of bread crumbs?"

She looked at the ground, got the smirk under control and executed a sharp turn. "Right this way."

I banged Gatt's door wide while knocking, and called out over his voice, "I got a problem here."

The door rebounded shut behind me.

"I'll call you back." Gatt slammed the receiver down. It didn't ring again, although the lights started twinkling frantically; Barbara must be holding the line, so to speak. "What the hell're you thinking? You don't knock?"

"I knocked. What the hell are *you* thinking? I told you, I need an office."

He did a quick paper shuffle. "I told them to set you up."

"Yeah, they set me up, all right. Whichever wise guy had the idea to make me Bob Cratchit in the tape dungeon gets a big hee-haw, Gatt. I need a desk and a phone and a door I can fucking close."

"Oh, Christ, not again," Gatt whined. "I'll try and talk to operations."

Both palms flat on his desk, I leaned in toward him. I could feel the grit of spilled sugar under my hands. "You do that."

"You get me anything to look at today?" he asked.

"No."

"You want to be a pain in the ass, O'Hara, you'd sure as hell better come across with something I can sell."

"No pain. No gain." I stood up and brushed my hands clean. "I'll get you a story. You get me an office."

Climbing your way up television's mythical ladder of success to the point you are—*ta da!*—Someone is a hell of a lot of work. The effort it takes to hold your ground, continue being Someone, is worse. I wanted an office to get my job done, but I *needed* the office to rate some respect.

Flashbacks of Schmed's killer handshake and the good doctor's voice and Sheriff Curzon's death-ray eyes all spliced into one lousy day, and the paranoia started kicking in. Was everyone in this suburban backwoods salivating at the thought of my crash and burn?

Barbara was doing some life-or-death typing as I passed her desk. I noticed the extralarge jug of ibuprofen sitting beside her elbow.

"You mind?" I asked, reaching for the bottle.

"Help yourself." She opened another drawer and passed me a packet of soup crackers. "I like four on a saltine this time of day."

"Tasty. Thanks."

She raised her hand to wave away my gratitude.

So. Not everyone was rooting against me.

All right then. Back to work.

The minute College and I finished logging photos, my cell phone rang. Jenny's teacher, a Mrs. Horner, was calling to ask if I would stop by her classroom. "I'll be here at school until six tonight. I'm very concerned, Ms. O'Hara. Please make sure to stop in and see me this evening."

Of course, I told her.

Ainsley must have seen me blanch because he chucked me on the arm and said, "It can't be that bad. It's Friday, remember?"

"And what exactly does that fact mean to you, College?"

"Beer." He shrugged. "All-night videos. All-day nap."

The blue glow of the monitors in the darkened room

made it harder to read facial expressions. I leaned back in my chair to make sure he didn't miss mine. "We have ninety seconds of usable material, to fill six minutes of national airtime on a story I don't even know is gonna *work*."

"No problem. It's not due 'til Wednesday—that gives us both Monday and Tuesday to work on it."

"And Saturday. And Sunday."

"Oh."

"That's right, College. Beer and video all night if you want, but I want you in the truck, in my driveway by—" he looked so horrified, I decided not to ruin both our days completely "—noon tomorrow. We'll start by picking up Melton's research on our mysterious Amish fireman."

5:46:60 p.m.

School was the one place I didn't have to worry about Jenny. Or so I thought.

"The art teacher didn't take attendance. Jenny wasn't missed for almost an hour. I think she was sitting in the girls' bathroom the whole time. Jenny refused to talk to me about it."

"I don't get it." My sigh was embarrassingly loud. "She ditched *art?*"

Jenny's school was a bright white labyrinth of wide halls and darkened classrooms. I'd found her teacher, Mrs. Horner, before collecting the kid from the after-school gig. Had to leave my driving gloves on to shake the woman's hand; my palms went slick the minute I walked through the front door. Catholic school didn't leave a parade of fond memories through my elementary education.

"I don't really understand either, Ms. O'Hara. She told the art teacher she didn't want to make pictures. This kind of defiant, secretive behavior isn't like Jenny. She's always been a pleasure to have in class." Mrs. Horner was a third-grade teacher straight from central casting: the careful coif, the Talbot's wardrobe and the friendly, direct manner—sort of a cross between Martha Stewart and a Zen Buddhist—a rigorously satisfied, female perfectionist. She offered me another pained smile. "Is everything at home…all right?"

"Her mom died a few months ago. I don't see how anything could be right." I rubbed my forehead where the pounding was the worst, mostly talking to myself.

"Ah. Yes, of course." Mrs. Horner discreetly studied her hands. "Is she getting any kind of counseling?"

"Counseling?"

"With a therapist. Grief counseling can be so helpful."

"Uh, no. Not right now."

The woman nodded, her expression so concerned and earnest, I felt like sticking out my tongue at her.

"I appreciate the heads-up. I'll talk to Jenny." I pumped reasonableness into my voice, until it was thick as sugar syrup. "Believe me, Mrs. Horner, Jenny is priority one right now. I'll do whatever it takes to make this right."

Maybe if I kept saying it, somebody would start believing me.

She nodded again and finally agreed to lead me through the school to find Jenny.

The after-school program was held in the gymnasium. It didn't look that bad. The kids had games and craft supplies. There was a low din of hustle-bustle to the place. Nobody was making them sit in perfect rows with their hands folded and their heads on their desks or anything.

We found Jenny sitting by herself at one of those plastic mini-picnic tables, watching the other kids play. I still couldn't understand the problem. The kid ditched *art?*

"Hey, Jen. Time to go."

She dug her backpack from the bottom of a sloppy pile against the wall and trailed me out of the place without making eye contact once.

"Heard you had a bad day."

I got the slantwise nod. We walked to the parking lot

and I tried draping my arm over her shoulder. She was so small. I expected the gesture to pull her closer, but it felt like I had too much arm to make it work.

"Thought you liked art."

Jenny sighed. "We were making flowers."

"Huh," I said as if I knew what the hell she was talking about.

"Caryn said she had to have the pink paper because that would match her mother's wallpaper. She just, like, took mine."

"Yeah?"

"Caryn was like "cause you don't need it.""

Little bitch. "Huh," I grunted again.

"I didn't care," Jenny tossed at me, her voice clear and fragile as glass. "I didn't feel like making flowers anyway."

We'd walked all the way across the parking lot before the girl managed to spill those five sentences. I handed her a helmet and balanced the bike between my legs, while Jenny scrambled onto the buddy seat.

"Watch your legs."

"I know."

The pipes were still hot. I'd burned myself plenty of times riding behind my dad, but my warnings were redundant to Jenny's cautious soul.

The neighborhood got pretty lively this hour of the day. Kids screaming all over the place with the joy of Friday's freedom, driveways suddenly sporting Dad's shiny four-door beside Mom's dinged-up van, and drifting on the breeze, the hungry smell of barbecue grills firing up the last of summer's feast.

I took the long way home, feeling Jenny's hands wrapped around my middle, her helmet pressed hard between my shoulder blades. It's too noisy to talk while riding. The kid's head barely clears my elbows.

"Hang on," I shouted, as we leaned into the last turn. "Hang on tight."

What else was there to say?

Jenny followed her aunt into the house and went to hang up her jacket. She noticed what was wrong right away. It made her feel creepy. "Aunt Maddy?"

Her aunt popped her head around the kitchen door. She'd gone straight in there to pull something from the freezer for dinner.

"The door's open."

"Yeah? I unlocked it."

"No. Mommy's door." Jenny tried to say it loudly but her throat was too tight. "Mom's door is open."

"Lasagne or chicken?" Holding two boxes of Lean Cuisine, her aunt walked into the hall. She saw Jenny staring.

The door at the end of the hall, the one that led to her mother's bedroom, was standing wide open.

"That's weird," Aunt Maddy said. "Did you go in there?"

Jenny shook her head no. "Did you?"

"No," Aunt Maddy said.

They both stared at the open door. Her aunt frowned.

"It must have blown open or something. I left a window cracked in my room today. That's probably it. Pull it shut for me when you go down there, would you?" Her aunt went back to the kitchen.

Jenny walked down the hall toward the room. She stopped in the doorway. Her heart was beating fast. She looked around. Empty. The room looked...ordinary in the daylight. Not the way it did at night. She took hold of the door knob, feeling calmer.

As she turned her head, she noticed it. The drawer was open.

Her mother's picture drawer in the bedside table was hanging open. Empty. All the pictures were gone.

"What's wrong?" Aunt Maddy asked. Like magic, her aunt was suddenly standing right behind her.

Jenny felt her body fly out in all directions at once.

"Whoa." Aunt Maddy touched her shoulder. "Easy, kiddo. I didn't mean to scare you. What's up?"

Guilt stuck in Jenny's throat. Where did the pictures go? If she told her aunt about the pictures, she'd have to tell her about being in the room. She didn't want to talk about that.

"You haven't been messing around in here, have you?"

"No. Not me," Jenny answered.

She wasn't lying. It was more like a wish.

(DR. GRAHAM ON-SCREEN): "Tom Jost's suicide might not be so surprising considering the statistics. There are patterns of inherited depression among Amish. There are patterns of depression in emergency service workers as well."

SATURDAY

9:55:00 a.m.

"She's here!" Jenny called.

I heard the door open and my friend Tonya Brown made her usual entrance.

"Mmm-mmm. That's what I needed this morning. How does someone so tiny give such good hugging? Your auntie awake yet?"

"She's awake. Did you bring polish?"

"I did."

Their feet clomped above me, then echoed on the wooden steps down into the basement.

"Hey," I called from the treadmill.

Tonya marched over and clicked off the CNN. "Non-business hours, honey. It's music time." She popped a best of En Vogue CD into the player and winked at Jenny.

The first time Tonya Brown made the trip out to my little ranch was the day after my sister's funeral. She'd brought her gym bag and my entire free-weight set, scavenged from my north-side apartment. The suspension on her drag-ass POS car would never be the same.

God, was I glad to see her.

Every Saturday morning since, she'd come to work

out and hang out with Jenny and me. Jenny liked her, too. A lot.

Tonya was an E.R. nurse at County Hospital when I first met her. I'd been hired to develop a story on inner-city emergency-room medicine. It wasn't that far from my usual material. The executive who did the hiring had used me several times that year. Maybe he liked my eye for stills, or maybe someone tipped him off that I needed downtime after Afghanistan. That was the summer I drove Peg into a sidewalk mailbox near the intersection of Sheridan Road and Jonquil, two days before the Fourth of July. Kids were playing with fireworks; I thought somebody was shooting at me.

Anyway, Tonya and I hit it off. Whenever I was home for a few days, T and I got together at my apartment on Saturdays. We lifted weights in the morning, drank margaritas until dinner and spent the rest of the night in a quiet restaurant complaining about work or men, or work and men.

When my life changed, Tonya found a way to keep the healthy part of our tradition going. We still worked out on Saturday mornings, Jenny fiddling with something nearby. Lately, the two of them had bonded over hair and nails. Tonya is the only weight lifter I know who maintains her relaxed grip on the bar by virtue of three-inch fingernails. Today, they were painted electric green.

Jenny was impressed. "Tonya, could you bring the green nail polish for me next week? It's awesome."

"Sure, baby." The bar clanged as she finished a set. "This girl's got sophisticated taste, Maddy. Not everybody appreciates my green."

Or her chartreuse unitard. Or the matching beads

clackety-clacking as her extensions swung above her shoulders. Of course, only an idiot would fail to appreciate the entire package.

"Huh," seemed a safe enough answer. I timed it to an exhale on my leg press.

Tonya twisted one elbow high beside her ear for a triceps stretch, while fishing around in her giant bag with the other arm. She grabbed a handful of something prescription level and chased it with water. "Don't eyeball me, Maddy O'Hara. I'm clean and legal here."

"Wouldn't think of it." I shifted the pin on the weight stack for my last set of reps, cleverly looking the other way. "How's the back?"

"Oh, just shitty. Sorry, baby, don't listen to that nasty talk." She must have told Jenny not to listen fifty times a day. "I may have to take another promotion if it keeps acting up."

"Why are you lifting if your back is bothering you—"

"Please." She cut me off in her Top Administrator voice. "I'm a trained professional. Biceps curls are good for me."

"What's with the meds?"

"Pain slows healing." She winked at Jenny, who was trying not to be noticed watching us. "I take a couple of these and feel no pain at all."

When T left the E.R. to become Director of Nursing, part of the reason was the added challenge. Most of the reason was the disc she'd blown rolling a road worker off a bed onto a gurney. Another reason T and I were friends—she understood pushing harder than made sense.

Sweat popped everywhere as I cranked out my last two presses. *I can do this. I can do this.*

"I think I'll need two coats of purple," Jenny announced. "I like them really dark. Next time though, I want to try orange and green."

"I think that'd be very…autumn. Now I'm going to do one more set of curls, baby, so I can still beat your auntie arm wrestling, and then we'll see about braiding your hair. Sound good?"

Jenny gave Tonya a pressed-tight smile, the one that always seemed to me as if she was hoarding her happiness.

I swung my legs around the bench and sat up. Exhaustion hit me hard.

All Tonya had to say was, "Would you go run and get me some more water, baby?" and we had a moment to speak privately.

"Thanks for coming out today and hanging with the kid," I offered.

"Daylight hours are no problem. It's those midnight runs that kill me."

"Uhn," was the best answer I could manage.

"Any more bad nights?"

"Not since the last time I called."

Things had calmed down since the school routine had gone into effect. Midsummer, I'd had a bad spell. I started slipping out at night when the kid was sleeping. At first, I'd walk to the mailbox and come right back. Then I went all the way to the corner and back. One night I walked all the way to the highway and back. That night, I got back just before dawn. Jenny was still sleeping peacefully.

But I knew we had a problem.

The next time I had the urge to walk away, I called
Tonya after Jenny fell asleep. She came, no questions
asked. I always returned before Jenny woke.

"Work's helping?" Tonya asked.

"Yeah. Sort of."

"Talk to me, Mad-dee." Tonya teased my name out.

I had hung a clock on the wall across from my treadmill, so I didn't have to feel the clock in my head while
I worked out. It's always there, :60, :30, :10, bumper,
commercial, joiner. Out. How much time did we have to
talk privately? Minutes, if I was lucky. I usually worked
myself up to these kinds of conversations, over hours
and an entire pitcher of margaritas. Another lifestyle
change: pruning my emotional life into the time limit
that fit around Jenny.

Tonya leaned back against the wall and patted her face
with a towel as if we had all the time in the world.

"This story I'm working on. It's got something. At
first, I was afraid it was pretty run-of-the-mill creepy
sex stuff, you know. But there's something else there."
I tried to shake it off. Make it seem less significant.

She gave me her careful eyebrow look, the one that
indicates concern mixed with you-crazy-white-girl.

I don't know why I tried to explain; I'm sure she's
right. "I spent the last few years in the field doing nothing but war and disaster. Half the time, I'd end up talking to the head guys because nobody worried about
talking to a girl."

We shared a long suffering eye-roll.

"And even though I sucked at first, figuring out how
to ask questions and get answers, wearing masks to
hide my disgust, hiding my fear—I wanted to do it. I
believed."

She nodded and picked up the barbell I'd just finished using, adding ten pounds to either end. She needed all the strength she could muster. Cynicism and hope were the left and right ventricles of a nurse's heart and soul.

"Sometimes, I was so afraid." Muscle memory caused a familiar burning roil below my diaphragm. "But I didn't want to stop. The stories mattered. They mattered to me."

Tonya gave me the blank look. "You are going to have to spell this one out. You're losing me."

"I'm just saying there's something in the stuff I get attached to that kind of worries me. You know—with Jenny around now." I popped my last three curls, breathing fast. My skin tingled, warm from the effort. "Damn. I'll shut up now."

"No. Say it."

"In my head, I hear my J-school profs yelling, 'You interview experts, you aren't the expert. You report the news, you aren't the news.' So I try not to get involved, but there's something underneath the stories I want to do that scares me."

"Sounds normal to me. You want to know what's under the rock. Remember how you obsessed about Dr. N?" Dr. Norman was part of my emergency-room story. He'd been in and out of recovery programs. He was good at two things that should have been mutually exclusive, high-pressure healing and drinking. My theory was he used them both the same way—full-body forgetting. "And it made a great story."

"If I was in a hurry, I could do something with the lead I've already got on this story. Splice in some network research on deviant sex and I'm done. No-brainer."

"So why don't you?" The words puffed out as Tonya curled.

I shrugged.

The weight clanged back into a resting position. Tonya took one deep breath, studying my face the whole time. "Then be about your business. Investigate. Report. Figure it out, baby. Figure it out. For yourself and the rest of us."

Upstairs, the doorbell rang.

We both looked up, listening to Jenny's feet run across the floor upstairs. Her voice filtered down to us. "I'll get it."

"How's she doing?" Tonya asked softly.

"Okay, I guess." I dropped my bar and everything sagged. Resistance was the better part of what kept me upright lately. "She ditched a class yesterday. Teacher asked me if she's getting any 'help.'"

"Like a shrink?"

"I guess."

"Shit." Tonya sighed. Therapists would not have been widely utilized in Tonya's childhood neighborhood. Too hard to do therapy on somebody who doesn't eat regularly. "You know any shrinks?" she asked.

"No."

"You want me to ask around? Get you the name of someone good?" People who work in a hospital know better than anyone that they call the guy who finished last in his class at medical school "doctor," the same as all the rest.

I sucked a long swallow of water. "I think she just needs some time. Her mother *died*. She ought to feel shitty. I do."

"Yeah." Tonya plopped her butt on the bench press and looked at me. "How bad is it?"

I stalled to get the bite at the back of my throat under control. "I got a six-minute story due in four days, jack-all in the can and my backup is Opie the Boy Wonder. Jenny still wakes up screaming once a week. This house I'm living in is triggering flashbacks to my misspent youth and my prescription for Xanax has expired. I'm great. Just great."

"I can help you out with the Xanax."

"You're a pal." The only towel I could find this morning was embroidered with daisies. It made my sweat feel especially dirty.

Tonya smiled. "There's always boarding school."

That got a grunt.

One of those nights I'd run for it, I returned with a half-baked plan to sell my sister's house and pack Jenny off to boarding school. My frugal sister had managed to build some decent equity. In the current market, I figured I could get the kid all the way through high school on that money. Summers, I'd let her stay with me, or she could go to friends. She'd make lots of friends at school, right?

Tonya had listened to the whole plan, one eyebrow cocked, television on in the background rattling on some typical morning news about a kid who'd gone missing and parents who were frantic. She'd clucked her tongue and dragged me up the hall to look in at Jenny dreaming. The room was warm with sleep, and smelled of what I knew to be Jenny and thought might be my sister, or even mother.

"No boarding school, yet. Thanks."

"You're welcome," Tonya answered. "Only one of us is allowed to have a breakdown at a time."

"I'm not having a breakdown."

"Uh-huh."

"I'm fine."

"Fucked-up. Insecure. Neurotic. Emotional. Yeah, you're *F-I-N-E,* all right."

There was the sound of footsteps on the stairs and who should appear? Ainsley's happy head popped around the corner. "Hi, there."

Jenny hadn't followed him. I could still hear her feet shuffling around upstairs.

"Hi yourself. Who's this?" Tonya drawled. Her posture altered and her chameleon-colored unitard suddenly took on that queenly nonchalance that only black women can pull off in lycra. Ainsley was suitably impressed.

"Meet my Boy Wonder," I grumbled. "Ainsley Prescott. Tonya Brown."

He reached out to shake her hand. Ainsley's version of weekend casual wear consisted of a gray T-shirt— tucked in—and ironed blue jeans. The shirt hung loosely across his shoulders, his collar bone and shoulder blades cutting into the drape of the cloth at the back. Ah, young-boy bones.

"And what a wonder he is. Very pretty. He gay?"

"Not sure," I said to rile him. "Never came up."

"Not," Ainsley replied drily. "I give demos, if you'd like to resolve any doubts." He pressed a palm over his heart and smoothed it down his chest, stopping when his fingertips tucked in his waistband.

Tonya cackled. "Ooh, I like him."

Uncle Rich would not be amused.

"Back upstairs, College." I inserted my sweaty self

between them, herding him toward the steps. "You're early."

"No beer. No videos. I woke early."

As I hit the top of the stairs, Jenny came stumping out of the kitchen with a can of pop in her hand and cotton stuffed between her toes to protect her polish.

"Give me five minutes to change," I told Ainsley. "Then we can run and meet Melton."

"Are you going somewhere?" Jenny's voice stretched to a squeak. Lately, even walking out to the road to get the mail out of the box, I'd heard that same question, in the same tone of voice.

Come on, kid. Keep it together. I answered slow and steady. "I've got to go pick up some stuff from the local newspaper. Tonya's going to stay here with you."

"How long will you be gone?" Tonya stepped behind Jenny, using her whole body to soothe. No hands, just a solid presence at the girl's back.

Why couldn't I do that, give her comfort automatically? How do you learn that?

"Not real long." I saw the raised eyebrows of skepticism. T had offered to stay all day, if I needed it. Until that minute, I hadn't realized how much I did.

"Okay," Jenny mumbled. She wrapped her arms around her ribs and her shoulders rolled forward into two sharp points. Her chest seemed to cave in at the center.

"You and Tonya'll have a good time," I insisted.

Jenny stared back at me, blank faced and big eyed.

Everybody nodded. Nobody cared. I didn't even try to hug her goodbye.

11:48:21 a.m.

It was a twenty-minute drive to the Clarion News-paper Worldwide Headquarters. The red brick shoebox that held offices and press machinery was in a very industrial neighborhood surrounded by car dealerships, auto-repair shops and a no-tell motel with a flashing sign promoting: All Parking in Rear.

Interesting zoning code.

Ainsley seemed relieved the newspaper had its parking right out front. Before we got out of the truck, I decided to say something.

"For the record, College, I like to keep my personal life out of the office. I'd appreciate it if you'd forget whatever you know about my home life."

"You got it," he chirped, very sincerely.

Gratitude makes me sheepish, but my thanks were equally sincere.

As I planned, we arrived a few minutes early. Through the glass double doors, I could see the reception-ist packing up. She came over to lock the front and looked suspiciously in our direction.

"Don't." I cautioned Ainsley against knocking. People started filtering out the back doors and heading for the cars parked nearby. I made a show of looking around as if we were there to pick someone up. "I think Melton wants to keep this meeting private. She'll be gone in a minute."

"How do you know?" he asked.

"All the papers I've ever known roll up the welcome mat at noon on the dot on Saturdays. I'm guessing that's why Melton told us to be sure to come *after* twelve."

"What papers have you worked at?" Ainsley asked, dangling his preposition like a good Midwesterner.

"I started taking pictures for the *Cook County Register* back in high school, then did news photography all the way through college." He looked impressed; I shrugged. "Paid for my books."

"They say print is really different from TV news."

"Some of it's the same—the low pay, crappy hours, psycho egos everywhere. The motives are different, though."

The lights went out in the lobby. I tried not to look impatient.

"Motives?"

"People go into newspaper work for the stories, usually. They get a thrill out of knowing stuff nobody else knows. Knowing stuff first." I glanced at my watch again. "TV people want to know stuff first, too. But it's mostly because they want you to notice them—they like the glam. They're attracted to the glow of the set, like a bug to a flame."

Ainsley leaned against the glass and tested his come-hither smile. "Is that why you went into television? The 'glam'?"

"I said 'mostly.'" I could see his questions percolating. I answered an easy one. "There are a lot more people watching television these days, than reading newspapers. I prefer to swim in the big pond."

"So you like the competition."

"Partly." I snuck a glance at his face and added, "Also, greater opportunity for impact."

His brow furrowed. I figured I'd lost him, until he said, "Impact won't be much of an option at WWST, will it?"

Damn. He was with me after all. I shrugged. "Could be worse."

Melton appeared, looking furtive but smiling. He snapped open the door and bustled us through the waiting area.

"This way." The buzz coming off him was palpable. He must have found something interesting.

The *Clarion*'s interior was remarkably similar to WWST. Brown on brown. The fourth estate is not renowned for the decor and gardens. Beyond the reception area, we passed through the semipublic classified area and on into the antipublic newsroom. We wound our way through a maze of desks, randomly personalized with widgety clutter, family photos and the all-pervasive paper mosaic of shorthand notes, Post-its and newsprint. Some of the computer monitors looked older than Ainsley. The space was democratically at-large but mostly deserted. Here and there somebody sat typing or talking on the phone.

Melton paid no attention and made a beeline for the back hall. He'd cultivated a slouching sort of amble that almost made him seem as if he wasn't hurrying. "Plate room's right through here. Jeff's at lunch so we can talk without—" his voice dropped to conspiracy levels "—you know…interruptions."

The plate room is sort of a demilitarized zone between The Press and the press—the people who think up the words and the people who actually ink them onto paper. Nobody hangs out there. Melton was taking no chances we'd be interrupted.

We crowded behind an old relic A-frame into a far corner, where the light tables had been left on, burning through the page proofs with that particular shade of pale gray and fluorescent glow I recognized. I could smell the developer from the nearby darkroom. I crossed my arms over my chest and smiled, feeling right at home.

This was going to be good.

Melton handed me an eight-by-eleven envelope, wiggling like a puppy. "I got him. Employment info, adoption history…"

"Spill it."

"…and, did I mention, his *arrest record?*" Excellent instincts; Melton knew his lead.

"Curzon busted the guy?" I asked with more than a reasonable amount of glee.

"Not the sheriff. His cousin."

"Ha! And now I got *him*." I laughed and put up a palm. "Can I get a witness?"

Ainsley slapped my hand.

"Let it be a lesson to you, College. Give us the short version, Mel."

"It's an unusual situation because the Amish don't register births like we do. What I found was Tom Jost's real father left the area with his son when the kid was young. He went west—California, New Mexico— somewhere like that. The next thing we know, Mr. Jost is petitioning to remove the kid—he's ten years old by now—from an Arizona foster home, bring him back to Illinois. Kid's dad is listed as deceased."

"Fast-forward to the good stuff, please."

"Right, right." Melton waved a hand, shuffling through papers. "The next bit of paper I found on him is his application for the fire service. He'd just graduated from a fire school in Elmhurst. That was three years ago. Nothing else interesting happens 'til last August, about a month before his death. When fireman Tom gets pulled over with a minor in the car. Cop writes it up—"

"Curzon's cousin?"

"Right—as contributing to a minor's curfew violation. I think there was some kind of scuffle, couldn't confirm that, but Officer Curzon ended up putting them both in the backseat and giving them a ride to the station. Jost's car was towed and—get this, the tow driver 'happened to notice' the trunk was full of porno magazines."

"'Happened to notice'?" Ainsley repeated.

"Them tow-truck drivers got X-ray eyes," I mocked. "Go on."

"Apparently, Curzon-the-cousin wrote that part up as well, and sent it to Jost's lieutenant at the fire station."

"How'd you find that out?"

Melton crooked a bashful shrug. "Buddy of mine at the fire station."

"Not very discreet." Ainsley tsked.

"'Telephone, telegraph or tell a fireman,'" Melton said. "Those men sleep together two nights a week. There are no secrets."

"But why tell you?"

"I get the feeling none of them really liked Jost, for some reason. Bad blood." Melton shrugged. He seemed convinced the guy had been telling the truth.

"Any idea who the minor was?" I asked.

"No. But the record mentioned Amish clothing."

Ainsley flashed me a look.

"Female?"

"Yeah," Melton said.

"Rachel." Ainsley said aloud what we were both thinking.

I was grinning like an idiot. I love these moments. "Got anything else for us, Mel?"

"Nothing really. The girl was shipped home. The guy was given some kind of write-up. His employment record is sealed. I couldn't get anything on how it impacted him at the fire station."

"Your friend didn't have anything to add about what happened with his shift buddies?" That seemed odd to me, considering the gossip fest we'd had so far.

"Nope." Melton shook his head. "He said it all blew over."

"Except the guy killed himself a couple weeks later."

"Yeah. Except that."

1:03:11 p.m.

Fire station number six was out in the middle of nowhere. Couple of guys were giving a big red engine a bath on the driveway. Behind the station a three-story brick building with smoke smears around the windows sat alone in a parking lot. A training tower, maybe?

Several old junkers were lined up on the tarmac below the tower. We watched someone pull another barely drivable vehicle around and park it. The driver got out and walked toward us, your typical hulking, Midwest beefeater.

I opened my door and waved.

Ainsley followed me out of the van but didn't make a move to pull a camera. "These guys aren't gonna tell us anything."

"Why do you think it's not worth trying?" I pulled off my sunglasses before delivering the bad news. "Listen, College, if I gave up every time I thought I wouldn't get an interview, I'd be selling Mary Kay cosmetics right now. You want to sell cosmetics, leave the camera in the van."

Ainsley shook his head, his lips tight.

Stories always feel like something at the start—a texture, a shape, even a temperature. Once I recognize it, the whole thing falls together quickly. Occasionally, I get a story I don't understand right away. I have to back up and feel my way around the edges. Crack it open. Stick my hands in deep, take hold and turn it around a few times. Those messy, ambiguous stories are the ones that don't come easy. They're also the ones that keep me coming back for more.

Two days ago, I thought this was going to be a straight salacious sex-death; the kind of story that reveals in intimate detail exactly how strange your neighbor is. With Melton's research—on top of Amish oddities and sheriff tantrums—I knew things were about to get messy in a very good way.

"Relax, College. This is the fun part. We're living the dream. Right now." I smiled at the guy with the soapy sponge.

He smiled back until I flashed my credential and said my name. "I'll get the captain. Hang on." He disappeared into the station without another word.

"What do *you* want?" the beefy one asked. Up close, he was ruddy skinned. Bright eyed. Good looking. And young.

Lately, I've noticed there seem to be a lot of near-children doing grown-up jobs like fighting fires.

I tried casual. "We'd like to talk to someone about Tom Jost. He worked here, right?"

"Yeah." He pulled off a pair of work gloves and tucked them in his back pocket. The patch on his shirt was embroidered with the slogan *Prevent & Protect*.

"Did you know him?"

The guy folded his arms over his chest, looked at Ainsley, looked back at me. "Yeah. I knew Tom."

"You all work together pretty closely, know each other pretty well, don't you? Did he have any family? Girlfriend, maybe?"

"Tommy was a loner," he mumbled.

He stared at me, willing me to shut up and go away.

"I've heard it's like having another family when you work for fire service."

His eyes narrowed suspiciously. *Yeah*.

"Maybe the guys on his shift were like his family?" I asked.

The eye contact I got for that question crossed over from annoyed to odd. Maybe the guy had issues with family.

"Maybe," was all he had to say.

"Was it like losing a brother when he died?" Ainsley asked.

The guy spun around to stare at Ainsley now, as if some kind of insult had been implied. He looked down at his hands, out to the street, everywhere but at us.

"What's going on here?" A big fella with a respectable gut came out from around the fire trucks in the garage.

"Hey, Captain. We've got a TV reporter here, asking questions about Tom."

"Thanks, Pat. I'll handle it from here," the captain replied.

Sometimes it's hard to tell with men and their patented empty expressions, but the captain seemed genuinely concerned. He gave the younger man a bracing upper-arm squeeze and sent him inside.

"Just a few routine questions. We're looking for background mainly."

"Sure. Sure."

Ainsley got the camera rolling. The captain re-tucked his shirt. You don't usually get the top job unless you can talk the talk. The incident with Jost was a "tragedy." They were all "saddened." Employment records were "of course, private."

"We have a letter written by a police officer documenting some trouble that Mr. Jost got into with a minor." I threw that fact out there, fishing. "Do you think the situation contributed to his state of mind before the suicide?"

"Son of a…how the…? Never mind." The man winced and rubbed one hand across his bald head. "No way. No more questions."

I had so little to go on, I nodded to Ainsley. He took the camera off his shoulder.

"Off the record?" I smiled. "I don't want to bring it up, if it doesn't matter."

The smile always helps. "That letter should never have been written. Cop was out of line." The captain pointed his finger at me. "I had to talk to Tom about it. Had to. We weren't going to fire him or anything. We couldn't have, legally."

"How did Jost react?"

"Deer in the headlights. He seemed stunned. Oh, he was pissed, I could tell. But Tommy wasn't the kind to just blow off steam. He held it in, you know? I told him the whole situation would pass if he'd put it behind him. Forget about it." He waved the whole thing away with both hands. "The kid needed to get out more. I offered to take him out myself to a real bar. Meet some women. Set him on the right track, so to speak. That's how much I respected him. As a firefighter, of course. The kid had stones."

"Did he catch flack from the other firefighters about the letter, or the incident?"

"Probably." Captain shrugged. "The boys give each other grief for farting on the toilet."

"And Tom was just one of the boys before the trouble. Got along with everyone?"

"I wouldn't say that—exactly." Captain puckered up

with consideration. "Tommy was different. He had his ways, you know."

"Because of the Amish background?"

"Yeah. Wouldn't watch TV. Except the Weather Channel. Always had to take a moment, you know, when he sat down to eat. Praying and shit. Me, I got no problem with that. Doesn't bother me. Some of the other guys, it took 'em a while getting used to that kinda thing. Vegas helped him fit in." The captain tipped his head in the direction he'd dismissed the younger man.

"The other man we were talking with, he was a friend of Tom's?"

"More than a friend. They partnered on the ambulance."

Maybe that explained the odd expression when I'd mentioned family. Tom's partner was definitely someone we would want to speak with again.

"Pat's last name is Vegas?"

"No." The chief shook his head. "Vegas is his nickname. Everybody in the station's got one."

"He's a Las Vegas fan?"

"Doubt he's ever been there. Pat's a dealer." The captain snorted a little chuckle. "Always got something going on, you know?"

Ainsley went ahead and put the camera back on his shoulder. "This isn't privileged info, is it, Captain? Could I get one more shot? I'm not sure about the last one."

The captain gave him the Big Man's affirmative. "Tommy and Pat rode the ambulance together. Both of them are…were paramedics—EMS." He sighed and stepped back. "That all you need to know?"

I smiled some more. "Were they friends?"

"Yeah, sure. Pat had been here awhile already when Tommy got hired. Kind of took him under his wing. Tommy was small for a firefighter, you know. Some of the boys had trouble with that at the start. But he was a good man. Fearless. He'd do things nobody else would, you know?"

"Yeah. Sure." Fearlessness is the first requirement of unbalanced competition. "Tom ever go into a fire?"

"Oh, yeah. Did it not one month ago. House fire. Got a sticker in the window, says there's a kid in there. I'm about to call for volunteers, Tommy's already suited up. The guy had stones, I'm telling you. He came to us better trained than most of those babies out of fire school, 'cause he'd worked VFD for the Amish. He knew fire. Unafraid."

"How does it work out there, if there's a fire on Amish land?"

"If? Shit, they get them all the time. They've got barns full of sawdust and kerosene lamps. They live in wood buildings and use candles. And wood-fucking-stoves! I'm surprised there aren't more fires out there."

"Do you get a lot of calls out there?"

He pursed his lips and shook a no. "Most of them are too isolated. By the time we hear about it, not much we can do. If it's bad and it's not too far out—and some-body calls us—we'll send a pumper. That's what they usually need. Sometimes, a guy in full gear will go in after someone. The Amish VFD don't use air tanks."

"Why?"

"Mask won't fit over the beards."

"How's somebody do that?" Ainsley piped up. "How do you actually walk into a fire, even with a tank?"

"Most of the good ones, they think about it ahead a

time. Get it set in their head, who they're going in for—their wife, their kids, their mother." The captain leaned back against the shiny fire truck, just another old salt waxing poetical. "Tommy had that and something else. He was the kind of guy who liked a test."

I cocked my head and wrinkled my brow, keeping my voice off the recording. My face said it all, *explain that*.

"He was always setting tests for himself. Asking how many runs did that guy do? Pushing himself. The other guys on his shift, they saw right away he was a man who'd do the job. That meant a lot to him. Tommy cared what the guys thought. That letter from the cop—" Captain frowned, his jowls shaking with discouragement "—knowing what people were thinking about him, after that letter, it messed him up. Maybe just about the worst thing could've happened to him, you know?"

"What did people think about Tommy," Ainsley asked before I could, "after the letter?"

The captain had warmed up. He seemed almost relieved to tell his side of the story. Sometimes that happens. Usually, it's where you find a guilty conscience.

"Hell, they thought he was a pervert! All this time, Tommy was never anything but a paramedic and a firefighter—a damn good one—but he seemed to have no life, no…urges—you know? He was a robot, a shiny robot. That's how he got his name—" one side of his mouth crooked in a half-forgotten smile of genuine fondness "—guys called him Tinman."

"Tinman?" I repeated, hoping to draw out more detail.

"From *The Wizard of Oz?*" Ainsley prompted. "The Tinman had no heart."

"Thank you. I get it now," I ground out before turning to the captain to ask, "So your Tinman got busted for copping a feel on Dorothy?"

"Can you believe?" The captain opened his hands, all shocked innocence. "We were pretty surprised. He caught some grief about that, too."

"Any idea who the girl was?"

"He never talked about her."

Ainsley tried again. "Um, Captain? What sort of 'grief' did the guys give Jost, exactly?"

The captain waved it off. "No more than the usual. Few jokes. Put stuff in his locker, you know? Just grief."

Just grief.

"How did Pat handle it?"Ainsley asked.

"What?" The question startled him. He was suddenly self-conscious, trying to remember how much he'd said.

"How did Pat handle Tom's trouble?" I said. "You mentioned they rode the ambulance together."

"Oh, they were fine mostly. Yeah. No problems. They had words now and then, maybe, like anybody working together. Nothing unusual. I'm sure it was a coincidence they argued before—" The words came to a sudden halt. He turned his shoulder to the camera as if he'd forgotten something behind him. "Listen, I've got to get back to work now."

"You think Pat might be willing to talk to us?"

"No. Can't help you there. Against department regulations." The captain was back in charge. He held up a hand, like a crossing guard warning of a stop. "That's all now."

"Anyone else you know I should talk to? Any other friends of Tom's?"

"No. Nobody—except that school teacher. He used to go see her, have Sunday dinner or something. That's it." He stepped back, both hands up now as if he'd push us away if we tried to follow him. He backed up, two steps, turned and hustled off into the cavern of the firehouse.

"Thanks," I called.

"That was weird," Ainsley summed up as the camera came down.

"That, my boy, was not weirdness. That was guilt."

"I don't know if this is such a good idea," Ainsley said again.

"I heard you the first time."

Traffic was a mess. We crawled past town hall for the second time. It was smack in the center of the main drag. From the front, it looked like the live location shots used half a century ago for *Mayberry, R.F.D.* Wide stone steps led to a columned portico. Doors tall enough to accommodate NBA superstars. Surrounding the building was a park that extended a full city block behind the place. As we circled the area looking for a place to park, I could see banners and booths advertising for the animal shelter, the art league, Republicans and various other gun nuts.

"What is all this?"

"City's celebrating the 150th anniversary of incorporation," Ainsley said. "They've been planning it for two years. It's a pretty big deal."

"I'll bet." I felt a sudden whoosh of relief, as I realized how close I'd come to being ordered to do a story on sesquicentennial weekend for network television. All due respect to Charles Kuralt.

"There's produce and animals in that big tent, like a mini state-fair market. City hall's open for tours. Carnival rides in the Catholic church parking lot. I heard there'll be Amish here for the market. I figured that would be the place for us to get those filler shots."

Not bad; the boy had come through with a plan for getting the Amish on camera. However, his parking karma was the pits. Even the spots reserved for Town

Hall Business Only were taken by huge Lexus-style sedans straddling two spaces. Damn lawyers.

"Maybe we should stick to the sesquicentennial party," Ainsley repeated. "Leave Sheriff Curzon alone for a while?"

Here in the boondocks, the county seat was also the sheriff's palace. So it just so happened that Curzon had an office in the old downtown town hall courthouse; although the jail itself was in the modern extension grafted onto the back of the building.

"We're here anyway. We need to ask about the letter." I tried to keep the edge out of my voice. I like my work. I like asking people hard questions. "Don't worry. Curzon's going to get a big kick out of seeing us again. I promise to make every effort not to piss him off. All I want is five minutes of clean interview with the letter-writing cousin." I dreamed aloud. "Park right there."

"It's marked Deliveries Only."

"I know." I gave the boy a friendly shot to the arm. "Good reason to go see the sheriff. We'll ask for a press pass."

Ainsley looked a little bug-eyed, but he didn't argue.

I think he was getting used to me.

Inside the town hall, the air was old-stone cool. We followed a clump of modern signs glued to the marble, directing us to the sheriff's office. The place was bustling with activity. Folding tables were set up with handouts, balloons, people educating the citizens about programs for recycling hazardous waste, invader bugs eating local trees and how to fingerprint your kids for their protection.

The hallway swarmed with people, dressed casually

and talking loudly, many using the building as a cut through to the park area out back. A pair of kids darted around us with balloons in tow.

"Ainsley!" a woman in a suit called from across the hall.

College hissed something under his breath, then answered her with a big, welcoming smile. "Hi, Mom."

That turned my head.

"Maddy O'Hara meet Phyllis Prescott, my mother—" Ainsley coughed "—the mayor-elect."

"How do you do?" I said. What else is there to say to a mayor-elect?

"I'm so glad you came to our little celebration today, Ms. O'Hara. You are planning on taking a tour of the mayor's office, I hope." Phyllis Prescott struck me as the kind of woman who maintains a narrow standard deviation of appearance. Her hair was a widely available chemical gold, styled and sprayed solid. Nice open smile, decent handshake. She wore slacks with a suede jacket that sported appliqué leaves, pumpkins and Indian corn.

"Ainsley was saying perhaps you could arrange a special tour for us." I smiled at our college boy. He was not an idiot; he encouraged her with a nod.

"Did he?" She looked pleased. "Well, certainly. I'd enjoy that. I'm busy for at least another hour. But hopefully we can meet—"

There was a shout and a sudden interruption of feet pounding toward us, echoing against the stone up into the high-ceiling hallway. My heart jumped. Low threshold for startle response.

A big teenage boy in Amish clothes shoved past

us, bumping Mrs. Prescott against a table in his hurry. "Pardon, ma'am," he called.

"Hey!" Ainsley called, steadying his mother with one hand.

I caught a bright line of blood down the boy's face, from his nose to his chin. He didn't stop. He sprinted toward the bright light of the main doors, lunging around the crowd toward the exit, like a critter on the wrong end of the hunt. His fan club appeared down the other end of the hall. There were five of them.

The Amish boy had already cleared a path through the crowd, so the boys chasing him were able to move quickly up the hall.

It flashed through me so fast, I couldn't say how I went from angry to action. I put my best boot forward and turned the boys running toward us into a split of bowling pins: three in front toppled, two in the back still wobbling.

Ainsley had stepped forward to shield his mother. I stepped back, swung my camera off my shoulder and started shooting photos.

"What the hell!"

"Quit taking my picture, bitch!"

"That's enough!" Mrs. Prescott snapped. "You watch your mouth, mister, or you'll be in more trouble than you can handle."

As the two boys in front scrambled to their feet, a swarm of uniformed cops hustled up the hall. I hadn't seen them coming, being too busy looking through the lens. All the men were very concerned about Mrs. Prescott and very unconcerned about the tumbled teenagers. One of the cops put a heavy hand at my

back and directed me up the hall toward a door labeled
Sheriff's Department.

We all trooped past the front desk, to an open desk
zone, full of busy people and the constant under-hum
of electronic services: a scanner, two-way radio buzzer
going off, telephones. The usual. Felt like a newsroom
to me—except the men were more butch.

The Amish boy had been nabbed as well. He was
sitting in a wooden armchair, with a paper towel full of
ice melting against his nose. He looked like a kid waiting to see the principal.

"I'd better go with Maddy," Ainsley told his mother
after the paperwork had been organized. She waved
him on, deep into a tête-à-tête with one of the officers.
Sounded like the boys would be picking up tot-park litter
until they graduated college if she had her way. Power
used for good is so appealing.

Curzon appeared in the doorway next to where the
Amish kid sat waiting. He stepped back and thumbed
the kid into his office. Before he shut the door, he shot
a glance my way.

Guess who was next for the principal's office.

"You still plan on asking Curzon for a press pass?"
Ainsley sounded sorry for me.

"Sure. No harm in asking," I answered. "So your
uncle runs the local television station and your mom is
the mayor-elect. Any other family members you want
to tell me about?"

"Um…no?" Ainsley waved at one of the cops who'd
raised a hand in greeting.

Shit, my boy was better connected than a Daley
democrat.

I crossed my arms and propped my butt against the

desk behind me. "What does being mayor-elect get you in this town anyway?"

"A parking place. Free rides on fire trucks." He smoothed his sunny hair back off his brow with a casual brush that mimicked a cartoon *whew*. "Oh, and a cable television show."

"Maybe I should ask your mom for the press pass." I would have laughed out loud if there weren't men everywhere. "Cable, huh?"

"Everybody's got to start somewhere." He stuffed his hands in his pockets, elbows locked.

"What's it called?" I asked.

Cable shows are the pulp fiction of television. I concede a secret fascination for them.

"One Heartbeat Away." Ainsley's grin stretched another inch. He cocked a shoulder in half a shrug. "I was into Tom Clancy at the time."

The sheriff's office door opened and the Amish boy shuffled out, Curzon behind him. The boy was hunched over, elbows pressed to his sides, the brim of his hat clutched between his hands as if that black anachronism were the lifeline to his identity.

Curzon pointed toward the way out. A man in uniform with a freshly shaved skull guided the boy away. Curzon's back was to me. That world-weary slump wasn't his usual stance. One hand came up to rub his forehead in that classic masculine indication of simultaneous feeling and thinking. Always looks to me as though it gives them a headache. Suddenly he snapped around to look at me. I expected hostility, but his expression was mostly wary, as if he wondered, *what do you see?*

I didn't look away, which was the only answer I knew.

The things we see change us. I know this in my bones as much as in my head. I wouldn't do what I do if I didn't believe it. That old saying, "the eyes are the window to the soul," means more than just a view from the outside; it's a way to enter someone's soul as well.

The thing is, Sheriff Curzon and I probably had a lot in common. We both made a living walking through shadows looking at stuff nobody wants to see. Neither of our souls were all that shiny anymore.

Of course, when I felt threatened and shot at things in the dark, nobody died.

The sheriff signaled *get in here* with a snap of his head. I waved back.

"I'll go with you," Ainsley said.

"Oh, most definitely," I replied, grabbing a handful of his jacket above the elbow to keep him close.

Curzon held the office door open and I slipped past. Ainsley was stopped at the threshold.

"Rick," Curzon called. "Show Prescott's kid the break room."

Rick was the skinhead cop who'd escorted the Amish boy. He had a chest circumference that would have matched Ainsley's and mine combined. I could feel his voice, like bass notes through a subwoofer, when he reverberated, "Do they let you drink coffee yet, kid?"

Ainsley answered with a long-suffering sigh as Rick led him away. He shot me a look over his shoulder that was part woe, part vengeance.

"Trade with you," I called out. I freely admit it's easier to play hard-ass on home territory. I was not looking forward to a private meet in the sheriff's inner sanctum.

The wood blinds clacked against the office door glass as it shut behind him.

"Talk," Curzon rumbled.

"Nice place you got here."

His office had an old-world gangbuster air. Dark, paneled walls, designed to muffle everything from shady deals to gunshots and a mahogany desk larger than some of the parking spaces downtown. On top of the desk sat a stack of files, a pad of paper and a phone. Everything was laid out in parallel precision to the desk's edges. Including the shiny, brass plaque that faced a pair of parochial wooden chairs. It read Sheriff J. Curzon.

The man himself took a seat behind the desk. "What're you doing here, Ms. O'Hara?"

"I came in for a press parking pass. There was a little altercation in the hall, and…" The intro sounded lame, even to my ears. I cut to the chase. "I heard your cousin is connected to Tom Jost's suicide."

He folded both arms across his chest. "Says who?"

Tough talk is a variation of playground rhetoric; to do it right you have to get in touch with your inner child.

"Says me."

"They had an interaction almost a month before his suicide," Curzon stated.

"Which led to an 'interaction' with his boss over at station six. And further 'interactions' with his co-workers. You heard about any of that?"

He smiled at me curiously. He wasn't a bad-looking man under the right circumstances. But I didn't like the glow behind those green eyes. Didn't like the timing either. According to playground rules, he shouldn't be smiling.

"Where are you going with this, Ms. O'Hara?"

"Wherever it leads, Sheriff."

"Uh-huh." He opened a file on his desk and in an extremely polite tone of voice asked, "How is your niece—Jennifer—getting along these days? She doing all right?"

My hands clamped down around the wooden armrests. "I beg your pardon?"

Curzon looked frighteningly sincere. "I'm sure it must be hard for both of you."

"How do you know anything about 'both' of us?"

"According to the file, we never found the man who ran your sister down."

Double shit. "No. You didn't."

He spread his arms wide along the edge of his desk and pushed himself back, assuming the immovable object position. His weapon bulged in a highly visible lump beneath the shadow of his armpit.

The black handle caught me up short. I don't know why. I've been around guns.

They have a lot in common, guns and cameras. Most people have enough sense to be scared at first. Very few realize how bad it can get until the damage is done.

"Why do you ask?" I snapped.

"It seems relevant."

In a very calm voice I asked, "Do you think there is a conflict of interest? That I might be pursuing this story as a way of getting back at your fine—" *useless, Mayberry* "—department?"

"I think you have legitimate frustrations."

"I have legitimate questions, Sheriff Curzon. Such as, is it department policy to rat out somebody to their employer for minor violations of the civil code?"

"No."

"Then why'd your cousin send Tom Jost's boss a note, tattling that he'd been caught—what?—with dirty pictures and a high-school sweetie past curfew?"

"A letter was sent. It shouldn't have happened. Nicky thought he was doing the right thing."

"Do you think he was doing the right thing?"

Curzon made a face. "What does that matter? Nicky took his reprimand and moved on. It's over and done."

"Then why are you still trying to protect him?"

"I'm not protecting anybody here. I'm telling you, Nicky's a good kid." Curzon's voice was getting loud. "And a good cop."

"What about Tom Jost? What kind of kid was he?"

"I can't help the fact that Tom Jost didn't have people watching out for him." The volume dropped abruptly. He leaned forward, crumpling paperwork in his effort to close the space between us. "Nicky is a member of the team, like everybody else. I treat him the same as anyone. I don't turn my back on somebody for making a reasonable mistake."

Translation: whatever anyone else thought, Curzon didn't believe his cousin had done wrong. And he'd kick the ass of anyone who said different.

"Is that what happened to Jost? He made a mistake and people turned their backs on him?"

"Jost's life sucked," Curzon summarized curtly, then started rubbing his forehead the way I'd seen earlier. "I can't do anything about that. Nicky crossed a line and took his lumps for it. As his superior I see *no* justice in ruining his career over this."

"I'm not trying to ruin your cousin's career." I was starting to feel indignant. "I'm not looking for a scapegoat, Sheriff."

He stood up and the sheer size of him looming over me was enough to shut my mouth for the moment. He walked slowly around the desk, propped one hip on the corner and stared down into my face. "What exactly are you looking for then?"

I stood up, my chair raking the floor with a screech. "I want to understand what the hell happened. *Something* happened here. Something more than cheap thrills."

"Such as?"

"Such as, what it's like to always be different, no matter what you do. Such as, risking everything and then—giving up." I was riffing, with no firm sense my story would end up being about any of those things. Maybe it would be about all of them.

Curzon locked on to me with a brain freeze of a look. Then, he nodded sharply.

I decided that was a go-ahead. "How you are characterizing Jost's death? Suicide?"

For a moment, I wasn't sure he'd answer. He blinked twice and the tired lines beneath his eyes revealed the flicker of tension he tried to hide. "What else would it be?"

"Accident."

"No. The report won't call it that."

Which wasn't what I'd said, of course. "Why not?"

"No reason to. Jost wasn't on duty. He wasn't vested in his pension yet. There's no insurance. Why do that? Guy has a family. Such as it is."

"But if that's the truth?" I didn't believe Jost had killed himself accidentally in the throes of a sex act. But a sheriff must have a reason not to believe. "Wouldn't you have to report it?"

Curzon snarfed loudly. His expression was quite the

cocktail of dry humor and skepticism. "What's this? A reporter who's concerned about *truth?*"

"Yeah." I laughed along, irritation locking my back teeth. "About as rare as a cop who's interested in *justice.*"

Both of us spontaneously leaned backward. Sarcasm like that'll scar at a close range. Curzon relaxed his arms and fiddled with the papers on his desk. He started to say something and stopped, then like a bolt from the blue, he asked, "Would you like to come to my father's for dinner tomorrow?"

"Excuse me?"

"My family's getting together for a cookout. It's casual. Nicky will be there. You two can…talk."

"Yeah, sure," I answered, trying not to sound suspicious. "That would be great. Can I bring a camera?"

"No. But you can bring your niece. There'll be other kids there."

"Well." I stood up. I couldn't think what to do next. I knew it wasn't, but I felt like he'd just asked me for a date.

"Funny." He tilted his head and that reluctant smile crooked his mouth again. He was back to studying me like a specimen, hardly blinking. Days gone by, mobs would drown people with eyes his shade of spooky green.

"What?" I did a quick visual check down the front.

"The way you do that."

"Do what?"

"Come on like a lightbulb when there's an audience, but here, the two of us behind closed doors, it's all frosty—" he sliced a finger through the air "—back off. "

It wasn't his comment, so much as the implication that threw me. I slid sideways toward the door, opened it and threw back over my shoulder the first playground defense that came to mind. "Yeah, well, I think you're cute when you're pissed off, too, Sheriff."

Somebody heard me and whistled. Some other joker called, "Ooh—so do we, Sheriff."

I could feel the heat in my face.

Should have kept it simple and gone with *oh, yeah?*

5:27:54 p.m.

"Are you okay?" Ainsley asked me for the third time.

"Same answer. Stop asking," I said. Town hall was not where I wanted to be. "We've got work to do. Let's blow."

"Not much of an afternoon person either." Ainsley amused himself. "Follow me."

My funk made it hard to appreciate either the tour by the mayor-elect or *Our Town*'s sesquicentennial celebration. College seemed to have a vision, so I let him go with it. He shot general footage and some distance shots of Amish mingling with the crowds, selling vegetables and sizing up livestock. I interviewed a couple geezers in plaid shirts about how the town gets along with the Amish community. Unraveling a story with so little of the groundwork prepped was tricky. The whole thing could end up flat, dull or predictably salacious. After an hour of shooting B-roll we had decided to call it quits.

While Ainsley packed the truck, I phoned home. Tonya reported she and Jenny were on their way out to Sally's Discount Beauty Supply—no need to hurry back. She also told me they'd taken a weird call an hour before.

"I think it was a kid," T explained. "Said her name was Rachel and you were expecting her to phone. Told me she'd wait in the Buona Beef parking lot until sundown."

"Until sundown?"

"Yeah. Sounded like she'd been watching too many old movies."

More like living them. I'd be willing to bet Rachel Jost didn't own a watch. "Thanks, T. See you back at the house."

Two hours had passed since Ainsley had last put food in his mouth, which meant the boy's blood sugar was plummeting. He whined about making another stop until I told him where we were going. Buona Beef is a Taylor Street original, straight from the downtown Chicago neighborhood where real Italians have lived and cooked since before the city had indoor plumbing. The suburban copy isn't totally authentic, but they serve a decent beef sandwich "joo-zee, wid peppas." It was one of the few signs I'd seen that civilization had crept west with the population.

"There she is." Ainsley pointed as we rolled into the lot.

Rachel Jost was sitting at a picnic table in the dusty grass that edged the parking area. She'd changed from her dark gown, white apron and bonnet, into jeans and a shirt that would blend at any mall. Her braid was tucked down the back of her collar, disguising the length. But everything she wore was a size too big, and her shirt was misbuttoned; the tail long on one side, collar cockeyed at her neck. Her feet were bare, her heavy farm boots abandoned nearby. She looked like a runaway in stolen clothes. I doubted it was ignorance of modern clothing that rumpled her. It looked to me like grief, that great disheveler.

Ainsley brought both cameras from the van. Rachel eyed them as if they were attack dogs.

"What are those?" she asked bluntly.

"This is my assistant, Ainsley Prescott. He helps me make the TV show." I sat down beside her on the wooden bench. Ainsley sat down at the second table with the cameras. I settled in for a wait. Sometimes an interview only happens if you're willing to sit first. I doubted we'd get any footage but maybe I'd get an idea about where to go next.

Ainsley was rapt. He stared at the girl with the expression of a big-game hunter on his first safari. I wasn't sure if he had work or recreation in mind. The girl was pretty enough. She made me think of that statue of *The Little Mermaid*—classic features, solid feminine curves, all frozen forever in a permanent state of yearning.

She glanced at Ainsley and blushed.

"College, how about you get us some Cokes?"

"Sure. Do you drink Coke?" he asked her tentatively.

Rachel nodded without making eye contact. Her arms were wrapped tight around her middle in the teen-girl hunch that disguised the shelf of the bust, while otherwise fortifying the heart. I wondered if she'd called my house today hiding in the same bush where I'd first seen her.

Together, we watched Ainsley walk into the restaurant.

I started with the simplest question. "Why did you call, Rachel?"

"My father won't tell me what happened." She straightened and took a breath. "To Thomas."

"You mean yesterday, after the fire truck took him down?"

"The fire truck that was on the other side of the field?" She wrinkled her nose in confusion.

"Yes." I drew the word out, hoping to see comprehension. No such luck.

"Before that." She blinked at me and looked away. "My father wouldn't let us watch. He ordered everyone to stay away from the fence for the day. The younger children weren't even allowed out of the house."

"Oh."

She waited for me to say it.

"You want me to tell you?"

She nodded, fast.

"It won't be easy to hear."

Her eyes were dark and wide and wiser than I'd have wagered. "If I wanted easy, Miss O'Hara, I would have stayed at home."

True enough.

"He killed himself," I told her softly, pretending to be completely absorbed by the coming and going of cars through the parking lot.

She didn't move at all. I glanced over every five seconds or so, watching her face shift to whiter and whiter shades of pale. There was the sound of air moving, a whiny hiss. I couldn't say if it was going in or out.

"You still with me, Rachel?"

"Ja," she whispered. "My fault."

We'd never come to terms on metaphysics, but I tried anyway. "What happened to Tom was a terrible thing. But how could it be your fault?"

"So many wrongs. I don't know how—" She spoke simply, her voice thin and high. "I am alone. Help me."

"How?"

"My father and the bishop, they speak of love and forgiveness but do not offer it." She started to squirm, looking at me, looking away, twisting where she sat. "It is not *gess*. But how can I obey? How can I be humble before those who break the laws?"

Talking to people for a living makes for curious dichotomies. I've interviewed a thousand people, most of whom are still a mystery to me, but every now and then, I'll have a moment of perfect understanding with a total stranger.

"The world is unfair, Rachel. You find a way to live with it. That's all you can do."

"How?" She looked at me, really studied my face as if I was saying something new. Something she hadn't heard before. Her face was almost unreal, it was so fresh, clear of makeup, earrings, hair doodads. She still had a hint of baby-fat double chin, a last trace of innocence.

"How do we live with unfairness?" I repeated, rejecting the accurate, inappropriate answers flashing across my mental big screen: alcohol—sex—drugs. "People are different. You kinda have to feel your way along. Fall down a few times. Try again." I laughed at myself. My ineptness. "Sounds like learning to ride a bike, doesn't it?"

"No," was all she said over and over. The teenager's anthem.

Could you blame 'em?

Across the restaurant parking lot, Ainsley was jockeying with the door, holding it open as an older couple entered. Nice manners.

Wish I had been the one sent for drinks.

I felt as if something had locked me down, forcing me to search for words that might connect with Rachel. "I guess I survive unfairness by listening to other people's stories. I bear witness. Then, I'm not alone."

She didn't say anything, but I caught the tiniest nod of recognition.

"Cokes all around!" Ainsley announced.

Rachel looked up at him as if he'd just beamed down onto the planet.

"Great timing, College."

Rachel held her drink with two hands and ducked her head to sip. There was a furious sort of concentration on her face.

"Hungry?" Ainsley asked, exactly like they do at Irish wakes.

"No one but you, is my guess."

He waggled his eyebrows and shoveled another handful of fries in his mouth.

"Get your camera box," Rachel said. "I will tell you a story."

"You want us to interview you on camera?"

"No way," Ainsley whispered.

Rachel made a pinched-lip nod. The look on her face explained everything. Every teenager who'd ever lived had worn that expression, *I'll get you yet, oh mighty parent.*

"No," I interjected. "Besides the fact that you're a minor, your father will have a cow."

"He has many cows," she replied with a frown. "It cannot be worse between us. I am eighteen now, a month ago. Thomas told me I'm free to make all my own choices with this age. Is this true?"

"Yes."

"I didn't believe him. It didn't seem possible. To decide such important things, without others, without question." She did an odd sideways duck of her face that turned into a sip of her drink. I'd seen her do it twice and suddenly realized it must be the way she hid her face behind the stiff brim of her bonnet. It wasn't only shyness. She seemed ashamed. I wondered if the camera were a punishment she meant for herself, as well as her dad.

She straightened her spine and announced, "I am ready."

Ainsley raised eyebrows of concern in my direction.

"Are you sure?" I asked her, soft and serious.

"Yes. Do not look so worried," Rachel assured me. "I am not confirmed. It is not so bad. I will tell you what I know of Tom. In return, someday, you will tell me what you know. We have a bargain?"

"All right. Set us up," I told Ainsley. "I'll dig up a release form."

The parking lot backed up to a field of autumn-tall weeds. There wasn't much wind, and the road traffic was shielded by the building. With the right mic and a lot of luck, we might get something decent.

"Tell me about how Tom came to live with your family." I moved across the picnic table from Rachel, putting Ainsley behind my right shoulder, forcing him to frame her tight.

"He...Thomas was the son of a man who worked on our farm many years, a good friend to my father. He married an Amish girl. The year I was born, there was an accident. A fire." Rachel stared at me. "Terrible. Several died. My mother and Thomas's mother both. His father left our community shortly after that and took little Tom with him. He wished to return to the place where he was raised. Along the way, there was an accident. Thomas never spoke of it to me. I do not even know what kind of accident. Such a little boy and he was orphaned.

"Thomas told me once he thought there had been a mistake—he should have passed on then, to be with his mother. Well, I often reminded him, the Lord does not make mistakes. His life was spared for a reason." The words faded into her thoughts with a sigh. "It was a long time before the members of our community learned that his father died as well, and longer still before they were able to discover where the little boy had gone. Foster care." She made it sound as dire as it probably was.

"How long?" I asked.

"Too long." Rachel shook her head and sighed. "My father never remarried after my mother died. He asked to adopt the boy. Some said it was a blessing for us, as Father had no other children. Thomas would be raised Amish with the family he might have had. But when Thomas finally came to us, there were many difficulties," Rachel summarized bluntly. "He was no longer Plain. But neither was he quite an *Englischer.*" It was clear by her tone, the meaning of the word was something closer to "outsider," than a Merrie Olde import. "Everyone was *ferhoodled*…um, mixed-up, crazy. Thomas had it worst. He was afraid. It is hard to live within the *Ordnung,* to be… *gelassen,* when there is so much fear inside." Her frustration was clear. We didn't just speak different languages; we spoke different life experiences.

"I don't understand—*gelassen.*"

"Peaceful? But more, to give over. To yield yourself to higher authority," she tried to explain. "Yield to God and the community. It is a peaceful feeling."

"He couldn't yield?"

"Sometimes he was *grenklich*…um, sick?" she translated. "Upset."

I didn't mind that she was having a hard time sticking to English; it was a sign that she was talking from the heart, talking truth in the words that came first. I'd seen people who spoke six languages fluently revert to their native speech in the midst of a crisis when no one could understand a word they said.

"So Thomas felt sick when he had to follow the community rules?"

Rachel shook her head and pinched her mouth tight for a moment. "He wanted to follow. He wanted to be good. But maybe, I don't think Thomas ever left that place—in between." Her eyes and the tip of her nose began to glow pink with Technicolor teenage empathy. "Not Plain. Not English. Not ever."

"Is that why he finally left the community?"

"I can't say," she mumbled.

"How did your father feel about Tom leaving? What did he say?"

"To me?" She sounded surprised. "Nothing, of course. I suppose Father had many feelings when Thomas left. He was angry, of course, but also…disappointed, ashamed. He had tried to do the right thing and somehow, it came out wrong." She clammed up and swung her feet to skim the stubble of grass.

"Tell me more about Tom. What was he like?"

That brought out the smile. "Oh, he liked the animals. The dogs all slept in his room. Barn cat would come to him if he—" She flipped her fingers against her pants, and then again in the air for Ainsley's benefit, as if she were fluttering hello. "He even made pets of mice."

"Mice?" I returned her smile.

"Thomas could be very…still. Animals appreciate that. But he could move quick, too. Especially, when he was afraid. Then he moved—quick. Without thinking." Her eyes drifted out of focus as a memory seemed to flash through her mind. Her words stalled.

"Tell me about a time he moved quick."

"I…don't remember," she mumbled. A flush spread up her neck into her face.

"Okay. Tell me about a time he was with the animals."

She thought a moment. "He was always in the barn when he was supposed to be working the field. He liked to be around the animals, pet them, curry the horses' hair. Once, for my birthday, he braided Foxglove's mane and put flowers in her hair. It was a Sunday. I took her to church that way."

"Pretty."

"We were punished for it," she added, matter-of-factly. "Father thought it was prideful, showing off. It is hard for me to turn away from pretty things," she admitted as if it were a terrible fault.

My empathy meter kicked into overdrive. I kept flashing back on my own heartfelt confessions: age seven, eight, nine. *Bless me, Father, for I have sinned. I lied five times. I broke the glass on purpose…stole the bottle…started the fight.*

"After Thomas left, I missed him greatly. Once I was sixteen, we found a way to meet in the town. He took me to see things. The zoo, the mall, movie theaters. Have you ever been to the O'Hare International Airport?"

"Yes."

"Have you seen the great hall of lights that sing above the moving walkway?"

That would be the tunnel that connects the two wings of the United Airlines tunnel. There's a light sculpture above, glowing paneled walls and a new wave music audio track.

"Yeah, I've been there."

"Isn't it wonderful?" Her voice breathed awe. "We spent the whole day at the airport once."

"So that was a good day. When was that?"

"Right after he first went away. Before I finished school."

Melton's research figured Tom had left his Amish home about four years ago. "When did you finish school, Rachel?"

"When I was thirteen."

"Thirteen? What about high school?"

"It's not *Ordnung,*" she said. Absolute is the only way to describe the tone that word invoked.

"You mentioned *Ordnung* before. Could you explain it?"

"Most do not attend high school because it's not *Ordnung,* um, not according to the community's rules."

I kept my face blank. "Ah. Well, then the airport was a long time ago. What did you and Tom do more recently?"

"My father would not be happy that I see Thomas." She ducked her chin. "Not so much time for trips to the airport these days. We stayed closer to home."

"Your father didn't know you saw Tom?"

"No."

The change was so abrupt, I could almost feel her guilt swell between us, big and dark, swimming right beneath the surface. The small hairs on my arm prickled.

"It's not forbidden yet," she assured me. "I have not been baptized. The *rumspringa*," she confided.

"Sorry, I don't know."

"It's the time between childhood and being baptized in the community. It is a time between—of adult choosing. I must choose."

I looked at the girl sitting in front of me. Reporters have a voice that comes out when they ask the questions that mask a strong opinion. I could hear the voice when I asked her, "How long have you been an adult, Rachel?"

"Since my sixteenth birthday."

"That long?" I said. "But then why were you surprised when I said you could make your own choice about being interviewed at age eighteen?"

It flustered her. "Well, I may choose to do things that please me, but I must think if they affect others. If others are affected, they ought to be considered. Yes?" She said it with such simple sincerity, we took a minute of silence before I could think of my next question.

"Makes sense to me. What sort of things did you and Tom do 'closer to home'?"

Her eyes flashed up and away. "Oh, things…you know," she lilted with an elaborate shrug.

'Til now, Rachel Jost had reminded of my farm-raised grandma. Lots of straight talk, in short declarative sentences. We must be getting to the good stuff; Rachel suddenly sounded like a teenager. She glanced past the camera at Ainsley's bright head, his eyes down, discreetly monitoring the recording.

"College, is that your stomach I hear again?" I called out. "How about you take a break for a minute and go get all of us some fries?"

The boy didn't argue. He nodded, pulled out his earpiece, fiddled with the tripod lockdown and left.

"Now that we're a little more private…what sort of 'you know, things'?"

Give the girl credit. She didn't dodge twice. "We have a custom called *bundling*."

"As in keeping warm in winter?"

She squirmed where she sat. "Between people."

"I don't think I know about that." After a long silence, I added, "Would you tell me about it?"

"People…when they are of an age to marry, sometimes… It is good to marry. To have children."

"Sure."

"And when you think of marrying, it is very important to choose rightly. There is no divorce for us. We remain together until death."

"You'd definitely want to choose the right guy."

Rachel studied the hole her toe was making in a scruffy tuft of grass. "Sometimes, you must get to know him."

"'Get to know him'? In what way?"

She met my gaze with a look that was twenty percent guilt and a surprising eighty percent wit. Rachel Jost had a sense of humor.

"Ah. *That* way."

Neither of us rushed to elaborate.

I tried again. "You and Tom have been spending time 'getting to know one another' to help you decide whether to marry?"

"Oh, Thomas wanted to marry me," she admitted, face turned away.

"But you weren't sure."

Slowly, she brought herself to look at me. Her mouth was pressed tight, holding back words and tears. The effort had mottled her face into a raw blotch.

Oh, shit. Teenagers are a danger to themselves and others. All that emoting from full-grown hearts without any adult-acquired immunity to suffering.

"Lots of people have trouble being sure," I said, as if I knew.

"To marry Thomas," she began, "and live with him in the world, I would have to accept *Meidung*—leave my community, leave my father forever. To marry and be Thomas's—" She seemed to be struggling for the right word.

"Wife?" I suggested.

"Amish wife," she answered firmly. "Then he would have to leave the world forever. How could that be right either?" She looked at me with a helpless expression. "There was a disagreement between us. Thomas thought that more would convince me." The pain in Rachel's voice put a kink in my neck.

"What kind of 'more'? More time? More money?"

She looked confused for a moment. "No, no. Can you remember, Miss O'Hara, what it was like *before*, before you knew there was something else?"

Riddles inside of riddles, but I didn't want to interrupt her flow. I shook my head.

Rachel sighed a little. "I don't remember anymore, what it was like not wanting to be different, to be with Thomas. Oh, and kissing," she whispered. "How much easier it would be, not to know. My father says true sin is not done in ignorance. We must have knowledge to sin. I understand now. That's why Thomas was always between. He knew both worlds. It surrounded him." Her voice was small as a child's. "He was lost and he needed me. If my faith had been stronger, perhaps."

"You could have saved him?"

"He asked me to marry him. And I refused him."

The kid had eighteen years of experience, an eighth-grade education and some of the damndest questions of the human experience to digest. Twice her age and double her education, I hadn't come up with anything better than Life Isn't Fair. As a motto, it wasn't much comfort. For me or Jenny.

The only remedy I know is to put the worst into words. "You think Tom killed himself because you wouldn't marry him?"

She nodded, so tight-lipped I was afraid she might implode. An ill-timed flashback to Jenny's face this morning caught me in an empathy ambush. I could see it in Rachel's eyes; she was disappearing down the well hole. Sinking into crushing, septic darkness. Sometimes, if you throw the right distraction, a person will try to save themselves.

"People aren't that easy to control, Rachel. There was more on Tom's mind than just marrying you. That much I can say for sure." Thanks to Curzon's cousin, Tom had been embarrassed at work, reprimanded by his boss and fought with his more-than-a-friend Pat. Rachel was only part of what pushed Jost over the edge. "I've got one last question for you." My voice went cool, *enough emotional crap, back to business.* "Who owns the binoculars? You, or your dad?"

"What?" She blinked back into herself.

"Do you or your father own a pair of long-range binoculars?"

"No. No," she said quickly. "I think maybe Mrs. Peachy owns a pair. Her grandson gave them to her for watching birds on the feeder. The bad leg keeps her inside most days."

"Ah, right. Does your dad have people helping him with the farm, since Tom left?"

"Of course. Always."

That didn't narrow down who might have been watching when I took the photo of Tom coming down from the tree. Nothing like real life to keep the story messy. "How could I get your dad to talk to me, Rachel?"

"Heaven only knows," she answered quietly. "I don't. I must go now."

Those last minutes of an interview are often awkward. The camera seems to rematerialize. Everyone becomes self-conscious. Most people fumble their farewells. Some shake my hand and ask me to call; some duck and cover. Rachel ran.

With a quick goodbye, she picked up her clunky boots and walked away. She wouldn't accept a ride, even halfway. Someone was meeting her in the Wal-Mart parking lot, she knew a shortcut, needed to walk. In other words, *leave me alone.*

I didn't push.

She picked her way across the traffic, carrying the clothes of her other life under her arm. The sun was low and sinking fast. I wondered if she'd make it home before dark.

Ainsley wandered out across the parking lot. "She gone?"

"Yeah." I sat down and made some notes for later.

Photos: iso Rachel boots? (Juxta. Firehouse boots.)
Need schoolhouse.
Airport pickups? (Stock/news library might carry.)

Ainsley checked the images before breaking down the tripod.

"How'd that last bit look? Enough light?" I asked. "Did she stay in frame?"

"Of course I kept her in frame." He snorted indignantly.

"What about after you left?"

"After I left?" Ainsley repeated. Slowly. "I turned the camera off when I left."

"You *what?*" I felt a sick sort of lurch, the kind you get on a downhill.

"I thought you wanted privacy."

"From you, you bonehead! Not the camera. Never, never from the camera."

I sank down onto the picnic bench and tried to give myself the pep talk. *It's not brain surgery. It's only television.* Unfortunately, the *you are fucked* voice was too loud for me to hear anything reassuring.

"Sorry," Ainsley offered, sinking down next to me. "I misunderstood. I didn't think she'd want to talk on camera if she didn't want to talk in front of me."

"Not again, that's for sure."

"What did we lose?"

At least he said "we." "Oh, stuff like she was pretty much sleeping with Tom Jost and if she'd agreed to marry him, he wouldn't have killed himself."

"No way." He was so full of Disney-earnest shock, the sick feeling in my stomach doubled. "She looks so innocent."

"She is innocent." I couldn't decide whether to laugh or punch him. This business makes it very clear: what you think you know, based on what you think you see, tells more about who you are, than what you saw.

"Listen up, College Boy." I rolled my head and cracked off the tension building in my right cross. "That was one. You get to three, I tell Uncle Richie you and I are breaking up, and you are going back to baby J-school classes. Got it?" Journalism school would beat the impulse for privacy out of him.

"Yeah. I got it."

"Good. Here's rule *numero uno:* never, ever turn the camera off. You hear me? You're walking backward into traffic or running for your life—I don't give a shit—you keep taking pictures. You work for me, you will die with your finger on the trigger. Are we clear?"

"Clear." He didn't sound too upset. Either Ainsley was one of those kids who didn't let much bother him or he got yelled at so often, he was immune. "Anything else?"

"You know the old saying, 'seeing is believing'?"

"Yeah, sure."

"Well, here's a clue, it means believing as in faith." Ainsley frowned. "I don't follow you."

"What you see is you, College. Whether you're looking in a mirror, or at some Amish girl-next-door, whatever you see, describes the inside of *you.*"

He took the hint, pulled in his chin, packed the equipment without a word and drove home the same way. Every so often he'd give me a sideways glare.

He was mulling it over.

My whole career has been about making pictures that would break enough hearts to change the world. All I ever saw were tragedies.

Tonya rushed out to meet me as soon as Ainsley pulled into the driveway back at the house. As much as you can rush in heels.

"Hot date?" I asked, getting out of the truck.

"We'll see. Tell you about it next week." She smiled toward Ainsley but he didn't bite. "Baby's out back." She tossed her evening knapsack into the backseat of her car and blew me a careful air kiss, so as not to ruin her lipstick. "You watch her close, you hear?"

"I'm on it."

How she folds those long legs, in those high heels, into that midget Escort is an eternal mystery.

That was all the goodbye I got from either of them. Ainsley roared off.

The party lights hanging around the living room window were plugged in. The TV was on. I could see everything because I'd pulled the curtains down the day I moved in. Unlike my sister, I never could stand my mother's old Woolworth's lace anywhere in sight.

My father was a drunk. I know most people say alcoholic nowadays, but he was old-fashioned. *Drunk* suited him. Friday nights, he liked to hit Pete's Tap on the way home from work. If he made it to the door, he'd inevitably drop his keys, curl up on the front stoop and nap. In the morning, Mother'd open the door to take in the milk and call, "Come grab his ankles, Magdelena. Let's get him inside before the neighbors see." Mom always claimed I got the ankle end because it was lighter. I think it was because half the time he'd pissed himself. Once we'd lugged him inside behind a closed door, she'd go to the window and peek around the lace sheer, checking up and down the street to see if we'd gotten away with it.

I never put curtains on my windows.

Once I got inside the house, the first thing I did was check the thermostat. Even living in this house for months, all through the dry blaze of a Midwestern August, walking into the place still made me shiver. It was still my sister's house—her dopey chili-pepper party lights, her basket of nursing magazines, her crocheted granny blanket over the back of the couch. The place was a hash of hand-me-downs and modest extravagances. Personally, a decent-sized television didn't count as extravagance, but for her it did.

The living room walls were thumbtacked with Jenny's art projects, some so old they'd dried and yellowed at the edge. Fragments would occasionally drop off if someone brushed the wall by accident. Once an entire sheet cracked and crumbled to the ground, a painting of two stick figures and a pair of stick flowers; Jenny cried in her room for hours afterward.

I walk carefully through this house.

The light from the television bounced across the unlit living room and gave everything the familiar blue flicker of the electronic hearth. Tonya liked to have the TV on, whether she was in the room, watching or not. She lived alone in a little apartment in Wrigleyville and I suppose the voices and the flickering lights masked neighbor noise and made the place feel lived-in safe. The white noise of the machine did not comfort or bother me. Surrounded by stimulation all day long, the ability to ignore it was part of my job description.

Jenny had not learned that trick yet. Whenever I saw

her cross a room with the TV on, she'd lock eyes on the screen and freeze midstep. My sister had set all kind of rules about television time for her—how much, what channels, what time of day. Those rules had evaporated since I'd arrived. They were ancient history whenever Tonya took the remote in hand. Sometimes Jenny's reaction bothered me, which was why I'd started getting her to count commercials and promos. I figured she'd grow out of it. I did notice after Tonya spent time with us, Jenny often chose to play on her own out in the yard or in the driveway.

Through the glass door to the patio, I looked for Jenny. It was nearly dark outside and colder than it looked. No sign of her. I thought of Rachel. Who would be looking for her as dusk settled?

I buttoned my jacket and wandered into the backyard. Found her sitting in the birch tree—a big old tree, with papery white bark and leaves that September's chilly nights had recast in sunlight yellow. In the gloaming, the white tree stood apart from the rest of the yard, melting into the dusk. The thickest bottom branch had grown almost horizontal to the ground. It'd be an easy climber.

"Hey. I'm home."

Jenny looked down at me. "Hey. You're home."

"Kinda late to be climbing trees, isn't it?"

No answer.

I switched to the imperative. "Time to come in. I've got to go into the station tonight and do some work. Pack up something to keep you busy and we'll head over. I'll show you around. Make some popcorn. There's a video player. You'll like it."

"Okay." She flipped onto her stomach and her feet

twitched in the air, looking for a place to land. "Tonya's leg was really hurting today. Why does her leg hurt because of her back?"

"The injured nerve starts in her back. It's all connected."

"That guy who died, the one in your picture, remember? Do you think it hurt?" She slipped down to the lowest limb and jumped.

"Huh?" I caught a breath, nervous and suddenly aware of dangers everywhere, the sharp stick pointing toward her face, the rock right behind her head, the smallness of her bones. My threshold for fearlessness had shifted; it made me irritable. "When?"

"You know, when he got dead."

"Sure. I think it hurt." I herded her toward the chili-pepper lights surrounding the back door. This line of questioning was definitely creeping me out.

"Yeah, me too." Jenny didn't sound surprised. "Once, I had to get this shot. A really big one 'cause I fell and there was this rusty can right there. Mom said I bled like a stuck pig."

"Really? I never saw a stuck pig."

Birch bark had left white streaks down her jeans and when she brushed her hood back, a chalky smear of white appeared on her temple and forehead, as well. Tonya had braided her hair as promised, and added a bead and feather frill to the plait beside her ear. She looked like an elf in the middle of some night-forest ritual. The thought gave me an urge to cross myself, something I hadn't felt in years.

"Mom said it was a lot of blood. The shot was huge and I was scared, so the doctor was like holding my arm really tight, and then Mom said 'Jenny?' and pinched my leg really hard."

"What'd you do?"

"Said 'ow.'"

Conversations with eight-year-olds can be very Zen.

"Right. Why'd your mom pinch you?"

"She said it's impossible to feel more than one pain at a time." Jenny bumped me with her shoulder as we walked along. "Do you think that's really true?"

"Impossible to feel more than one pain at a time?" *Un-fucking-likely.* "Your mom was the nurse, she should know." My skin started to prickle. "Why're you asking?"

"Just thinking," she answered and wouldn't look me in the eye.

We passed under the red twinkle of lights and into the cool glare of the television.

Jenny froze, mesmerized by the screen. My hand floated over her head and settled between her shoulders near the top of her spine as if we were caught in slow-pause.

No pinch could camouflage what she felt. What Rachel felt. What we all felt.

I patted her gently instead. The words echoing back to me, *it's all connected.*

7:51:43 p.m.

"My mom used to take me to work with her all the time," Jenny called to her aunt from the backseat.

It was dark outside. The radio was off. Aunt Maddy turned it off. She was trying to think. Jenny was trying not to think. The car door was too cold to lean on. Jenny'd packed her pillow and her Nintendo and her softie pig in her backpack, but Aunt Maddy had put everything in the trunk.

"Used to take you to work, huh?" her aunt repeated eventually.

"Yeah. It was fun. There were machines with food and ice cream and stuff. And a cafeteria, too." Jenny looked out the window. At a stop light, the pretty lady in the car next to them smiled at her. It was so surprising Jenny didn't smile back quick enough; the light changed and the lady drove away.

"Sounds like an Ainsley Prescott tour."

"Huh?"

"Nothing."

"How long do you have to work?" Jenny asked.

"We'll see."

"Do you like work?"

"Yeah."

Jenny was quiet after that. She picked her finger and bit the skin next to the nail. Nobody ever told her not to anymore, so all her fingers had rough spots that were good for catching between her front teeth. Aunt Maddy didn't like to talk. She liked to ask questions. She liked to listen sometimes and watch people. She wasn't too chatty, though.

The TV station was far away in an empty place. The antenna had a red light that Jenny could see. Slowly, they got closer.

"I got to ride in an ambulance once. When I went to meet my mom at work," she mentioned. "It was a special deal."

"Really?"

Jenny could tell she didn't care. She bit her thumb skin until she felt a warm prickle of blood. It never hurt when she made it bleed. Sometimes it hurt later though. Lots of things were like that.

Aunt Maddy parked and popped the trunk. Jenny felt better when she had her backpack in her hands.

"I want to carry it," she said. "Don't put it in the trunk anymore. Please."

"Sure, Jen, whatever," her aunt said.

Inside the station was actually not so bad. No weird people. All the lights were on, so it wasn't scary. And there were TVs everywhere. Every room had one; some had more than one. The editing room where Aunt Maddy had to do her work had a whole mess of them, but they were all mini-sized.

"Come on." Her aunt led the way down the hall. Jenny hurried to keep up. "There's a couch in the break room and a VCR. You can watch a movie."

"Where are you going to be?"

The break room had a cabinet with snacks next to the fridge. Her aunt grabbed a package of popcorn. "I'll be in the editing room. Where I just showed you."

"Can't I watch in there with you?" Jenny asked. The couch looked pretty scuzzy.

"No." Maddy slammed the microwave door and hit

the power button. "You'll be fine here, kiddo. I'll be right down the hall."

Jenny didn't answer. Her heart started beating really hard, like she'd been running a monster lap in gym.

Aunt Maddy fumbled around with the video. The preview started and the familiar music helped Jenny catch her breath. She looked over at the screen and nodded.

"Look, the faster I get to work, the sooner we can go home. Here's the popcorn. I'm right down the hall. Okay?"

"Okay." She repeated the word because it was what her aunt wanted and sometimes if you did what a grown-up wanted for a while, they would give in and do what you wanted for once.

Jenny didn't watch her leave, but she did slip over to the doorway and peek down the hall to be sure which room her aunt was going into.

The previews ended and the movie started. Jenny went to the couch and let the story take her mind away. She'd watched it almost every day since her mother was gone. The girl in the story didn't even have a mother. Sometimes Aunt Maddy said, "This one? Again?" but she never made her choose something else.

Jenny hadn't been watching very long when she heard voices, loud voices. She hit the pause button and listened.

"…and I don't have time to play any fucking sales games tonight, Schmed. I'm working here."

Jenny's face got hot. That was the baddest word there was. She'd only heard it in school twice. She went over to the doorway, backpack in hand, and tucked herself into the doorjamb close enough to hear and see what was happening.

A tall man was talking. "…like I'm not? It's practically my office you're getting."

"Get over it."

He snorted before he spoke again. "All I'm asking is you go talk to him. Is that too much to ask? A little cooperation between departments."

"Take it up with Gatt." Her aunt sounded more than angry. She sounded mean.

"Fine. I will."

The man stepped out of the room and looked up the hall. His clothes reminded Jenny of this one neighbor on the block who was always playing golf.

When he caught her watching, Jenny froze.

"Hello? Who's this?" he called out. His voice was icky-happy. "You have a kid with you, O'Hara?"

Aunt Maddy came back into the hall. She turned toward Jenny with a look that meant *everything all right?* "Yeah. She's with me. Come here, Jenny."

Jenny walked slowly at first, then faster, up the hall. She kept her eyes on the man as she slid in beside her aunt.

"Jenny, this is Mr. Schmed. He works at the television station." Her aunt sounded angry.

"Hi there, honey." He smiled a big white grin at Jenny. His eyes creeped her out, even more than his teeth. "You're working late, aren't you?"

Jenny didn't say anything. She tried to smile but her lips felt too stiff.

"Pretty girl, O'Hara. You should put her on TV," he said.

"You're just full of good ideas tonight aren't you, Jim?" Aunt Maddy answered. She put her arm around

Jenny and directed her into the little editing room. "Nice chatting with you. I'm going back to work now."

"We'll talk Monday, O'Hara. After I see Gatt."

"Great," she said, but Jenny could tell she was lying. Maddy shut the door and added, "Bite me."

"Whaaat?" Jenny giggled. She didn't even know what that one meant.

"Technical talk, kiddo." Her aunt rubbed her face with her hand. She looked tired, like she was trying to scrub herself awake. "Movie over?"

Jenny shook her head no.

"Oh. You want to stay in here with me for a while?"

Jenny nodded yes. She sat down in one of the spinner chairs and tried to pay attention to the mini-screens flashing around them. Her aunt stopped noticing everything but the picture in front of her. She watched the screens while both hands moved over something that looked like a giant computer keyboard and a PlayStation controller. The picture on the screen would stop, go back, play, go back, play, stop, go faster, stop again. It made Jenny dizzy. Every now and then, her aunt would write something down or lean back and hit a button that made a bunch of machines all clunk and whir at once.

It was boring. All Jenny had to do was sit and spin and think. After a while, she had to ask. "Were you fighting with that guy?"

"Don't worry about it," Aunt Maddy mumbled.

That was one of those things grown-ups said all the time that Jenny really hated. Things like *how are you?* or *see you later.* Things that didn't mean anything. Did they think she was stupid? If Aunt Maddy wasn't getting along with the people at work, Jenny knew she wouldn't want to stay in this job. Where would they go? What would they do?

Inside, Jenny got that scary feeling again. It felt like shrinking, like all her guts were disappearing. Jenny felt if she breathed too hard, her hollow inside might pop and she'd vanish, like a bubble. Forever. She bit her finger where the blood had come out before but it didn't help.

"Aunt Maddy?" she said, real soft and quiet. "Aunt Maddy, I feel shrinky inside again."

Her aunt leaned closer to the screens, straining to see or hear something Jenny didn't understand.

"Damn," Maddy whispered. The picture flashed. Stop. Go again. "What? Sorry, Jen, I gotta work here. Don't talk to me unless it's an emergency."

Jenny stood up and walked to the door, dragging her backpack. She didn't try to be especially quiet. She didn't have to.

(Rachel, V.O./Audio only): "Thomas said something once, when I first visited him and I was stiff about the Englischer. 'The closer you look at Plain people, the more you see that things are not always so good. And the closer you look at the Englischer, the more you see it is not all so bad.'"

SUNDAY

8:55:12 a.m.

I could feel the blood tickling its way down my leg into my shoe.

"Where have you been?" Jenny demanded the second she opened the front door. "You were running."

She sounded like a high-court judge. I pushed past her and limped toward the kitchen. *Squish, squish.*

"Is that blood?" The icy, early morning wind snapped her nightgown around her legs. Jenny didn't budge. She stood there in bare feet, scowling at me. Kids have no sense of self-preservation.

"Close the door, you'll freeze to death," I said.

Cold water from the kitchen faucet dulled the throb in my palms and cleared the dust off my face.

She followed me as far as the kitchen door. "What happened?"

"I fell." My eyes wouldn't stop watering. Because of the dust. That's my story and I'm sticking to it. "Go get dressed."

Jenny took a giant step away from me, eyes wide.

"Wait, Jen—find me the phone, would you?"

She nodded, then vanished.

I don't run every morning. For one thing, running's boring. For another, Jenny's not too fond of the idea. But sometimes, when my brain is too thick, the only thing that clears my head is running. Pounding it out through my feet—down and out, step, breath, step, breath—somewhere along the way, the picture in my head focuses and I can see again.

I'd spent half the night on the computer researching everything I could find about the Amish and my new hometown. I'd filtered out a list of local experts I could interview about the Amish culture, relevant local history and once again reread the stuff Melton gave us on Jost's time in foster care. I was missing something.

Around eight minutes past six, I threw on a sweat suit and slipped out into the predawn dark to run the story loose.

So far, I had a suicide that could have been an accident, a firefighter who would have been an Amish guy, and a girl who should have been a bride. Coulda. Woulda. Shoulda. I'm onto something all right. It's the road to hell.

Right on schedule, some underworld hound comes roaring up on my heels, driving a silver SUV.

"Son of a bitch!"

The car roared up alongside me, riding the shoulder and spitting gravel. I jerked right and misjudged the slope into the drainage ditch. My ankle buckled. My knee popped. My ass went down.

The guy slammed on his brakes, skidding to a stop twenty feet ahead of me. I scrambled upright, favoring the knee and flipping him the bird with every finger I've got available—not to mention providing plenty of audio—when the jerk-off guns it, fishtails gravel all over me and takes off. I got the first letter of the license before the dust hit my eyes.

Six months ago I was one of the toughest videographers in the business. Now, I'm the Joe Atlas wimp getting sand kicked in my face.

What the hell has happened here?

Jenny was of the same opinion. She stood there in the kitchen doorway, fists on her bony hips.

I slid down onto the cold ceramic floor and braced my back against the sink cabinet. I could tell it was going to be a few minutes before I could even make a call; my teeth were chattering too hard to speak clearly. Typical aftereffects of adrenaline: chills, shivering, lightheadedness. All completely normal.

Eyes narrowed, Jenny peeked around the corner cabinet.

"I'm not dead, Jen. I'm just sitting on the floor." The words set off another bout of chills.

Jenny remained skeptical. "Why?" she asked.

"Felt like it."

With a huffy snort, she came over to sit beside me and check out my leg. I must of hit a rock when I went down. There was a gash near my knee about four inches long. I'd used my sock to slow the bleeding, but it was still seeping down my calf. I'm fine with other people's blood; mine bothers me.

"I bet you need stitches."

"Probably."

"I got stitches once."

"Yeah?"

"It hurt."

"Your mom pinch you for those, too?"

"No. She had to hold me down."

"Oh."

"I'll be right back." Jenny patted me on the head, once, and scrambled out.

Inside, my muscles registered full of juice, ready to fly. Outside, I was crusting over with drying sweat and dust. A wobbly drip of bright red blood clung to the rivulet that streaked my calf. I flexed my toes inside my running shoe and watched the drop release—*splash, splash*—quickly followed by two more. The white ceramic tile made a dramatic contrast where it landed.

Everything tunneled down to breathing. Slow, in through the nose. Out through the mouth.

A few months ago my sister had a car roar up behind her. But she didn't slide down a ravine to safety. I opened my mouth and gulped air, trying to settle my stomach.

Do not think. Do not puke.

No way could I tell Jenny a car was involved. Neither of us would survive the resulting panic loop.

Work. Work was the way out of this, away from this feeling. Work brought calm.

Calm would help Jenny.

I hit the autodialer. Ainsley picked it up in one ring.

"You got the morning off, College." I'd made arrangements for Ainsley and me to go in and rough cut with the engineer. "Call Mick and ask him if he can meet us tonight for a few hours, instead of this morning."

"Sweet. Why?"

I checked for Jenny before I answered. "Some asshole in an SUV didn't want to share the road."

"No way."

"Way. I'm headed over to the emergency room."

"Are you hurt?"

"Add insult to injury, College. Ask me another stupid question."

"Geez, how bad? You need a hand?"

I slumped lower against the kitchen cabinet, closed my eyes and pictured my choices of worst-case scenarios: totaling the Subaru as I lost consciousness and spun out of control, versus Ainsley holding me down for stitches in the emergency room.

"No, thanks. I've got it under control," I told him.

"This stuff might help." Jenny appeared carrying her mother's Rubbermaid tub of all-purpose medical repair. My sister had been an emergency-room nurse. If anyone was prepared for trouble, it was her. "Worst-case scenario, first-case scenario," I used to tease.

Too bad I was right.

"Where'd you find that?"

"The little one stays in the linen closet. The big one was in the garage. Mom kept it in the car for emergencies."

Hunkered down beside me, Jenny started digging through the tubs, passing right by the latex gloves, bottles of pain relief and piles of unlabeled foil blister packets. I tried to keep my voice nonchalant as the supplies appeared: one box of princess Band-Aids, rubbing alcohol, three ace bandages, a stethoscope and a rubber tourniquet.

"Make sure we have an engineer tonight, College." I spoke very deliberately into the phone. "And I've got a new list of pickups we should go after. I want to go back to Jost's apartment and try his partner, Pat, again. See if we can catch him off duty."

"You got it, boss." I could hear him fluffing his pillow

in preparation for another few hours of sleep. "I'm yours to command."

Jenny took a rubber strap between both hands.

"What's that?" I asked.

"This will stop the bleeding by cutting off your circulation."

"Anything else?" Ainsley asked.

"These are for pain." Jenny held out the giant bottle of acetaminophen and a foil blister pack. "Or maybe it's these?"

The only words stamped on the back read "Sample, Not For Resale."

"I'll stick with the usual." I tossed the packet back into the bucket. Jenny shook out two tablets. "Get me some water would you, kiddo?"

"I'll meet you at the station tonight," Ainsley said. "What time?"

"I need you earlier, but don't panic. It involves food. How'd you like to go picnic with the sheriff today?"

"Uh…"

"Great. Pick us up at noon."

Socializing at a garden party after stitches in the emergency room is like eating brussels sprouts after army-issue MRE's. Some improvements aren't worth the wait. Unfortunately, the Curzon family picnic wasn't a meal I could skip.

It took forever to haul ourselves less than ten miles through small-town traffic to the old neighborhood where the Curzon family manse was located. We got caught behind two freight trains going opposite directions. The old Subaru wagon I'd inherited had a cassette *prey-er,* no tape ever ejected with its guts still intact, so Ainsley and Jenny sang to the radio Top 40 countdown. I was safely insulated by the meds they'd given me for the stitches.

According to Ainsley, the houses in Curzon's neighborhood were built back in the days when middle-class families hired architects who would build-to-suit. We passed cottages and castles, Tudor beside Victorian, and the occasional practical brick bungalow, all on lots big enough to require gardeners. From what I'd heard, the area was mostly interchangeable old-money Protestants and new-money Republicans. Broad lawns and narrow minds, as the saying goes.

Ainsley parked the wagon at the back of a line of cars half a block away. The house was a big faux-French cottage built of yellow Midwest limestone. Tall windows. Iron fence. A string of Curzon for Sheriff signs across the yard. And a cement duck dressed in a pumpkin costume.

Jenny took my hand as we wandered toward the front

door. As we came around the cubist shrubbery, I could see the garage door and hear the sounds of battle. The Curzon men were engaged in our local blood sport: man-on-man driveway hoop.

Worth watching.

The sheriff's face was dripping sweat. The younger guy—I knew he must be related, same coloring—wasn't as sweaty but blood marked his face, from nose to cheek. In Chicago Land, backyard basketball is nothing like the long-court ballet of the NBA. Whether it's cement playgrounds with chain nets or blacktop driveways with acrylic backboards, the game is played rough and up under the net—hustle, push, hip-check. Make that elbow connect! Whip the ball around your opponent, bounce once, shoot, grab, twist—do it again. No blood, no foul.

Jenny, Ainsley and I stood there admiring the action for a while.

An older guy with a face that made you think basset hound was watching from the raised bluestone patio that surrounded the house. Waving a crystal highball glass in one hand, he leaned out over the wall to shout at the players, "Come on, you old fart. Can't you do better than that? That's it! Ooh, Nicky, you gonna take that?"

The sideline razz didn't seem to bother the guys too much. Nicky might have youthful speed working for him, but Curzon had experience and attitude. He played like a son of a bitch.

The last shot went into the air and Nicky jumped to block half a second too late. The ball tipped the rim and dunked. Nicky cursed.

"Hey—watch your mouth, you. There're ladies around," the old guy snapped.

"Sorry," Nicky replied automatically. He dropped his hands to his knees, bent over to suck in air.

Curzon looked around, saw Jenny and me, gave Nicky a friendly smack upside the head, and hustled over.

"You're here," he said, a little surprised. "You met my father?"

"No. Not yet."

The old guy stood up and leaned over the wall to shake hands. He had gold wire-rim glasses so thick they magnified those tabby-cat Curzon eyes to new dimensions. His scalp was as ruddy as his droopy face and he wore a short-sleeve button-down and ironed shorts. We got through introductions and Nicky went off to clean his bloody nose. Curzon Senior called one of the younger females, just old enough to be equally dazzling to Jenny and Ainsley.

"Tria, sweetheart, show these two where they can get a Coke and a hamburger, eh?"

"Sure, Grandpa." The girl wore a Notre Dame sweater and a neat French braid. She held out her hand and smiled at Jenny, and it shocked me how easily the kid went for it. "We're all gonna play touch football as soon as my brother's done with his food. You want to play?"

"Sure." Jenny tried hard to sound casual.

Ainsley gave a modest shrug of agreement, and as soon as Tria looked away he shot me a fox-in-the-henhouse eyebrow.

Just like that, I was deserted.

"So, now, tell me about yourself," Senior said as he waved a cheerful goodbye to my chaperones. "Jack tells me you make television shows." It didn't take me long to realize he thought I was there for nonprofessional reasons. If I'd have been a guy, he'd have asked what my intentions were regarding the sheriff.

A little crowd congregated around us. Most everyone else at the party was family. Sisters, uncles, cousins, even the grandma was there. Donna, Curzon's mother, introduced herself. Grandma didn't bother.

"This the girl you invited, Jack?" White-haired, hawk-nosed and wearing a velour pantsuit, Curzon's grandma was sharp—of dress, of mind and of tongue. I liked her.

"This is the one, Nana."

"She's not as skinny as the other one." Sounded like that was the nicest thing she could think to say. "Get me an ashtray, would you, Jack? Your father thinks I'm gonna flick my ashes on the patio like a tramp."

Curzon went inside to find Nana an ashtray.

"You like my Jack?" she asked.

"Seems like a good guy."

"You two work together?"

"Not exactly."

She puffed a cloud of smoke off to one side. "What's that mean?"

"I'm a reporter. We kind of—" I tried to finesse it with my hands "—work against each other."

That got a laugh. "Good. That's what he needs. Girl who'll come straight at him, not stab him in the back like a damned sneaky—"

"Damned sneaky what, Nana?" Curzon crossed the patio in three long strides. He wasn't hurrying, but he plopped the glass ashtray into her hand with obvious irritation. Curzon Senior laughed.

"Damned sneaky yourself, Jack-over. And I don't want to hear any of that 'you shouldn't be smoking at

your age' crap. Damned few enough pleasures left at
my age, I oughta know." There was a patter to it, like a
comedian's routine. Everybody seemed to have heard
it before.

"Nana," Curzon's mother chided. Donna Curzon
struck me as one of those round, settled women who
read sad novels in their spare time and always wore the
wrong color lipstick.

"Keep it up, Ma. Jack's gonna buy you a case of
cigarettes for your birthday." The old guy laughed at his
own joke. I saw one hand reach for his wife's ass, give
her a squeeze.

Donna didn't seem to mind. She shifted her weight
toward him, leaning until her shoulder touched the
whole length of his body. His hand popped into view at
the small of her waist, holding her close.

That seemed to be the cue for Donna to take charge
of the conversation. Had I ever met Barbara Walters?
Was Peter Jennings handsome in person? In between
the small talk, I nudged the sheriff twice about talking
to his cousin. He continued giving me the brush-off. To
make matters worse, I could see Jenny across the way,
smiling and talking with some of the older kids. Even
though I was itching to get the interview and get out, I
wasn't looking forward to dragging her away, now that
she seemed to be having fun. I couldn't remember ever
seeing her have fun.

The whole scene felt odd as hell. I am not familiar
with adjusting my schedule to someone else's good time.
I needed how-to training in standing around watching.
Not to mention, the feeling that Curzon was being more
than merely helpful by inviting me here. Richard Gatt
had it right when he said small-town business wasn't

that different from the Chicago neighborhood politics I remembered. My clan instincts were all atingle.

Across the lawn, a pair of Curzon women were chatting up a pair of guests who stuck out as nonfamily. The older man was early forties, tall, with a jawline as chiseled as a comic book hero's. His lanky body contrasted with a head of thick silver hair for that youthful-but-mature look. The other man I knew. Mr. Vegas himself. Pat. Tom Jost's ambulance partner.

Interesting. I entertained the fantasy of grabbing a quick interview and crossing him off my pickup list.

"Who's Dick Tracy over there?" I asked Curzon. "The guy with the chin."

"That's Marcus Wilt. We went to law school together. He and my sister are—"

"Don't remind me," Nana interrupted.

"Law school?" I prodded.

Curzon shrugged. "Didn't stick for either of us. Marcus ended up going to work for his father's construction company."

"You guys are friends?" I asked.

"Not close."

Senior hacked out one of those old-man gargle sounds. "Keep your friends close and your enemies closer."

"Dad." It was a warning.

Too late.

"So you guys are enemies?" I repeated with the same cheerfulness.

"Marcus is running for sheriff," Curzon answered in a bland voice.

"Why shouldn't he? You aren't putting up a fight," his father accused. "Shit or get off the pot, son. If you don't, the dogs'll get you with your pants around your ankles."

"You want another drink?" Curzon asked me politely. "I'm going to the bar, Dad. You want something?"

"No." Senior flapped a hand in dismissal. "Fine. Go on then."

"*Phaw.* You tell me 'keep it up.'" Nana jut her jaw forward and blew a stream of smoke straight up.

"Give it a rest, Ma."

Curzon took hold of my elbow and walked us toward the patio serving area. Clearly, they didn't need an audience to enjoy themselves.

"So what's Pat doing here?"

"Pat who?"

"Pat, Tom Jost's buddy, who is right now sidled up to your frenemy Marcus. That's who."

"Marc's got a contract with the hospital. Those two know each other."

I looked back at Marcus Wilt. He was dapper enough to be entertaining a gentleman caller. "Are they like, together?"

"Christ. I'll give you twenty bucks to ask Marc that question." Curson laughed. "No. It was my mother's idea. She asked Marc to invite the guy. And here's Nicky. Perfect timing," Curzon grumbled. "Now you can ferret out the rest of the family secrets. I'll leave you to him." Another brief introduction and Curzon marched off in the direction of the bar.

I tried to think of Nicky Curzon as the bad-cop type, but it just wouldn't stick. A couple inches shorter and a couple years younger than the sheriff, he had the same width in the chest and shoulder. Cop-sized. He'd changed into a red-on-black Be Like Mike T-shirt which, given his earlier net loss, seemed kind of cute.

"Sorry to keep you waiting." He shook my hand—not squishy, not stiff.

I didn't want to launch straight into the Jost thing. Rarely does the best stuff flow at the start of an interview. I glanced across the patio at Senior. "Seems like your uncle's pretty annoyed with the sheriff."

Nicky shrugged. "It happens."

Occupational hazard of mine—with only a taste of information, I felt compelled to feed him another opening. Something vague and open-ended like, "He doesn't think Jack's fighting for it?"

Nicky shot me a skeptical look. "Jack talked to you about the election?"

"More or less." Curzon would gut me with a spoon if he caught me wheedling personal secrets out of his cousin. I smiled casually.

"Jack told me to watch myself around you." Nicky gave me a smug once-over. "Guess that's because you got to him first, huh?"

I feigned a little maidenly modesty.

Nicky plopped down on the bench beside me and stretched his legs out in front of him, making himself comfortable. He had the blunt body of so many cops. Not clumsy, but stiff. Made to be in motion, they never seemed quite happy at rest.

"I have to agree with Uncle Mike. Jack's not trying very hard. I think he wants to lose."

"Really? Why?"

"Don't know. I do know the work's a part of him. Being sheriff, law enforcement, all of it. Part of his heritage. You can't just walk away from that."

"Not easily." I took a stab. "Do you think the divorce had something to do with it? It's not uncommon. Guy splits with his wife, wants to make some changes across the board."

Nicky stared hard at me. "Jack talked to you about that, too?" He exhaled as if he were blowing off steam. "It's been two years since the She-bitch left. Guess it depends on whether the change improves things or makes it worse. He's a good sheriff. He knows the job. Marcus—" The look I saw was long-suffering and skeptical. "I don't want Jack to lose. None of us do. Some good press would help."

Ah-ha. My invitation to the party suddenly made sense.

"Good press can be hard to come by. Tell me about your letter to Jost's commander at the fire station."

Nicky was ready for my question. "Maybe I was trying to keep things from getting worse."

"Tell me."

There was no camera running. There was no one to hear but the two of us. Sometimes, guy has a problem, all it takes is someone asking nicely.

"What did the girl say to you?" he asked.

"Rachel Jost said you interrupted a clinch. She sounded ashamed and worried for Tom."

"For him? Jesus. Why?" He shifted around, aggravation coming through in his body language. "She didn't have a thing to be ashamed about. He was the one acting like a dick."

"How so?"

"They'd already steamed up the windows when I rolled up on them but Jost must of opened something to keep the air circulating, because I heard her 'No,' clear as you and me talking right here. More than once she said it. 'No, *please* no.'" He said it quick and rough and absolutely flat, in a rumbly baritone. On his face, it was clear that wasn't how he'd heard it.

I pulled in a deep breath and let it out slow.

"And I heard his answer, too." Nicky upended his beer bottle and chugged like he was washing out his mouth. "'Stay,' he told her. 'Stay!' Like he was talking to a dog."

He was lost. He asked me to stay, I turned him away.

"And then he says, 'If we do it, you'll stay with me. I know you will.' Word for word, my hand to God, that's what Jost said—right before I dropped on his ass," Nicky added, grim and satisfied.

"You think he was about to rape her?"

"Girl said no."

"Fuck," I said softly.

"Exactly."

"More 'paraphilia of a sacrificial type.'" I sighed. Tom Jost was desperate enough to pressure Rachel physically in order to coerce her into marriage. He knew Rachel was conflicted enough about her feelings and conservative enough about sex that losing her virginity to him would seal the deal. She'd marry him.

"What?"

"Rachel was Tom's sexual sacrifice. Tell me about the memo."

"They were gonna let him walk. No record. No report," Nicky confessed. "Firefighter. One of the brotherhood. Nobody got hurt—no real crime. You know what I'm talking about."

"Sure."

"I seen guys like that before. Goes right back to his life. Eventually, it's gonna happen again. You know it. I know it. He's gonna hurt somebody. Some woman probably."

He was playing for my sympathy and I was having a hard time resisting.

"Maybe."

"I kept thinking about her and what Jost had said in the car. I made a couple calls. The guy was no angel. I decided somebody ought to know." He sucked back another quick swallow of beer. "I wrote his chief and put it on the record. I knew there was a chance I'd take shit for it." He looked me in the eye and shrugged. Nice eyes. Curzon eyes.

"They reprimanded you for sending the letter?"

"Yeah."

"What about the guys at the firehouse? Did they give you a hard time?"

"Let's just say, I better hope nothing near me catches fire anytime soon." Nicky smiled that feral, humorless grin that stands for *bring it on*.

Police and fire service are boy-gangs-for-good. They may fight the bad guys, but they live the same code. Fuck with a brother, get fucked back. No firefighter ever had to fear a speeding ticket in his hometown. No cop had to carry out a dead body, even if he made it dead. Especially if he made it dead.

Pat the fireman was twitching his way toward the exit, saying his goodbyes. He was full of nervous tension, glancing around, checking his watch. Donna Curzon tried to slow him down, gesturing toward Nicky and I. Pat shook his head and took a backward step.

"I heard Jost was getting a lot of grief back at the firehouse."

"Guess we both got our share."

"Anyone in particular?"

Donna crossed her arms and watched Pat head down the driveway. Her husband slipped up behind her. His face said, *let him go*.

Obviously, Curzon's mother was a politician as well. If Nicky was getting shit from the men at the firehouse, who better to make peace than Tom's pal?

Nicky laughed. "Why? You gonna go beat him up for me?"

"You don't think I can?" We were easing out of it now, using the jokes to back away from something that was still pretty raw.

"I'd like to see you try," Nicky said. "Especially in those shoes."

We both took a moment to admire my sandals. Not the kind of footwear that inspires fear in your enemy. Or maybe it was the pedicure. Jenny had insisted on helping me feel better by polishing my toes with bubble-gum-pink-and-extra-glitter after the emergency-room staff held me down for the stitches. I had some fine painkillers on board by then.

Nicky ceased with the admiration when we noticed cousin Jack headed our way. "You must be tougher than you look, if Jack's interested."

"He's not interested in me. I'm a useful irritant."

"Don't tell Nana. This is the first peace he's had from the nagging since Sharon left."

"Sharon? The 'She-bitch'?"

"Shh," he whispered. "Family pet name Jack never appreciated."

Right about then, the sheriff himself came striding into the conversation with all the tact of a cop breaking up a house party. "You're done. Dad wants you inside."

"Guess I'm done." Nicky flashed me a grin but asked his cousin seriously, "Trouble?"

Curzon shrugged, noncommittal.

Nicky crossed the patio in a hurry, his voice drifting as he closed the French door behind him, "Whaa-at?"

I shot Curzon a look and he was smiling, too.

"Family."

He nodded. "The food's ready. Brats are done." He pronounced it like a good Midwesterner. *Brahtzs*. Sausages. "Dad promised him first pick since he lost the ball game."

"Doesn't the winner get first pick?"

"Of dessert."

I laughed. What was it about being gathered in a family unit that made people revert to their prehistoric patterns? Big man. Little man. Boss lady. She-bitch. I looked over at Jenny and my momentary bubble of equilibrium popped. Who was I to her?

Somehow, Curzon managed to slip a question into that breach. Then another, and another. Questions about how long the drive had taken us, and how long I'd been working out and how long I'd been away from Chicago Land. I knew he was pumping me. At first, I answered with the thought, *give a little, get a little*. Maybe I'd get a little something about Tom Jost out of him. Much later along the way, I realized I was giving more than I could reasonably expect to get, but the conversation continued. I told him things about work, about me, that I hadn't told anyone.

"Holy shit," Curzon marveled. "You gotta be kidding me."

"That was about the worst."

Some of the things I'd turned into pictures haunted me. Most of them weren't frightening exactly. The danger had passed.

They were only bones. Bones can't hurt you. Even rows and rows of bones. Human skeletons. And me, picking my way across the ground, stepping oh, so carefully. In dreams, it always ended the same. I choose a skull and turn it in my hand, considering the best angle for my camera's eye. I am trying to find a way to get the light to shine inside behind the empty sockets. No matter how I twist it, nothing ever works. The skull stares back at me, eyes so black they give me vertigo.

That's the dream that wakes me in a sweat. Curzon took a long drag on his Anchor Steam beer. "The shit people do to one another," he said philosophically.

"And to themselves," I added, thinking of Tom Jost.

The kids were organizing a game on the lawn. Ainsley put up a token resistance to being dragged in to play, pulling Jenny along with him. Their voices crossed the space in little sound bites of high-note happiness.

We watched them play as Curzon talked about the things a cop sees.

Work stories. War stories. Everybody has them. I've probably got it easier than the sheriff in one respect. My stories might be on a bigger scale but they originated far, far away; his hit closer to home. Maybe it was calculated to charm me. Maybe.

If so, it was working.

"Right. That's enough, you two clams. Come join the

party." Donna Curzon came with a trayful of glasses, filled with an iced yellow liquid topped by two inches of white froth. "Maddy, you have to try this. It's lemonade beer. Really nummy."

"What the hell have you done to that perfectly good beer, Mom?" Curzon said. "Ice *and* lemonade? I'm going to have to issue you a warning for indecent mixing."

She gave me the long-suffering look but otherwise ignored her son. "Go ahead, Maddy. Have a taste."

"I'm not much of a drinker."

"That's not much of a drink," Curzon said.

"Your father likes it."

I accepted a glass to keep peace with the hostess. She smiled at me and wandered off to sell the rest to other guests. I took a sip. "Your dad must be a politician, too."

"Only when it comes to my mother," Curzon answered. "My job would drive him crazy. He's all cop. Married to the same woman, living in the same place, going to the same barbershop over thirty years. Drives a Crown Vic. Always has a hundred dollar bill in his wallet for emergencies. Upright guy."

Nicky came out of the house carrying a plate piled with enough food to feed Jenny and me for a week. Curzon noticed he was headed our way and pointed out across the lawn. "You want to walk?"

"Sure."

He stopped in a quiet spot beside the half wall that banked steps leading down to the cellar. We could still see the touch football game, but the rest of the gang was out of our line of sight—or we were out of their's.

"Except for politics, you and your dad sound like two of a kind to me."

"No way." He sucked back a swallow of beer. "My wife left before we'd marked a nickel. My car's foreign and I got nothing in my wallet but plastic."

That's the problem with sharing war stories. It brings you down. If there's one thing I dread, it's decent guys flaying themselves for an audience. Time to change the subject.

"Any word on that police report you promised me?"

He looked the other way, irritated with himself. "What do you want to know?"

"Everything."

He made an effort to laugh. "Cause of death, gross displacement of spinal cord and cervical vertebra—"

"Translate."

"Broken neck. Time of death was approximately nine o'clock—"

"No shit, 9:00 *a.m.?*"

"Guy died about a half hour before we got there." He sounded matter-of-fact, but I could see him questioning my reaction. I waved it off.

"How'd you hear about it?" I asked.

"Phone tip. Somebody saw him setting up, I guess. We ran the plate and knew it was Jost by the time we sent guys to the scene."

"Phone tip called in the license plate?"

"Yeah."

That seemed weird to me, given the off-road nature of Jost's parking job. His little car had been parked parallel to the road in the ditch. The person who called it in would have to have driven right by the car.

"Coroner thinks Jost must have been out there awhile,

setting himself up. There was a lot of foot traffic between his car and the site." Curzon shifted back to a recline against the patio wall. Sipped his beer. Nothing like a little shoptalk to make you forget your troubles. "He used rope from the ambulance rig. Stacked the boxes he had in his trunk to get the lift he needed, kicked the top box out from under him...or it slipped."

"Does the coroner have an opinion?"

Curzon hesitated. "Off the record?"

"Why not? Everyone else is." I took a sip of lemonade beer to wash the bitter out of my voice. On the fourth sip, I decided Mrs. Curzon was right. It was nummy.

"Evidence is contradictory. I assume you saw what was inside those boxes?" he asked.

"Porno magazines."

"Yeah. Same ones found in the trunk of his car the night he was brought in." He said it as if it might not mean a thing, but the silence that followed said otherwise.

Figuring people was a skill that improved with experience. Tracking people, tracking behavior, the more you knew of the possibilities the more likely you could imagine a solution to a scenario. Things fit or they didn't. I figured Curzon was one of the lucky few who could keep up with me when it came to tracking someone into the dark of uncharted, unhappy possibilities.

I threw out a suggestion. "Everybody already knew about the mags, so why bother to take them out of the car?"

Curzon crooked one of those black eyebrows in disbelief. Didn't sound right to me either. A guy like Jost wouldn't leave them in his car once they'd been discovered. He'd have the guys at work asking to see what he had in his trunk every damn day.

"He used the same magazines that got him busted to hang himself. Could be remorse. Self-punishment." I sipped my lemonade. "What's 'contradictory' about the evidence?"

"The magazines suggest a sexual—" Curzon finally settled on "—intent. But there's no other evidence to support that assumption. No pertinent body fluids. Guy had his clothes on. In fact, those clothes he was wearing? The pants don't even have a fly."

"How...awkward for him."

Curzon acknowledged this with a tip of his beer. "Exactly. On the other hand, judging by the time of death, and the mud on the sides of the box, he had to have been standing out there a while. Probably standing up on the boxes for a while. Looking at pictures, maybe? We don't know." He shook his head.

Weirdness.

"Trying to get up his courage?" Was courage what it took to face that moment?

"Possibly," Curzon answered vaguely. "Guy was no Boy Scout. Maybe he couldn't figure out how to tie the knot." That thought generated a frown and shrug. "On the other hand—how many hands is that now?—there was no note."

Another indication of autoerotic asphyxiation, according to Dr. Graham.

I shook my head. "Contradictory evidence."

"You got it." Curzon sounded stoical, in a pissed-off sort of way.

"Any other witnesses," I asked as casually as I could manage, "besides the phone tip?"

"No." He turned to face me and consider the possibilities my question suggested. "None."

I nodded, *ah*.

"You'd report any pertinent information to the proper authorities, wouldn't you, Maddy O'Hara?"

The use of my whole name—a sure sign of trouble.

"Of course I would, Sheriff Curzon."

He smiled and the glow in those eyes understood exactly how little we really knew of each other. "I see you brought your boy along today." He wasn't looking at Ainsley; he was looking at me.

Ainsley was thick into the game of touch football with the underage Curzons. The females seemed to be tackling him whether he had the ball or not.

"I didn't think you'd mind."

"Not at all," he assured me. Eyes still trained on the game, he added, "I'm glad."

"Gives the kids someone to play with?"

Curzon smiled as a gang of mostly girls brought Ainsley down again. The boy stood up and shook himself off when Marcus Wilt called out a hello. Ainsley ran a couple of loping steps that direction and shook hello, all charm. PK—politician's kid—probably knew three quarters of the people in town. Beside me, Curzon tensed.

The kids called Ainsley back to the game.

"I'd say the fact you brought your escort looks good for me."

"Don't hold your breath, Sheriff."

"Jack," he said.

"What?"

"Jack Curzon. It's my name. You're a guest in my father's house, eating my mother's food. Drinking her—" he curled his lip and pointed at my glass "—drink. You ought to be calling me Jack…"

"How about I call you jack—"

"…not to mention the fact, I'm about to get familiar with you."

Without so much as a glance in my direction, I felt his hand shift from my elbow, to my waist, to the small of my back. The cold of the wall behind me was suddenly replaced with the heat of his palm.

Jenny squealed with laughter as she went down under a pig pile of ballplayers.

All those painkillers on board, I should have had no trouble staying cool. Numb, even. "Uh," was the best I could do.

Lame. Maybe lemonade beer was stronger than I thought.

That spot of warmth quickly slipped lower, tucking under the hem of my blouse. Skin to skin at the small of my back, warm became hot. All the blood left my head.

I hissed, sidestepped away from him with my bad leg, and sang a stinging little song of the profane.

Curzon grabbed my arm when I bobbled. "Whoa. What's the problem?"

"Your town's full of crazy-fucking drivers is what." I backed out of his grip and boosted my butt up onto the concrete wall. Gingerly, I swung my leg up in front of me and hiked up the split cuff of my capris. The white patch of bandage sported a brown stain that I hoped was peroxide. I decided not to peel it back and check.

"How'd that happen?"

I grumbled out the short version of my brush with the SUV.

"You report it?" he asked in the work voice.

"No. Are you kidding? Not that big a deal. Besides, the emergency room ate up my free time. I had to get to this swell party."

"Come in tomorrow and fill out a complaint." It wasn't an order; orders presuppose a future compliant will. This was more like old news. A done deal.

"Why bother?" I snapped. "You people couldn't catch the guy when the victim was all the way dead."

Oops. Where did that come from?

"And how is that conflict of interest going?" he replied smoothly.

"Sorry," I mumbled. "That came out rougher than I meant. Blame the Vicodin."

Both his eyebrows lifted. He was working to manage no smile. God help me, if he laughed.

"Legal, totally legal," I said. "Twelve stitches under there."

Curzon had that cop way with his hands, momentum held in check that could suddenly turn physical. He took hold of my calf, and before I could think to stop him, he'd carefully extended the knee for closer inspection. "Hmm. Looks like what you need is somebody to kiss it better."

His hands were a good five degrees warmer than my leg. When he leaned forward, the air around us moved and I caught a clear whiff of him, all boy and healthy sweat.

Perched on top of the wall where I was, it was obvious the rest of the Curzon clan had a good view of this exchange.

I know everybody has more than one reason for doing anything. But sometimes the best way to get along is to concentrate on one motive at a time. Maybe this little show was nothing personal. Maybe Jack Curzon was laying down a cover of suitable female interest. He might not wiggle all the way off the hook, but his nana would quit harassing him about his post-divorce solitude as long as he was busy elsewhere.

On those grounds, I could play along.

"Yeah, sure," I agreed. "In fact, why don't you start by sucking that foot clean? I had a little trouble reaching down so far in the shower this morning."

It was my favorite type of man-eater reply, perfectly suited to discouraging barely legal soldier boys who hadn't even learned to appreciate the taste of vegetables.

Curzon's leer made it obvious real quick; I'd miscalculated. He skewered me with a look that offered a peek in his bedroom window. Toe sucking was only one of the activities on his menu.

It had been a long time since I'd had to deal with a guy like this. Out of practice and out of ammo, I faked a cough to cover the blood rushing to my face.

"Another time maybe," he replied after due consideration. One hand slid up and down the underside of my calf. "Come to the station tomorrow. File a complaint."

"Mmm."

He let go. I sat up, jerked my pant leg back in place and picked up my near-empty glass of lemonade beer. He took a sip of his drink. I took a sip of mine. Just a couple of calm, collected characters having a polite discussion of probabilities.

"I hope I'm not interrupting?" Marcus Wilt smiled at me. No teeth, plenty of eyebrow.

"Marc. Have you met Maddy O'Hara?"

"I haven't. Yet."

Wilt's hand came out and I shook it, even though it was awkward the way I was perched on the wall. He was the kind of good-looking man who puts a lot of effort into the first two and a half seconds he meets a woman: *yes or no?*

He read my *no,* loud and clear, and shifted his attention immediately to Curzon. "Heard you had to reprimand Nicky."

There was a long silence.

Wilt leaned against the wall beside me, hands in his pockets. He wore beautifully tailored linen slacks, a dusty-blue silk shirt and Italian woven loafers without socks. Probably had the lifetime subscription to *Esquire* magazine. If Curzon was the basketball gladiator, Wilt was doing his best to rank as garden-party senator.

"Too bad about the suicide," he said seriously. "Reopens that whole can of worms, doesn't it?"

Generations of controversy had time to be considered before Curzon finally answered, "No."

Wilt nodded as if he'd heard paragraphs of rationale. "Hope you're right," he replied sincerely. Donna Curzon was waving frantically from across the patio. Wilt pushed off from the wall. "I'm being summoned. Nice meeting you, Ms. O'Hara."

We watched him walk away and I asked, "Why's he busting your ass?"

Curzon cracked a smile, then shook his finger at me. "No family business on the first date. It's a rule."

"This isn't a date. This is work."

He countered with a frown but his good humor didn't fade. "In that case, I believe Marc is indicating that should Jost's suicide become publicized, Nicky's reprimand will be fair game in the race for sheriff."

"All that from three sentences?"

"We've known each other awhile."

"And what do you want me to do about it?"

"Nothing."

"Then why am I here?"

Green-eyed death glare. Before he could fire off another one of those scintillating one-word answers, Jenny obliged him by crashing into the conversation, red-faced and breathless. I'd never seen her so charged up.

"Hey, kid, nice timing."

"Why don't you come see me at the station around lunchtime tomorrow?" Curzon threw out suddenly. "Leave your boy. Come hungry."

"Did you see me?" Jenny asked. "Wasn't that great? Come hungry where? What are you talking about?"

"You can't be hungry, kid." I slipped off the wall, careful of how my weight landed. "I saw that hamburger you ate."

"Remind your aunt tomorrow morning, she's having lunch with me, so she can tell me all about her incident," Curzon said to Jenny, with a head nod toward my bad leg.

Jenny's face squinched suspiciously. "What does he mean 'incident'?"

He answered before I thought to stop him. "With the car, when she hurt her leg."

"What car?" Jenny rounded on me with all the drama of a soap diva. "You *said* you fell."

"I did fall." I glared at Curzon, even though—

technically—this wasn't his fault. "A car made me fall."

All the fun visible on Jenny's face vanished.

Hit-and-run. It happens just that fast.

"We need to make a stop, College." I looked over my shoulder into the backseat. "That fine with you, Jen?"

She managed the effort of a single shoulder shrug while staring grimly out the window.

I really needed to work. We needed more material if we were going to squeeze out six decent minutes. The desire to be in the studio—in the dark and absorbed by my process—bubbled in my blood like a junkie's addiction.

My hands even shook a little at the thought of going straight home, straight back to my sister's empty house with Jenny. She had not said one word to me since Curzon dropped the bomb. Mistake after mistake, I was piling them on as fast as Tom Jost did in his last weeks.

For some reason my brain kept replaying Curzon's comment that Jost must have stood on those boxes a while before he died.

What had he been doing? The Amish clothes and his choice of location suggested he was spitting in his father's eye. But the fact that he wanted to marry Rachel in the Amish church also suggested the costume was for her benefit.

Is it date rape if the guy is trying to compel you to marry him?

Or is it kidnapping?

Ainsley glanced in his rearview mirror, monitoring Jenny's mood. "Where're we stopping?"

"Let's try Tom Jost's apartment building again. It's

Sunday afternoon. The neighbors should be home. Maybe we can talk to the super or something."

"Tom's apartment." Ainsley hooked the turn that would put us closer to Jost's apartment on the fringe of town. "I'm on it."

Jenny said nothing. Every so often, I'd catch a snap of anger in her eyes right before everything stiffened into the child zombie routine.

"What's the problem, Jenny? You've been sulking since we left the party."

"No problem," she mumbled.

"You can see I'm fine. I didn't say anything about the stupid car because I thought it would bother you, okay?"

"Okay," she said.

"Okay," I said.

Ainsley raised both eyebrows.

This time the drive seemed to take forever, even without the whole Top 40 sing-along. It was close to sunset when we finally pulled into Jost's parking lot. There were windows open in several apartments and more cars in the lot than the last time we visited. I could smell a charcoal grill. Good signs. The All Stressed Out and No One To Choke bumper sticker showed a certain amount of ambient hostility, but who am I to criticize?

"You want to come in with us?" I asked Jenny over my shoulder. "Or wait here in the car?"

"Car."

"Fine."

"Okay," Ainsley added.

I'm not entirely sure he wasn't making fun of us. I slammed my car door before opening the back hatch.

We'd packed cameras, of course. Ainsley had loaded

the car without a repeat of the we-sleep-with-equipment speech. At least the boy retained new information.

"Let's carry cameras to the door this time." I pulled my press card out of my messenger bag and clipped it to my shirt.

We aren't supposed to be class snobs in the good ol' U.S. of A., but there's a certain segment of the population that still got so tickled at the thought of seeing their faces on television, they'd say or do just about anything to get there. Perhaps even give a lady a tour of an apartment that might normally be considered off-limits.

I could see Jenny was busy not watching us from the car.

It took two rings before we got an answer.

The intercom buzzed. "Whozzit?"

"Looking for the building manager?"

There was a long pause and then the electric click and hum of the lock release.

No one came out to greet us but I gravitated toward the only door in the hall that had a buzzer button. Someone had posted a line of notices down the door that included a shiny Volunteer Fire Department sticker and Solicitors Will Be Shot on Sight.

I could hear voices coming from inside the apartment, raised over the sound of the television.

"…they want?"

"…the hell should I know?"

The door popped open and a fine native specimen in a Chicago Bears T-shirt announced, "I'm the manager. What d'ya need?" He had a round face, belly and shiny spot on top where the hair was missing. He'd make a terrific contrast to our first interview, Farmer Lowe, and even better one to Old Mr. Jost, if I could ever get the Amish man on film.

"Sorry to bother you. I'm Maddy O'Hara from WWST and we're working on a story about someone who used to live in this building. Guy named Tom Jost?"

"Television?"

"That's right." I smiled. Moments like these always feel a bit like I'm holding out the dog biscuit with one hand, while the net dangles behind my back in the other.

"You want to put me on television?" he said with a grin. He sucked in his gut and puffed out his chest *a la* Fred Flintstone. He didn't sound surprised, more like his moment had finally arrived.

"If you aren't too busy." More smiling.

"Hold on a minute." He shut the door in our faces.

Ainsley set the camera case on the ground and scratched his head. In a bad-news tone, he told me, "Uh, Maddy, I didn't bring enough lighting to shoot an interior interview."

"What?"

"Sorry. You said it was a picnic. Picnics are outside. I can do docudrama style."

"'Docudrama style'? That's two, College."

He rolled his eyes up to heaven hoping for a second opinion.

"Maybe we can shoot the manager on Jost's patio."

The sound of a ball game on television mingled with the voices inside.

"…no shit?" a woman's voice asked.

"…clean fuckin' shirt?" answered our Fred Flintstone with the potty mouth.

"Not as if lighting is going to make the difference for this guy," I had to concede.

Fred reemerged a few minutes later in a clean knit shirt, with very unfortunate horizontal stripes, and the word Manager embroidered above the pocket. He'd clipped a carabiner full of keys to his belt loop that gave him a jingle as he walked.

"Tom's place is right down here. You want to see inside?"

"That would be great."

"Cops were here last week but they didn't say nothing about it being off-limits. I can let you in. No problem." He had one eye on Ainsley's camera box. "Am I gonna be on TV?"

"I was hoping you might agree to let us interview you if you've got a minute? We'd like to ask a few questions about Mr. Jost."

Ainsley unsnapped the case and had the camera on his shoulder ready to roll faster than I've ever seen.

"Did the police remove much from the apartment?"

"Nothing to take," he assured me. "Guy lived like a hermit. Cops walked through Took some pictures, a few personal papers. That was it."

"Did you know Tom?"

"Yeah, sure. I manage this building so he had to come through me for everything. Keys, lightbulbs, shower clogs, I do it all. I think he had one clog, once. Odd guy. Nice enough, sure, but something about him. Wasn't right, you know?" He tapped his temple with his finger. "Guy was a firefighter for the city though. You knew that, right? I'm local VFD myself, so when this guy calls saying there's a fellow fireman looking for a place, I'm gonna help him out, you know, Amish or whatever." He unlocked the door and waved us through.

Jost's apartment was as spare as I remembered. Ainsley set up with a flood lamp attachment, which would probably look crappy, but was the best choice given the circumstances. I walked around pointing out the pickups I wanted: the lonely bed, the uniform fresh from the cleaner, the photo of Tom and Rachel at the carnival.

"Tell me more about Tom."

He crossed his arms above his gut and propped himself against the table, the picture of authority. "Well, he was real quiet. Never heard him coming in, going out. Most of the people in this building, I know when they come and go. Not Tom. Never drank beer, either, and I offered plenty of times. Never took me up on it. Then, there was the problem with the animals. Couple times, I had to give him warnings about that. No pets allowed, you know."

"What about the dog sign out front?" Ainsley pointed out.

"That's a guard dog."

Ah. "What kind of pets did Jost keep?"

"They weren't pets. They were pests. Baby birds that made a nest in the firehouse and had to be fed like every commercial break, you know? No one in the firehouse would take them so he did. Shit like that, pardon my French." He glanced at the camera. "Sorry."

A woman with straw-colored hair and freshly applied lipstick popped her head around the corner. "Honey? Mrs. B is on the phone."

"I'm busy here," Fred replied.

"She says it's an emergency." She whined at him, but

smiled at me. "They never leave him alone. Especially on weekends."

Fred heaved a gusty sigh. "This'll only take a minute."

"No problem."

I was afraid the wife would stay to supervise, but Fred pulled her into a hotly whispered argument on his way out, the gist of which seemed to be if he couldn't stay to be on TV, neither would she.

"Leave the setup," I told Ainsley the minute the door closed. "Let's look around."

Ainsley made a face like he'd swallowed something nasty and shook his head *no*. I got busy opening kitchen cabinets, the utility closet, the fridge.

"Don't panic. I'm not going to ask you to roll camera on his underwear drawer."

In a worry-whisper, he asked, "What are you looking for?"

"You'll know when you see it."

The best thing about my college boy was he mostly did as he was told. The camera came with him. In most camera jocks, this would be because the camera is as much a part of them as some people see their shoes, their keys, their wallets. Ainsley wanted it for his cover story, in case we got busted searching the place.

Exploring Jost's place did not take long. If there was anything interesting to find, we'd have found it. The only halfway remarkable item was the sheer mass of strawberry jam—at least two dozen jars in the cabinet.

"How much jam can a guy eat?"

"Don't knock it. This is really good stuff." Ainsley pulled down a jar and held it out for me. "You ever had Amish fruit spread?"

"Focus, College. Stay focused."

I grabbed the jam jar and looked more closely at the label. The handwriting on the front was a thin, slanted script that seemed to barely touch the paper. It made me wonder if Tom's taste for preserves had more to do with the strawberries or the girl who made them.

"Let's try the bedroom."

Empty, except for a full-sized box spring and mattress. I looked under the bed. "Nothing."

"Why do you say it like that?" Ainsley asked. "Is being neat such a crime?"

"Guy had a trunk full of pornography, remember?"

"So?"

"It occurs to me, College, there are more convenient places to peruse your porno collection than the car."

"Oh. I get you." Ainsley ducked behind the viewfinder.

There was nowhere in the room to hide anything. The guy didn't even have a nightstand. His phone charger sat empty on the floor, plugged into the outlet closest to the bed. The closet was as sparsely arranged as the kitchen cupboards. I shuffled the few hanging items over to the far side of the closet. A tool belt hung on a hook above a set of construction boots. There was something tucked behind his boots in the back corner, an empty box for a pair of brand-new, long-range binoculars.

"Check this out," I called.

"This guy doesn't even have a stereo," Ainsley pointed out. "Why's he got those?"

"Watching the neighbors?"

Ainsley peeked out around the camera. "You've got a bad opinion of humans for the most part."

"You think?"

"Maybe Jost was a bird-watcher," Ainsley suggested, hopefully.

"I'm back," Fred called.

I stood up and faced the door.

"Oh, here you are." He gave a little self-effacing chuckle and then bluntly asked, "Look my wife's wondering if you can put her on TV, too?"

"Sure. Great idea."

An hour's worth of interview with Fred and his wife and I was generating spin-offs for future stories: Dangers of Rural Housing Developments.

"We are on a roll, College," I reported as we pulled out of Jost's parking lot. "We scored background and meat on the same day. Things are looking up."

The sun was at the hard edge of the horizon and setting the sky on fire. The green-white light of the streetlamps burned like spot flares above Butterfield Road's five lanes of strip mall flow. Everything looks better when the work goes well.

The empty binocular box kept running through my head. According to Manager Fred, the cops hadn't removed anything from the place. "What's there to take?" he'd scoffed.

The cops wouldn't make the connection to the death scene I was making because they hadn't seen my photos. At this point, I was the only one who knew someone had been watching Jost hang through binoculars. Unfortunately, I couldn't ask the cops if they knew anything that might explain the empty box or the watcher in the barn without Curzon requesting full disclosure.

Technically, there was no crime here—a broken heart, a soiled reputation, the hell of a public shame. Nope. That's no crime.

Could Tom Jost have arranged for someone to be looking through binoculars when he kicked that box out from under him? Or did he figure his father would want to check it out after the fact, when the commotion of police and fire trucks arrived on the scene?

Rachel told us her father wouldn't let her watch. Was that because her father knew exactly what she'd see? Nothing quite made sense.

"Let's make one more stop, College."

There might have been a sigh but it was a small one. The Boy Wonder was getting used to me.

"Where?"

"That sporting-goods store up ahead, where 355 meets Butterfield."

A plan started percolating, based on my curiosity and a chink of suspected guilt. There's more than one way to squeeze info from a situation. Sometimes it's a question of the right tool.

Ainsley parked but left it running. Swearing I didn't need a lot of time, I slipped into the store as the manager was locking up. Nobody remembered Jost. I found what I needed and was out in less than ten.

The sky had already faded to twilight-black. I opened my car door. Ainsley and Jenny hit the mute button. They'd been talking, I could hear the silence in Ainsley's sudden smile.

"What's in the bag?" he asked.

"Project for tomorrow morning."

All the stores were closing and it took a while to maneuver through the glut of cars in the parking lot. Ainsley was watching his mirrors closely. I should have known something was up. Boys don't check their mir-

rors when they drive; everything important is in front
of them.

At the second stoplight, he leaned toward me, speaking softly, "What sort of car was it gave you trouble?"

"This morning? Silver SUV."

"Crap." Ainsley jerked his chin, toward the rearview
mirror. I twisted to look out the back window.

One lane over, one car back, hummed a silver SUV
with tinted windows.

"How long has he been back there?"

"First noticed him when we left Jost's place." Ainsley
was watching the guy in the side mirror. "I didn't think
anything of it, except he followed us into the parking lot.
I never saw anybody get out of the car and then when we
pulled out of the lot, suddenly he's behind us again."

The left turn arrow went green. I had half a minute,
maybe.

Something happened to me a long time ago, wires got
crossed that were never meant to be crossed. When most
people are frightened of something, they back away. I
run straight at it.

"Maddy—" Ainsley called. "Jee-zus. Wait!"

Too late. I'd flung open my door and started stalking
my way through the traffic. The headlights of the cars I
crossed in front of flared like spotlights. A horn blew.

"Okay! You little shithead," I announced, loud enough
the old lady in the Bonneville rolled up her window,
speedy quick. "You want to conference with me? Let's
do it. Right here. Right now."

Another horn blew, longer this time.

"Maddy, no!" Ainsley stood in the gap of the open
driver's door.

Jenny'd crawled out of her seat belt and had her palm

pressed against the glass at the back window of the station wagon as if she were trapped inside. Her small pale face had no expression in the white glare of the headlights; nothing but stillness and round eyes.

The SUV's passenger windows were tinted and the early night shadows made it impossible to see more than the shape of a head behind the steering wheel. I pointed at him and then reached for the passenger side door handle. Suddenly, the asshole cut out of the waiting line of cars straight into the oncoming lanes, then gunned a U.

Gone.

The riot of horns and Ainsley waving *come on!* snapped my attention in line. I threw my hands in the air and forced a smile. Must have been a fairly scary-looking smile; the guy in the car next to me stared like I was some kind of zoo exhibit.

"What?"

He pulled in his chin and faced the traffic ahead.

I walked back to the Subaru and got in.

Ainsley and Jenny were giving me the same look.

"It's fine," I told them. "We're fine, okay? Drive."

"Where to?" Ainsley asked, the words clipped hard.

"Office. I got stuff to pick up," I snapped back. I caught a glimpse of Jenny in the rearview mirror. She was staring out her window without blinking, tearing at her fingernails with fast, nipping motions.

My knee started throbbing like a son of a bitch. "Give me a sip of your pop," I ordered Ainsley, using it to swallow another pain med. I shut my eyes and waited—for pain to pass and temper to cool.

I needed time. I needed more time than I had. As usual.

"Was it the same guy?" Ainsley asked, his voice low.

"Maybe. I don't know. Maybe I just terrorized some unsuspecting SUV driver who happened to have an errand at the mall the same time we did."

"How could anyone have followed us? We didn't plan to go to Jost's place."

I looked at him. "I'd say they'd have to have followed us from the sheriff's party."

"You don't think—?"

"I don't know. Jack—Curzon—seemed awful hot for me to make a report, so I doubt he had anything to do with it, but his cousin? I don't know. Too much I don't know here." I looked back into the backseat. Jenny was half-asleep, slumped against her door. Adrenaline does that sometimes.

"But why?" Ainsley sounded as mystified as I felt. "What do they want?"

"Hell if I know."

After the office stop, Ainsley decided to talk to me again. "What's the worst thing you've ever seen?"

I couldn't resist a high drama sound. "What kind of bullshit question is that?"

"No bullshit. I'm really asking."

"Fox News."

Ainsley blew a gust of exasperation.

"Look, College, it's a personal-fucking-question. Ask me my cup size, I'd be more inclined to answer."

"Really?"

"Every man in the television business I've ever met can estimate stats on a woman within fifteen seconds of meeting her. What's your problem?" After five minutes, I couldn't take the pout. "Fine. What do you mean by worst? Worst destruction? Worst suffering? Worst smell?"

Ainsley's face crunched tighter with each question. Obviously, he hadn't considered all the possible permutations.

"First thing that comes to mind, I guess," he answered.

"I don't feel like doing an ugliness Rorschach for you, College. What's your point?"

"Okay. I'll tell you the worst thing I ever saw. There was this guy I knew in school who used to—" he caught his breath before saying it "—cut himself. On his hands, arms, chest, everywhere."

"How?"

"Razor blades. Pens. Pushpins. Everybody thought he was psycho. Once he did it with a fork in the lunchroom." His pretty face wrinkled with disgust and he shagged a hand through his hair, smoothing everything back into place.

"That's it? That's your *worst?*" Now he was depressing me.

"Well, no." He got defensive. "One night, it was late on a Saturday night, I walked into the bathroom in the dorm, you know—"

"I know what bathrooms are, yes."

Ainsley coughed. "Anyway, he was in there. On the floor. With blood. Lots of it."

Long breath. I finally understood where this was going. "Dead?"

"Just about. He died at the hospital, I guess."

"What did you do?"

"Puke," he admitted with a grimace. "Then, I called somebody."

Silence, except motor sounds and the wind, the sound of time passing.

"Here's the thing," Ainsley continued with a reasonable imitation of backbone, "since I was the one that found him, it always seemed like maybe, if I'd have gone to the bathroom sooner, you know? He wouldn't have died."

"You found him, so it was your fault?"

"Yeah." He rolled his palms up on the steering wheel in a sort of baffled partial shrug. "We weren't even friends. Still. I wish I hadn't waited so long to brush my teeth that night."

All I needed. Goading parables by innocent savants. "Who is it you think I can save, College Boy?"

He didn't answer.

I stared out the window into the dark and the ghost of my own reflection.

Ainsley looked over at me, once, twice. Obviously, he wasn't done.

"What?"

"Remember how you said, what we see when we look at something is ourselves? I can't help wondering what an Amish person looks like to you." He sounded curious, hardly flustered by my bad attitude.

We were still a good twenty minutes from civilization, such as you'll find between a television station and suburbia. Streetlights were few and far between but the autumn moon was fat and high. I could see the stumps of a broken, harvested field whip past my window and the darker ruffle of trees beyond. Farther out, almost at the horizon, I could see the glowing creep of monochrome homes, all constructed in the same shape like a Monopoly game run amok.

Empty farmland, or expanding homeland, I'm not sure which image depressed me more. Without a disaster or a battle underway, I didn't belong in either scene.

I never did answer him.

None of his damn business, anyway.

Stupid bitch! What was she thinking? An open confrontation where anyone could see? Anyone could be watching?

He popped the glove box and pulled out one of the blister packs he stashed for himself. He clutched the tablet in his hand and stared out the window at the darkened house.

What if a patrol car had rolled up in the middle of her little demonstration?

That's all he needed. Curzon was all over him now for bullshitting his way onto the police lot to search Tom's car. If Curzon had the slightest reason to think he was linked to Maddy O'Hara, there'd be a shit storm of questions.

He would have it out with Maddy O'Hara when *he* was ready.

Right now, he needed to find the things that belonged to him. He'd searched everywhere he could think, anywhere even remotely possible. He was nearly out of time.

Had he missed something when he searched Tom's apartment? Unfortunately, that fat-assed VFD building super of Tom's hadn't called with the heads-up until after O'Hara and her gay boyfriend were already in there. She'd looked so satisfied, so fucking smug when she walked out. It made him itch to floor the accelerator again. He wasn't going to run her down or anything, just put the fear of God into her. Remind her that everything can change in a second, just press a button and *boom!*

Christ, his head was pounding! He got out of the car and walked toward the house.

He needed to calm down. Get on track. He tightened his grip on the tablet in his hand.

There were no streetlights in the neighborhood and the light by the front door was on a timer. He'd watched it blink off a while ago. Nothing but dark out there.

There was a garden hose hanging near the garage door. The faucet squealed when he opened the valve. The rush of flowing water could probably be heard inside the house. It might even wake someone. He popped the pill and drank from the hose.

No lights came on. No one woke.

He stared at the empty windows, mapping the house in his head: bathroom, bedroom, another bedroom. That's when he realized—there *was* someone who could help him, someone who would know Gina's hiding places.

Jenny.

3:19:06 a.m.

Must have been close to 3:00 a.m. when Jenny came screaming awake. She hadn't done it in awhile, but I was on my feet and in her room before my head recognized what was happening.

"Don't go! Don't go. Don't go." Eyes popping with fear, she leapt out of the bed into my arms, half football tackle, half baby monkey in long-john pajamas.

"Easy, Jenny. Easy." My hand went up and down her back on autopilot. She'd lost weight since I'd come. I could feel the vertebrae of her spine. It gave me a hollow, sinking feeling.

I forced myself to speak softly. "Calm down. I'm here. I'm here."

Clutching my T-shirt in her hands, the rest of her body relaxed. I stretched out beside her on the bed. My heart was thudding hard with the adrenaline rush of being woken from a sound sleep by terror. Jenny didn't seem to notice. When my hand began to prickle from a lack of blood circulation, I pulled back slightly to shift her weight and she mewled a cry of despair that didn't stop until I had my arm around her again.

We lay glued together most of the night, while I listened to her sleep and wrestled my familiar demons of fight and flight to the mat.

All I'd ever done was watch and point. I'd never had to fix anything.

Insecurities never hit harder than when they're spliced into the black between dreams. Over and over, my head played an endless loop of mortification, *you are fucking up. You are blowing it. Do something.*

"Be okay," I ordered Jenny through the darkness. "Please be okay."

Wide shot Amish family selling veggies, Centennial Park; boy licks ice cream.

If you take a young teen, pull them out of school, concentrate their world experience into farm life, marriage and parenthood—it fundamentally changes the possibilities of their future.

The life that looks like happiness to them will have a certain shape.

MONDAY

9:23:14 a.m.

"Good thing we worked so hard to make up with the sheriff yesterday," Ainsley remarked. Our feet crunched on the crushed stone as we marched up the long driveway.

I was surprised he got out of the van at all, after the stink he'd thrown. "Why?"

"After they arrest us, Curzon'll have to go easy on us."

Worst thing first, is my motto. Quick stop at the office and back out this morning, straight to a visit at the Jost farm. Farmers kept early hours, right? I shifted the binocular box under my arm to the other side.

"You think?"

"He certainly won't want to tell his granny he just put his new girlfriend in jail."

"Right," I drawled. "Quit your whining. It's not like Uncle Richie would let you rot."

"He would if Mom told him to." Ainsley made it sound likely. "If Jost calls the police, I'm running for the truck."

"How's he gonna call the police, College Boy? He's got to go all the way out to the phone hut on the other side of the yard. Give us plenty of time to sprint to our getaway vehicle. Not that we'll need to," I added with all the shiny confidence of a well-practiced bluff.

"Don't remind me. I cannot run on an empty stomach."

Ainsley hadn't been employed long enough to realize Monday is the workday most likely to exceed safe-living speeds.

I had a list that started at my hairline and ended where my trouser-cuff broke. We'd managed to finagle another interview with the Amish psychologist, so I could ask her about Rachel Jost's situation. We needed to squeeze in another attempt to speak with Pat-the-fireman. And I had a conference call with New York scheduled, along with rumors of another GM visit.

Ainsley's to-do list seemed to hold one item at a time. Currently, it read doughnuts.

"Tell you what. If there's time, we'll get doughnuts before we hit the hospital."

"If we have time?" he said. "We had time to run Jenny to school."

It was still early and I was feeling mature, so I chose not to shoot back. Points for me.

Getting Jenny to school had been even harder than

usual this morning. She was slow, then she was sick, then she was "bored with school. It sucks." I heard all about how her mother would leave her home alone if she promised to just lie on the couch and watch TV.

Right. My bullshit meter was pinging *red-red-red,* then she missed the bus and I saw *red-red-red.* I don't really remember my mom hollering at me before eighth grade. Jenny won't remember either.

The Jost farmhouse appeared as Ainsley and I rounded the tree line, exactly as white as the sun on a cloud, except for the windows. Glare made the glass a one-way mirror to interior shadows. I scanned the windows and continued walking. As we passed the chicken hut, there was a burst of cackling clucks and crows.

"That's weird." Ainsley jabbed at me with his elbow.

"The watch-chickens?"

"No. That." A car was parked almost out of sight, around the side of the house that led to the barn. It was a modest gray Toyota—about as Amish as you could get in a car.

We both stopped to stare. Then the front door of the farmhouse banged open and out comes a guy in a suit coat with a briefcase the size of a dog kennel and a wad of manila folders. He's clearly pissed and rushing to get out. So naturally, the folders slip and stuff shoots everywhere in a papery blizzard of fifty-two pickup.

The guy shouted something fairly common, but definitely not Plain language.

"Go help him. See what you can find out."

"Me?"

"I'm going in to see Mr. Jost." I held out the box in my hands.

"Trespassing, breaking and entering—" Ainsley ticked off the words on his fingers.

"Not 'breaking.' Guy left the door open, see?"

"—being a public nuisance."

I blew him a kiss and stepped around the mess to get to the front door.

Behind me, I heard Ainsley offer, "Let me give you a hand."

The door swung open with the slightest push. I could hear Rachel's voice in the room beyond the entrance hall.

"—don't understand."

"Understand this!" her father shouted back. "I will have nothing of *his*. Nothing."

I wonder sometimes why other people back away in retreat when they hear the sounds of an argument. Is it fear? It can't be only that. I am something like afraid when I walk toward trouble. But I still can't turn away. As a kid, I slept with the closet door open and staged routine falls off the bed to stare into the dark beneath.

The world is too full of things to fear. A fight gives you a chance, at least.

From the doorway of the dining room, I saw Rachel gather her apron in both hands and cover her face. She looked like a small child hiding her eyes in the hope of not being seen.

Jost was the opposite. He wore no hat now and the blunt cut of his hair and wiry beard made me think of old photos of Rasputin. His face was burning, blotchy red, squeezed in a vise-grip of strong emotion. When he looked over and saw me, I thought he'd blow his last gasket.

"What are you doing here? Get out of my house!"

Rachel dropped her apron in shock. She covered her mouth with her hand and gave the smallest shake of her head.

"I brought you something," I said. The room was an echo chamber of flat, reflective surfaces: hardwood floors, bare walls, a long dining table with bench seating. My voice sounded loud and hollow.

Jost looked at me like I was a lunatic. "I want nothing of yours."

"It's not mine. It's yours."

10:47:41 a.m.

"The *rumspringa*. It's a fascinating contradiction. Follow me. We have to be quick, I have a patient coming in fifteen minutes." Dr. Graham pointed us up the corridor, making us work for every second we recorded. "The Amish way of turning teenagers into responsible adults is to set them free. One day they are completely under the rule of their parents and then they turn sixteen and suddenly, they aren't."

Ainsley danced around trying to stay ahead of her, or at least in profile. I was lugging the separate audio track. It was a good test of College Boy's mobility skills. But I hated traipsing through the hospital. The place gave me the creeps.

"Both the boys and girls?" I asked.

"For the most part. The commitment to their church must be made by an adult. Parents cannot force children to enter the church. In a way, it's also a test of the parents."

"If I were sixteen and somebody said I could do all the crap I'd ever wanted, I'd have been gone."

"That's how a lot of boys feel," Dr. Graham said. She stopped to let a gurney pass and smiled at Ainsley. "I knew a boy about your age who acted out quite a bit when he turned sixteen. He even bought a truck so he could be the one to haul kegs to their parties."

"What happened?"

"He's married. His wife gave birth to their third child last May. Cute little girl."

Ainsley looked horrified. "Are you kidding me?"

"No." She laughed. "That young man, everyone he knows—his family and friends, his peers—they're all Amish. He fell in love. But there is no marriage in the Amish church until both members commit themselves to the community. The truck was sold. The keg-hauling stopped. He started a family. Life went on."

Hospital people stopped to stare as we bumbled along the hall. The doctor walked slowly, enjoying her moment of fame. She may not care about television in general, but she enjoyed showing her colleagues that she was TV material. More power to her.

I couldn't help wondering which of the people we passed might have known my sister, worked with her, spoken to her in this very hall only a few months ago. Focusing on the doctor, I pulled an imaginary string with my fingers, reminding her to speak in full sentences. "What about Tom and Rachel? Could they have gotten married outside the church?"

"A couple who married outside the community would be put in the *bann*. They would be shunned by other Amish, a very different life from the one Rachel expected. Normally, a young couple lives with their parents until a child is born, then they move to a separate household."

"No way," Ainsley said.

"Enough with the commentary." I had a hand free, so I smacked him. Quietly.

"While they live with their parents, working the farm, they receive a share of any profit and save for a home or farm of their own. If it's a dairy operation like the Jost family runs, young couples will often build on the same farmstead, so they can be nearby to help."

Jost's family farm was a dairy operation. But Tom was not invited to work the farm and build a home there. He'd gone off and made the fire service his home.

In the end, both families had turned on him.

The corridor the doctor led us down seemed impossibly long. On camera, it would read like the Flintstone's house. I held that image in my head to ward off the shivers. The smell of the place reminded me of my sister's house. She must have used the same cleaning liquid.

"Can they leave the community during the *rumspringa?*" I asked. "Go live in the city for a while?"

"Certainly. Many do. Especially the boys."

"Really?" That confused me. "A man could leave the community before being baptized, go make a living in the world and then return, years later?"

"It's possible," Dr. Graham said. "But experience changes everything. One of the paradoxes that the community creates for itself is raising people of such strong convictions that when they choose to stand apart, it can be very difficult to heal a breach."

Tom's ghost must have hovered nearby. I felt the tickle of hair rising on the back of my neck.

"Especially after they've had cars, broadband and safety razors," Ainsley said.

"True. The experiences of the early teen years fundamentally affect the possibilities of a person's future. The life that looks like happiness takes on a certain shape."

I shook off my unease. "Sounds like living in the Amish community stunts your growth."

She stopped walking. "Don't play ignorant with me, Ms. O'Hara. Obviously, we benefit by the choices available to us. Although, personally I can't say I'm happier, or even more useful to the world because of them." She pointed a scolding finger my way, although if Ainsley had the shot framed correctly, it would look as if she were pointing to the viewer. "Can you?"

As soon as we stopped, the camera drew a crowd. I felt my hackles rise again. I was monitoring the audio levels, watching the cables that tethered Ainsley to me and trying to maintain eye contact with the doctor while she lectured me. It was hard to get a good look at the people around us. Last night's adventure had me paranoid. I could swear someone was following us. Following me.

"This is it." The doctor stopped in front of a padlocked set of metal doors. She looked around at the people who had stopped to watch. "I'll be signing autographs in my office later, for anyone interested."

I heard a few chuckles. Her comments had the desired effect. The crowd moved on. Dr. Graham jangled a ring of keys, searching for the right one.

"Come on, Doctor, as a woman, would you choose that environment?"

"I agree, it's a sexist, masculine hierarchy. But that exists everywhere. My chosen career environment for example." She popped the lock off the cabinet. "And yours perhaps?"

"Perhaps."

"Amish women work the system, just like you and I. Many find balance—mates, family who appreciate them, rewarding kinds of work that they enjoy. Is it really that different?"

Academic arguments only go so far with me. "Rachel had to stop attending school after eighth grade," I said. "She told us how she enjoyed the museums and the airport and the library and the movies. It seems as if she wanted—wants—a bigger world."

"Sadly, she can't have both. To accept an outsider's offer of marriage and live in this world, she'd have to leave everything behind—her father, her home, the only life she's ever known." The doctor glanced at her watch. "On the other hand, accepting her community's rule means giving up the wider world forever."

"A devil's bargain."

She frowned. "Only if you think in terms of this life and not the afterlife the Amish believe in. Any Amish girl has been raised to consider the eternity after death as her highest priority."

"Eighth grade." I frowned, too. My dad died the summer after eighth grade.

"A very formative time," the good doctor said. "I really must say goodbye."

"One more question? About the *bann,* how does it work? What does it do to you?"

She sighed. It wasn't an easy question. "*Bann* is the term for prescribed shunning. Sometimes it is done as a punishment, for a term of days, to remind the one who has broken the rules what it would feel like to be left out of heaven. When the time ends the person is welcomed back into the community. Under the *bann* the person shunned may not speak to or eat with anyone in good standing in the church. They must sleep in a separate space, like a cot in the barn or the basement, and no one can accept money or work done of their hands. It is a state of almost complete isolation. Every schoolchild knows how it works. And how it feels. 'You are not one of us. You can't play. We don't want you.'"

"Does it work? Does it really make someone change?" Ainsley chipped in.

She nodded seriously. No question was too stupid when it came to the boy. "Human beings are social animals. It's not simply a question of wanting company, we need it. The same way we need food, water and rest."

"People die if they don't get food and water."

"Exactly."

"Tom Jost didn't die of shunning."

"There are stages. Like the stages of malnutrition. You don't fall over from missing one meal, even a small amount can keep you going for a very long while. Since we are of a religious bent today, think of the monks who choose to go into retreat. They often describe a God so personal, he's capable of conversations, touch, even sharing a meal. Not to mention the tendency to anthropomorphize their pets, the birds they feed, even the plants around them."

Rachel had said Tom was always sneaking off to talk with the animals. Poor lonely kid.

"You're saying, where there's no human contact, we work to create it."

"Exactly. People will go to great lengths to make those connections. Without them, it gets harder and harder to interact 'normally.'" She put the little quotes around the word with her fingers. "That is, in a way which is predictable and compatible with the people around you."

Only psychologists have to define normal.

"Believing the people around you would never respond, that you would always be an unwelcome outsider?" She grimaced and her whole body tightened with a suppressed shudder. "That would be like living death."

Her words conjured the image of Tom standing on the pile of boxes, knowing he was being watched. The cold of that thought was enough to stop my breath.

His father, his work, his girl…how many times had Tom died inside, before he finally surrendered to the dark?

"I'm sorry." The doctor jingled her keys like an alarm bell. "I'll be late for my next appointment."

"Right, right. Thank you. College, shut us down."

Ainsley and I broke down the equipment enough to make the transport back to the truck easier.

I popped my head around the door to say goodbye and thanks again. "What is this room?" I couldn't help but ask.

"Just a storage locker for my office."

"What have you got there? What are those?" I pointed to a plastic bucket that held a few opened foil blister packs like the ones I'd seen in my sister's emergency kit, the kit Jenny had dragged out of the garage to bandage me after my fall.

"These?" The doctor held up several of the small boxes she had obviously come to retrieve. "Medical samples provided by the pharmaceutical companies. You really shouldn't be in here, Ms. O'Hara."

"Sorry." I said thanks again—despite the cold prickles her words gave me.

What was my sister doing with a bucketful of medical samples normally kept under lock and key?

Back in the truck, work was the best way to improve my mood.

"Make yourself useful, College. Figure out how to get me another Amish interview and the all-doughnut lunch is yours."

"Amish on-camera interview? No way."

"'No' doesn't get the job done." Another hidden downside to training newbies—every once in a while, I sounded like my mother. "I worked the story over hard Saturday night. We still need meat on Tom Jost. Somebody who can explain him, build us a little sympathy."

The shots from the sesquicentennial gave us visuals, but I needed audio. Walking, talking Amish, not just wide shots of guys in beards and hats. I wanted to understand how the Amish felt, what they thought about Tom and Rachel and all of us *Englischers*.

That was part of the piece I was thinking of spinning out—the blessing and danger of perspective. We know ourselves better when we look from the outside. Unfortunately, as Tom discovered, the view is not always all that flattering.

"Won't Dr. Graham's interview build sympathy?"

"No. She comes across as an outsider, an expert." Empathy was the missing element. "The problem we have here is that people revere firemen. Fireman does something weird—like kill himself in Amish clothes— people are so pissed that their hero isn't perfect, the tendency is to swing the other way and vilify him.

Tom Jost, evil-weirdo, would be easy. We could stop today."

"Why don't we?"

Was he kidding? I wasn't adverse to a little sex teaser, but I wasn't going to hang a cheap resolution on Tom Jost any more than I would hang a half-assed rap on Curzon's precious cousin.

"Easy sucks," I said.

Ainsley's smiling *huh* of approval was exactly that sort of throaty sound that drives teenage girls to their knees in adoration.

"Fuck you," I grumbled, reaching for my notebook.

"Nice try." He might have passed for cool—if he hadn't turned pink paying me the compliment. "You're rough, Maddy O'Hara, but you're not all bad."

What do you say to that?

Ainsley went back to making faces at the road and slapping his thigh to the music. Thinking was a full-body experience for my college boy.

"Does it have to be on a farm or just talking to an Amish person?"

"It's a visual medium, College. I want the farm." I flipped back through my shot list notes. "But we're fairly desperate here. Compromise is possible."

"I got an idea. The fire chief mentioned that Tom Jost used to have dinner with a teacher of his?"

"Yeah?"

"What if I know that teacher? I think it might be Grace Ott. She grew up Amish." He glanced at me and shrugged. "I told you, it's a small town."

"Why didn't you say something sooner? Pull off at the next doughnut factory. We'll make a few calls."

My notes slid to the floor as Ainsley cut into the turn

lane to bang a U. The kid was like a universal locator for bakeries. I tried to gather all my spilled papers in one hand and that reminded me. "Hey, who was that guy on Jost's front porch anyway?"

"Man! I can't believe I forgot to tell you about him. He was from some bank in town. When we finished picking up his stuff he goes, 'That old man's crazy.' I said we knew the daughter and she was nice."

"Smooth."

"Then he says, 'Tell Rachel to come see us at the bank. It's her money now. She needs to come talk to me.'"

"Her money now? What money?"

Ainsley shrugged. "Weird, huh?"

"Holy shit. Do you think Tom left money to Rachel?" Out loud, it didn't sound like much. In my head, something snapped together. "How much money?"

"Guy didn't say."

"We need to find out."

"Sure. I'll just add that to my list of calls," Ainsley tossed off.

"Great."

I swear he rolled his eyes. Did he think I was kidding?

The sight of Grace Ott's home reminded me, I'm on the verge of old. I fight the slide of downhill acceleration every day: increase exercise, decrease calories. Increase sleep, decrease expectations. Occasionally, it makes me cranky. Being cooped up in a remote truck with the Boy Wonder doesn't help. But standing on the doorstep at Grace Ott's house did, strangely enough.

This was the house you look for when you go over the

river and through the woods. The frame was a simple white clapboard saltbox. The driveway was gravel. The garage was detached with old-style sliding barn doors.

Hanging from the doorknob was a weather-faded paper daffodil. I could barely read the printing on one of the leaves. "Happy Spring! Mrs. Ott! We Love you!" On the stoop of a house like this, we were all youngsters.

Ainsley knocked.

With one glance, it was obvious Grace Ott was the kind of woman who had butter in the house and knew how to use it. Her round, sweet face contrasted nicely with the no-nonsense chin. Her hair was white, neatly curled and pinned. She studied me through the mesh of her screen door and turned to Ainsley.

He raised the wattage on his smile to tanning-bed levels.

"Come in then, Ainsley Prescott." She sounded amused, but not fooled. I got a nod. "You come, too."

We followed her up the hall that divided her tiny house. In my sister's neighborhood, the garages were bigger than this house. Grace's place smelled of time and detergent.

I kept an eye out for photos. I've always liked the display of past and present in an oldie's house, but there was only one picture out—an eight-and-a-half-by-eleven black and white of a young man with a '50s haircut that showed way too much ear.

"That's Mr. Ott," Grace said. "He keeps me company."

The kitchen would have seemed smaller if it hadn't been so spare. White cabinets. Yellow Formica. No knickknacks. No pasta-espresso-processor gadgets. No mess at all. There was a drop-leaf table and chairs, a wall-mounted phone with two yards of well-stretched spiral cord, and a calendar with a farm scene.

"I've got lemonade in the icebox. Sit right down." Grace's heavy-soled shoes clunked across the tile. "Television, hmm? Didn't I warn you you'd come to no good without another year of history?"

"Yes, Mrs. Ott." College hunched his shoulders humbly. She turned her back to get the lemonade out of the fridge, and he grinned at me. Thumbs-up!

"So what's all this about Thomas?" she asked.

"We'd like to do a story on him," I explained.

"Have you heard—" Ainsley started.

"I heard."

Even in profile, I could see how the thought stiffened her entire body. You live as many years as Grace, you've got to take a surrender like Tom's personally.

"We understand from his captain at the fire station that he visited you now and then."

"Sure. Amish leaves the community around here, they'll need to get their GED, sometimes take tests for college and such. I help with all that." She busied around the cabinets, taking out glasses and setting up a tray.

"How long have you been teaching over at North, Mrs. Ott?" Ainsley asked politely.

"Since before you were born."

"You still teaching high school?" I asked.

"They put me in administration two years ago. Part-time. I do the GED paperwork for the district. Used to teach history. And German. Ainsley knows about that."

"*Ja. Himmel,*" he answered.

She gave a snort at that. "What do you want to know about Thomas?"

"Whatever you can tell us," Ainsley answered.

Preparation of the lemonade tray continued without comment. Ainsley looked at me and shrugged.

Interviewing people for a living can be a bit like burglary. What the Boy Wonder didn't understand yet was how to slip into someone's house. You aren't selling vacuums. You don't necessarily go in the front door.

"Tom seems like a good guy who got stuck." I struggled to phrase it right. "So stuck that life ended up crushing him from opposite sides. I want to know why."

"Oh, do you?" She turned those old eyes on me and looked hard enough to make me nervous. After a minute, like a soft dissolve, I realized she wasn't looking at me anymore, she was looking into her own head. "It wasn't really opposite sides, you know, more like from the inside out."

The lemonade came to the table on a tray with extra sugar and long spoons for stirring. There was a fruit bread and jam in a lumpy glass jar. Good omens.

"Did Ainsley tell you I grew up Amish?" Grace asked. She sipped her drink with a frown, once, twice, then finally approved. "Youngest of ten. Things were different for me than for my eldest sister, of course. My mother was barely eighteen when my sister was born and nearly forty when I came along. I'll save you the trouble of calculating. My eldest brother was sent to jail for a short while for refusing to fight in the Second World War. My husband and I both were jailed for participating in a protest against the Vietnamese War. Times change even for the Amish."

"I thought the point was not to change."

"The point is to stay humble, and focus on something besides yourself," she said. Not angry, more like a teacher pinpointing the danger of a little bit of knowledge.

Ainsley coughed. "Speaking of times changing, I've seen guys drag racing that empty stretch of 39 in the middle of the night. They go out in horse buggies with boom boxes blaring and high-power flashlights."

That won him a twinkle of a smile. "Sure. Those are courting buggies. Shine a light into a girls' room at midnight, she might climb out and join you for a ride. In my day, it was pebbles against the glass. There's another change for you."

"I don't get it. No electricity but halogen flashlights are acceptable?"

"Oh, heavens, I can see your hackles rising all the way over here." Grace waved at me. "People are never as simple as rules, Ms. O'Hara. You're old enough to know that by now. That's why everyone has to make their own peace with the contradictions."

"What about Tom? Did he make his peace?"

The question deflated her. "Tom was the kind of boy who needed the rules. Not because he didn't want to do good. He needed rules to be at peace. He wasn't like some of the ones who go away from the community. They stretch and try new things—they experiment. Tom didn't do that. He held the *Ordnung* inside as a shield, and kept to much of it. The fire service was the same for him. Rules to a greater purpose. A sense of order, routine. He would have liked the military, I think, except for the fighting. Only man Tom ever hurt was himself."

She took off her glasses and pulled a tissue from up her sleeve.

Ainsley sipped his lemonade. I shook my head at the waste, of both Tom and the image of the moment. I'd never get her to tear up again, even if I could convince her to repeat the interview for the camera.

"Tom liked structure," I restated to keep her talking. "He played by the rules."

"Yes. It's prideful to analyze a person too much. We can never know someone's heart without walking in their shoes, but maybe…" She sighed in speculation. "Tom's childhood shook him. He had good reason to wish for security. When he first came to me, I could hardly imagine how he lay down to sleep, he was so stiff."

"Did he visit you often?"

"More so in the beginning. I gave him a list of chores I needed done and told him what time dinner would be on the table—'If you're late,' I says to him, I said, 'might be nothing left.' He was raised on a dairy farm. He wasn't late."

Ainsley laughed, but Grace could see I didn't get the joke.

"All farmers aren't the same, you know. Dairy farmers have a schedule to keep, every twelve hours. Those cows got to be milked. Now a seed farmer, what with the equipment people have today, they barely have to show up once a week." She curled her knobby fingers in front of her mouth and pressed, holding a memory back. She nodded until she was calm again. "Thomas would have made a good dairy farmer."

All together, we preserved the quiet for a moment, imagining a good life unlived.

Finally I had to ask, "Why do you think he did it?"

We locked eyes. I've seen the same look in women's eyes in every part of the world I've stood upon—fire, flood or fighting—the pain of failing the one you've tended.

"I keep asking myself, why didn't he come to me?" Grace leaned back in her chair and rested her hands in her lap. Her cotton print blouse was buttoned all the way to the neck. She was built wiry, and her collar gaped at her throat. The soft loose skin that circled her neck made her look fragile, exhausted by time. "Something happened to Thomas at the fire station, oh some weeks back. I'm sure it was before school started. I was bringing in tomatoes that day. Most of those firemen, Tom revered them. I don't know exactly what all went on, but somebody on his shift did something that put Thomas in a real twist. Wouldn't say much to me, but I gathered some fellow broke a rule. Something that put a terrible weight on Tom's conscience."

"What rule? Why Tom's conscience?"

Grace winced as she shrugged, embarrassed or hurt not to know the answer. "He was so upset. It's hard for *Englischers* to understand the feeling—"

"What feeling?"

"An Amish community watches over each other. We have the elders, yes, but we also have each other. We are each responsible and we are all responsible."

I nodded to encourage her. Did she know she used the inclusive "we"?

"After all—" she reached out and patted Ainsley's knee with a gnarled hand "—what would heaven be without all your loved ones around you? When someone is no longer at peace with himself, he must seek public confession. I think, maybe the fighting, even the things that happened later, maybe it was Thomas's mixed-up way to make the problem public."

"Uh-oh," Ainsley summarized.

"Yes. Public confession is not *sod,* not the worldly way. The last night I saw him, Thomas said he didn't know if he could belong anymore."

"At the fire station?"

"I thought he meant there, with the *Englischers.* I always wondered if perhaps, Thomas might wish to return to Amish ways someday. He'd hinted as much to me. Perhaps he meant something else."

"Then what happened?"

"He left after dinner as usual." She pressed her lips together, frustrated. "The world looked different to Thomas than it does to most. It was all a bit darker, more unpredictable. He expected bad things. They never surprised him. Rules helped keep him—" She stopped and searched for the right word.

I thought about saying "sane" but changed it to "—on track?"

"Yes. That's just it. When this fellow he trusted broke the rules, poor Thomas was at a loss. He seemed to feel anything could happen and all of it would be bad."

"Did he tell you about how he was getting along with the men at the firehouse after that? Or about an incident he might have had with the police?"

"Thomas? No. Of course not." The denial came first because that was fundamentally how Grace thought of Tom, not because she was out to fluff me. I didn't enjoy watching her perception change. "Did something happen with police?"

"An officer found him with a girl in a parked car," I

said. "They were taken to the station because the girl appeared to be breaking curfew. And she was Amish."

"Rachel."

I took a breath. I liked Grace. I didn't want her to agree to be part of this story without knowing the whole story. Being civilized was a professional liability, but there it is.

"They also found magazines in his trunk."

"Magazines?"

"Can I have a piece of that fruit bread now?" I asked.

Grace served. It gave me a good excuse to keep my eyes on my plate.

"They were adult magazines," I told her. "Someone at the police station found out and there was some gossip. It seemed to affect how his colleagues were treating him."

"Mercy." She said it softly to herself. Loud and firm, she said, "If you are here to gather information to slander that boy further, I'll ask you to leave right now."

"No, Mrs. Ott. I don't want to slander anyone. I wouldn't be here if I thought that part of the story was the whole truth."

I looked over at Ainsley, mostly because I was wishing he wasn't there. Right at that moment, I didn't like doing this interview in front of him. It felt uncomfortable. I took a breath and spoke the truth, despite the audience.

"Help me understand what happened. Lots of people know what it feels like to be stuck between old ways and new ways."

Grace stared at me, eyes large behind glasses. Her

face wore a mask of age, but I sensed the empathy of recognition behind it.

"I know what it feels like," I confessed. "Help me understand why he gave up trying."

3:30:58 p.m.

We finished way past lunch. Since we were expected back at the office already, Ainsley was driving like a high-school boy after dark. The tires screamed at every stoplight.

Bits and pieces were flying around in my head, I needed quiet to sort through the whirl.

"I can't believe you talked her into that interview. I never thought she'd go for it." Ainsley rattled along, doing the ten o'clock football recap. *Let's see that play again. Wasn't that great?*

"Yeah."

"I thought we'd never get it. But you talked her into it. Man. That was great. Great stuff. The farm and teaching. Maybe I should call the high school tomorrow? I bet I can get yearbook photos of Mrs. Ott from way back. What do you think? Maddy?"

"Yeah, great."

"What's wrong?"

"Timing's not right."

"What timing? On the track?"

"No," I snapped. "Think about this. Grace said Tom came to her to complain about feeling betrayed before school started, but he was arrested after that. Rachel said the same thing. He was upset before they got caught in the car."

"So?"

"So something must have happened at the fire station first. Tom gets all worked up about it. He goes out with his girl—he's frantic, he's pushing her to marry him, give him some reason to return to the Amish—not only does she turn him down, he also gets busted with jack-off material in the trunk. Doesn't that sound funky to you?"

"You mean like funky luck?"

"I mean like a funky-fucking-setup. Somebody set him up with those magazines. That's the only thing that makes sense."

"Why?"

"To ruin his reputation?" As soon as I said it, I knew it felt right. "To make him look like a sneaky, untrustworthy bastard? To distract him? Revenge, maybe? It has to be something to do with that fight at the fire station."

The chief had said Tom and Pat were fighting right before he died. Was that what put Tom "in a twist" before he saw Rachel? Or did the boys fight later, over the magazines in the trunk? Talking to Pat just moved to the top of my list.

I jumped to Tom's death and started playing with another idea. "How much do you think a firefighter makes a year?"

"I don't know. Maybe 40K?"

"How much would that cheesy apartment he lived in cost a year?"

"Maybe five hundred. At most."

"Used car. Cheap-o housing. No drugs, no expenses. He's been working four or five years in the fire service. He could have forty, fifty grand saved. Maybe more. That might rate a personal visit from a banker."

"Whoa." Ainsley shook his head. "Never thought of that."

"Oh, it's diabolical." I cackled as I pieced possibilities together. "Tom makes it up to his girl and sticks it to his old man all in one blow. Fucking ingenious."

"What?" Ainsley flashed quick looks between the road and my grin. "Why is that good?"

"He's left all that cash in Rachel's hands. She can do whatever she wants now. If we're right about the money, she could choose to leave her father's farm. Buy her own place. Or go to college. Now, she has a choice."

I sat up straight, leaning against the strap of the seat belt. If the money went to split Rachel from her father, the binoculars went to split him from what? Peace of mind? His community? I crammed that thought under-cover. Would my story make it worse for him? No room for that guilt. I had to produce a piece for television and Rachel Jost would be appearing in it. If Old Man Jost had to take the hot seat with his Amish neighbors over six minutes of pre-prime, well, maybe he deserved it.

"Tom Jost wasn't shunned. Rachel told us that," I calculated aloud. "He left the community and didn't take vows."

"Sort of the same difference, isn't it? He never went back."

"He never left." It all spilled into place, his apartment, his relationship with the other firefighters, his relation-ship with Rachel. "That's why Rachel said, 'I would be his Amish.'"

What's a guy who follows rules to do, when nobody else will play fair? The words of an Amish school ditty I'd found in my research came rushing back:

I must be a Christian child
Gentle, patient, meek and mild;
Must be honest, simple, true

In my words and actions too...
Must remember God can view
All I think, and all I do.

"'God can view all I think, and all I do,'" I quoted for Ainsley's benefit. Picturing those binoculars in Jost's closet, I shivered. Could Jost have been trying to get the old man arrested? "Remind me to call our favorite sheriff when we get in. I need a little instruction on Samaritan law in this fair county."

Ainsley looked confused, but hopeful.

Just the way I like 'em.

3:38:25 p.m.

Jenny usually walked around the playground during outside time. The school aides didn't pay much attention to her when she walked. They were too busy yelling at the big kids.

"One at a time!"

"No chicken on the monkey bars."

"Mulch stays on the ground."

It was a good day to walk. Sunny, but cold. With her hands in her pockets, Jenny stopped under the twisty slide. It was shadowy there, like a cave. She could see out but it was hard for other people to see her.

There was a man watching the playground. He leaned against the hood of his big shiny car, arms across his chest.

Jenny couldn't stop staring. Was it him?

His car was parked at the curb where other moms sometimes waited for kids after school. He looked like he was waiting for somebody.

She wasn't sure if it was him. She decided to climb the slide tower for a better view.

She was only a second grader the last time she saw him. He came to The Funeral. He stayed at the back of the church though. One time, she waved hello but he turned his face away. She didn't see him again after that.

Jenny thought he must be mad at her, maybe even hated her. It wasn't her fault that Aunt Maddy moved in and took over. Thinking about it made Jenny feel like crying and wrecking something. If she thought about it too long, she got that shrinky feeling inside and couldn't eat, until she smelled the inside of Mama's closet for a long time.

From up on top of the slide, she could see pretty well. There were some trees and Dumpsters and the grass field and then sidewalk.

He smiled at her and waved with one hand.

Jenny was surprised by how good she felt seeing him recognize her, like a happy memory coming back for no reason. She waved back at him with a small, secret bend of her wrist that hid the motion from everybody else. She smiled, too.

The kid behind her at the top of the ladder was getting impatient. "Go!"

Jenny pushed off and leaned back, speeding faster through the tunnel than she expected. Her stomach felt afraid and excited and sick and happy all at the same time.

The bell rang right as she shot off the slide onto the mulch.

Jenny looked at the blacktop where the other kids were running to line up. She looked back at him. He called her with a wave.

What a relief!

Usually grown-ups came to the door to sign out the kids who were going home. If the kids were on the playground though, parents usually signed them out first and then took kids home from the playground.

He probably signed her out already. Jenny was glad. She didn't want to go back inside. She wanted to leave. Right now. She walked straight out to the curb across the grass.

He used to pick her up all the time, before. It wasn't like he was a stranger or something. She knew not to get in a car with strangers. She wasn't a baby. He knew it. too. He even let her sit in the front seat.

"Hi."

"Look at you. You've been growing."

"Yeah."

His car was so big, it felt like sitting on top of the world. He told her to buckle up and she did. They started driving and for a long while he didn't say anything. He only looked at her, quick, and then looked back at the road.

Was she supposed to talk? She bit her fingernail instead.

When they were almost at her house, he started asking her the usual stuff about school and how her fish was doing and if she still liked Scooby-Doo. He kept driving right past her house. Did he forget where she lived?

"Um? You passed it. That was my house."

She got a weird feeling inside, bad weird. What could she do? She couldn't think of one good thing. Pretty soon the worried feeling was a fuzzy feeling, almost sleepy. She wiped her hands on her jeans.

"Seen any movies lately?" he asked.

"Where're we going?"

"You'll see," he answered. "I need you to understand something, Jen. Something really important. Something your mother would want you to understand."

"Okay," she said. Nobody talked to her about her mother. Quickly, without looking at him, she asked, "Do you think about her ever?"

He pulled over to the side of the road and snapped the stick thing between them into the slot marked *P*. Jenny stayed very still, wondering if she'd made him mad.

"Do I think about your mom?" Very quietly he said, "All the time."

Jenny sighed. "Me, too."

He turned in his seat and stared at her. "Look around. You know where you are?"

They were on the edge of the neighborhood, somewhere. She recognized the fence up the road a ways, that went around the old cemetery. She and Aunt Maddy passed it when they took walks on the Prairie Path last summer. Jenny had never gone in there.

She said *yes* with a tiny nod.

"You ever say anything to your aunt about me?" he demanded all of a sudden.

"Like what?"

"Like anything." He said it in a funny tight voice.

"No." Suddenly, it hurt her throat to say even that one word.

"Good. That's good. I didn't want any of this, you know." He banged one fist against the steering wheel.

Jenny jumped. Her seat belt got really tight. It was hard to breathe.

"Look at what I got here." He pulled a shiny silver square out of his pocket. It was one of those medicine things with the pills in little bubbles. "You ever seen these before?"

Jenny nodded. They looked just like the ones that Tonya had for her hurting leg.

"In your house? Where?"

Jenny knew where medicine should be. "The medicine bucket?"

"No. They aren't there." He sounded pretty sure about that. "Where else could they be? A whole bunch of them."

Jenny raised her shoulders up around her ears. She didn't know. Really.

He threw the medicine in the air and said a bad word. "Okay. This is really important, Jenny. Are you listening? Don't say anything to your aunt about me and your mother. Do you hear me? Something bad might happen if you do."

His hand reached out, like he was going to touch her or something, and she squeezed herself against the car door. He leaned across her body to jerk her door latch. Jenny's fingers fidgeted for her seat belt button.

"Get out," he said.

Jenny didn't argue. She scrambled out, pulling at her jacket where it caught on the seat belt.

"Take a look around. You know where you are? It's a dangerous road. Cars everywhere. None of us are safe, Jenny."

She shook her head *yes, yes, yes,* but all she could think about was getting out of that car. Her feet crunched on the gravel as she practically fell out the door. There wasn't any sidewalk. The shoulder of the road was white gravel and weeds. The car pulled onto the road. Jenny took a few giant steps backward and fell into a tangle of bushes, poking, scratching, tearing at her clothes. The car drove away.

Jenny watched him go. She looked down at her feet and saw the packet, the silver square carrying white bubbles of medicine. It must have fallen out of the car when she opened the door.

A car whooshed by. Jenny's heart jumped.

She picked up the medicine, turned and ran. She didn't run toward anything. She ran away from the car, away from him. When she was tired and out of breath she stopped, sat down hard and put her head on her knees.

More cars passed. They were loud and windy and scary. Cars could hit you and kill you. They were like dinosaurs or alligators. Big, dangerous, stupid cars. Jenny crawled backward, away from the road until she bumped into a fence. She hid in a cave of branches between two big bushes.

Safe.

4:25:00 p.m.

It was one thing to see Tom Jost's story begin to make sense. It was another thing entirely to turn what I knew into commercial television. The high that came with understanding made the crash back to WWST reality all the more painful.

"What the hell? No office?"

Barbara squinted at me over the top of her cat-eye glasses. Glasses like hers are the secretarial equivalent of a bleeding-dagger tattoo and a gold front tooth. "You got no call to use that kind of language with me."

"What kind of language do I need to use to get an office with a fucking phone? French? I have a New York conference call coming in ten minutes. Am I supposed to take that in the lobby?"

Barbara hit the intercom. "I'm not dealing with this, Richard. She's using the F-word again."

"Goddamn it!" Gatt shouted in stereo. The sound of his voice came through the intercom and the wall at the same time.

The door to the inner sanctum banged open and Gatt hollered, "Get in here, O'Hara." He stumped back behind his desk. "This, I do not need today."

Schmed was in the office lounging in one of the faux-leather chairs. He shot me his signature snarky smile. Unpleasant memories of Saturday night's conversation came rushing back. It was pretty clear what he and Gatt had been busy discussing. Schmed leaned back, crossing his ankle over one knee. The chair sounded like it was gasping its last fart.

"Say excuse me," I told him.

"Why? You're the one interrupting."

"Quit acting like a couple of juvies," Gatt said. "We got five minutes to resolve this. You've got a conference call, don't you?"

"As a matter of fact."

"Okay. Here's the deal. Jim gives up one of his people's office spots and you do his story on what—?"

Schmed jumped in right on cue. "Local car dealerships."

"No way—"

"—I'm thinking something along the lines—'The Industry that Saved the West or maybe Rotten Reputation, Respectable Reality.' I'll give you a list of contact names."

A hairball of disgust formed at the back of my throat. I considered hocking it at Schmed. Instead I asked him, "What kind of car do you drive?"

"Like I'd tell you. You planning on putting sugar in my gas tank, O'Hara?"

Not a bad idea. "No. I'm asking what model. I'll bet you're an SUV man."

"Stay away from my car," Schmed said.

"I knew it. You and your dealership buddies are going to have to find another way to lure the suckers." This conversation was not taking me to my happy place. I went for the door. "You'll never sell that to Network."

"Come on, O'Hara," Gatt whined. "Don't bust my balls here."

"Selling it to Network is your job, honey," Schmed said.

"No way."

"Phone in your complaints," he tossed back at me. "Lines are always open."

Gatt heaved a high-drama sigh even though I didn't bother to answer. Men with buffed nails have no power in my universe. But his jab pushed a button, and a light came on.

I spun around to stare at Gatt. "Tell me again about the Amish story. When did the tip come in?"

TV people are better than most at following quick cuts between subject matter. Gatt thought for a few seconds and said, "Right before I met with you on Thursday. Barbara passed me the call. Male. Guy said there was 'something to see.' Said fire and sheriff had been called. I assumed he was a bystander."

"Why?"

"Cell phone call. Sounded like he was outside."

"Traffic sounds?" I asked skeptically. There weren't any cars on that road.

"No. Bugs and wind." Gatt had a producer's ear for audio.

"Got it. Thanks." I turned on my heel and headed toward Barbara's desk.

"Does this mean you're not quitting?" Gatt called sweetly.

I raised my right hand and waved goodbye with the single most appropriate digit.

At Barbara's desk, I stopped. She continued to ignore me, mouth in a lemon pucker.

"If I promise never again to use the F-word against you, would you please let me have four Excedrin on a pair of Tums?" Might as well take some calcium with my caffeine.

She handed me the pills but the face didn't change. This time there was no offer of a cracker.

"Is there a phone in the big conference room?"

"Yes."

"That's where I'll be."

I'd written up a shot list for Ainsley to run down at his convenience, by tomorrow morning. I needed pickups logged, library materials, things we needed to review before next week's story. My main thought was to keep him out of my hair, give me time to think. Luckily, I had a two-hour conference call ahead of me.

Part of the fun of working in television is learning to break down the world's constant stimulus. I can block out the sight of six monitors and focus on one. I can hear both a speaking voice and the hum of an air conditioner that might ruin the audio track. To do the job right, I have to be able to see all the parts, separately, before reassembling them into something meaningful.

Having a flexible attention span is critical. Which is exactly what made conference call time so productive.

"Maddy O'Hara, this is the operator. Are you on the line?"

"Here."

"You are the last caller being connected. Everyone is present. Your conference may begin."

There was some opening bullshit where everyone pretended to be so glad I was "on board," and I had to say something cheerful. As soon as that was done, I clicked on the phone's privacy feature and took out my cell phone.

"This is Maddy O'Hara. I need to speak to Corporal Curzon—Nicky Curzon, please."

Ainsley pushed the AV cart with the HD8 through the door. "Where do ya want it, lady?" He made a face when he realized I was engaging in teleconference bigamy.

"Park it where I can reach it," I told him. "Yeah, I'm

still holding," I said to the woman at the police station. "College, I've got a new to-do list for you."

The speakerphone called for me and I shot Ainsley a finger *shh*. "Sorry, I missed that. They've got me working in a temporary space that's noisy as hell. Say again?"

"We've got a suggestion on the table for theme weeks, set in advance that you'd customize a story for in your market. Can you get behind that, O'Hara?"

"Who decides the themes?"

"Good question," New York answered.

"Ms. O'Hara? Are you still there?" the police operator asked.

I popped the mute on the conference speaker. "Here!" I answered and then rotated the cell phone one-hundred-eighty degrees on my ear. "Plug me in would you, College?"

"Transferring you to Corporal Curzon at extension 2-2-8."

The speakerphone crackled. "All the producers participating will agree on themes. New York has the final say."

Typical. I hit the voice button. "As long as they don't ream us during sweeps with crap like Sexual Perversion in the Vatican, I'm in." There were a few grumbled affirmatives. Somebody decided to bear witness on the topic. Mute on.

"I'm in, too," Nicky answered. "What's going on?"

Ainsley held up two cassettes.

"Run the stuff we shot this morning." I twisted the cell phone down in front of my mouth. "Hey, Nicky. Thinking about something you said yesterday, that I forgot to follow up on—do you mind?"

"Shoot."

"Is that safe to say in a police station?"

"Funny. Don't quit your day job."

The speakerphone called my name. "O'Hara? You with us?"

Press a button. I chided all the fellas at once. "I'm not going anywhere."

Local and long distance—they all grumbled.

Ainsley was the only one who fully appreciated the show.

The conference call continued with the mute on, topic—satellite problems—while I continued speaking to Nicky Curzon. "I heard you say you 'did some checking' before you sent the letter on Jost. I haven't found anything to support the freaky image of Jost that the magazines suggest. Can you help me out?" I let it hang for a second. "Who'd you talk to?"

"I talked to the guy's partner at the fire station. Friend of the family knows him."

"Really? What'd he say?"

"Said Jost was a closet kink, hiding mags everywhere, all the time. Also said he'd had girl trouble before. Jost told the guys in the firehouse he'd left the Amish community over a girl."

Ainsley hit Play on the stuff we'd shot earlier.

"What the hell? You kidding me?" I said, mostly to my college boy. He'd played with the angle, zoom and the registration. I had the doctor in black and white as well as colorized like a bad hallucination.

"No, I'm not kidding," Nicky said. His voice dropped. He didn't like me getting excited about something he'd said. "Look, I gotta go, Maddy."

"Transfer me to the sheriff, would you? I got questions for him, too." I went into transfer limbo.

On the conference call, a sales himbo was stroking himself over the marketing presales.

"College, didn't I tell you to quit screwing around with the artsy-fartsy shit?"

"It's only the early stuff," Ainsley assured me. "I was experimenting." He hit the FF button until the picture was recognizable.

"Well, cut it out. You're making me nervous."

"If I'm making you nervous, why would I cut it out?" Jack Curzon asked.

Shit. I hadn't heard the pickup. "Hello, Sheriff. How's your day?"

"Fine. Very open over the lunch hour. My appointment didn't show."

"Really? Listen, Jane Citizen would like to ask a question about Samaritan law in this fair county. How's it work?"

"That's state law, actually. Protects a citizen who tries to help from legal action. Requires anyone who is licensed as fire, police or medical personnel to assist if they see a person who needs help."

"And that's all?"

"Yep."

"Ah." So Tom Jost wasn't trying to get his father in trouble for being a "bad Samaritan" by providing him that timely set of binoculars.

"Why does Jane want to know?" the sheriff asked.

"Jane likes to be informed."

"Jane needs to get her ass in here to make a report if she wants to get any more cooperation from the sheriff's office."

If SUV-guy was trying to scare me, the last thing I wanted to do was look like I was running to the cops. Running encourages a bully to chase you.

It'd be nice to hang the whole thing on Schmed. I figured I better throw Curzon a bone to get him off my back about the reckless driving report. "Yeah, about that—I'm fairly certain the driver was a guy from the office." Ainsley gave me a sharp glance over the shoulder. "I'm rethinking the whole situation. Maybe I should try and resolve it in-house. I got to work with the guy every day, you know what I mean? I'm sure we can come to some kind of peace pact."

Curzon remained silent.

Ainsley paused the audio on the interview. The conference call expanded to fill the dead air. Voices droned on about local issues, each market forecasting inevitable success. The bullshit factor was ten-plus.

"Fine." Curzon blinked first. "I'll let you slide. For now."

"That's all I got for this week," said the guy in Boston.

I hit the speaker button and answered them both. "Great." New York still had to give a report, so I hung in there with Curzon. "Jane's got one more question for you, Sheriff."

He sniffed a laugh. "Jane doesn't give up."

"Admit it, you love that about her."

Ainsley rolled his eyes in disgust. I shrugged, *what?*

"I don't remember you mentioning, did Tom Jost have a phone with him when you found him?"

"A cell phone?" He thought about it and answered me with the question, "Why do you ask?"

"Curiosity."

Another silence followed. The kind of silence that squeezes between moves when old guys play chess.

When Curzon committed to his response there was no hesitation. "We didn't find a phone."

"Really? Too bad. I had my next question all lined up. Thanks, Sheriff. I owe you one."

"You owe me more than one. You're running a tab now."

"Bull. I got you off the hook with Grandma and the rest of the clan yesterday. I think you still owe me." Best defense: be offensive. "And next time you need a beard, warn me so I can dress the part."

"What you wore yesterday was fine." His voice dropped into that dark place where whispers take root. "But I'd love to see how you'd dress the part."

"Whoops! Boss just walked in. Gotta go."

I could hear the man laughing as I hung up, which was bad enough, then Ainsley gave me a know-it-all look that was totally inappropriate from someone his age.

"Shut up." I pointed at his face. "You do not have time." I flapped the shot list at him.

He skimmed my notes, top to bottom. His expression made it clear when he got to the one requiring the *Dawn—pickup. Need long, wide, establishing shot of tree where Tom died.*

"Dawn? How am I going to get that?"

"I find if I set the alarm for 3:00 a.m. I can get camera ready in plenty of time. If I skip breakfast."

"You're kidding?"

"This afternoon I want you to concentrate on the firehouse. Your mom left a message that we had permission to go in and shoot interiors—his locker, his bed, whatever." There was a definite advantage to working with someone hooked into the power loop. Not that Richard Gatt was going to hear it from me. "See if you can set up a couple match dissolves to what we've already got from his apartment."

"Got it." Ainsley nodded.

The shock of a 3:00 a.m. call time was passing; he was starting to get excited again which was a good sign. If he didn't love it enough for 3:00 a.m., he didn't love it enough. There are worse things about the business than an early call. Lots of them.

"I want nice clean shots, College. Nothing funky. Think journalism, not art."

"Yeah, yeah."

"Text me if you run into trouble. I'll be here. Working." I tipped a nod at the conference call. Sounded like they'd almost finished driveling through the LA rep's report. My agenda had no name listed for the next spiel. Maybe they would wrap early and I could squeeze in a little studio time. "Warn Mick I might be late, would you?"

Ainsley looked wistful at the thought of the next editing session. "I'll tell him."

"Don't worry. There'll be plenty to do tomorrow."

He smiled at the thought. "Yeah. That's true."

"Get out of here, College. You're making my teeth ache."

I went back to buzzing through the shots of Grace and Dr. Graham, looking for sound bites and jotting down times.

The conference call was still going strong. A couple major players from the top-ten markets had been invited, so the grunts kept interrupting with clever comments.

Whatever. I had enough to keep me occupied.

There were a few bits I could pull out of the doctor's interview, but even less of what Grace Ott had given me would make sense in the story I had roughly sculpted. I'd given up the salacious sex angle, but I needed something that would fit with the program. Much as I'd like to paint a picture of human isolation, Mysterious Death of an Amish Outlaw was probably my best television premise.

This is not a public service, I lectured myself. Television is a business. The purpose of business is to make money.

"O'Hara, I've got that office cleared for you," Schmed wheedled from the doorway.

Speak of the devil and in he walks.

"My hero." I had a sudden premonition I'd be carrying antacid in my wallet from now on.

"I'll have the list of dealerships to interview on your new desk by tomorrow morning." He winked. "Thanks, hon."

"Getting tired of telling you to bite me, Jim. Go away."

"GM's in the building, by the way. She's looking for you."

I mumbled something creative. Schmed exited with a snicker.

New action item on my list—end Schmed's good mood.

With the conference call as white noise, I focused on the monitor, committing some pieces to memory, watching for glitches, listening for audio errors I'd need to cut around. My brain knows how to do this stuff on autopilot. Almost like driving—there's a part of your mind that's totally focused and another part that's free. I'm better at the pieces than I am at the big picture. That's why I prefer stills to video, editing to previewing.

When it came to Tom Jost's death, I could almost see the bits I didn't understand coming together, spread like a collage in front of me.

I wished I had the time to follow College to the firehouse. Maybe talk to Tom's partner Pat again. If Grace was right, Tom's problem began there.

I still didn't have an explanation for who'd called the station the day of Tom's death. What kind of Samaritan would call, but not stop? If they'd only called the cops—maybe. But why call the cops and the local television station?

According to the sheriff, Tom had no phone with him. I know Tom owned a phone; we saw the empty charger in his apartment. What happened to it? I thought of Rachel sitting in the bushes with the phone pressed to her ear. She hadn't known Tom was dead, hadn't seen the body. She couldn't have been the Samaritan.

I picked up my cell phone and hit the new *Clarion* speed dial for the private extension of Mr. Melton Shotter.

"News."

"Hey, Melton. What news?"

"Maddy?" He sounded surprised. "How's that story on Jost going?"

"Not bad. Question for you. How'd you get the tip on Jost? Was it off the police band or what?"

"I got called on my way into work that morning. Can you hold? I'll check."

"No problem." I hit Rewind and toggled the mute

button on the conference call to vote fine with me on a local weather graphic preceding local stories.

The guy from Dallas added, "People watch TV to find out what tomorrow's weather will be. Give them what they want. Get them hooked. This ain't brain surgery."

Melton came back on the line with interesting news. "Someone called the paper with a tip. Said there were cop cars and fire trucks along the road. The receptionist who took the call knew I'd pass that exit on my way into work. She phoned me at home."

"What time?"

"Must have been around ten. That's when I leave for the office."

I blew some exasperation his way. "Nice work if you can get it."

"Hey, I work 'til we go to press on Thursdays. I'm here 'til midnight sometimes."

"Midnight? That's all?"

Melton and I traded poor-me stories until we were both sleeping on desktops, surviving on Tic Tacs and tap water.

The conference call got around to taking another vote.

"Thanks for the help, Melton. I got another call." I hung up before he could pump me for more on Jost.

After I weighed in on title graphics, I tried to call Ainsley in the truck and got no answer. Either he wasn't in the truck or couldn't hear the ring over the downbeat of WKiSS-FM. Guess which one I was betting?

"Ms. O'Hara? I've been looking for you." Shirley Shayla, my new general mother, stood there, hands on hips. She was almost eye level with me, if I slumped in my chair. Aggravation or a long day had crumpled her Donna Karan suit. Not a good sign.

"You found me." I waved to the line of empty conference room chairs. The machine clucked into standby and the speakerphone suddenly cracked out an "O'Hara?"

I held up a one-minute finger to Shayla and answered, "Yeah. I've got a couple stories on the burner right now. For the first week, I like this piece on a local suicide."

"Details," the New York guy barked.

"Guy was a refugee from a local Amish community. The suicide had signs of being autoerotic asphyxiation."

Bits and pieces of my colleagues' opinions popped through: a snort, a chuckle, a drawn out *shiiiit*. "Sounds good," was the final answer.

What followed was a sequence of feelings that were fairly familiar when I sold a story based on salacious spin—relief, shame, and as I met Shayla's gaze, guilt hunkered down for the long haul.

I hit the mute. "What can I do you for?"

"*That's* the story you're putting together for the premiere?" She made a firm nod in the direction of Grace's sweet image on my monitor cart, twitching rhythmically in freeze-frame. "Former Amish Sex-Death?"

"Actually, I'm not sure what the story will be yet." Guilt made me sound grumpier than was polite for a new boss. Thumbing toward the phone call, I tried to work the charm as I admitted, "You know how it goes. These conference calls are fairly, um, promotional. Until I have it in the can…" I let it drift into a long pause.

"That topic would certainly sell ads." Her arms were folded across her bosom and her feet were planted wide and toe out. She was not smiling. "Although, I have to say I'm surprised. It's not what I expected from you. Rather predictable."

Amish autoerotic asphyxiation was predictable? Where had she been living?

I opened my mouth, hesitating to stick my foot straight back in there, when the cell phone vibrated. Saved by the bell. "Yeah?"

"Maddy? It's me," Ainsley whispered in his undercover voice. "I'm at the fire station."

"Great." I started talking, hoping Shayla would lighten up on the hairy-eyeball she was giving me. "Here's my—"

"You won't believe the visuals! They're training on car fires. Torching old beaters in the back lot. It's incredible. We can totally work it in. Tom-the-Amish-firefighter lighting a car on fire? Get it? And Pat just came in to pick up his check."

"What? Ask—"

Ainsley would not shut up. His whispering got fierce. "Pat got all over me when I told them about the bank guy out at the Jost farm."

"Really?" I went to full stop.

"I'm going to try for an interview."

"With Pat? He wants to give you an interview?"

"I can handle it. Leave time in the story. I'll call you later."

"Wait!" Too late. I hit ring-back and the guy at the firehouse who answered laughed loudly as he passed the phone back to Ainsley.

"That's three, College Boy. You're grounded. Never, *ever* hang up before I do."

"Right, right. Can I go now?"

"No. Pat's in this thing deep. Watch yourself. Ask

what he fought with Tom about and find out when—before or after Rachel. Ask what he said to Nicky Curzon. And find out how the fire service call came in about Jost. Did they hear through the cops or was it direct?"

"Okay. I can handle this, Boss."

The words "I can handle it" were a little too scary to let slide. "Don't get fancy on me, College. Get your shots and get back here. Don't make me give you the J-school speech again."

"Anything else?"

He was being such a pain in the ass, I snapped, "Yeah. I need you to pick up Jenny on your way back." Too late, I thought of Shayla and the fact that I really didn't want to spread the word I was permanently responsible for a kid these days.

"From school?" Ainsley asked.

"Yeah," I mumbled. It wasn't in me to ask for a personal favor without justification but it felt tricky explaining my motives to Ainsley. "I'm going to check something out at the Jost farm and I may run late. If you get her by six, we can rendezvous back at my place and watch whatever you get at the firehouse."

Silence.

Conference call went lull.

Shayla tapped her foot.

"You want to talk to Mr. Jost again, don't you?" Ainsley's mental wheels were turning. "Don't go back there, Maddy. He's going to call the cops or something this time."

"He might talk now that he's had all day to think about what I dropped off this morning." Quietly I added, "And there's something I need to say to him."

"Oh, man." Ainsley sounded worried. "Don't make me give you the J-school speech."

"Ha. Funny."

Shayla stood there watching me with one eyebrow cocked, so I could only penalize the boy with the silent treatment. The conference call droned on. A close-up image of Grace flickered before me on the monitor, waiting. I felt caught in a paused moment, waiting for someone to press the button that would release me from the sameness of it all. Something had to change.

"I'll pick up Jenny by six," Ainsley relented. "No problem. Maybe call a pizza, too? Delivery to your place?"

Pizza, the ultimate Prescott peace offering.

All I could say was, "Thanks. I'm hanging up now. Get back to work."

"Do I rate your attention, yet, Ms. O'Hara?" Shayla drawled.

"Absolutely." I stood to face her.

The conference call shouted, "O'Hara?"

I tapped the mute button. "Yeah?"

It was the voice of my New York production counterpart. "Are you going to uplink your story for everybody to preview?"

"No."

"We'd really like to see it," the shark from Dallas cooed.

"Oh well, in that case, *hell no,*" I said with a smile. Shayla can vouch for me.

There was a laugh or two and then someone started to argue about how the stories would be previewed and I was off the hook again, for half a second anyway.

"Sorry. This may go on awhile." I waved at the

speakerphone. "Can we schedule something later? We could preview tomorrow before the uplink."

She wasn't fooled, but she wasn't a time-wasting moron either. I was hired to do a job, and she'd been doing her job long enough to recognize when to stay out of the way. "Fine. I'd prefer to see what you do for us, before we talk anyway. So, 'get back to work,'" she mimicked.

I shot her with my pointer finger and nodded.

That I could do.

The sun was all the way down and it was really cold now. It hadn't even been warm when she got out of the car. Jenny pressed farther under the cover of the bushes. She pulled her knees against her chest.

School was really far away. Home was probably closer. Maybe.

She'd lied. She really wasn't all that sure where she was. Luckily, she'd gotten pretty good at waiting, giving herself time to figure things out.

If she went home, Aunt Maddy would ask her why she wasn't at school. What could she say? She had to think of something. She had to have an answer. Something bad would happen if she didn't think of a way to explain.

Her head hurt.

Everyone at school would be mad at her, too, now. Worse than when she hid in the bathroom.

She was gonna be in trouble.

Now her stomach felt horrible, too.

Why was this happening? It was all wrong. She didn't used to get in trouble. She used to believe she was a good kid. Her mom always said it—like every day.

But that couldn't be true, could it? Because she was the same kid, and now she was always in trouble and everybody hated her. Being a good kid must be when other people thought you were good.

Grown-ups were so tricky.

Why did he do it? Why did he make everybody mad at her? She thought he was nice. He used to bring her stuff, like candy, and tell her mom to order her a pizza with plain cheese, nothing on it. He even gave her a piggyback ride to bed that one time and everyone laughed.

Jenny felt her nose tickle because of another drip. She looked for a dry spot on her jacket sleeve.

Stranger danger was such a joke. The people she knew were the scary ones.

Her fingers were getting stiff. Jenny tried to push them into the front pockets of her jeans to warm them up and touched the square of medicine tablets. She took it out and looked at it. It was exactly like the one that Tonya had. The thought gave her such a rush of guilt and excitement she stuffed it back in her pocket and shut her eyes.

What would it be like to feel no pain?

A tornado started whirling in her stomach. The inside of her throat got all thick and sticky. If she swallowed she might even vomit.

Her mother always told her to use the word vomit. Not puke or barf. Vomit was a medical word. People got sick sometimes; it was normal. People got hurt, too. And sometimes they needed medicine to get better. Her mother told her that, too.

What time was it? The sun hadn't quite gone down, but it was so low in the sky the tall trees made it seem like night where she sat. She couldn't even see lights from houses or anything, only trees and fences and road.

Nothing looked the same. A car passed her on the road, fast and loud.

Jenny pressed her forehead to her knees and folded her arms tight around her legs. She sniffed and rubbed her nose on her sleeve again. It burned.

She was in so much trouble she couldn't even think

what would come next. It was like trying to imagine fifth grade. Those kids had hardcover books and homework, like, every day.

How could she ever do it all by herself?

Jenny wiggled her fingers in her pocket and felt the medicine move under fingers.

What would it be like to feel no pain?

That part wasn't so hard to imagine.

She could try to remember.

Or she could take some medicine.

6:14:46 p.m.

I was on Peg, so there was no hiding my arrival at the Jost farm. Older bikes, like the Super X, had very little covering around the engine and pipes. Peg roared.

I shut the engine down before I turned into the driveway. I left the bike propped on the far side of the road near the cow fence. Yes, Ainsley, I can be taught.

It was third-world dark out there. No streetlights. No landscape highlighting. One window in the entire house showed a glow. Anywhere else in the state of Illinois, you'd think the family had gone out, leaving nothing but a kitchen light to guide their return.

In this house it was a sign someone must be home.

I knocked hard on the front door and called out, "Mr. Jost? It's Maddy O'Hara."

My metabolism rarely lets me cool down, but tonight my hands felt frozen stiff. I tried stamping my feet to throw off the nervy chill creeping up my back. I knocked again with the side of my fist, *bam, bam, bam.*

"Mr. Jost? It's important. It's about Rachel."

His face appeared through the small square of window. The white skin around his eyes and the sharp profile of his nose was all I could see.

"What about my daughter?" he said.

"Open the door, Mr. Jost. I'm not going to talk to you through a door." The ridiculousness of the situation took some of the edge off.

The door opened slowly. He wasn't wearing his hat or his jacket. His suspenders followed the line of his chest to the forward hunch of an older man's shoulders. He didn't step back. Didn't invite me in. He was being so obvious about it, I almost laughed. Why was I so afraid of this guy?

"Look, Mr. Jost. I thought you ought to know, your daughter came and spoke to me last Friday. She seemed pretty upset." I didn't like narcing on Rachel, but Ainsley was right. I'd feel better knowing that somebody understood how deep she was in. The only one I could think to tell was her father. "I thought you should know, she and Tom were still pretty close. She blames herself for his death."

"What are you saying to me? What is this?" His voice was aggressive but his eyes winced with confusion. That wiry gray hair, ringing his head from skull to chin, had a life all its own.

"Help her. She's too young. Don't let her blame herself." I looked him in the eye and said it out loud—the thing he feared, the thing I feared. "You were more to blame than she was."

He stared at me, silent.

I don't know why I waited.

"I would do most anything for her," he told me quietly. "For my daughter."

"Talk to her. Let her talk to you. Did you and Tom fight before he died?"

He closed his eyes and shook his head, no. Quietly, as if he were talking to himself or thought I couldn't understand, he mumbled, "The sinning comes with knowing."

"You think you can avoid the sin through ignorance?"

"The road is hard enough. Turn away. Be separate. That is the choice we make."

"But once you know, what then?" He wouldn't answer. His whole way of understanding the world made me hot. "Once Tom knew things that no one else around him knew, what could he do? Did he tell you what it was like to be a kid and watch the whole world dissolve or did you make him hold it in to protect your separateness?"

"Not so well enough," the old man growled. "Oh *ja*, it came out, all right." His accent gave the sarcasm an edge. "How could I keep him in this house with Rachel? I had to keep her safe."

"You brought him here. You were the only father he knew."

"My pride brought him here. That is my shame. And my error to put right."

"So you sent Tom away. You banished him."

Silently, the man who gave Tom Jost a name, shook his head. *No.*

I couldn't believe he would deny it. He might not have said the words out loud, but Tom had known he wasn't welcome. I lost it. Couldn't listen anymore, couldn't hear his side of it. I got furious and something clicked. "The sin comes with knowing." The next thought was whispered. "You *knew*. You saw him standing there on those boxes. Alone. For how long? You watched him die, didn't you?"

His eyes popped and his whiskers twitched all directions. Then he growled at me in non-English, stepped back and slammed the door in my face.

My phone rang about three seconds later. I was still standing there facing a closed door.

"What?"

"It's Ainsley, Maddy. I'm at the school. You won't believe this. They can't find Jenny."

6:51:23 p.m.

I tried calling home, stopped there first, hoping there was some mistake, some kid-confusing explanation for why she wasn't where I expected.

No luck.

I got to the school and all they could tell me was Jenny hadn't been checked out of the program. The last people remembered, she was on the playground. They had tried to call me at the station and at home. Apparently, the number in the file for my cell phone was wrong. When Ainsley showed up at closing time, almost all the other kids had been picked up. The only clue they had to what happened was the word of one of the kids from the playground, who claimed Jenny had walked off the playground toward a shiny car.

"I think we should call the police," one of the teachers suggested tentatively. "That's the procedure at this point, isn't it?"

I already had two of the babysitters in tears and Ainsley threatening to lock me in the car, I needed to get out there and start searching.

"I stopped at the house on my way here," I said. "She's not at the house."

Ainsley interrupted. "What about friends? Could she have walked to someone else's house?"

"Whose? There's nobody," I said. "Kid doesn't have any friends."

"One of us should wait at the house," I told Ainsley, "and one should go out looking."

"You want to look, right?" he answered. "I'll go wait."

"Thanks," I said, stiff with gratitude. The women were conferring among themselves about what to do. "Call the police. I'm going out to look. You've got the right number to reach me now, yes?"

"Yes, yes," one of them mumbled guilty, but with an edge of evil eye.

"Good." That made two of us.

It was maybe a mile and a half from the school to the house. There were two routes Jen and I generally took to get home, a third that the bus followed. I'd followed Ainsley back to the house, searched the backyard and racked my brain for ideas. Nothing useful came to mind. Consequently, I was out of my mind.

Twenty minutes later, I pulled over and called Curzon.

"I need a favor."

"My lucky day." The shift of his attention, from work to me, was as clear as a car changing gear.

"Jenny's gone." It didn't take long to explain. Curzon put me on hold twice, checking with the guys at the station about what had already been done. A car had been dispatched to the school minutes before.

"Come to the station," Curzon ordered. "We'll go out together in my car. I'll have paperwork ready you can sign when you get here."

"What paperwork?" I know I sounded irritated.

"The stuff we need to get a wider search going. Description for the radio, that kind of thing."

"All right. Be there as soon as I can."

The station was hustling when I arrived. I remembered the way to Curzon's office and walked straight through. The door was open. He sat behind his computer, wearing a pair of executive-style wireless-frame glasses and a white button-down that was creased and damp at the back from long hours in the big chair. Smart and hardworking looked good on him.

"You didn't speed on the way here did you?" he asked without looking up. "I'll be one more minute. Sit down."

I was hoping the first thing out of his mouth would be something like, *don't worry, we'll find her, she's fine*.

Unfortunately, Curzon was the kind of guy who didn't do platitudes.

I didn't sit.

From the doorway, I had an excellent view of the action in the station. There were cops going about their business with plodding intensity, and a couple of secretarial types hanging up their cardigan sweaters and putting on their jackets. Sulking against the wall were a pair of Goth hoodlums in full-length black capes. Beside a desk, hunched an old man with a bloody head. At the farthest end of the room, four burly guys were dragging an eight-foot-high chunk of concrete up the hall on a cart.

Police stations are surrealism on testosterone.

"What's with the roadwork?" I asked for distraction. "Putting in a patio out back?"

He handed me paperwork on a clipboard, pen attached. "Guy's garage floor. Evidence."

Translation: somebody died—bloody—on that slab of concrete.

A bolus of sick bubbled up my throat. "All this on a Monday night? Why would you ever want to leave this job?"

Curzon pointed at the paper. "Write. Give details under 'last seen wearing.'"

There was too much pumping through my head. I had to force myself to think, to write.

Purple jacket. Jeans. White tennis shoes, pink laces.

It was impossible to believe what was happening. Less than two hours ago, I was standing in front of Tom Jost's father, accusing him of parenting failures.

"I got a question for you." Even to my ears, my voice shredded the words. "Do you think people have to separate to be good?"

Addresses: home, school…friends?

Had I failed Jenny already?

Curzon mumbled, *"Mmduhknow."*

Names: parent or guardian. Guardian. What a terrible word for it.

A woman stuck her head in the door. Curzon stopped typing.

"Amber Alert's been issued," she said without looking at me.

"We'll have the rest for you in under five."

She walked out. Curzon went back to typing.

"I've always thought there's good and bad in all of us. Everybody's capable of going one way or another at any time."

"Are *you* more capable of the 'bad' because you see it," I asked him, "because it's around you all the time?"

Without hesitation, he answered, "Yes."

"Really?" I was unprepared for how vulnerable his honesty made me—with no camera between us. I crossed my arms over my chest and tried to argue. "I'm not so sure."

"Yes, you are. You agree. Those Amish people agree.

Pretty much everybody agrees. Same reason people move to the suburbs. It's why we build prisons in the middle of nowhere. It's why you live alone."

"What?" I spluttered. "What's my living alone got to do with anything?"

"Who'd understand what you've got inside your head? You said you hadn't had a date since Sierra Leone. My guess is that's because you can't picture chatting your way through a meal with some guy, then going into a bedroom with him, taking off your clothes, but never being able to show—" he snorted to himself "—to *talk about* what's inside."

This conversation was rapidly deteriorating. Direct eye contact seemed dangerously inappropriate, but Curzon wouldn't look away, so I couldn't either.

"How would it feel to lie beside someone, go to sleep, with that innocent mind on the pillow beside you?" He turned away from me just like that, and returned to typing paperwork. His last words were not speculative at all. They were hard with personal conviction. "It'd be a sort of punishment, wouldn't it? Hiding a part of yourself all the time. Forever."

"Does hiding it make you more capable of wrong, badness?" I floundered looking for the right word. "Evil?"

"Like I would know? I'm on the protection-cleanup detail." He blew me off. "One thing I do know, once you realize how bad a human being can be, once you can imagine it—" he shook his head as if the rest were obvious "—you can imagine hitting back. You can imagine hurting that person sleeping next to you. You can imagine all sorts of things."

I was imagining all sorts of bad things right now with Jenny missing.

"Aren't you just the Philosopher King?" I tossed off after too long a silence. This conversation was not helping me worry less. Topic change. "Living alone didn't protect Tom Jost."

"Tom Jost didn't want to be alone. His problem was reaching for the wrong companions. Classic mistake." Curzon laid out his version of the facts without hesitation.

"You think so?"

"Absolutely. So says the King." He gave me a cock-eyed grin that took the edge off the certainty in his voice. "Did you bring a picture?"

"In my wallet."

"Good."

"Aren't you gonna say we probably won't need it?"

"You want me to?"

"Yeah."

"I hope we don't need it," he answered carefully. "I want to know about the SUV."

"Don't start. It's nothing, I'm sure." It was my problem for now.

The SUV run-ins had to be connected to my job. Someone at the station or someone connected to the story on Tom Jost. If I dragged Curzon in at this point, he'd slap a gag on the story. I'd never make the satellite feed.

Twenty-four hours from now, I could come clean.

"It's work related. Got nothing to do with Jenny."

Curzon fixed me with the stare. He didn't agree. He didn't disagree. "So you got people from your office trying to run you down. Work is going pretty well then?"

"Work is great. Especially being here, which means I am getting jack-all done on a piece that will probably be seen by an eight share of Nielsen homes nationally, which is to say, *no one,* and completely submarine my career." Saying it aloud actually made the urge to puke worse. *Jenny. Jenny, where the hell are you?* "Have I mentioned I'm going to kill that kid when we find her? You got any Tums?"

Curzon slid a drawer open and lobbed a bottle across the room. He didn't prompt, didn't offer any consolation. He waited, silent.

I knew the trick of silence, but couldn't stop myself from saying, "It feels like I've stepped into a time machine."

"Because of the Amish?"

"Of course." The Tums dried the inside of my mouth like road salt. "And Jenny. And my sister. That house of hers." I quit rubbing my forehead to glare at him. "You, too."

"Me?" He sounded pleased. "Why me?"

"I don't know." More rubbing, less glaring. "This place, I guess."

"Ahh. You've been in trouble with the law before."

"Ha."

He surrendered with both hands.

I tried to stay seated. Couldn't.

"Two more minutes," Curzon soothed. He ran Jenny's picture through a machine at the back of his desk. No wasted motions. "Almost there."

"I wasn't meant for kids." I paced the tiny rectangle

of space in front of his desk. "I can't do this anymore. It's crazy."

"You can," he replied, totally calm.

To me, it sounded like, *you have to.* "I stink at this. I swear, when we find her—" I kicked my heel against the leg of one of the wooden chairs in frustration. "I did not ask for any of this."

Curzon looked up from his computer, nodded pleasantly. "Done?"

"Fuck you."

"Sure."

I wasn't ready to laugh, so that pissed me off, too.

He spread his hands and tilted his head exactly like a dashboard Jesus. Men rarely open their hands and show their palms. Curzon's looked smooth and ruddy. Alive. I remembered how warm they felt and my skin prickled.

"You can't turn your back on family," Curzon said. "Not and keep your self-respect. There it is. Nobody said it would be easy."

Pompous, asshole, know-it-all.

"No shit, Sheriff," I said. "Tell me about it. Why don't you start with your divorce from the She-bitch."

He didn't move an inch but suddenly the man I'd been talking to disappeared. Where does a man go when he hides behind his eyes? Curzon had retreated to that dark interior before. It came easily. His eyes narrowed. His face became impenetrable from the inside out and I watched myself change in his view.

The hurt it caused me was another surprise.

"My bad. I shouldn't— You don't—" I closed my eyes to escape his stare, to hide from myself. My own callused hands reached out, pleading for retraction. "Sorry,

Jack. Nothing you've said is untrue." I realized as I said it, how much that meant to me.

Long time ago, I gave up trying to figure out the mystery of what makes human beings connect. Friends. Neighbors. Lovers. I couldn't say if it was dumb luck or fine timing or the science of body smells the conscious brain has no control over, somehow Curzon knew how to read me. He knew what I meant. Maybe he knew the words I didn't say as well.

"I'm not talking about Sharon here," he said slowly. His hands laced together and the knuckles whitened with the force of his grip. "But I know what it's like. All that business on Sunday with Marcus and my father—it's the same for me. What I want. What my family wants." He pulled his hands apart. "Sometimes it's hard to separate them."

I don't even know if he realized, but his right hand tightened into a fist and his left wrapped around it. I thought of that kids' game—*paper covers rock*. I felt the force of his will in his eyes, hoping for my understanding. I remembered Jenny running, laughing, playing in his family's backyard.

All I could think to say was, "Please, Curzon—Jack, please, I've got to find her."

He nodded. No false promises. *We'll find her, she'll be fine*.

I was right; nothing he said to me would be untrue.

"We'll take my car." He stood up and pointed me to the door.

Couple of serious-looking men in uniforms called "good luck," as they punched the clock. Curzon raised a hand.

I was going to owe him big for this. The boss did not,

as a rule, drop everything for a kid missing less than two hours. Something else to worry about. Later.

In less than ten minutes, we were on our way. Probably the fastest completion of police paperwork in history, but I was still crazed. I'd have sprinted to his car if I'd have known which one it was. Instead, I trailed at his elbow.

"There's my car." He pointed me toward an older Audi.

"What about those?" I pointed. Two rows over sat at least five matching silver SUVs. They had no visible police markings.

"Special transport. We got a grant," he said. "Is that the kind of car that gave you trouble?"

The parking lot was suddenly colder. I met Curzon's narrow gaze and thought about the darkness he closed himself into so easily.

"Maybe."

"There are a lot of silver SUVs out there." His voice had a bland edge that wasn't there a minute ago.

"Yeah, sure. Let's just go."

We were in his car and on the road in a matter of moments but Curzon wouldn't stop glancing over to check on me. "You cold?"

"I'm fine."

He reached over and grabbed my fingers, then let go before I could make anything of it. "Those still bend?" he asked, while punching buttons on the dash to fire up the heat.

"How's this?" I curled my hand into a fist and shook it lightly.

"Hey! Look, kids, it's Feisty the Snowman. Where to first?"

I resisted the smile, but his silliness struck a spark that the car's heat built into warmth. "Let's go back to the school."

We drove in silence. Curzon didn't even need directions.

What is it about the inside of a car at night? He was watching the road and I was looking out the window, eyes burning for a glimpse of purple jacket. The car wrapped a cave of safety around us. I was too worried about Jenny to resist—the comfort or the intimacy.

We cruised the neighborhood, stopping anywhere I could think Jenny might have walked so I could get out and shout her name. I saw at least two other police cars slowly driving around, which pleased me at first but gradually sent the anxiety creeping up, up, up. A lot of people were looking.

Where the hell had she gone?

"So. Only you and your sister in the family?" Curzon's tone was an injection of calm.

"Just the two of us."

"What neighborhood you from?"

Neighborhood, parish, high school—I gave him all the standard Chicago-locator coordinates, answered every question and more. I don't usually talk so much. Must have been the car.

"Can we follow the bus route?" I asked. "Maybe she tried to walk home that way."

"Good idea," he said. "I'll go back to the school and we'll start from there."

I did a couple head rolls and shoulder drops. With every zap of the police radio, I twitched. Curzon was right of course; we needed to be systematic. Systematic was taking too damn long.

"Tell me about this story you're working on. Why'd you ask me about Samaritan law?"

It was hard shifting my brain to thinking about work, shifting tectonic plates hard. I wasn't sure whether to call the result a headache or a headquake.

"I think somebody may have seen Jost at the tree. Setting up. Doing the deed. The whole thing."

"He did it by the side of the road," Curzon pointed out matter-of-factly. He flicked a glance my way. "You feeling all right?"

"Great," I said, with one eye closed. "Don't you think that's weird?"

"What, the tree? No. He picked a tree on his daddy's front lawn."

"Okay, classic protest suicide—look what you made me do. But the more I've talked to people, the weirder that part seems. Amish people don't do protest, much less suicide. And wouldn't he have gotten the same effect if he did it in his apartment and wrote a note? So why the tree? What was he thinking?"

Curzon slowed to a stop at a yellow light. "You're asking, what did he get by doing it in *that* tree?"

"Exactly."

Curzon's cell phone rang. He answered, "Sheriff."

Time stopped. The streetlight was red.

Still red.

My night vision dissolved. All the grays of the shadows around us went black. In the distance, car headlights flashed and turned away.

Red.

"Yeah, got it. Tell them five minutes." He snapped the phone shut with a flick, dropped it into the space beside the gearbox. "They found her."

"She's okay, right?" *Don't bury the lead, you sadist.*

The answer was hard to hear over the sudden blare of his siren.

"She's alive."

8:47:59 p.m.

I doubt it took us three whole minutes to get to her. Curzon drove like a bat out of hell. I was numb enough to admire the bright streak of lights we passed and the sensation of gentle compression into the Audi's butt-warming leather seat.

As soon as he turned onto Orchard Road, I knew where we were going. Past the flashing yellow, where the edge of a golf course became a cemetery, lay the Prairie Path—an old railroad route that had been turned into a safe path for pedestrians, bikers, joggers. The Path crossed the busiest part of the road here. Cars against people.

I'd been to see the place myself several times this summer on my late-night jaunts. It was the spot where my sister died.

A squad car, wigwag lights flashing, and an ambulance were parked perpendicular to the road. Curzon pulled in next to the police cruiser. I had my door open before he'd even geared all the way down.

The night air near this narrow patch of woods had cooled faster; my breath fogged out ahead of me. I pushed between the cars, hands in my jacket pockets, cold and nervy to the core.

Trees and ancient bushes blocked most of the light around us from the houses. I could hardly see where I was walking. Dry leaves were heaped ankle high in the ditch. The crunch of my feet hustling toward the clump of emergency people was inappropriately silly.

"Jenny? Where is she? What happened?"

The cop got in my face. The paramedics were so busy they didn't even look up.

"She's alive." He came toward me hands wide. "She's unconscious. They need to know if she has a drug problem."

"A *what?*" Someone moved, I could barely see her legs. "She's eight years old!"

"Easy." The cop body-blocked me.

I would have shoved him aside if Curzon hadn't come up behind me and put a solid hand on my shoulder, calming, restraining. I'm too big for that move to work most of the time. It caught me off guard.

"I'm on it," Curzon assured the guy. "Let her through."

I shoved past the junior cop, took two steps and suddenly, I could see everything. The paramedic reaching for a hypodermic. Jenny's face—so white it was hard to believe she was alive. Her closed eyes smudged with dirt or something darker. Leaves blanketing the edges of her body. She looked so tiny, something the wind could carry off, like the rest of autumn's refuse.

"Oh Lord," slipped out.

Curzon was talking and the paramedic was saying something, and all I could hear was my one, single thought: *no.*

She was dead. My sister was dead.

I see. I can see it now.

Memories began to flip on the screen in my head and I pressed the heels of my hands against my eyes.

Stop. Stop it. My sister's in her crib, holding on to the rail, screaming. My parents may, or may not hear her. The TV is on and they are screaming over the sound of music and gunshots and other happy voices. I'm not allowed to get my sister out of her bed. I watch her face, wetter and redder by the moment. She isn't looking at the door, she is looking at me.

My stomach curdles. I walk the long hall, one foot at a time…*um, baby's crying?*

Get back in your bed!

The pain is fast and sharp, but gone quick as a doctor's needle. One fight ends. My father slams a door on his way out. My mother goes to the baby. I lie on the rug listening to commercials until my nausea is gone. I'm so calm, I'm invisible. I float back to my bed and…

My father laid out, dead this time, in his box. My mother is somewhere, speaking to strangers. My sister stands beside me. She is crying. This time her head is down. There is a line of white scalp where her hair parts. It is exactly the same color as the streaks her tears make on the front of her uniform blouse.

She fumbles for my hand—half my height, almost half my age—and in her face, I see all the sorrow I should feel but I am empty. Blank. I take her hand and…

They all look at me, the faces of my work. Brown skin, black skin. Hungry eyes. Haunted. They come from everywhere.

Listen to me!

I pound the heels of my hands against my eyes. *Stop. Stop. Stop.*

Worst of all, my family's small pains were nothing—nothing!—in comparison to some of what I'd seen—the worst on earth. All my common pains, all Jenny's. Not worth a photo or a sound bite's worth of time.

Now, here in front of me, my sister's eyes in my

niece's face. And I still felt the pain, exactly the same. Despite all I'd seen.

"Oh God," I croaked. My stomach folded in on itself with pain.

"Maddy!" Curzon shouted through the interference. He was behind me, holding me back, or up, one arm across my chest and a hand gripping my shoulder. "She's alive. Don't bail. Get your ass in that ambulance."

I did.

Doctors jabbered at me in the emergency room. Their voices were hard to hold on to. The sounds of buzzers and elevator bells and metal carts kept jumping to the foreground, as if my internal audio B-track had a mind of its own. I kept nodding, hoping they'd just get the hell away from me or shut up for a minute. The last three hours had been hell.

"We're going to transfer her to peds ICU, Ms. O'Hara. Her oxygen levels are still pretty low. The seizures will probably pass but she has to stay under observation."

"I understand."

"She's all right for now. Everything seems to be stabilizing. The paramedics found the blister pack. It was some kind of trial pack of antianxiety medicine. Nasty stuff for a kid. Any idea where she got it?"

"No."

"Do you take any medications?"

"I had something prescribed for my knee on Sunday. I had stitches, in the emergency room. Could she have—?"

The doctor rejected that idea. He showed me the foil packet. "This is a sample. Doctors give them out to test a medication, to see if it's effective for a specific patient. The drug companies often provide them free of charge. This particular drug is the rage on the club scene right now. Mixed with alcohol it creates a very uninhibited evening."

"Where did she get something like that?" I recognized the blister packaging. Tonya had something similar for her back medicine. And I'd seen some in the emergency bucket Jenny had pulled out of the garage. "A friend of mine had been visiting this weekend. She has back problems. I know Jenny saw her take something, heard us talking about painkillers."

"...the pleasant land of counter pane."

A grinding nausea returned to my stomach. All those questions about pain. Tonya was going to freak.

"Jenny didn't take painkillers," he said. "She took something a lot harder to find."

"My sister is—was—a nurse. Here, actually. She's got a huge bucket of medicine and stuff." I rubbed my head. I should have taken the bucket away from Jenny. Put it somewhere safe. It never even occurred to me. "I'll have to check. That might be where Jenny found them. How many did she take?"

"Not many. More than a couple and her liver—" He frowned, shook his head. He was a young guy with the ashy complexion of doctors indentured to the emergency room. Pale blue eyes behind glasses, he didn't make eye contact easily; he kept looking toward the window. "She's going to need more than my kind of doctoring when she comes around. You do understand that?"

"Her mother died a couple months ago." There was too much to explain. It would take too long for both of us. His impatience to move along to the next patient, next crisis was like the buzz of a live current between us.

"I'll have to report this to a social worker. She'll be able to get you a referral."

"I understand." Tiredness swamped me all of a sudden. "I need to stay here. Jenny gets nightmares. I want to stay with her."

"Of course. We're moving her up to a room. You can

stay as long as you want." He made the effort to meet my eyes and I realized that some of the awkwardness was meant as empathy. He nodded at Curzon and left us alone. Finally.

Curzon announced he was headed down to the cafeteria and promised to return with some warm caffeine-alive, fully sugared for both of us.

Jenny was moved upstairs to a small double room with two empty beds. The last time I spent any time in a hospital, there were crucifixes over every bed. My mother was comforted by the statued suffering hanging on the wall. Jenny's bed was surrounded by cables, electronics, tubes and sound effects. A television was mounted high on the opposite wall. I left it off, but I had to fight a constant urge to stare at the distorted gray reflection it created.

Nurses clucked in and out, double checking all Jenny's monitors. They told me she was fine, better, not to worry.

I sat down on the second bed and watched the girl sleep, wondering how she could look so much the same after all that had happened in the last few hours.

Curzon returned with coffee, as well as cups of salty chicken soup and oyster crackers. I made room for him beside me on the bed and when he sat it was a comfort, not an intrusion.

"She's gonna be all right," I said, as if I'd always believed.

"That's good." He sipped his soup.

"Yeah." I smiled. "Thanks. For…everything."

We were having a moment. It's been a long time since I made a friend. My instincts aren't always good in that department. I wasn't quite sure what should happen next.

Jenny's breathing changed and it caught my attention. Her eyes shifted back and forth beneath the lids, her head twitching with tiny vibrations. Unconscious, she was on the lookout for trouble. The words Grace Ott had spoken to me earlier would not stop looping through my head.

"Do you think Jenny expects bad things to happen to her?" I asked. "Do you think she believes good things won't ever come again?"

"Kids learn from what they see around them," Curzon answered. "How about you? Do you expect the worst? Or something better?"

A ripple of something like panic hit me low and deep, but I pushed it off. Who was I to judge Old Man Jost? I had watched while bad things happened my whole career. My whole life.

I picked up our empty cups, stood and tossed them into the trash. He stood, too, as if those kind of manners were his habit, and faced me.

"I believe there's something better," he said. And then he reached across the space between us. All I could see was that fine warm hand coming toward me...almost... barely, his fingertips touched my cheek.

Perhaps, I closed my eyes.

Maybe I turned my head into his hand.

It's possible I wanted to feel him against my cheek, my lips. Touching me.

But I never asked for what I saw when my eyes opened.

Longing.

"Jack?" I whispered. "Oh, come on now—"

And he did. He scooped me into the wall of his body, arms and thighs and chest making contact, following my clumsy retreat, pressing until I was against the window, nowhere else to go, the metal sill behind my thighs, cold glass at my back. His body was solid and more real than anything I'd felt in months, years, forever.

He pushed his fingers through my hair and tilted my head, my face, my lips up to him.

"You," he whispered, and then took away those last few molecules of separation.

Mouth soft, everything else hard. What a contrast. *Kissing*…how long since I'd been kissed? Soft, so softly. *Please?* Pleasing. Hard as in inevitable. Deal with me. *Now*.

Just like that, I'm gone.

I don't even know what happened next. Honestly. I couldn't tell you. My brain reverted to something lower than lizard-level function. I was all the way back to spineless protoplasm.

Next thing I know, Curzon's pushing himself back, eyes locked on me. The look on his face—oh! I'm not Maddy. I'm like food.

I'm survival.

I'm *it*.

Nobody's ever looked at me like that. Every small hair on my skin lifted. I stood there like an idiot, mouth gaping, lips burning.

Which is right about when I realized Curzon's cell was ringing, and here comes a nurse shoving her way through the door. I shuffled sideways, the sheriff and I still staring, not even blinking.

"Somebody's phone is ringing," the nurse said, glancing back and forth between us. "They will kill you dead if they catch you with that thing turned on anywhere near the telemetry machines. Sign outside says *all* phones off."

"Turning it off. Right now." Curzon pulled out his phone. Breaking the law every now and then was a law-enforcement perk, after all. "Sheriff here."

The nurse bustled around the room, checking Jenny's gadgets for her temperature and pulse, while I focused on getting my own vital signs back into the normal range.

"Christ, you gotta be kidding me. Who responded?" Curzon asked. He continued staring at me while listening. "On the way." He snapped the phone shut. "I've got to go."

"Okay," I mumbled like a half-wit. "Thanks—"

For everything? The words stuck in my throat, blocking some key artery and causing my face to flush with heat. Junior-high social gaff #101.

Curzon raised his hand once again and pointed at me.

You.

He turned and walked out.

I stood there. The nurse did some fiddling with Jenny's IV. She told me they were pushing fluids to help her body flush the toxic stuff faster. I lay down on the second bed and watched it bubble and drip, counting the seconds, measuring out increments of guilt and confusion.

One one-thousand,
Two one-thousand,
Three one-thousand,
drip.

One—not again,
Two—not today,
Three—not now,
drip.

Jenny slept on. When the ten o'clock news started, I went looking for a can of pop and called Tonya. She was out, so I left a message with the bare bones of what had happened. I knew she'd probably come flying out to the hospital as soon as she heard it, but there was no holding back on this kind of info.

I went back to the room and lay down on the second bed. When pressure ratchets my world down to an impossibly narrow range of positives, my body hums with something that's a cross between dreaming and a downhill bike ride. I'm hollow inside. My chest echoes with each heartbeat. My eyes burn the world to a soft-focus haze. As a kid it felt like going to heaven, the empty quiet gave me such relief. It still gives me relief, although it never lasts.

My head has been trained to keep busy. All my work is broken into increasingly smaller increments: quarterly, monthly, weekly. *Critical.* Six minutes. :30 seconds. *Out.*

One one-thousand,
Two one-thousand,
Three one-thousand,
drip.

Lists of things undone began to crowd my mind. I'd have to cobble together the final piece for the satellite feed tomorrow, tomorrow night latest. Network does not stop for me. Maybe Ainsley could bring the equipment to me so I wouldn't have to leave Jenny.

A small noise, soft as a lover's altered breath, came from the bed beside me. Jenny twitched. Her chin thrust up, then froze stiff and still. Without warning, her eyes snapped open. She looked straight up at the ceiling.

One step put me within reach. I touched her wrist with my fingertips.

"I was pretty worried about you." My voice sounded like I smoked a pack a day.

Jenny blinked. I had no idea how blank-faced a child could look. I rubbed up and down her forearm, warming her skin, keeping her with me. The blank face melted as I watched, first the mouth sagged, then the eyes welled with tears.

There was that look again, the one I'd seen flash across Curzon's face—need.

I was it.

Me? The thought echoed between my awe and panic for two, three, a dozen heartbeats. Is this what a woman feels like when she becomes a mother? When someone hands her a baby and just like that, who she's been and who she must become are measured in the eyes of her child?

I dropped the guardrail on the bed and dragged her as close to me as the rubber tubes and strapping would allow. Something started beeping. I ignored it.

"We'll figure this out. We'll figure something out. You hear me?"

Her head bumped against my shoulder. I pulled back so I could see her face. Her eyes had rolled back and the whites were all that was visible. Her body shook from inside. It lasted just long enough for me to register what was happening.

Before I could panic, the nurse was standing there. "She's had another seizure. It's not unusual." After checking the monitors, she helped me straighten Jenny in the bed and smooth her covers. On the way out, she added, "Why don't you try to rest, too?"

"This is me—resting."

As soon as the nurse was out the door, I crawled into bed with Jenny on her tubeless side. She was so slight, it was easy enough to shove her over and make a little room. I put one arm around the top of her head and propped the extra pillow behind me. Our bodies touched all down the side.

I couldn't create the white calm of resting. It was too quiet. When I was a kid I used to pray at times like these, repeating words of comfort over and over. Without thinking, the lonely perjury of a *please God* slipped out. Once upon a time, I was a good Catholic girl. Until I grew up and saw what havoc it wrecked on the people around me. Total abstinence has been my answer. No more guardian angels. No more saints. No mass. No confession. No absolution. And no prayer. Still, sometimes I crave it like a junkie—just a taste of heaven, so to speak.

Listening to Rachel the other day had whetted my appetite for some reason. I thought of the pictures I'd taken of the Amish, their faces turning away even as they saw my camera. I would never use them without consent. I snapped those pictures for myself, to keep, to look at later. Sometimes pictures help me figure things out.

I got my first camera when I was eleven. Took pictures

of everything—my sister's baby toys, the tree stump in our yard, the rust on our Pinto wagon, my mom in front of the sewing machine, my dad in his work clothes, my dad on the floor. I kept them all. When things got worse, I took more. I kept those, too.

This is what I know about pictures—they can be like water, sixty percent of you, if they get inside your head. With all the things I'd seen in my career, my contents label must read at least that much in human toxins.

What had Jenny seen that had led her here?

Was it something in me?

"Want to watch a little TV?" I whispered.

The mumbling of late-night syndication emptied my head at last. Politics and laugh tracks and Old Navy, still promoting their sale. Commercial breaks—the modern consumer's mindlessly repeated prayers.

This is what I know about words—they can be like air, everything and nothing. Hot enough to choke. Cold enough to bite. Invisible but absolutely necessary.

Why couldn't I find the words Jenny needed?

Did I even have them in me anymore?

I drifted off, comforted by a little girl's even breathing and the modulated sound of happy, grown-up voices coming from the television.

I'm not sure how much later the faint trill of my phone had me up and scrambling. I grabbed for my messenger bag, trying to answer it quick, before the nurses caught me with my cell phone still turned on.

"O'Hara?" Gatt's gravelly voice was even rougher than usual. "Did you send Ainsley off on a shoot alone?"

"What?" It took me a minute to organize my head. "Yeah. Yeah, I did."

"I'm not paying you to send the kid out by himself, O'Hara," he said in a voice rising in volume with every sentence. "I'm paying you to work with him."

"I am working with him. He's on a shoot for me."

"And you are—" Gatt finished the question himself "—in bed?"

I was sitting on the edge of Jenny's hospital bed actually. No way was I ready to tell that to him. Personal problems are not welcome in my workplace. "Get to the point, Gatt. What are you asking me?"

"I just got a call from my sister. She wants to know why Ainsley is out there on his own, when he's only done two shoots in his frigging life. So my point is this—get your ass out of bed and supervise him, or you can assume I won't be requiring your services any longer. Got it?"

"Got it," I said. He hung up. I hit phone-off.

The door swooshed and Tonya entered, her footsteps soundless. Her green neon tracksuit glowing loudly. "Hey, baby," she said. "How's it going?"

"She's asleep. They said she'll probably sleep through the night."

"Tell me everything. What happened?"

The recap didn't take long. I remained sitting on the edge of the bed, the phone in one hand. Tonya stood towering over me, eyes shifting between Jenny's monitor equipment and her face. As I filled her in, her frown deepened, then she added the slow head shake and the crossed arms, and finally, the *mmmghh* of disapproval.

"And to top it off, Gatt just called," I said.

"The new boss?"

"Right. He told me not to come in tomorrow if I don't

go out and hold Ainsley's hand for a simple dawn pickup shot. One lousy shot!"

"Shh." Tonya pointed at Jenny.

"The man didn't even ask me for the details."

She must have followed my line of sight. "Does he know about Jenny?"

"No."

"You should tell him."

If anything, my feelings now were even more complicated. I could barely admit it to myself, much less aloud to my boss. I was ashamed.

"You need this job, Maddy."

"I know it."

With helpful enthusiasm, Tonya said, "Go. Check on Ainsley. I'll stay here with Jenny."

"No. Thanks. If Gatt decides to fire me—" I blanked. I'd never faced this kind of work dilemma before. I didn't even have a vocabulary for this kind of scenario. "I guess I'll figure something out. I want to stay. I want to be here when Jenny wakes up. She might need to see a friendly face, you know?"

"Sure, baby." She didn't smile but I heard warmth in her voice and the next thing I knew, she'd grabbed my head with her two hands and planted a big kiss on the top of my forehead. "You're gonna do all right. You'll do fine."

Half a smile crooked my lips. "Took me long enough."

"That's true," she admitted.

"The least you could do is argue a little."

She took up residence in the sleeping chair and I curled up on the empty bed. And we waited.

When the phone rang the second time, it was with the brutally unfamiliar jangle of the hospital phone.

"What?" I answered in a hiss. It was still pitch dark around the curtained window and I had that nauseous disorientation that lack of sleep brings.

Across the room I could see Tonya staring. Jenny, thank goodness, didn't budge.

"Maddy? You won't believe it—"

"Ainsley, is that you? What the hell time is it?" My eyes were burning. My brain wouldn't compute the numbers on my watch into anything meaningful.

"How's Jenny?"

"She's still asleep. They say she may sleep for hours. Where are you?"

"I'm at the Jost farm. I'm ready to go. I've got the camera all set and, you won't believe this, there's a car at the end of the driveway."

"A car?"

"*A silver SUV.*" Ainsley made the words a sibilant tease. "And I saw someone get out and go around the backside of the house. What should I do? Should I go check it out?"

"No! Absolutely not. You keep recording and—" I considered and discarded a couple of options before I settled on, "Call the cops. Call Curzon."

"What if this guy's up to something? There are other people in there. Rachel. Her dad."

"Call the police, Ainsley! You stay right where you are."

"Good idea. You call Sheriff Curzon—he likes you. I'll try to get a little closer, so I can make sure that nothing bad is happening. I'm turning off my phone now, so I can be quiet. I'll call you back as soon as I know something."

"Wait! No!"

Too late. He'd clicked off.

"What is it?" Tonya asked.

"Ainsley's at the Jost farm," I said. "He saw somebody drive up and creep around the back."

"Who'd be driving up to an Amish house?"

"Somebody not Amish." I started digging through my bag for my phone. "I'm calling the cops." I tried the number I had for Curzon, got voice mail and left a message. I called emergency, made a report to the woman who answered. She seemed skeptical and definitely unconvinced of the urgency I was feeling.

"I'll make a report to the sheriff," she said blandly. "They'll send a car to do a drive-by."

"When?"

"I'm sure they will get to it as soon as possible," she assured me.

"Crap," I said the minute I hung up. I speed-dialed Ainsley's phone but got no answer.

"Well?" Tonya asked. She looked worried. Maybe I looked worried, too.

"I don't like this." I started to pace the small length of floor to the end of the bed and back. "The car he saw at the house, Ainsley said it was an SUV."

"Same kind of car ran you off the road," Tonya said.

"And followed us that night we went to Tom's apartment." Car references flipped through my head and another one clicked. "'A shiny car.' The little boy that saw Jenny walk off the playground today, he said she got into a 'shiny car.'"

"Shiny meaning silver?" Tonya guessed exactly where I was going.

"Whoever he is, if he did this to Jenny, he's dangerous.

Ainsley's in trouble. Maybe Rachel and Mr. Jost, too." I looked at Jenny. I looked at Tonya. I felt petrified.

Jenny and Ainsley—they both needed me.

"What do I do?" I said.

"Jenny is safe here," Tonya said. I understood her offer even before she added, "And I'm not going anywhere."

"I don't want Jenny to wake up without me."

Tonya nodded. "Then hurry back."

AUDIO (V.O.): "Tom Jost got lost somewhere between a land of black-and-white, good and evil, simple and worldly."

TUESDAY

7:36:09 a.m.

It took me forever to get out to the Jost farm. Tonya's Escort was not made for high-speed maneuvers.

The smell of smoke was apparent miles away. The first red lick of dawn was beginning to give way to a weak gray sky that was part smoke and part nasty weather.

When it finally came into view, the house was a shock. That perfect image of country life was a wreck of blackened timber bones. Smoke rose in drifting towers, solid yet impermanent.

The front porch and most of the entrance facade were intact, like an old movie soundstage. Straight through to the back, there were timbers still smoldering. The smell was intense. There was no escaping it, no shift of air current made a bit of difference. It clung to the inside of my throat and nose, rough and bitter. Coughing didn't help. Neither did spitting. There was a low hum in the air, part buzzing subwoofer and part baby-cry. It took me a while to figure out what I was hearing. The cows wanted milking, crisis or not.

People were everywhere. The Amish neighbors seemed focused on the animals. They moved deliberately, going about work that was as foreign to me as my camera would be to them. The county volunteer fire department had sent a pumper truck. Fire service types, easy to identify in their bulky uniforms, were raking out smoking clumps and spraying down others. I momentarily wished I had a camera in my hand when I saw a tired, dirty fireman in fifty pounds of gear standing near Rachel's chicken shed while a rooster on the gable crowed the arrival of dawn—exhausted modern man glaring at old-time alarm clock.

I grabbed the arm of the first firefighter who passed me. "Ainsley Prescott? Have you seen him? Young, blond guy—not Amish."

"The one who went into the fire? They've got him over by the ambulance."

"Into the fire?"

The flash of the ambulance's warning light led me over the grass, my footsteps tumbling faster and faster.

I found Ainsley sitting on the ambulance tailgate, having his hands wrapped.

"They keep slipping off," he told the paramedic. The long shock of blond hair he usually combed so neatly off his face drooped over his eyes. He reached up to flip it back.

"Stop using your hands," the paramedic said.

"Yeah," I interrupted. "Try using your head."

"Maddy!" Relief was all over his face. "What are you doing here?"

Looking at his hands bandaged like The Mummy, turned all my fear into anger. With all the trouble he was in, he should not be glad to see me. I did not understand this kid.

"How's Jenny?" he asked, his face full of concern.

It was hard to launch into lecture mode with Jenny as

the lead. "Fine. She's going to be fine. She hasn't woken yet. It may be a while—later this morning."

"Good. That's great."

"What the hell happened to your hands, College Boy?"

He looked down at his wrappings, looked up at me and smile-shrugged. He was about as filthy as a fellow can appear in khakis and a Brooks Brothers button-down. The smear of ash on his cheek looked like the makeup department had arranged it for maximum cute with minimum muss.

The paramedic helping with his bandages jumped in. "Not to worry. Only second degree. And this guy's a hero. Went in there and dragged the old man out." Mr. Paramedic clapped him on the shoulder.

"I'm no hero." Ainsley shook his head.

"Old guy might not make it," the paramedic said to me. "Smoke. Really hard on the heart at that age. Took him to the hospital a few minutes ago."

"Great. That's where I'm headed next. What about Rachel?"

"She wasn't in the house," Ainsley answered. "It's weird, Maddy. Nobody seems to know where she is. But nobody seems worried either."

"That is weird," I whispered, suddenly very aware of all the ears nearby.

"No shit," Ainsley repeated, all seriousness.

I flashed back to the day I was hired and Uncle Richie's concern. If teaching the kid street-French was a problem, second-degree burns acquired during un-supervised location shoots were going to be a hanging offense.

I sat down next to him and rubbed my throbbing

head. "What happened here? You didn't mention a fire on the phone. How'd it start?"

"Not sure yet," the medic answered. "Looks like the kerosene stove had something to do with it. Everybody's saying it started in the kitchen." He tied off the last bandage. "No operating any heavy machinery today, got it? In a few hours, those puppies are gonna smart a bit." For my benefit, he added, "I'd have someone at the E.R. give him the once-over. They can give him something for pain as well."

"I'll make sure he checks back."

"Not yet," Ainsley complained. "There's stuff to do here."

"Get there before nine. The wait won't be as long," the medic offered, before heading off to pack his gear. One guy's emergency was another guy's average day. I could relate.

I crossed my arms over my chest. "Well?" I asked.

Ainsley held up the swaddled palm of his right hand. "I used this one to open the door." He pantomimed reaching for a doorknob, metal no doubt, and snatching back a burned hand. "This one—" he blocked with the back of his left hand "—kept something from falling on Jost."

"As you were dragging him out of the house?" I said, marveling at my own calm.

"But don't worry, I remembered to leave the camera rolling. I've looked at some of it, Maddy, and it's not bad. I've got this great idea for a dissolve. Fire into dawn? Sort of re-create a time-lapse look?" He was so excited he stood up and waved his thickly padded hands in the air.

"Go on."

"As soon as we hung up, I saw weird lights moving around inside the house. Not the same kind of lights though. Upstairs, the light was a muted yellow-red. Downstairs it was a blue-white light." His eyebrows emphasized the point. "Really hot."

"Halogen?"

"Definitely. Mondo flashlight, I'd bet. Remember, the kind Mrs. Ott said they used for courting?"

"Somebody was coming for Rachel?"

I could tell he was thinking the same thing, but he shrugged. "The blue light went out. And then I saw a yellow glow downstairs. It was a fire, Maddy, I could tell by the color and the smell the minute the wind turned. So I called 9-1-1 and ran across the yard, climbed the fence, got into the house as fast as I could."

I started shaking my head. I felt sick again—the way I had when I found Jenny in the ditch.

"As I was going in the front door, I heard a car pull out. Gravel. I know I did."

"Did you tell the police?"

"Yeah. They acted like I was the suspect. What was I doing there? Did I have permission? All these other questions."

"They think somebody set the fire on purpose?"

"Yeah. But why?" His voice cracked. "Why would anyone want to hurt these people? These are good people."

My sister. Jenny. Saint Ainsley the Hero. Goodness was no shield.

"Ainsley, Ainsley, Ainsley." I interrupted that line of thought. "What's the rule? *What is the rule?*"

"Rule?" He blinked, welcoming the chance to refocus his emotions before the tears dropped. "You mean about the camera? I left it on the tripod, running the whole time. Everything's wide, but I checked it, Maddy. We've got some amazing stuff. Really."

"Not that rule."

"Huh?"

"The one that says you report the news." I grabbed his closest hand and held it up between us. "You don't become the news."

He looked confused. "What do you mean? There were people in there. They could have died."

"You could have died. You were there to do a job. Your uncle was counting on you. I was counting on you. By all means call for backup. Call fire. Call police. Call your mom—but I can't have you rushing into burning buildings every time I send you out. My nerves can't take it."

"Your nerves? That old guy may still die." He might look like spun sugar, but it was all grit now. "What about him?"

"The rule is you stay on your side of the camera, and they stay on the other. If you can't handle that simple instruction, I can't work with you." My voice got loud enough to make some crows in the trees take flight. Nice Amish country people probably never shouted loud enough to scare birds.

"That how you handle it?" Ainsley leaned into my face.

"We aren't talking about me, College Boy."

"Right. Television is about entertainment, Ms. O'Hara. Even I know that." His voice stiffened. He sounded older. "Nobody dies for entertainment."

A mental flip chart of images appeared, one I was glad he couldn't see. "People die for it all the time, kid,"

I admitted. The smoky air surrounding us felt like a rasp down my throat. "*You* have to be careful."

"Careful?" He took two big steps backward. "Careful? Right. Now explain to me how I live with myself the next day?"

"If you're alive the next day, I'm good with that." My vision was blurring and my nose was stinging. I blinked about a hundred times to keep the view cleared.

Ainsley shook his head in disgust and backed even farther away.

"I'll get you back to the hospital as soon as the gear's packed," I told him.

"Don't bother. I'd rather go with the ambulance." He waved a clublike hand in dismissal, turned his back and stomped off.

Damn, I hate it when other people have a point. My phone rang and it gave me an excuse to put off chasing him down and apologizing.

"Miss O'Hara?" The voice was familiar—older, female.

The first person I thought of was the nurse who'd been helping Jenny and my heart stopped for a second. "Yes?"

"This is Grace Ott. We met the other day at my house. You recall?"

I pressed my shoulders back down, out of the hunch-of-dread. "Sure. What'd you need, Mrs. Ott?"

"Oh, nothing. No, I'm fine. I'm sorry to call so early but you seemed like the type that wouldn't lay about come morning."

"You didn't wake me."

"Good. I thought you should know, Rachel Jost is here with me."

"With you? Where?" I blurted out the next thought as the light came on, "She's left the community."

"Yes. I think so. She's going to stay with me awhile anyway."

"Mrs. Ott?" I closed my eyes, ostrich-style. "I have some bad news. There's been a fire."

"Yah. We know," Grace replied, her accent coming through heavily. In a hushed voice, as if she were talking to herself, came the whispered words, "Patience. Patience."

How long since I had stood on the porch talking to Jost? "When did she come to you, Mrs. Ott?"

"Yesterday. She and her father had a bit of a to-do." She stopped all of a sudden. "Rachel wants to talk with you. I can't convince her to wait. The only way I could get her to rest at all was by promising you would come soon. Is that possible?"

"Um, that could be tricky. Maybe tomorrow?"

"I was hoping we might come and meet you."

"I'm actually out at the Jost farm right now." I did a full three-sixty, scanning the view—singed barn, ruined house, and resisted the urge to add the obvious, *what's left of it.*

"Goodness." Grace laughed. "I will never get used to these phones."

It seemed an odd thing to say, until I caught sight of a bundled gnome in the distance. She was near the road that led to the driveway, wearing one of those plastic rain hats old ladies always seem to have in their purses.

"Is that you?" I asked. My brain took a second to adjust. I had seen her image frozen on-screen for hours yesterday. Here in this place, the real person was disconcertingly out of context.

"We're parked across the road." She pointed as she spoke. "I had to get out of the car to make this silly thing work. Now, what good is that?"

"Here I come." I snapped my phone shut and walked toward the apparition of Grace at the end of the road.

She didn't wait. At a surprisingly fast clip, she marched down the drive past the line of horse-powered vehicles parked along the country road, head down as she passed the buggies.

About a half mile up the road, an antique Ford Galaxie was parked on the shoulder. It was tan, of course, and more of a tank than a car—mostly hood and trunk, it must have packed enough steel to keep the Gary mills in business for a week. Grace got in on the driver's side. Someone was sitting on the passenger side.

I knocked on the window.

Rachel.

She was sitting in the car. That's why Ainsley had noticed no one was worried. Someone had seen her sitting in Grace's car. They must have guessed that Rachel was leaving the community.

She popped the door latch and slid to the middle of the bench seat.

I climbed in beside her.

Grace didn't speak. Rachel didn't speak. We all sat shoulder to shoulder and stared straight out the front window.

Parochial school manners prompted my words. "Sorry for your trouble, Rachel."

"I have something for you."

Grace passed her the phone. Rachel passed it to me.

"A cell phone?"

"And this, too." Rachel had wrapped herself in a giant triangle of black shawl. It covered her bonnet, her shoulders and the bulk of her plum-colored dress. She opened the shawl to reveal a pair of binoculars lying in her lap.

"Is this the phone I saw you holding that day in the bushes?"

She nodded.

"Where did you get these," I asked gently, "the phone and the binoculars?"

"My father had them hidden in the barn. I found them both the day Thomas died." She spoke without turning her head toward me. Her profile wore the stiff mask that covers heart-core panic.

"Do you know why he hid them?"

For a moment, her lip trembled. She reached out and took hold of Grace's hand. "I was afraid to ask. The morning Thomas died, there was a call to the dairy. It was for my father. After that, he was gone awhile. I found him in the barn, *grenklich*—not so good looking. So I asked, what's the matter? He shouted me away, off to the house. 'Back to your chores,' he yells.

"I was pretty unhappy about that, the way he talked to me. I'm not a child anymore," she insisted earnestly, her eyes glassy. "I went back to the house and then we all heard that big fuss with the sirens and car engines. That's when they told us stay in the kitchen because there was *Englischers* everywhere with a fire truck, too." She sniffed and raised the back of her hand against the end of her nose.

Grace clucked and dug her pocketbook from under the seat. She unsnapped the latch and passed Rachel a cloth handkerchief.

Rachel nodded her thanks. "I wasn't so happy there were hard words between my father and me, but I wanted to know what was all that business with the fire truck. I thought maybe I would see Thomas." She wasn't crying yet, but her voice had gone high and light enough to break glass.

"I knew Father wasn't in that barn anymore. He'd gone to help with cleaning the milking equipment. I went up to the loft window. From up there, I could see the lights sparkling, the fire truck, all those people. My foot kicked that—" she nodded at the binoculars "—and I found the phone buried next to it under some hay.

"I knew it was Thomas's phone. He let me use it once. I couldn't think how it got into the barn. I took the phone and went to call his fire station so I could leave the message I had this phone. I thought he must be working with the others over in the field. Maybe that's what had made Father so angry."

"That's when I found you under the bush."

She nodded in agreement. "I was afraid someone might find me using it if I stayed in the barn."

Grace squeezed her hand. All three of us did some more staring out the windshield. The hood of the Galaxie stretched almost to the horizon from where I was sitting.

"How do you suppose your dad ended up with Tom's phone?" I asked.

"Father must have seen Thomas. That's all I can think."

"Seen him?"

"Yah. Maybe in town? Friday is farmer's market."

"Maybe." I didn't have the heart to point out she didn't

believe it herself. "Has the phone been on the whole time?" There was enough power to read the LCD.

"No. We only turned it on to call you."

I took a deep breath and scanned the menu for the calling record. My cell number was first, with the date and time of Grace's call noted in the corners of the tiny screen. I hit the menu button to see previous calls, going back once, twice, and then some.

"Oh, man." I started to shake with the full-body willies.

Seven calls were stored in the phone's memory. On a guess, I'd say they were all placed within minutes of Tom Jost's death. I searched my pockets for a pen and scrap of paper from Jenny's hospital admittance. I copied all the numbers down, so I wouldn't lose anything to the phone's waning charge. The first and last numbers were the same. Maybe it had been busy?

One of the numbers, I didn't need to write down. It was the number for WWST.

Rachel watched me making the list. She pointed to the number that had been called second. "That's the number for our phone at the dairy."

"Do you know any of the others?"

She shook her head.

I put Tom's phone back in Rachel's lap and took out my own.

"This'll only take a minute." I called each number and made a note of who answered.

The *Clarion*.

Police nonemergency.

Firehouse, station six.

And one number identified as no longer in service.

Television, news, police, his partners in fire—this wasn't a call for help. This was a staged media event.

Tom himself placed the calls that brought everyone to the scene. But how had the phone gotten into his father's hands? I mumbled to myself for a while. Yucky thoughts. It was hard to tell if Grace and Rachel were concerned or disgusted. I waited to be asked something, anything.

Nothing.

Coming up with questions is never my problem. "Rachel, why give these things to me?"

She bowed her head. "I saw the box you brought my father that day. You knew already."

"Knew what?"

"My father had those binoculars in the barn. I think he saw Thomas die." She was crying now, jagged glassy tears. "And he sent me off to do my chores."

She surprised me. Naive doesn't mean stupid, but I didn't expect her to be able to visualize the ugliness of the situation.

"I didn't know. I only guessed," I whispered. "Neither of us knows what happened—not really. How your dad got the phone. Or how he felt inside."

Grace clutched Rachel's hand in a grip that made the knobby knuckles of her old hands bulge. "Leave God's business in God's hands," she chided.

Rachel's face showed the struggle to calm herself. "You asked me about the binoculars before, when the camera was there. I didn't speak the whole truth. I don't want to hide from things I know. If I will begin a new life now, I will begin right."

Every wrinkle on Grace's face was tight with concern.

"I'll do what I can. To make it right." I wanted to offer Rachel some sign of comfort but I was afraid to touch her bare hand. She seemed so new to the world I occupied, I feared the contact of my bare hand on hers might pass some unseen ruin, some *Englischer* pox, invisible and deadly to those historically unprotected. Instead, I leaned into her shoulder. Just for a moment.

Then I got out of the car.

Grace called out, "Wait." She maneuvered herself out of the vehicle more slowly, no surprise. That old steel car door had to weigh more than she did.

I walked around to the trunk end and propped my butt against a back fin. Grace came around the back fender, her chin tilted high to look at me through glasses speckled with raindrops. "Rachel told me about that business with the television camera. I certainly hope we can trust you to use your better judgment regarding that recording. It wouldn't be too good for this girl to have her private things on the TV right now."

My "better judgment"? That would give Ainsley a laugh.

I heard the *splat* and *ping* before I felt anything. I looked up. It was raining again. I started to laugh, one of those private, unhinged sounds that cause most folks to back away. With my face raised to the drizzle, I managed the words, "I understand."

Her thank-you was crisp and perhaps, a little dubious.

"I don't understand, Grace. What was Tom Jost trying to do? This wasn't your typical depressive slide into suicide. He planned something. He was making a point." My lack-of-sleep headache was becoming a full-frontal-pain lobotomy. "Wasn't he?"

"Maybe the bad things that happen in this world aren't something we can understand. Maybe all we can do is keep walking."

"Walking away doesn't help. Look at the mess they got into when Tom walked away. Rachel, her dad, Tom—they had this whole community looking out for them. People keeping them in line, keeping them connected."

Grace made a soft exhalation, the sound of someone exhausted by irony. "And so do we, Miss O'Hara. So do we. Look at all the trouble we still get into. But each time we fail, we always have the chance to start again." Her crumpled, arthritic hand took hold of my sleeve, slid down to my fingers and gripped me there. She gave my hand a shake. "Use my old face all you want, but be careful of Rachel, you hear me?"

I did my best to nod.

I hiked back toward the grassy space where the camera sat resting on a tripod. It didn't take long to break down the equipment for transport. A couple of fire-guys stomped into range, one of them clanking along in fifty pounds of cutting-edge fire apparatus, the other wearing only knee-high rubber boots, a heavy canvas coat and six inches of beard. Mutual aid requested and provided. I hefted the camera into place and got the shot of them walking past the smoldering ruins of the house.

It was all I could take. I shut the camera down and packed it in.

Another time, another place, I'd be rolling gobs of tape. I'd be smooth-talking the guy in charge for personal interviews. This time, the ashes of another man's life were sticking in my throat, and all I could think of was where I'd rather be.

The hospital. Jenny.

My phone rang. Never fails. The mundane knows no rest.

"What?" I snapped the last of the camera box buckles closed.

"Don't give me that 'what?' bullshit," Richard Gatt roared right through the terrible cell signal. "Where the hell are you and why is my nephew on his way to the hospital with second-degree burns?"

At last, someone who spoke my language. "Because he thinks he's Dudley Frickin' Do-Right and doesn't follow directions."

"You're the one who sent him there. Why weren't you on the *frickin'* scene? This is totally unacceptable…" Gatt raved on for a while.

He was right. My being there would have made a difference. My being there would have made a difference to Jenny, too. I imagined Tom Jost making those calls, calling for witnesses, right before he jumped—and I had to sit down.

The grass was wet and cool under my pants. It felt so good, I laid down. The inside of my skull pounded at the shift of altitude, then eased with the chill. The air smelled a little better down here, too. Less smoky.

Cows made noises nearby. I concentrated on the cows.

As soon as Gatt took a breath, I told him, "I'll have a story on your desk tomorrow morning. Consider it my resignation."

"Shut the hell up, O'Hara, I'm not finished talking. And you aren't going anywhere until my story is one hundred percent in the can, if you ever want to work again in this business…"

Blah, blah, blah. Heard all of this before. Nice cosmic irony, though. "'Isolation is a powerful tool for behavior modification,'" I quoted.

"Don't try to change the subject," Gatt yelled right back. "What the shit am I supposed to tell my sister?"

"Tell her—her son's a hero. Tell her I'm sorry. Tell her I quit."

I could hear the television through the door when I finally made it back to Jenny's room at the hospital. Relief and regret hit me together. Jenny had woken and I'd missed it.

I should be so lucky.

"Where have you been?" Tonya sat propped up on the second bed, reading *People* magazine.

I swear her lime-green sweats were glowing. They hurt my eyes.

With relief, I saw Jenny was still flat out, shut-eyed, unconscious in the bed.

The television, mounted high in the corner of the room, was tuned to reruns of *Little House on the Prairie*.

I laughed. "Are you watching PAX channel?"

"Shut up, you. Don't even start with me." Tonya snapped her words like a nun's ruler crack. "You've been gone for hours. Where've you been?"

"There was a fire at the farm. Everything took longer than I expected." I considered elaborating but the details were not likely to help my case.

"A fire?"

"The Jost house burned to the ground. Ainsley went in and pulled the old man out. The doofus managed to burn his hands pretty badly in the process."

"Oh Lord."

"And then Gatt called while I was out there." I plopped down on the foot of the bed. "Then I quit."

"You *what?*" Tonya said. "I thought the point in sending you out there was to keep you from losing the job?"

I'd had three hours of sleep. I stunk of smoke. My favorite black pants were covered in mud, my shoes in cow shit. My motorcycle was still sitting in Curzon's parking lot—in the rain. And both my young charges were currently receiving emergency medical attention. I think it's fair to say my judgment was not operating at peak performance.

On the television, Laura and Pa casually led a cow up a grassy hill. With all the things on my mind, what came out of my mouth was, "When I was a kid, I loved this show."

"What is the matter with you!" Tonya flapped an all-inclusive hand. "How could you let this happen?"

"Let what happen?"

"That poor baby—"

"Which one?"

"That is the most lame-ass—"

"They weren't *my* drugs," I pointed out.

"What is that supposed to mean?"

"They were antianxiety meds. And they were in a free sample pack."

"Are you serious? Where did she get something like that?"

"I don't know! You had a sample pack of meds in your gym bag. The stuff for your back, remember? Where did you get those?"

"From my doctor. That's the only place you can get them." Her voice dropped. "Oh Lord, did Jenny think she was taking something for pain?"

"That would be my bet."

Tonya was paralyzed by the thought of contributing to Jenny's condition. Her voice was a monotone. "I'd never forgive myself—"

"It's not—" *your fault,* I started to say.

"Of course it is! Yours and mine—this child has no one else."

"*That* I am fully aware of," I said. Loudly.

We both turned and looked at Jenny. She kept right on sleeping.

"I do not understand you." Tonya's voice dropped to a steamy whisper. "Why do you prefer living in hell?"

How did she do that? Stick me where I never expect, and bleed a wound I didn't even realize was open. I clapped my mouth shut and started counting to one hundred, while gesturing in large useless motions.

Tonya went into nurse mode, fluffing pillows with double-fisted punches, snapping the sheets smooth and tucking them under the mattress with a kung-fu chop. Normally, she was the kind of person who flowed in motion, never looked off-balance or clumsy. At that moment, she looked like dry sticks animated. I didn't get up from the bed. I made her work around me. As she jerked the blanket into position, I nearly fell off the edge.

"You have a life, a beautiful, precious girl-child put in your hands. Something other people would die for." She waved at Jenny, laid out like an effigy. I knew she was speaking of herself. Tonya would have gladly accepted Jenny into her life. Through me, she already had.

"What else am I supposed to do, T? I don't know how to be the mom."

"There are only two requirements," she said with all the patience of someone explaining the how-to of bar soap. "You commit to the long haul. And you consider her needs first. She won't always get top priority, but she always gets first consideration."

"I'm committed."

"You haven't even moved out of your apartment yet! How committed is that?" Tonya's voice amplified with every word.

My eyes kept drifting toward the television screen. It was impossible to turn away from the flash and comfort of those familiar images—the smiling faces and sugary landscapes, figments of our collective, mass-consuming unconscious. Even knowing all that I know, doing all that I do, I sighed. *Little House* had shimmered before me in childhood reruns, like the mirage of heaven hammered into me on Sunday mornings. There was the wise, kind father, the patient, loving mother, and the sisters who all lived together in a land where truth was known, justice was served and love begat love, never suffering.

Behind me, Tonya spat, "If you don't stop looking at that God-*damned* television and pay attention to me!" She whipped the plastic cup from Jenny's bed-side tray at my head. It clipped me, took a high bounce and smacked the bottom of the set. Must have caught the power button. The picture popped off; the screen a sudden darkling glass.

Empty.

Everything went out of me in the breath that followed. Busted, sucking comfort from a little house on the prairie. I swung my legs around to the side of the bed. The vent was blowing hospital AC right in my face. The cold burned the wet lines on my cheeks.

Tonya moved toward me, looking like she regretted every step.

"Careful," I told her. "I stink."

"Yeah, you do." She put her arms around me anyway. I felt her shaking her head, her cheek pressed to my scalp.

Again, it was impossible to turn away.

Jenny woke up around lunchtime. There was a bit of bedlam at first—thrashing, tubes coming undone, machines beeping like crazy, but it didn't last long.

The nurse said we got off easy. "Usually we see some projectile vomiting when they come around."

Possible sign my life was on the rebound?

Hold that thought.

We had a visit from the doctor making rounds. Tonya sat in while we heard that they would probably keep her one more night "to see what happened with the seizures." Jenny accepted it all with big eyes and nodding; she didn't start to cry until the woman got to the part about the social worker who would be visiting before Jenny could check out of the hospital.

"Why did you leave school yesterday?" the nice-lady doctor asked.

Jenny shot me a worried look and shrugged.

"Where did you get the medicine?"

"Found it."

"Where?"

"Mommy's medicine box?" Jenny's eyes filled with tears.

My sister was spinning in her grave. I could feel the breeze.

"Tell me about why you took it, honey."

"I just…" Jenny started off strong, as if there was a way she could explain, but her voice faded "…thought they'd make me feel better. That's all. Really," she added for my benefit.

"This is very serious, Jenny," the doctor said. "Everyone here is worried about you. That's why we're going to have the social worker come talk to you. We all need to understand what happened so we can make sure it won't happen again."

"It won't. I swear," Jenny pleaded.

"Don't panic, kid." I squeezed her hand. "You don't have to go alone if you don't want to. I'll go with you."

"You will?" Jenny's voice sounded awful. She was choked up and the tubes had scratched her throat pretty good.

"If you want."

"I think we ought to meet this social worker before there is any talking," Tonya said, casting serious doubt on the title social worker. "All of us."

"Certainly," the nice-lady doctor replied.

"Good thinking," I said.

Tonya gave a tight-lipped nod. Everybody was in agreement.

The rest of the day was busy. Tonya yelled at me about changing channels too much, while we took turns playing cards and reading to Jenny. I pretended to nap but couldn't stop myself from checking out the competition's news magazine shows.

I tried not to think about work. It was impossible. Employed or unemployed, the story rattled through my head.

A long time ago, I learned that truth isn't relative. It's quantum. The closer you get, the smaller and infinitely more complex the related elements become. The modern world lives in smaller and smaller segments. There's Coke, Diet Coke, Caffeine Free and Cherry. We added to G, PG, PG-13, R, NR and NC-17 with Gens X, Y and Z on the way. Television isn't so different from life. It's built from bits and pieces, strung together over time, and repeated on the endless reruns of the mind.

Except for the part about things making sense by the end.

Part of my problem is that I've gotten too good at seeing parts. Finding a way to tell the story without exploiting Rachel, without using Nicky Curzon's off-the-record explanation for Tom's arrest, without relying on a little salacious conjecture about all those porn maga-zines…it seemed impossible. Not to mention the fact that any story I produced might become fodder against Curzon's reelection for sheriff, which would never stop me from reporting on the story, but might qualify as a speed bump.

Editing a story together is similar to taking a photo. Shadows determine form; the light source determines the shadows. I couldn't figure out where to shine the light on this.

"Maybe I'll go and see about some caffeine."

"Bring me something." Tonya waved at the breakfast tray.

"Me, too," Jenny agreed. Her mushy fruit sat aban-doned, a spoon poking out from under a paper napkin shroud.

"Caffeine and 'somethings' all around. I'll be back."

I wandered the halls, people-watching and mulling. After twenty minutes or so, it appeared the cafeteria had lost itself. The hospital had some renovation project going on and all the maps were either wrong or led to dead-ends of orange mesh. I came out of an elevator, turned a corner and found myself in a hall facing a circle of women and men in Amish dress. Two medical types were talking with them in the waiting area.

I recognized one of the men. It was the guy who'd tromped through Jost's kitchen in knee-high dairy boots ordering me to vamoose.

The nurse behind the counter saw me gawking. "They're Amish," she offered. "A friend of theirs was in a fire."

It wasn't easy to keep it to, "Really? That's a bummer. Was he burned?"

"No," she assured me with a kindly, vacant frown.

"A little smoke inhalation is all. Can I help you find something?"

With an opening like that, how could I not ask? I gave her Jost's name and she didn't appear to make the connection. She checked a chart, directed me to his room and returned to her paperwork.

The sight line between Jost's door and the waiting area where the other Amish were listening to the doctors was blocked by the privacy curtain surrounding the nurses' station. He was under close observation. I knocked before I entered.

Old Mr. Jost was under the clear plastic covering of an oxygen tent. They had him in a hospital gown but the whiskers still set him apart.

I stood and watched him for a while, thinking of Jenny mostly. I had no plan to ask him questions. Nothing to say to the old fart, really. I think I just wanted to look at him one more time; like the accident off to the side of the road, reminding me to slow down, wear my seat belt and quit flipping off the other drivers.

What happened here won't happen to me.

I wished I had my camera between us, but I forced myself to stand there and look through my own eyes.

He blinked awake. That didn't bother me. But when his fingers flicked against the plastic, I jumped. He wanted me to lift the curtain.

"What?" I asked. I leaned over so my ear was right above his mouth.

"—ay-chel?" The word was mostly exhale.

"She's all right."

"Wherrre?"

I thought about lying. "She's with Grace Ott."

His eyes closed. He looked dead. The color of his skin, the nearly imperceptible shallowness of his breathing, his eyes didn't even flicker. It was impossible to perceive any part of what he was thinking or feeling.

That's when my questions came. I couldn't stop myself. "Why did he do it, Mr. Jost? Why did Tom ask you to watch? Did he want you to stop him?"

"No." That word was soft but clear. His eyes stayed closed. With my ear hovering, he whispered, "Maybe, die a little bit…with him."

"The phone—how did you end up with the phone?"

"Shame," he whispered, "my shame."

"You took the phone from Tom."

His eyes barely opened. They were red with smoke irritation, the skin around them gray and sagging. "Tried. Run to him…too late. Too late." His eyes pooled with tears.

A nurse pushed into the room. "Uh-uh. Don't disturb the tent," she scolded. "Out, out, out of there!"

"I'm going. Sorry."

His fingers curled and tapped across my hand like the dance of a spider's legs, calling my attention back.

"Yes?"

"Resist not evil." They were the clearest words he'd spoken yet.

Miracle of miracle, I remembered that one. "Turn the other cheek. Overcome evil with good."

He tapped the back of my hand three times. *Yes, that's it.*

I nodded. I think he believed that taking the phone was a way to turn the other cheek. Perhaps he meant to confess to his community and explain what happened, or save Tom from the public shame of having acted in anger. But Rachel found the phone. And the protective, controlling father took over. Until now, the only scenarios I had been able to imagine were the ones motivated by a man's self-preservation and guilt. A hundred questions formed in my head. The nurse glared at me.

"Please, one last question. My colleague thinks there was someone in the house with you last night. Before the fire started. Did you see anyone?"

"Thought boy come for Rachel," he struggled to say. *"Englischer."*

"Did you see him?"

His eyes closed. Exhaustion or the need to keep his own council ended that line of talk.

"That's all," Nursey scolded. "You're disturbing the tent. He needs to rest."

"I'm done. I'm gone," I told her. I touched the back of his hand. "Thank you. Be well."

Slipping out was more nerve-racking than going in. Through the mesh at the top of the curtain, I could see Jost's friends and family three feet away and closing. I ducked around the curtain partition and followed it toward the nurses' station. Just ahead of me, I could hear men on the other side of the curtain. They were having a tight-throated discussion. I froze.

I'm pretty good with voices. To the careful ear, voices are as distinct as a walk, a form of handwriting, a style of dress. Still, it surprised me—was it really *that* small a town? There was something familiar in those voices.

Everyone has heard the research into pheromones that sync us up with mates. I sincerely doubt that's all the lizard brain can detect. I think we smell all sorts of crap, like lies and wickedness and trouble ahead. Maybe that explains why a person might freeze and listen to a conversation that makes very little sense at first.

Or maybe I'm just nosey.

"...tired of it, do you hear me?"

"I hear you. I'm trying—"

"I don't want to hear how hard you are trying. You've turned something very simple into something complicated. Am I going to have to find someone else to help me?"

"No. No."

"I hope not. I'll call you."

"Um, yeah, listen I have a new number. Old phone's gone."

Hello! The light went on. That was Pat talking. Fireman Pat, Tom Jost's partner, a.k.a. Mr. Vegas. Couldn't place the other voice. I slipped back two steps as a nurse came barging full steam around my curtain wall.

"Whoops—sorry," she said automatically. She followed it with a more hostile, "What are you doing here?"

"Lost." I grimaced and backed through the curtain into the open hall area. "Cafeteria?"

"That way." She pointed with a finger-gun toward the far end of the hall.

"Thanks."

I caught a glimpse of someone rounding the corner at a good clip, the reflectors on his uniform jacket flashing as he passed beneath the yellow-green light of each fluorescent ceiling fixture. I looked back the other way, no sign of the second man. The only door nearby that didn't seem to lead to a patient's room read Restricted.

"Hey Pat!" I hollered, taking a chance that he was the man disappearing around the corner. "Wait up!" On four hours sleep, subtle Miss Nancy Drew I'm not.

Lucky for me, Mr. Vegas had a lot of friends in the hospital.

"Looking for something?" a guy in scrubs asked.

"EMS guy named Pat?" I tried.

That brought an eye roll. "Figures. Never the ugly ones. Toward the cafeteria."

"Thanks."

Couple of nurses pointed me, "That way."

"Right. Thanks."

I turned a corner into an empty hall. Quiet. No sign of anyone. My heart was pumping with adrenaline and the sudden change of pace. I'd been race-walking the halls, trying to catch up. Mounted on the wall near a frosted glass door was a small, brass plaque.

Chapel. Open 24 Hours.

It felt like a trick. I pulled the door and peeked inside.

My breathing made a surf-roar in my ears. "Hello?"

No answer. I made myself quiet—hiding quiet—and entered.

The room was shoebox small, only a dozen chairs, and a solid table with glass votives at the front. The walls were bare, the wood trim spare and nothing but a pair of dim uplights shining on the curtained wall behind the altar table. I smelled hospital cleaner and the burning sweetness of beeswax candles.

I circled the room. It was empty and then some, as nondenominational as a place of worship could be. In the Amish world, simplicity came from sameness. Funny how in our world, it was diversity that bred simplicity.

Could anyone sink low enough to hide behind an altar table? I looked and realized there was a door behind the curtained wall.

Cold rushed through my blood. Calm took effort.

Ready—I opened the door as carefully, quietly, as possible. It swung inward.

Absolute dark. I slipped my hand past the doorjamb, feeling for a light switch.

Click!

The overhead blinked on. Room empty. It was a walk-in closet-*cum*-sacristy. A rack of vestments hung on the back wall, a small bookcase to one side. Nothing but a room.

I slipped all the way inside—

Boom!

The light snapped off as the door slammed, the sound mixing with what happened next. My face hit the wall, cheekbone first. The sudden reversal of light blinded me. My hand covered the switch, but his larger hand—sweaty and strong—pressed my palm into the toggle, biting into my skin.

Caught.

"Don't move."

There was nothing to move. I couldn't even twist my head. His jaw and neck locked the threat of his body right beneath my ear. His chin dug into the top of my scalp. We were both panting, strangely synchronized with each movement of chest, and that was the most coldly frightening thing of all.

"You," he whispered. "You smell like her."

"Who? Pat, what the hell—?"

"Shut up." He crushed his body against me. I stopped inhaling. "Questions don't help. Knowing won't help. It only makes things worse. Don't you get that?"

"No. I don't believe that."

"What's it take to teach you? They both died! Leave it alone."

"Both?" I said.

"Tom and Gina."

"Gina?" *You smell like her.* Confusion was all that kept me calm. Once again, my lizard brain jumped ahead to a place where logic feared to go. "Angelina? Do you mean my sister?"

My internal temperature dropped twenty degrees. It's a miracle my next breath didn't fog the air.

"You are making everything worse," he said. "You have to stop."

Resistance bubbled up, hot and sharp. I bucked and twisted. "Get off me."

He was as mad as I was, but a whole lot bigger. He slammed himself against me again, smashing us into the wall. All the body parts you never see, never think about, suddenly appeared on my mental map, tracing a line of vulnerability from the top of my spine, down the slope of my back, to the curve of my ass.

Nobody moved for a heavy second.

He seemed to lose track of the moment, anger suspended by a surge of hormones, or confusion, or something else. His body took over. He inhaled deeply, chest swelling, and I felt the barest suggestion of motion forward and back with his pelvis, a reaching out. His cock was big enough to make an impression. I kept very still.

"Stop," he repeated. "Just stop."

Too slowly, he withdrew contact with his lower body. The pressure of his hand over mine increased. It hurt.

Before I realized what he meant to do, he grabbed the back of my collar and bent my arm behind my back. With a twist, he shoved me hard from the center of my back toward the middle of the room.

I flew forward and face-planted, hands too slow to catch myself. My head rebounded off the industrial carpet.

Pat was already out the door.

Over the sound of my ears ringing, I heard the bad news, loud and clear.

He'd jammed a chair against the outside of the door. I was locked in.

"What took you so long? Where'd you go this time?" Tonya said in the usual way. Then she took a good look at me. "Oh Lord, what now?"

I stood in the doorway of Jenny's hospital room, not completely in my body, or my right mind. The urge to scream, hit something, throw something, had stiffened every muscle.

Jenny sat right up in the center of the bed with the rolling table pulled across her lap. There was a bunch of balloons tied to the water pitcher and a curly haired teddy bear leaning on her pillow. A "Get Well" card from some of the hospital people her mother had known was on the bedside table.

"Did you bring us food?" Jenny asked. She was concentrating hard, trying to bridge-shuffle a deck of playing cards.

"No food."

"Darn."

"What's wrong?" Tonya leaned toward me, her body alert. She'd pulled her braids behind her back and tied them with a piece of silver curling ribbon cut from the balloon streamers. Jenny wore a headband of the same ribbon. It looked like they were having a little party.

"I got lost. And I stopped to talk to someone. Remember Dr. Graham? The one I interviewed the other day. She said she'll come down and talk to Jenny later."

"She a social worker?" Tonya asked.

"No. The other kind."

Psychologist. Psychiatrist. Headshrinker. Whatever.

At least I knew her somewhat. She seemed normal, given her profession and all. I'd certainly trust Jenny with her, better than a stranger.

"No wonder you look a little worse for the wear," Tonya said.

It hadn't taken long to attract someone's attention and break out of the chapel lockup. It took longer to convince the guy we didn't need to call security. Afterward, I'd wandered the halls in a daze of muddy thinking.

When I recognized Dr. Graham's offices it seemed like fate. Here was a problem I could solve. I sat in her waiting area and gathered my thoughts until she was free. "How would you like to study the effect of small families on self-actualization?" I bantered as my lead. She waited for me to come clean with the real story. It wasn't easy. She turned those shrewd eyes on me and saw the things I didn't headline, like admitting I'd only been on the job with Jenny four months and I'd already crashed and burned.

Everywhere I turned, I was tanking on my own ignorance.

Pat-the-paramedic knew my sister. From the hospital maybe?

You smell like her.

More than just the hospital.

Part of me wanted to call Curzon and get the asshole arrested immediately. Unfortunately, that wouldn't get me what I wanted even more. Information.

They both died?

Turn Pat in and the sheriff would lock him up where I couldn't talk to him. End of story.

"Your boy called," T said. "He's going to stop in to see Jenny in a few minutes." She did a slide of the eyes over the shuffling cards. "You giving that boy a hard time?"

College interviewed Pat yesterday at the firehouse. I couldn't help salivating at the thought. What the hell did he say to my boy? I needed to see that interview.

Too bad I'd quit.

"Me?"

"I'm hungry," Jenny said again. She bounced as she waited for Tonya to finish passing out the cards. "Really hungry."

"How many people you planning on putting in the hospital today, Ms. Maddy?" Tonya asked. She turned over her first card and cackled.

"Keep it up. I'm sure they got room for one more," I answered. The second bed looked good. I stretched out flat and could feel the ghost of Pat's body behind me. Pressing. "Have I mentioned that I'm tired, really tired?"

Jenny's tongue poked out in concentration. She took another card from the deck and discarded slowly.

"What do you know?" T mumbled.

The question sunk into my silence.

Not much.

My guess was Tom Jost killed himself because he discovered Mr. Vegas scheming and scamming something big-time. They fought about it. Tom couldn't stop him and couldn't keep the secret inside.

Pat tried to ensure no one would believe Tom if—or when—he spilled the beans, by setting Tom up with a trunkful of porno. And the men at station six turned on Tom.

When Tom reached out for the girl he'd hung the last of his dreams on, he found himself more alone than ever and raging with despair. He phoned his father, the fire station and the fourth estate to witness his death. He went gunning for both Pat and his daddy, with his elaborate suicide setup—calls, binoculars, trust funds.

Tom wasn't a suicide victim. He was a suicide vigilante. This was para-misery of the sacrificial type.

And Rachel? Maybe Tom meant to give her choices by leaving Rachel all his savings. Maybe he meant to say sorry for the episode in the car, or worse, split her from her father forever.

Bits and pieces of conversations tumbled around in my head.

Number no longer in service.

Old phone's gone, I'd heard Pat say to the man behind the curtain.

Had Pat ditched his cell phone to try and cover for Tom's suicide calls? The first time we met, Pat seemed genuinely unhappy about Tom's death. Maybe he didn't mean to hurt Tom as badly as he did. For an extroverted loose screw like Pat, a trunkload of magazines was probably the kindest way he could imagine to ruin a man's reputation. That weird scenario in the chapel was all the proof I needed—in the planning department, Pat was an idiot.

That worried me most of all. Idiots could be tricky.

Was Pat the Player driving the silver car that College saw parked at the Jost farm, the silver car that had been following me?

What if Mr. Jost was right about Rachel having a gentleman caller?

They both died.

I traced the timeline in my head again. Pat knew my sister. She died. Player moved on. If Pat started seeing Rachel next, Tom would have been in quite a twist.

Rachel hadn't said anything about another guy. But

that girl was half clam. If she *was* seeing Pat, she would certainly know how to keep it to herself.

Had my story gotten between Pat and his girl?

"Anybody want a bagel?" Ainsley knocked once as he came through the door with a wave for Tonya and a full-blast smile for Jenny. He'd changed into clean clothes and his hands were freshly bandaged.

"Hallelujah and pass the bag," Tonya said. "Welcome to the real world, where people eat food. They don't just talk about it."

"You talking to me? I've seen the shoes you wear on Saturday night. You live nowhere near reality."

"And it ain't heaven either. Just look at these cards." She discarded a queen. Jenny snatched it, tucked it into her hand and threw down all of her cards.

Tonya shrieked and stamped her feet to Jenny's obvious delight.

"Want to play?" Jenny asked. "Four people are just right. It's crazy eights."

"Sure," College said. He dragged another uncomfortable chair to the side of the bed where Tonya was sitting. It took some arranging but he finally got his legs situated under the bed. What is it about long-legged boys? My legs are almost that long and you don't see me fussing like a debutante in a ball gown.

"What's your plan for today?" Ainsley asked.

"We're hanging out here."

"Jenny can't go home 'til tomorrow," Tonya said.

Ainsley looked at me.

"For observation," I said.

"My turn to deal." Jenny reached for the cards. The dark hair bordering her face exaggerated the shadows under her eyes. I wanted to carry her out into the sun and tell her every knock-knock joke I knew.

"Heard you quit," Ainsley said.

"Yeah."

Jenny froze, mid-deal. "I'll figure something out," I told her, gently pulling the card from her fingers. "Keep dealing."

"Why didn't you tell Uncle Rich anything about—the circumstances?"

"I was pressed for time." I gave Ainsley the shut-the-hell-up eyeball. "We're playing cards here, College. You in or you out?"

"In." His cheeks darkened with the flush of self-conscious emotion. "Somebody told me the only way to survive the bad days is to get back in the game."

Tonya snorted. I don't think it was the cards she was holding.

"I've got all our raw footage with me. And a monitor and some other stuff."

That would include Pat's interview at the firehouse. I wanted to throw my arms around him. I shifted my cards around.

"Other stuff? Editing equipment?"

"Enough to do a rough cut. We could set it up in here. Maybe fiddle around a little."

"Did your uncle send you?"

"No." He sighed. "This morning, maybe I misunderstood where you were coming from, you know?"

Tonya stared at me. Jenny stared at me. Ainsley stared at his feet.

"Yeah," I said. "Me, too."

"Uncle Rich said you promised him a story." Ainsley sounded hopeful.

"Did I? Maybe after I kick your butt in crazy eights, we'll get the tapes and give these two a private showing."

He held up his bandaged hands. His fingers were exposed from the second knuckle down. He demonstrated button pushing and dial twisting abilities. "Ready, boss."

"Finish the deal, Jen," I told her.

"Eat-your-ownies round."

Something changed in her face as she tossed cards at all of us. A shadow passed.

Finally, I'd done something right.

WEDNESDAY

8:49:16 a.m.

"You been at it all night?" Mick popped his head through the door of edit bay one. He had a cup of coffee in one hand. With the other, he patted himself down for cigarettes and lighter.

The fresh light sliced through our privacy. It made me wince. The editing bay is a cave, no telling day or night, sun or rain, when you're inside. Time is counted in hundredths of a second and passes without notice.

"Clock?" Ainsley asked.

"Almost nine-A," Mick told us. "The troops are gathering. I've been on since midnight. Headed out. There's a call for O'Hara on line three."

Jenny. The fear hit me hard as I realized how completely I'd been sucked into the work. "Yeah?"

"'Hello' is the way the rest of the world starts a phone conversation, O'Hara."

Curzon and relief didn't normally combine in my head. At least five seconds of dead airtime passed while my nerves settled.

I cleared my throat with, "Ha. Thanks for the tip, Sheriff. I love a public servant who provides good service for my tax dollars."

"How's Jenny?"

"Better," I said. "She's getting out this morning. I'm headed to the hospital as soon as I send this feed."

"And what will you be driving?"

"Holy shit! Quick, tell me. How's my other girl?"

Curzon clucked. "Motorcycle like that is not a girl. That one is all woman. And every guy in this place has a hard-on for her, judging from the requests I've been getting."

"Keep those animals away from Peg."

"I might be able to work something out for you in that regard," he agreed, his voice dripping the promise of slippery compromises. "With appropriate reciprocity."

What was I doing with a guy like Curzon? Apparently, my hormonal *coup* had put a figurehead Maddy in charge. She appeared to be a bit of a hussy. I shifted back in my chair. Bounced out a little rhythm. Had one of those stomach-crunching after-flashes that a good kiss will set off.

"Reciprocity, huh? What exactly are you looking for, Sheriff?"

"Seen any SUVs lately?"

Talk about the cold-shower effect. "No. Not me."

"What is it?" Ainsley whispered. His radar was up.

I clapped a hand over the mouthpiece. "Curzon wants a report on the SUV driver. You told the guys at the fire, right?"

"I told them," Ainsley mumbled. "For all the good it did."

"O'Hara? You still with me?" Curzon asked.

"I'm here." Too much at stake. Time to come clean. And the story was in the can. "You might be right, Sheriff. Maybe we should make out a report."

"We?"

"Me and my college boy. There was another possible sighting last night, out at the Jost farm? Not sure it's related, but my new motto is take no chances." I filled the sheriff in on what Ainsley had seen. And told him my theory on Jenny's shiny car as well. "If I'm paranoid, you've got only yourself to blame, Sheriff. You're the one that keeps nagging me about SUVs."

"Not paranoid enough I'd say," Curzon said. "I'll send a car to pick up your man Pat. See what he has to say. I still need you to come in and make a report."

"Can you give me the forms in a handy take-out bag? I could make a quick stop on the way home from the hospital. Make sure my poor Peg isn't subject to further harassment."

"It ain't harassment if she likes it. Tell you what? How about I run the paperwork out to your house later? I'll bring a pizza and give you and Jenny a lift back to the station afterward to get the bike?"

The cold shower of disappointment did a quick reversal. If it was only work, why invite himself over?

"Sounds good," I said. "We'll handle the pizza though. Jenny may want to eat as soon as they spring her from the joint. Come after five."

"You got it." Mr. Phone Manners didn't offer any goodbyes.

I shagged my fingers back through my hair, stretching and shaking off the work intoxication with the juice of Curzon's interest.

Mick appeared at the door of the edit bay again. "You all done in here? I need to check a discrepancy."

"We're done." I hit the rewind.

"Can I see it?"

I glanced at the clock. "There's time before the feed.

But I've got to run. Want to watch while we check the last dissolve?"

"Sure." Mick settled against the dark egg-crate foam.

Ainsley rolled his chair away from the counter to stretch his legs straight out in front of him and hit Play.

The piece timed out at nine seconds under the six-minute mark. Good thing a picture's worth a thousand words. How else could you tally the cost of isolated innocence against the price of emancipation in three hundred fifty-one seconds?

"Who wrote the copy on the voice-over?" Mick asked.

"I did."

"Different, but it works. You done that before?"

"No. Seen it done here and there."

Instead of the usual omniscient voice-over, I'd gone for a narrating voice that had an identity, an "I" voice— part Rod Steiger and part Laura Ingalls Wilder. Maddy O'Hara's alter ego.

On-screen, the house melted in reverse from flame to smoke. I matched the gray-whites to a close-up zoom-out we'd gathered of the Jost farm that first morning. Billowing sheets danced on a laundry line, the children weaving between. Magically, the house was restored.

Somehow the college boy had managed a racked-zoom centered on the old oak, with the children disappearing into the billowing laundry. It's a tricky maneuver with the camera on a track—almost impossible freehand. The camera moves away from the subject at the same rate the zoom magnifies the subject closer. The picture looks as if the world behind the subject shifts, while the subject remains still.

"Nice rack." Mick gave Ainsley a shot of praise, fist to top of the left biceps.

Ainsley mugged *aw shucks* and rubbed his arm with his bandaged hand.

The voice-over came in again.

"Tom Jost lost himself in that middle distance between good and evil, simple and worldly. His life served the fireman's motto Prevent and Protect. His death did the same, a signpost at the middle distance, where some mystery always remains."

As the children disappeared, the house and barn came into view, then the road and finally, the great old oak spreading its branches across the horizon line. Still standing.

"I didn't think that last shot was gonna work," Ainsley admitted. "Cutting back to the kids? But you were right. Sadder, but less depressing."

"Yeah." I punched the save button. "Send it."

I tried to make it out of the building before anyone noticed me. No such luck. The wide-eyed kid from the mail room came running up behind me as I walked out the dock exit.

"Mr. Gatt wants to see you."

"Tell him I left."

"He said if I don't bring you back he'll fire me and—"

"—you'll never work in this business again. Yeah,

yeah." I turned around. "You should take the deal, kid."

When I passed Barbara's desk on my way to Gatt's inner office, she was typing ninety words a minute from dictation. Without turning her head, she pushed a folded napkin across the desk toward me. Four ibuprofen and a stack of soda crackers.

Breakfast and absolution.

"You are the effing best," I told her sincerely.

Barbara never stopped typing, but the smug expression on her face was one of the friendliest I'd seen.

Gatt spewed a string of common and colorful obscenities as soon as I opened the door. He summed up, "Are you insane?"

"I had no idea you were in this early, Gatt. Satellites don't wait."

"Bullshit! Nothing gets sent unless I approve it." He waved the remote in the direction of the largest monitor. The screen was paused over the last few seconds of my piece. It must be running on the in-house channel. Without Gatt doing anything the image suddenly reversed and played again. He clicked on the audio.

"...where some mystery always remains."

"What the hell does that mean? Where's the auto-shit? Where's the erotic stuff? All I see are a bunch of kids playing with the wash."

"Did you watch the piece from the beginning?" I propped my butt on the arm of a chair. Two all-nighters in a row; I was trashed. If I sat down now, I might not get up again.

"No, I haven't watched the piece. Because you didn't

bother to show it to me. But I know this is not what we discussed."

"It's good stuff."

"Not for pre-prime, it isn't. Not against game shows."

"It's six minutes of programming, Gatt," I snapped back. "I'm sure Network has other material that can conquer the game show."

"I want to see it. Now. And I may have changes. So you'd better stick your ass to the chair and see what happens next."

I could see daylight through the window. The view was exactly the same as a week ago—parking lot to weed field to pasture. Today though, I wasn't looking at a horizon line. I was looking at a time line. Present and past laid flat, right in front of me. The rest of my life started now.

"What are you worried about, Gatt?" I had switched to crisis calm, but sales mode was hard to muster. The protective shell hadn't hardened over my work yet. I picked up a pencil and a piece of scrap paper lying on Gatt's enormous desk. "I'm telling you this piece has class. It's mysterious. It's metaphysical. It's tragic. The target demographics are going to eat it up."

"Network is not 'eating it up' after that pitch you fed them." Gatt dug inside his desk drawer for a fistful of sweetener. He ripped half a dozen sugar packets clean through the middle. Sugar crystals exploded all over his desk. Some of them must have made it into his cup. He gulped a swallow followed by, "Jesus God, I hate freelancers."

"You saw most of the raw stock before I cut it to-gether. Give me some credit." I rolled my neck and got a sound like something breaking. Deliberately, I jotted a short message on the scrap paper. "You're pissed at me because your nephew got his fingers burned."

"Bullshit!" he countered. There was a growing sheen to his head which was pumping red-and-white flashes of furious blood to his skin. "You should have shown me the finished version before you released it. Simple courtesy, even if nothing had changed. Those guys at Network are going to want your ass on a platter now. Your problem is you want it both ways. You want a team position but you act like a freelancer. Here today—gone tomorrow. No respect for the team!"

Same theme, new variation. "I've been up two days, Gatt. Speaking of bullshit, I'm too tired to take this right now." I stood up.

"You walk out that door, don't think you're coming back."

"No, I don't think I am." I pushed the note across the desk. Signed and dated, it read simply, *I resign.*

I turned around and Ainsley was standing in the doorway, wearing his goofiest grin, carrying a VHS cassette pinched between his bandaged fingers. His face was pale, his eyes glassy, and he had a hint of manic vibration about him. Six or seven hours in the booth, running on nothing but deadline adrenaline and diet pop, and my college boy was still standing. Don't ask me why, but I felt a little flash of pride.

Ainsley tilted his head to see around me. "Seen the story yet, Uncle Rich? It's great."

Gatt couldn't speak. He pointed. His eyebrows twitched. His nostrils flared.

"Go ahead and show him," I told Ainsley. "I'm gone."

I begged a ride off the mail-room courier to pick up the Subaru. Then drove back to the hospital, waited around for the doctor's discharge and suffered through forty minutes of paperwork, wherein I promised to turn my entire self over to accounts receivable for parts if I forfeited on my bill.

Tonya kissed us both goodbye and went back to the city. Jenny cried.

"I'll be back on the weekend, honey. You can count on it." Tonya always knew the right thing to say. For both of us.

At last, Jenny and I were on our way home. It was a quiet drive. We hadn't really been alone together since I'd shipped her off to school on Monday. The silence swirled between us, warping into an emotional black hole that sucked my energy. I wanted to pull over and slump into a long, dark nap.

I'm in this for the long haul, I reminded myself. *Consider Jenny first.*

As we pulled into the garage, I looked for her face in the rearview mirror. "Home at last."

"Yeah," she said. She didn't sound convinced. She climbed out of the car and into the house without a glance back. It took me longer to gather up the sack of stuff from the hospital and my camera bag.

"Remember that guy we met at the picnic on Sunday—Sheriff Curzon?" I followed her inside the house. "He's supposed to stop by later. Maybe share a pizza… what?"

She stood stock-still, four feet inside the doorway. I almost stepped on her.

When she tipped her head to look up at me, I could see her eyes had dilated, the black iris swallowing up the lighter brown of her eyes. Her lips moved barely making words.

"What?"

"Someone's here," she whispered.

My first instinct was straight out of a bad TV movie. *"Don't be silly."* We were only four feet inside the door. They'd told me Jenny might be jittery coming home, but this was more than I expected.

"Someone's in the house?"

Her head bobbed up and down, fast. "The TV was on when I first came in," she said. "And the light, too. But they turned off when I opened the door."

It sounded a little too specific to be a hallucination. I pushed her behind me.

"I put the lights on timers, remember? Wait here. I'll check it out. Stay by the door."

"No!" She grabbed my wrist.

"Jenny, calm down, babe. You don't want to wait?"

She shook her head.

"You want to come?"

Nod.

No one could be in the house. The fact that my heart was beating twenty percent faster was my irrational need for excitement.

I dropped all the junk I was carrying and took Jenny's cold hand in my warm, moist one. I led her over to the closet, quietly opened the door and removed the Midwest girl's weapon of choice—a solid oak, regulation, Louisville Slugger.

In sixteen-inch softball, the balls aren't the only things that run bigger.

Jenny appeared suitably impressed.

"Stay behind me," I said. "But watch my bat."

The main rooms of the house made a loop—entrance area to living room, family room, kitchen, dining room and back to the front. A hall off the living room led to the bedrooms. The garage led straight into the kitchen eating space. We walked all the way around the house once, turning on all the lights, before I said, "All clear."

"Let's check the bedrooms," she whispered. "Just in case."

Right. We walked up the hall and checked the bedrooms, too. Nothing.

Jenny tried a smile and took a big, deep breath. "Could we check the basement, too?"

I hoisted the wood onto my shoulder. "You bet. Let's go."

Basements can be creepy on the best of days, but ours was definitely intruder free. Jenny looked slightly embarrassed, but she was speaking to me in full sentences now, so I didn't mind.

We stopped in front of the spare fridge and I pulled out a frozen pizza.

"Would you take this up and turn the oven on, kiddo? I'm going to throw in a load of wash, before I throw myself in the shower."

I was still wearing the clothes I'd started with on Monday. Even black jeans can only take so much. I dropped my pants and stuffed them into the washer.

"Double-check I didn't leave anything in the oven," I called.

Jenny remained where I'd left her, right at the bottom of the steps. "Go upstairs…by myself?"

"I'll be less than two minutes. You want to take this with you?" I held out the bat.

Her mouth twisted in a rising grimace. That smile of hers needed work.

"It's heavy." She put the pizza box under one arm and carried the bat in front of her with both hands.

"Darn right it's heavy. What should we do tonight?" I kept talking as she went up the stairway, giving her a voice to hang on to as well. After I tossed my shirt in the washer, I dug through the hamper for other stuff that could stand a double wash. "Want to watch a movie? After Sheriff Curzon leaves, maybe we could watch some cartoons…Jen?" There were no sound effects upstairs—oven door squeaking, gas clicking as the oven fired—so I called louder, "Jenny?"

No answer.

A giant thud rocked the ceiling above my head.

My first thought was that she'd seized again and pitched a header on the kitchen floor.

I sprinted for the stairs, throwing on some old bathrobe hanging near the dryer, pounding up two at a time. As I rounded the top step, I hollered, "Jenny! What the hell was that?"

"Hello, Maddy."

Pat the fireman was standing in our kitchen. I caught him in the act of picking up the fallen bat. He let it swing from his fingers by the cap end. "Did you send her up here to club me with a baseball bat?"

"Softball," I corrected. Under duress, my primal nature reverts to know-it-all. "What are you doing here, Pat?"

Recognition took the edge off my shock and sharpened my anxiety until I tasted sour metal at the back of my tongue. He was wearing jeans, a leather jacket and a baseball cap—White Sox. Figures. My grandfather always said *Don't trust a White Sox fan.*

His eyes were glassy. The unblinking stare curdled my stomach.

"Where's Jenny?"

"She dropped the bat and ran." He seemed embarrassed by that thought. "I guess I scared her. I didn't mean to. Everything's gotten so complicated."

"Uh-huh. How'd you get in here, Pat?"

City girls always lock the door. In the back of my mind, I figured if he broke a window to get in, he was definitely dangerous. If he got in through some other means, he might still only qualify as an idiot with really bad boundaries.

When resisting the urge to panic, go with whatever rationale works.

Pat juggled the bat to his other hand and reached down into the pocket of his jeans. As he shifted, I realized the right-hand pocket of his jacket was bulging with something large and heavy.

"I have a key." He tossed it on the kitchen counter. It was a twin to the one I carried.

"Oh. How'd you get a key?"

"Your sister gave it to me."

"She did?" *You smell like her.* "You knew Angelina."

Pat huffed, a sad, ironic sort of laugh. The bat swung from his fingertips, side to side like a pendulum. "Jenny didn't tell. What a kid. What an amazing kid."

Jenny. Pat's intrigue went right out of my head. Where was Jenny? There were four ways out of the room: past me, past Pat, out the door or up the hall. I hadn't heard a door open or close and my ears had been primed. She must have run up the bedroom hallway. I stepped that direction.

"The wacky-intruder thing is getting old. You and my

sister were friends—I get it." My sister's taste in men sucked. "What do you want?"

"How did your TV story turn out? What did you say about Tom and everything?" He perked up as he said it, sounded more like the Mr. Vegas I'd met before.

"Good. It turned out good." I eased another step toward the hall.

"I heard about that fire. Heard you had your camera there. Did you put that in there? About the fire at the Jost farm?"

"Some. Yeah. Where were you that night?"

"I wasn't on call. I was busy. Somewhere else." He stacked the denials one on top of another.

"You know Rachel? Or her dad—Tom's dad?"

"No. Not really. A little. She's the one who got all Tom's stuff."

So much for my Tom-Rachel-Pat love triangle theory.

"Hey, did they ever find a note?" he rambled on. "A note from Tom? I was just wondering."

"No. No note. Were you hoping they would?"

It would be hard to swing the bat in the narrow width of the hall. I took a giant step back, into the hall so Pat had to pass me to get to Jenny. He followed.

"What exactly did you say about Tom on that TV show?"

"You'll have to wait until next Monday. Seven o'clock central time. Why don't you watch? See for yourself."

"Can't wait that long."

"Why not?" I asked.

The outer layer of my skin began to tingle with the rush of adrenaline. I backed into the hall. It was dark. Had Jenny hit the lights as she ran by? There was indirect light from the other room, but the black-

and-white photos of ancestors my sister had hung along the hall—Momma, Daddy, Papa, Gran, all dead, all gone—darkened the passage with the fierce faces of family ghosts.

Pat followed me, step for step, into the hall. "I've got to go now. Jenny's coming with me this time."

The words *this time* rolled through my head crushing all other thoughts.

"Don't worry. I'll watch out for her." He stopped advancing on me. Took off his baseball cap and rubbed a palm over his scalp. Hat in hand, he added, "I won't put her out on the roadside again, if that's what you're worried about." Hat went back on, backward. There was nothing shading those glassy eyes now. He was hopped up on something.

"You took Jenny off the playground." Everything clicked. "She knew you, because you'd been dating her mom. That's why she went with you."

His words popped into my head, *Jenny didn't tell.*

"You threatened her, didn't you?" I swallowed the *you son of a bitch.* The guy was still gripping my Louisville slugger by the cap end.

We were halfway down the hall and running out of real estate. There were three bedrooms at the end. I had a good idea which one Jenny had chosen to hide in.

"You threatened a little eight-year-old girl. What happened to 'prevent and protect'?"

Pat propped the bat in the notch of the bathroom door molding. Big, strong firefighter didn't need a softball bat to get what he wanted from a woman in a bathrobe.

"Don't shout," he cautioned me. "You'll scare her."

"I'm not the one she ran away from."

"Aren't you?"

The flip side of knowing how to charm someone was

knowing how to crush them. His words closed my throat. It felt like I'd fallen from a great height and landed flat on my back.

"Aunt Maddy?" a small voice called behind me. Jenny's bedroom was on my left, which meant she was either in my room or her mother's old bedroom.

"Jenny?" Pat called. "It's me. I'm sorry I scared you, honey. Will you come out so we can talk?"

"No!" I found my voice with a shout. "Stay where you are, Jenny. Don't come out."

"That doesn't help." Pat jabbed his finger at me, less than three feet from my face.

I lost it. I backhanded him at the wrist, knocking his arm into the wall. His jacket was swinging heavily on that side, and the overburdened pocket of his coat hit the wall half a second after his hand. There was a tearing shriek as the lining of his pocket split on impact. A large halogen flashlight dropped to the ground.

It was a Scooby-Doo moment: everybody looks down, everybody looks up. Maddy looks surprised. Pat looks guilty. Oh, those meddlesome kids.

"Ainsley told me he saw a light in the farmhouse the night of the fire." The words popped right out of my mouth. "That *was* you."

"I had to know if Tom left anything else." Pat grabbed the flashlight and stuffed it back in the opposite jacket pocket. "Any more surprises. Your camera boy came to the firehouse and told us all about the bank manager's visit to the farm, all about the papers being delivered. I thought maybe Tom left a note. That's all. Shit's sake, he left enough phone messages. The stupid ass."

"The fire?"

Pat looked disgusted. His Sox cap came off again; he was sweating now. He wiped his face with the inside of his elbow and propped his butt against the wall as if he needed to rest before putting his hat back on. I couldn't tell if he was tired, weak or strung out.

"It was an accident," Pat said. "Simple as that. How was I supposed to know the guy was making coffee in the middle of the night? I'll tell you something— six months ago, I never could have believed Tom could be such a selfish asshole. Mr. Holier-than-Thou. Those magazines I put in his car were nothing. So what? He could have passed them around at the station and been a hero. No, not Tom! Here I am, busting my ass trying to improve the situation for everybody and all he does is fuck the whole thing up." He rolled his eyes drama-queen style.

"You burned the Jost farm down—by accident?"

"Try and stay on track here, would you? Jenny and I are going someplace safe while you do something for me."

"What?"

"You're the one who likes finding shit. Find the bag that Gina hid from me."

"What bag?"

He leaned toward me and smiled. "Like you don't know. I promised I would make it right. But I'm not having a lotta luck here, so I think Jenny and I will take a little vaca-time and you can do the looking."

"I don't know what you're talking about."

He nodded like I'd agreed. "Gina found out how serious I can be. I tried to tell her to leave it alone but no, she's on a mission." His voice cracked. He closed his eyes and pinched the bridge of his nose between his fingers. "Nobody wanted it to end like that."

Conspiraces and madness, barely tinted by facts. "End like what?"

"Tom was good about it at first. He knew what it felt like to lose somebody. But when he found out—"

"What?"

"I didn't want it to go that way. It really was an accident. But she was going to the police. I had to stop her."

"You stopped her?"

"I had to!" He smashed his fist against the wall. All the family photos banged and tilted.

I felt just as off-balance. "You were driving the car that killed my sister?"

"Tom went totally insane when he found out. Said we'd both go to hell if I didn't make a public confession. He would find a way to bring us into the light. Like I had anything to do with his family problems." Pat put his back to the wall. Confessing drained the little bit of spine he had. "When I saw how he'd done himself, I knew. I knew he was going to try and take me down, too.

"And then you showed up!" He pointed at me with both hands and laughed. "What are the chances? I thought for sure Tom had set it up. I thought you were after me."

My brain continued to process. The rest of me was numb. I think I slurred my next words.

"You saw me at the tree the day Tom died."

Pat waved his hands like a professor repeating the facts for the slow kid. "Sure. Standing there with your camera, I recognized you right away. Gina had pictures. But there's a family resemblance, too."

The word *family* hit me like a shot to the head. Could Jenny hear him? If she made any noise, Pat would know where she was.

"You've been following me. You ran me off the road."

"Oh for God's sake, I did not." A hand on each knee, he pushed himself upright. "I was miles away when I passed you. You slipped on the gravel. You weren't hurt."

"Only twelve stitches." Pat the fireman was the fucking Moriarty of the Western Wasteland. "Jenny got the pills from you—that's what this bag business is all about."

"I didn't give that stuff to her." He seemed appalled at the suggestion. "She stole them from my car. Jenny?" he called out to her. "Tell your aunt how you took that medicine without asking."

"Don't answer him," I shouted. "Jenny ended up in the hospital. Same hospital Tom Jost's father is in. The old man saw your flashlight and thought Rachel was still in the house. Went searching for her and the smoke got him. If he dies, that'll make you a double murderer, won't it?"

"Shut up!" he screamed. "Shut up, shut up!" He pounded his fists against his forehead, and then squeezed them into his eye sockets. When he raised his head, he looked at me with wide, wild eyes. "I never meant for anyone to get hurt. That's why you've got to help me and Jenny get out of here, right away. Right now."

"Jenny is not going with you," I said slow and clear.

"She has to." He stepped forward and I stepped back, synchronized like Fred and Ginger, until we both stood in the center of my bedroom. "Nobody would want to hurt Jenny. Jenny is just a kid. If something happened to her, there'd be a lot of fuss."

He wanted Jenny as a shield.

"Who's after you, Pat?"

To my left, a nightstand held a paperback, a travel alarm and a glass of water. The water was in a nice, heavy glass. It might do some damage if I dropped it on his head. Nothing else weapon worthy.

Pat glanced left, right. Pulled the bedroom door out to see the pile of dirty clothes behind it. He moved one direction, I moved the other, circling.

"Jenny?" he called, leaning over to try and see under the bed.

There was a clear path to the door. I jumped forward, shoving his butt as I passed and enjoying the thud that followed. I jerked the door shut on my way out, dashed across the hall to my sister's room, got that door closed and locked before he slammed against it. The hollow-core door buckled like tin.

"Jenny? Jen! Come out," I whispered. I jerked a dresser toward me, while my butt braced the door. "Little help here."

Her face appeared, peeking around the bottom of the closet door.

"Find the phone! Quick."

"It's dead." She held it up. She must have carried it into the closet with her. Realizing I needed help, Jenny scrambled out of the closet, got behind the chest and pushed.

As soon as we had the door blocked, I grabbed her hand and dragged her to the window. "Outside. Go!"

Pat hit the door from the outside, rattling the dresser. Knobs and hinges tinkled metal on metal. The wood trim around the doorjamb cracked.

I cranked open the casement window with one hand and fumbled the latches that held the screen in place with the other.

"Hurry, hurry. Out you go. I'll keep him busy in here. You get to a neighbor's house and call Curzon—I mean, call 9-1-1. Run. Don't stop." I grabbed her by the waist and swung her up, feetfirst, over the window frame. It wasn't hard. Most of my shoes weighed more than Jenny.

She dropped into the shadowy space between the foundation hedge and the house with hardly a sound. I watched her get her bearings and skitter off.

"Good girl," I whispered. Like her momma in the emergency room, Jenny didn't freeze under pressure.

The chest of drawers gave a final creaking lurch and Pat's hand wrapped around the door, caught the jamb and shoved it wide enough to fit his shoulder sideways. His face appeared in the crack for less than half a second. He saw me by the window and *poof!* he was gone.

"Shit!" I leapt over the bed, squeezed around the chest and pinched my way through the opening.

I flung myself down the hall with one thought—*time*. Jenny needed time to get away.

Pat must have heard me coming. He'd grabbed the bat. But his expression, as he glanced over his shoulder, was something between confused and skeptical, when the one-hundred-and-fifty-pound woman in a housecoat did her best to drive her shoulder right through his rib cage.

I've seen people shot, crushed and run over. I've seen fistfights, bar fights and concert brawls. News flash: watching and doing—very different.

Pat's head hit the tile floor right where the hall carpet ended. Sound effects: the muffled *whump* of his body, followed by the melon crack of his head.

I bounced off him and landed with the small of my

back against the corner of the wall. Sound effects: the *oof* and *aaiee* from your typical chop-socky martial-arts movie.

The Slugger clattered to the floor on the far side of Pat, then rolled toward the front door.

Pat grunted and turned over slowly—elbows, to knees, then upright.

I clawed my fingertips into the back of his pants, the plan being either to pull him down or myself up. "She's not going anywhere with you."

Focus on me, I thought. With my head ducked tight against his back, I kept both arms wrapped around his waist and locked my fingers. *Run, Jenny, run.*

"Let go...you stupid—" he grunted "—cow." He took two steps, dragging me toward the door with him, then chopped at my hands and arms with the side of his fist. When he dug his thumbs into my wrists and twisted, my grip broke. I couldn't stop my eyes from welling up, the tip of my nose from burning.

He reached for the bat. I dropped back on my haunches, swiveled a one-eighty on the slick wood floor, and pictured my sister when I whip-kicked into the side of his knee. Sound effects: crunchy-snapping followed by a satisfyingly high scream.

Pat's whole body lurched in the direction of the hurt as he stumbled and fell.

Time shifted into slow motion. I couldn't move the way my mind insisted. An angry man in pain is not a good person to be underneath.

Roaring with animal pain, Pat grabbed for my ankles as I crab-crawled backward. He was babbling, repeating himself over and over. Saying things like, *I'll kill you. You are dead. Dead!*

My robe bunched up around my waist, flashing my

white, Monday underwear. For half a second covering my undies seemed like my top priority—until I saw the fist. He couldn't reach my head, so he aimed for my stomach. The thought alone was enough to give me a puking cramp.

I shut my eyes, muscled a turn trying to protect the soft parts and screamed.

"Stop…"

Time stopped. He froze. I froze. Nothing else happened, because we both recognized the voice.

Jenny.

"No!" I cried.

Boom. Pat connected.

Sound effects: air *whuffing,* gagging. I lost my visual completely for a few seconds.

"Don't!" Jenny finished, her tone more of a loud whine than a demand.

I blinked to clear my focus. Jenny was a shadowed silhouette against the open door. I could see she held the bat in the ready position—barely half his size and ready to fight.

"Jenny! You came back." Pat almost sobbed with relief.

His reaction surprised her. She cocked her head, as if to ask *why's he happy?*

A siren, getting louder by the second. Now I was the happy one.

Pat's fist changed to a grabbing claw. He snatched the bat from her hand, upended it and levered himself to standing using the bat like a cane. He hunched forward.

"Stop," Jenny squeaked.

Pushing up to hands and knees, past the pain, past the

consequences, past everything but the present moment. "Keep away from her."

Pat's face was a Halloween mask of human fears. "Jenny comes with me. You stay."

"No!"

He tried to nab her with his free hand. Jenny jolted past and into my arms. I twisted to push her behind me.

"I do not have time for this!" The siren was so loud I could hardly hear him. Pat drew back with the bat, aiming for my leg.

I covered Jenny with my body, worried he might hit her by mistake. I grabbed a shoe lying near the door, trying to block his swing.

He caught my right thigh muscle an inch above my knee and lit my entire side on fire. Nerves at the top of my head spasmed. Weird primordial sounds leaked out of my mouth. The first thing I saw, when I could see again, was Jenny's face. She was so unnaturally pale and stiff, she looked like a mannequin.

Damn him for scaring her.

I pressed up on my arms, rolled off Jenny and curled myself in a ball breathing in short, gasping outbursts.

"See what it feels like?" Pat screamed. He stepped closer and shouted into my face, "See?"

Behind us I heard the familiar *bam!* of the front door slamming open. A voice I recognized called, "County Sheriff!"

Curzon.

Startled, Pat turned to look and I took that opportunity to swing around again and uncurl my good leg with every ounce of force left in me. I connected right on the bull's-eye.

Pat screamed. Then he fell down.

Jenny screamed.

I didn't scream, even though I wanted to—real bad.

Curzon stepped into the melee and whipped out his phone. He called everyone but his grandmother to assist, while he pinned Pat's hands behind him in handcuffs.

"Maddy, Maddy, Mommy." Jenny rocked herself side to side on the floor. "Mommy, Mommy."

The sound of Jenny's panic made it hard to feel any pain, any relief.

"Help me, Jack. Help her." I crawled toward her. "It's all right, Jenny. It's all right."

Curzon scooped her up off the floor and carried her to the couch in the family room. I got myself upright but had to lean hard on Curzon to make it there.

"I got you now. I got you, Jenny." I pulled her into my arms. I didn't realize tears were slipping down my face until I tasted them on my lips.

Curzon dropped in front of me and examined my leg with a light touch. "How bad?"

A creepy, unhinged laugh came out of me. "Not as bad as him."

I pulled Jenny close. Less than half a minute after we started shivering, Curzon produced a bag of frozen peas for my leg and an afghan from my sister's bedroom.

The ice and warmth helped my insides calm, but my hands would not be still. I petted Jenny's back, her head, her shoulder, over and over. "So brave, you are so brave. You came to help me, didn't you? You are so brave," I told her. "Everything's safe now, Jenny. We did it. We did it together."

We shook and leaked and sniffed. And gradually, calmed.

Curzon bustled around in the kitchen. I thought I

heard the microwave beep. He appeared with two warm mugs. "Drink."

Jenny sipped hers and handed the cup back with a grimace.

I took a swig. It was warm, watered-down juice.

"I was hoping for something stronger."

"EMTs will set you up. Drink. It'll help."

"Where did you come from?" My body was in full stop, but my brain was still revving on the instant replays. "How did you know?"

"Jenny flagged me down. She came running into the street, saw my car at the corner and started hopping up and down, waving her hands."

Jenny smudged her face against my already wet robe front and dragged the afghan over her head, hiding beneath the familiar scent of comfort. It seemed to help, so I didn't stop her.

Curzon put a hand on my shoulder, gave it a squeeze. "Paramedics will be here any minute."

I thought he would walk away again, but he didn't. He let his hand fall on my head and he stroked my hair once, twice. It seemed to help, so I didn't stop him either.

The rest of our evening was a party of paperwork and helping professionals. I had to promise I'd go to the station tomorrow for more of the same.

The paramedics looked me over but nothing they said could convince me to get off the couch. The bruise was going to be awesome but nothing appeared broken. They packed me in ice and fed me eight hundred milligrams of my favorite snack. After Jenny was checked and rechecked, they took off with Pat strapped tight in the back of the ambulance. I heard the phone ring while the guys were loading. Curzon answered it.

"You want to talk to your boy at the office?" he called from the kitchen.

I held out my hands and Curzon tossed the phone to me.

"Maddy?" Ainsley sounded upset. "What's going on? Why are the police there? Is it bad?"

"Your camera work's passable, College, but your questioning skills suck." It took about ninety seconds to fill him in. He supplied the "no way's" and "oh man's."

"It's been a long day, College. What do you want?"

"Well, I have good news." Ainsley's voice went all breathy and excited. "I talked to Uncle Rich. Everything is copacetic with Network and everybody. It's totally cool."

"O'Hara?" Gatt's voice interrupted. I could hear Ainsley complaining in the background about the phone being grabbed from his hand. "Why the hell didn't you just tell me you had a kid in the hospital? Am I some kind of asshole, I can't make exceptions for somebody who's got a sick kid? What are you thinking?"

"Uhh—"

"That's what I thought! Christ! Get over yourself and start acting like a team player, you hear me, O'Hara? Do I look like I've got time for this kind of shit? I ripped up that stupid resignation and put it where it belonged— in the garbage. You're goddamn right, I did. Whoever heard of somebody resigning in pencil? Garbage!"

"Who's that, Aunt Maddy?" Jenny whispered right in my ear. With her head on my shoulder, I'm sure she could hear the whole thing, loud and clear.

"That's my boss."

"He's loud."

"Yeah." But not so bad.

Ainsley came back on the line. "There's someone else here who wants to speak to you."

"If you ever satellite something without my approval again I will fire you, blackball you and bad-mouth you at every ITVA convention I attend for the rest of my career. Clear?" Shirley Shayla said with the kind of cold-blooded lizard directness that left no doubt of bluff.

"Uh, yeah."

"How is your niece?"

General managers drive straight to the point.

"She's going to be all right." My awareness shifted from the phone conversation to the weight of Jenny fitting right against my side. It felt like having a secret, like I'd finally figured out the answer. "We're going to be fine."

"Good," Shayla said and I really think she meant it.

Ainsley came back on the line suddenly. "It was Uncle Rich who talked to the guys at Network. They were a bit freaked about the shift from the autoerotic angle. But everybody's cool now. Ms. Shayla really went to bat for you, too." His voice dropped to a half whisper. "They just walked out so I can tell you, Shayla really liked the final version. She said, 'Now that's what I was hoping to see.' After everyone talked, I only had to do a couple small changes—"

"What?" I stiffened. Jenny's head bounced lightly against my collar bone.

"—but I think you'll like them."

"You changed my story?"

"Only a little. Mostly audio."

"You changed my story?"

He blew out a rush of words. "We—they thought the end was sort of preachy. I took out a couple lines of voice-over and added some music. Some good music."

"You changed my story." I wondered for a minute if the pain in my leg was making me delirious.

"Yeah." Ainsley gave in. "I changed it."

"What 'good music'?"

"It's instrumental. Nothing canned. It's an old folk song that starts with a flute and ends with a full rock band. It's cool."

"I'm sorry? Did you say 'full rock band'? My funky, Amish-modern-world tragedy, *This American Life* meets *60 Minutes,* sure-bet-for-an-Emmy-nomination-at-least, now has a music video soundtrack?"

No answer.

"College, did you ever explain to me exactly why they kicked you out of school?"

"Ha." He laughed nervously. "Funny."

"We're going to talk about this later. I'm hanging up now. I think I may be hallucinating." My pride sluiced through a filter of relief. "Thanks, Ainsley. For handling stuff on the work front. I'll call you in the morning."

"You're welcome, Maddy."

Jenny decided she was hungry as soon as I got off the phone. Curzon volunteered to stick around and supervise the heating of the frozen pizza. Then he stayed while we watched a mind-numbing kids' movie on cable. When Jenny finally fell asleep on the couch, he was the one who carried her into her room while I limped along behind them. But he left me to do the tucking in.

"You did good today, kid," I whispered to the sleeping girl. If people in a coma can hear you, why not someone merely dreaming? I brushed the hair off her face and rubbed her forehead lightly with my thumb. Little by little the motion smoothed the furrows between her brows. "Don't give up on me."

She didn't answer. She slept. Peacefully. That was enough.

For the moment.

Before I went back into the family room, I went and found my messenger bag and the large plastic storage container that my sister had filled with medicine and supplies. The same one Jenny had pulled out to treat me after my fall. Hobbling back into the family room, I set the box on the coffee table in front of Curzon. Curious, he reached for the lid. I stopped him from lifting it.

"Did you know?" I asked.

"Know?"

"Pat. My sister. He drove the car—"

"He tell you that?" he interrupted, suddenly shifting forward on the couch.

I nodded. Holding so much inside, I lost the ability to verbalize. I was afraid I'd scream if I opened my mouth.

Curzon stared at me. "He's going to jail. For a long time."

I hit the top of the plastic box with the flat of my hand. The sting helped. "Did. You. Know."

"I suspected."

I heard my breath rush out as if I'd taken a hit. "Why...why didn't you say something?"

"I told you I hadn't given up investigating your sister's case." He was completely matter-of-fact about it. "I've been watching that guy for weeks."

"Why didn't you tell me!" It wasn't a question. It was an accusation.

"Same reason you didn't you tell me, until a few hours ago, you had an SUV following you all over town!" He stood up fast and sent the box skidding across the table. "You have secrets you need to keep, Maddy O'Hara? I have mine."

True enough. I hadn't told him half the things I should have.

Curzon tipped his head and winced, as if he didn't like the sound of his own words. "Nicky's letter had the fire-service people in an uproar. I couldn't go near Pat without a written complaint, something concrete to investigate. The IAFF filed a grievance against the police department that named every man at station six. Politics muddied the water."

I sat down on the edge of the table. "That's why you were nagging about reporting the car that ran me off the road? Politics?"

"Pat's connected. You know how things work."

"Where's the pressure coming from? The guy who brought Pat to your party? The one who's challenging you for Sheriff?"

"Got it in one."

"I'll witness a complaint. But I can do concrete, as well." I pulled the box close and took off the lid. Beneath the princess Band-Aids and the hot-water bottle sat a gallon-sized Baggie full of several dozen foil blister packs. "This is what Pat was looking for. Jenny found it out in the garage the other day. According to Pat, my sister took it from him. She was planning to turn him in."

Curzon squeezed the bag, smooshing the foil packets around inside. "They're samples. Handed out by the pharmaceutical companies to doctors as trial medicine for patients. Not tracked like other medication because they're supposedly available in limited quantities." He looked at the labels. "These are popular on the club scene."

We both took a few calming breaths. Curzon finally sat back down on the couch.

"I have one more thing to show you." From the bottom of my backpack I pulled out Tom Jost's cell phone and put it on the table. "Jane Q. Public wants to turn this in."

"Christ, O'Hara! I've been looking everywhere… Where did Jane get it?"

I thought of the old man in the plastic hospital tent and his daughter in Grace's car, both struggling to heal in isolation. Curzon was right. I needed to keep their secrets. "Jane doesn't remember."

The sheriff did not look happy with that answer, so I kept talking. "The phone numbers in memory show that Tom Jost called the authorities and invited them to his pending suicide. He also called his dad. And Pat."

Curzon nodded. "I looked those calls up with Dispatch after Jane gave me her last tip. Didn't know about the dad or Pat. But that fits."

"Fits how?"

"Am I still speaking to Jane? Or am I speaking to Maddy O'Hara?"

"Maddy's story is in the can. Jane is merely curious."

"Tom did write a note. He mailed it to the fire chief. Didn't say he was going to kill himself, but he confessed that he'd failed to discourage Pat from engaging in harmful activities and the fire chief might want to investigate." Curzon waved the sample packet in the air. "Figured it was something like this. I tried to use the note as leverage for a warrant but there was too much blowback. How could the judge trust the word of a guy who was obviously unstable?"

"Shit."

"Pretty much." Curzon flicked at the edge of the foil tablet packaging with his thumb, an angry, nervous gesture that reminded me of someone playing with a cigarette lighter. "In the letter, the guy apologized to the entire universe. Then he warned the chief they'd need someone to cover his shift days from now on."

A tired sigh deflated me. "No way."

"There are some things I will never understand." Curzon tossed the packet into the box. He held out his empty hand.

I took it.

"There's more to the story, isn't there? Pat's no evil genius. There's no way he got into this all by himself."

Curzon tried to stonewall but the man had just spent the last two hours eating pizza and insulting the intelligence of cartoon characters with me. The blank face no longer worked as a disguise.

"Am I wrong?"

"Press and police sit on opposite sides of the fence, O'Hara. Most of the time." He tugged my hand and pulled me beside him on the couch. The dip in the cushion rolled me toward him. "Your sister's death was a tragedy. The man responsible is going to jail. Don't get focused on the wrong thing here. What happens with you and Jenny now, that's the part you can do something about."

I thought about the fight with Pat. Jenny's safety, physical and mental, all that mattered. Still, "I want to know what happened. I want to know the rest of it."

"So do I." He said the words with quiet conviction.

I believed him. "Can I help?"

"No."

"Can you stop me from helping?"

"No?" he replied rhetorically, then leaned forward and oh, so gently touched my cheek. "I haven't done this sort of thing in a while."

"Me neither."

Overcome evil with good.

In Curzon's eyes, I saw goodness. It reminded me of something I didn't tell Ainsley. Sometimes what we see describes half-forgotten dreams of what might yet be.

"Kiss me?" he asked.

I thought of Curzon's words and the truth he'd told me so far. This was another part that mattered, another part that I could do something about.

Slowly, I felt myself tilt toward him in a motion both grand and imperceptible as the earth shifting on its axis.

Tomorrow would be soon enough for all the unasked questions.

All the untold stories.

About the Author

J. Wachowski writes stories, screenplays, school excuses and anything else that pays.

She lives with her family on the Midwestern edge of civilization, but is often sighted lurking at jwachowski.com.

REQUEST YOUR FREE BOOKS!

2 FREE NOVELS
PLUS 2 FREE GIFTS!

MYSTERY

W❁RLDWIDE LIBRARY®

TM

Your Partner in Crime

YES! Please send me 2 FREE novels from the Worldwide Library® series and my 2 FREE gifts (gifts are worth about $10). After receiving them, if I don't wish to receive any more books, I can return the shipping statement marked "cancel." If I don't cancel, I will receive 4 brand-new novels every month and be billed just $4.99 per book in the U.S. or $5.99 per book in Canada. That's a saving of at least 25% off the cover price. It's quite a bargain! Shipping and handling is just 50¢ per book in the U.S. and 75¢ per book in Canada.* I understand that accepting the 2 free books and gifts places me under no obligation to buy anything. I can always return a shipment and cancel at any time. Even if I never buy another book, the two free books and gifts are mine to keep forever.

414/424 WDN FDDT

Name _____ (PLEASE PRINT)

Address _____ Apt. #

City _____ State/Prov. _____ Zip/Postal Code

Signature (if under 18, a parent or guardian must sign)

Mail to the **Reader Service:**
IN U.S.A.: P.O. Box 1867, Buffalo, NY 14240-1867
IN CANADA: P.O. Box 609, Fort Erie, Ontario L2A 5X3

Not valid for current subscribers to the Worldwide Library series.

Want to try two free books from another line?
Call 1-800-873-8635 or visit www.ReaderService.com.

* Terms and prices subject to change without notice. Prices do not include applicable taxes. Sales tax applicable in N.Y. Canadian residents will be charged applicable taxes. Offer not valid in Quebec. This offer is limited to one order per household. All orders subject to credit approval. Credit or debit balances in a customer's account(s) may be offset by any other outstanding balance owed by or to the customer. Please allow 4 to 6 weeks for delivery. Offer available while quantities last.

Your Privacy—The Reader Service is committed to protecting your privacy. Our Privacy Policy is available online at www.ReaderService.com or upon request from the Reader Service.

We make a portion of our mailing list available to reputable third parties that offer products we believe may interest you. If you prefer that we not exchange your name with third parties, or if you wish to clarify or modify your communication preferences, please visit us at www.ReaderService.com/consumerchoice or write to us at Reader Service Preference Service, P.O. Box 9062, Buffalo, NY 14269. Include your complete name and address.

WWLII